TYLER WHITESIDES

JANITORS

HEROES OF THE DUSTBIN

TYLER WHITESIDES

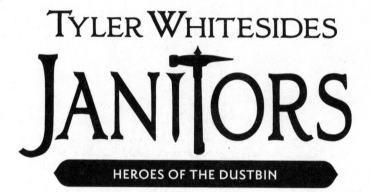

JANITORS

HEROES OF THE DUSTBIN

ILLUSTRATED BY
BRANDON DORMAN

SHADOW
MOUNTAIN

For friends and family
who stick with you to the end.

And for Jessica, Laura, Molly, and Clayton,
who stuck with me from the beginning.

© 2015 Tyler Whitesides

Illustrations © 2015 Brandon Dorman

Library of Congress Cataloging-in-Publication Data
Whitesides, Tyler, author.
  Heroes of the dustbin / Tyler Whitesides.
      pages cm. — (Janitors ; Book 5)
  Summary: Spencer and his team of Rebels must face the combined evil of the Founding Witches and the Sweepers, or the world is doomed to fall under the control of the sinister Bureau of Educational Maintenance.
  ISBN 978-1-62972-065-4 (hardbound : alk. paper)
  [1. Monsters—Fiction. 2. School custodians—Fiction. 3. Schools—Fiction. 4. Friendship—Fiction. 5. Magic—Fiction.] I. Title. II. Series: Whitesides, Tyler. Janitors ; bk. 5.
  PZ7.W58793He 2015
  [Fic]—dc23   2015005189

Printed in the United States of America
RR Donnelley, Harrisonburg, VA

10   9   8   7   6   5   4   3   2   1

CONTENTS

CONTENTS

Contents

CHAPTER 1

"JUST CAN'T KEEP UP."

Spencer Zumbro was supposed to spit. He didn't like spitting. It was typically disrespectful and totally unsanitary. But today, it was necessary. Today, in the janitorial closet at Welcher Elementary School, his spit was a secret weapon.

It was really the only thing keeping the Rebel Janitors going in their fight against the corrupt Bureau of Educational Maintenance. The BEM had Mr. Clean and his strike force of mutated Sweepers. They had Pluggers, trained to ride and control oversized Toxites. They even had the Founding Witches, who were masterful at Glopifying cleaning supplies even without their wands of power.

The Rebels had Spencer's spit.

Spencer glanced around the secret janitorial closet. The shelves were almost bare, the Rebels' stock of magical

1

JANITORS: HEROES OF THE DUSTBIN

cleaning supplies nearly depleted since Walter Jamison had died six weeks ago. What few supplies remained had been Glopified by Spencer's right hand and delivered around the country by Marv to the last of the loyal Rebels.

Spencer's attention turned to the open doorway. Daisy Gates had just appeared, framed by the hulking form of Marv behind her. Daisy was already wearing her blue Glopified coveralls, which fit loosely over the clothes she'd worn during school.

"Sorry we're late," Daisy said.

Just as they did every Monday, they were supposed to meet in the secret Rebel closet right after school ended. They couldn't slack off now, not even on the last week of school. Marv said the Toxites would be heading into a light hibernation for summer vacation. In preparation for the months of empty school, the potency of the Toxites' breath had increased. That surely explained why students seemed to grow more rowdy as summer break drew nearer.

Today, Daisy was nearly fifteen minutes late for their appointment in the janitor closet. "What happened?" Spencer asked.

"I was tap dancing in the cafeteria." Daisy shrugged with embarrassment.

"Another Grime?" Spencer asked.

"Two of them," Marv said. "They got away." He dropped an ordinary pushbroom onto the table in front of Spencer. It wasn't Glopified, which would explain why Marv hadn't been able to destroy the Grimes. The big janitor shook his head. "Just can't keep up."

The Toxites were making a terrible comeback at Welcher. Just the day before, Spencer had fallen asleep in class. And he knew his fatigue was brought on by more than Mrs. Natcher's boring lessons. Daisy said she'd seen a Filth bedding down in a dusty corner behind the door.

Marv rubbed a dirty hand through his shaggy beard and gestured at the pushbroom on the table before them. "Magic time."

Spencer nodded. "Are we keeping this one?" Marv only grunted in response, which prompted Spencer to press the matter. He pointed at the bare shelves in the Rebel closet. "There are at least three Grimes and a handful of Filths out there," Spencer remarked.

"Yeah," Daisy cut in. "And Dez said he saw a flock of Rubbishes, but I don't know if he was pulling my leg."

"We can't keep giving all the supplies away," Spencer urged. "We have to keep this pushbroom for Welcher!"

Marv's expression seemed to darken, and he shook his hairy head. When he spoke, his voice was a low rumble. "Think it's bad here? There's schools out there with three monsters for every kid. Good Rebel schools where the janitor has nothing but a maxed-out mop and a pinch of vac dust." Marv rested a hand on the bristles of the pushbroom. "This one's going to a school in Tennessee. Trust me, they need it more than we do."

Spencer lowered his head, ashamed to have thought so selfishly. He missed Walter Jamison's guidance, not to mention the old warlock's power to create new Glopified supplies with regularity. But the Witches had ordered

Walter's death, and Mr. Clean's Glopified rag had carried it out, reducing the kind old janitor to a mere wisp of vapor. Without Walter, the Rebels were left with only the weapons they had in stock. And most of those cleaning supplies had maxed out, becoming useless after destroying so many Toxites.

Spencer's spit was the only hope the Rebels had of receiving new Glopified supplies. But he could use his magic on only one item at a time, and it took a couple of days for his power to recharge. He was doing all he could.

Marv gestured to the pushbroom on the table. "That's going to save somebody," the janitor said, as though reading Spencer's mind. "Maybe even stop them from getting taken."

Marv didn't have to explain what he meant. Spencer knew that from the moment the Founding Witches had returned, the Rebel Janitors had begun disappearing. So many schools were defenseless now, the students' minds rotting from Toxite breath while the janitors vanished without a trace.

It was distressing news, and it shook the Rebels in the wake of Walter's sudden death. But the news turned worse as the disappearances increased. Spencer wondered again what might have happened to those loyal Rebel Janitors.

Then it became personal.

Meredith List, Welcher's own lunch lady, had gone missing four weeks ago. Then Earl Dodge, the cowboy janitor who had helped the Rebels in Colorado. Then Agnes

Maynard, a Rebel spy who had helped them gain entrance to the BEM's secret lab.

Then Penny.

Walter's daring red-headed niece, a veteran of so many Toxite battles, had been missing for over two weeks.

The Rebel Janitors who remained were scared and underprepared. Spencer wondered why he had been spared. So far, no apparent attempt had been made to abduct him, Daisy, or Marv. He felt almost insignificant, as if the BEM were ignoring him. But why?

Spencer looked at the ordinary pushbroom on the table. Marv was right. He needed to Glopify it, even if it would bring hope to only *one* person in this fight.

Spencer checked the zipper on his Glopified coveralls. He wasn't expecting trouble, but it was a habit for him to check whenever he had them on. The coveralls didn't defend against magical attacks, but as long as the zipper was pulled tight, they would protect the wearer from any physical impact.

Spencer held his right hand before his face, worked up a bit of saliva in his mouth, and spat onto his palm. He clapped his hands together, rubbing them briskly until a bright golden light spread from his wrists to the tips of his fingers. The magical Aura had once encompassed his entire body, introducing Glop into his bodily systems and transforming him into an ageless Auran.

Daisy giggled, and Spencer turned to look at her. She shrugged. "It's just ironic."

"What's ironic?" Spencer asked, his glowing hands outstretched.

"That you have magic spit," she said. "You hate spit."

"Tell me about it," Spencer muttered. He looked at his hands, the right one with the power to Glopify and the left with the power to de-Glopify.

He'd gotten quite good at it over the last six weeks. He knew how to let the magic flow through him, changing the ordinary cleaning supplies into magically charged weapons. Warlocks like Walter had to experiment with Glop formulas, sometimes taking days to find the right solution that would yield a magical result. Spencer could do it instantly. And unlike the warlocks' creations, Spencer's cleaning supplies could be used endlessly without maxing out.

There were no warlocks anymore. Their bronze hammers had been replaced by three evil Witches sequestered at New Forest Academy, experimenting with Glop formulas and sending Mr. Clean and the Sweepers in search of the bronze nails that were actually the Witches' wands.

Spencer lowered his right hand toward the table. He had to be careful to touch the pushbroom first, since the Glopifying power would go to work on the first thing it contacted. And the Aura took two days to recharge, so Spencer didn't want to waste it.

Spencer's hand was an inch from the pushbroom's bristles when a sound outside the closet drew his attention. A razorblade sword flicked open in Marv's hand, and Daisy drew a pinch of vacuum dust from her reserves. Spencer clenched his glowing hands into fists as someone appeared in the doorway of the secret Rebel closet.

"Don't touch that pushbroom!" the newcomer shouted.

Marv growled and pointed his razorblade at the intruder. "Who are you?"

But Spencer and Daisy knew exactly who had barged into the closet.

It was Rho.

Spencer stepped away from the table, his glowing hands raised so he wouldn't accidentally touch something.

Daisy's mouth opened in surprise. She seemed to forget about the pinch of vac dust in her hand, and it slipped out of her fingers, causing a suction force to grab her leg and pull her down.

Marv kept his razorblade pointed defensively at the white-haired girl in the doorway. "Know her?"

Spencer nodded. "This is Rho. She's an Auran."

"And she's Spencer's first crush," Daisy added, trying to sit up against her own vac dust suction. "But that was before we found out that she's really three hundred years old."

Spencer rolled his eyes at Daisy's brutal honesty. His face was definitely turning red. "Anything else you want to share about our history?"

"Well," Daisy said, oblivious to the sarcasm, "they met at New Forest Academy, but Spencer thought her name was Jenna. She was kind of flirty and pretty, but then we found out she was just spying on Spencer so she could trick him into going to the Broomstaff, where he'd have to wear a dustpan around his neck and live in a landfill forever."

Rho smiled awkwardly, then held out her hand to Marv. "Pleasure to meet you."

Marv didn't seem any more trusting, but he lowered the tip of his razorblade a few inches.

"What are you doing here?" Spencer finally asked. Rho lowered her hand when Marv didn't accept the handshake, instead turning her attention to Spencer.

"Don't touch anything," Rho ordered.

"Is there a problem?" Spencer asked. He hadn't seen her in months and she was already bossing him around.

"The boys are ready," said Rho.

Spencer felt a chill pass through him. He'd been waiting months to hear those words from Rho. The Dark Auran boys, cursed to wander the landfill with imprisoning dustpans around their necks, had told Spencer to wait for Rho. It had been so long, Spencer was beginning to lose hope. But Rho's sudden arrival at Welcher Elementary's janitorial closet could mean only one thing.

Rho nodded. "It's time for you to un-Pan them."

"Now hold on," Marv cut in. "Spencer's already got a job to do." He pointed his blade at the pushbroom on the table.

"That can wait," Rho said. "The Dark Aurans cannot."

"You don't come barging in here, telling us—" Marv began.

"She's right," Spencer cut him off. "Nothing is more important than getting the Pans off Olin, Sach, and Aryl."

"But what about V?" Daisy asked, dusting herself off as she stood once more.

"She's come around," Rho explained. "She's on our side now."

It was hard for Spencer to believe. V was the ringleader of the Auran girls. She had Panned the boys when they had stopped her from giving the *Manualis Custodem* to the BEM two centuries ago. V had been recycling Glop through a pump house, a process that only created more Toxites.

"V wanted the Witches to return more than anyone," Rho said. "When they finally arrived, V realized that they weren't the friends she thought they'd be."

"Yeah," Spencer muttered. "Join the club." He felt awkward, standing there with his golden hands outstretched.

"We should go," Rho said. "Gia has a garbage truck in the parking lot. We'll jump through the back and come out the dumpster portal at the landfill."

"We should get my dad," Spencer said. "He won't want to miss this."

"No time," said Rho. "General Clean could be here any moment."

"General?" Marv snorted.

Rho nodded. "That's what the Witches are calling him."

"General Clean is coming to our school?" Daisy yelped.

"Not sure where he's going," Rho said, "but we spied a team of Sweepers on the way into Welcher. General Clean was with them."

"That can't be good," Spencer muttered. It made him uneasy not to know the exact whereabouts of the Sweeper General. Spencer used to be able to touch bronze objects and see through the warlocks' eyes. Since the Witches had returned, there were no more warlocks. Now touching bronze did absolutely nothing.

"How long until he gets here?" Daisy asked.

Rho shrugged. "Sweepers move fast. They were out in the subdivisions. Looked like they were heading into a place called Hillside Estates."

Spencer reeled, his heart thumping. He tucked his glowing hands close to his chest and staggered around the table.

"Hillside Estates . . ." he muttered.

"What's wrong?" asked Rho.

It was Daisy who answered, since Spencer seemed to be going into shock. "That's where Spencer's family lives!"

CHAPTER 2

"HOW DO I LOOK?"

Spencer focused his shock and fear into something that might help. He needed to get home and warn his family! Perhaps it was already too late.

"Squeegee." Spencer pointed a glowing finger at a squeegee leaning up in the corner of the closet. "The other one's at my house."

Marv picked it up. The big janitor would be familiar with this particular squeegee. He had opened a portal to the Zumbros' house on many mornings when Spencer's mom was running behind and didn't want the kids to be late for school. Squeegees created an instant means of travel, but they only worked if someone swiped a matching squeegee at the desired destination.

Next, Spencer pointed to an item on a dusty shelf. "Can

somebody grab that walkie-talkie? My dad keeps his on channel 14."

Daisy grabbed the device and tuned it. She pressed the button and held it out for Spencer. He couldn't touch it for fear of releasing the Aura power that still surrounded his hands.

"Dad! Dad! Come in! I need you to use the squeegee and open a portal." Spencer nodded to Marv, who dragged his squeegee across a tall mirror in the janitorial closet. The magic fizzed and hissed a bright green, but the connection wasn't complete.

"Dad! I repeat, use the squeegee and open a portal!"

The radio went quiet in Daisy's hand, and Spencer held his breath. Then an image flickered, cutting through the magical fizz on the mirror and linking the two destinations. Spencer exhaled as he saw the Zumbro toy room above the garage. The room looked like an absolute disaster . . . which was just the way it always looked.

Spencer hurried to step through the portal, his shoe crunching on some scattered Legos. The magical entryway to his house had been formed in the large window above the driveway.

Daisy entered right behind him, and when Rho stepped through, Spencer was suddenly a little embarrassed by the disastrous state of his house. Then he remembered that Rho lived in a landfill, and he decided she was probably used to messes.

"Careful," Marv muttered, hiking up his pants to step through the portal.

"Hold back," Rho ordered him, a hand outstretched as Spencer scanned the toy room. "We need someone in Welcher to keep the portal open. Just in case."

Marv grunted in protest, but he obeyed. Rho's precautions were wise.

The Zumbro house was perfectly quiet. It was strange that Spencer's dad wasn't standing in the toy room. Whoever had opened the portal appeared to have vanished, and suddenly, the whole scenario was starting to smell very much like a trap.

Then Daisy squealed and Spencer whirled around in fear. But there was no danger. In fact, his friend seemed unusually happy.

"Oooo, Spencer!" Daisy fell to her knees amidst the toys. "I had no idea you had such a huge collection of Barbies!"

Spencer felt his face turn bright red. "They're my sisters'!" he said, his voice a little more forceful than he meant it to be. "You can look at them later. Now's not the time to get . . ." As he spoke, he realized what was happening. ". . . distracted."

He had scanned the toy room and found it safe. But there was one place he hadn't checked. Spencer's eyes turned up to the ceiling just as General Clean dropped from where he'd been clinging.

"Look out!" Spencer yelled. He and Rho scrambled backward through the toys, but Daisy was so distracted by Clean's potent Grime breath that she didn't even glance up.

She had moved on from the Barbies and was brushing the plastic hair of a toy dog.

General Clean landed silently in front of the portal. Marv's razorblade flashed through the opening, but the Sweeper tossed a pinch of vacuum dust into the janitorial closet, pinning the big man to the floor.

Clean squared his broad shoulders, standing firmly before the portal. He was a hideous sight: half man and half Grime. His white lab coat was discolored from the yellowish slime oozing off his dark skin. His black hair had grown longer since Spencer had last seen him, and the tight curls seemed to hold a filmy goo. Clean's eyes bulged, his snakelike tongue flicked out to taste the air, and a serpentine tail swished silently behind him.

The Sweeper's fingers were tipped with venomous suction pads, and one hand gripped a Glopified squeegee. Spencer swallowed hard, realizing that the item in General Clean's grasp likely meant that the Sweeper had opened the portal. If that were true, then where was Spencer's dad?

"They're gone," said the Sweeper, his voice a low rumble.

"Where?" Spencer demanded, his glowing hands clenched into angry fists of fire. If he could get close enough, a single touch from Spencer's left hand might knock the Sweeper powers out of General Clean.

As if anticipating such an attack, Clean reached into his lab coat and withdrew a dirty rag. Spencer felt a chill pass through him. That same rag had obliterated Walter Jamison, reducing the Rebel warlock to thin air.

"Your family is safe for now," General Clean said. "Safely out of the way. They tried to put up a fight, of course. But your little brothers and sisters came quite peacefully once your parents were unconscious."

"If you hurt them . . ." Spencer threatened, but his voice didn't sound half as brave as he'd hoped.

"Relax," said Clean. "Nothing but green spray. They won't remember a thing about it when they wake up."

"Spencer?" Daisy said, kneeling amidst the toys. She had a look of intense concentration on her face. "I know I'm supposed to be paying attention right now. But it's kind of hard. So many dress-ups . . ." Losing her focus, Daisy dove headlong into a pile of costumes.

"Let's get to the point here," said General Clean. "You tell me where the bronze nails are, and I'll tell you where your family is."

Walter Jamison had died protecting those nails. If the Witches got them, they'd have nearly unlimited power through their wands. Rho gave Spencer a sideways glance. He was suddenly grateful that he hadn't been trusted with that information.

"I don't know where they are." If he had known, Spencer might have spilled the secret to save his family.

"You," Clean said, pointing a slimy finger at Rho. "Where are the nails?"

"How should I know?" she retorted. "And if I did, I wouldn't tell you."

"Then the Zumbro family will rot with the rest of the Rebels," said Clean. "*Someone* must know the location of the bronze nails. And if we need to, we will abduct every Rebel for questioning."

"How do I look?" Daisy shouted from across the toy room. She had a Dracula cape tied around her neck and a shiny tiara on her head. She was wearing giant red clown shoes and a big foam hand that said "WE'RE NUMBER ONE!"

"I don't usually make house calls," General Clean said, ignoring Daisy. "But you paid a visit to my laboratory a month or two ago. I thought I should do the same."

With the squeegee slung casually over one shoulder, Clean reached with his other hand into the folds of his stained lab coat, stowing his deadly rag. When it withdrew, the pale suction bulbs on his fingertips were gripping a slender plastic jug.

Spencer squinted at the label. It was drain clog remover. The liquid's common purpose was familiar to him; it was a powerful chemical that would quickly dissolve anything clogging a drain. But Spencer had never come across a Glopified version.

With a single sticky hand, the Sweeper managed to twist off the cap while still gripping the jug. "You flood my house," General Clean said, "I flood yours." Then he paused, holding the drain cleaner outstretched. Clean glanced across the room at Daisy. "One more thing," he said to Spencer and Rho. "When your distracted friend regains her senses, give her a message for me." Clean's Sweeper eyes fixed on Spencer. "My socks are warm and fuzzy."

General Clean upended the jug of drain clog remover and threw it down against the toy room floor.

CHAPTER 3

"DID HE SAY ANYTHING TO ME?"

General Clean was gone in an instant. He made a single leap, his Grimelike characteristics allowing his body to compress through the narrow crack under the door. He had vanished before anyone could blink. But Spencer's attention was not on the fleeing Sweeper. It was on Clean's final message.

My socks are warm and fuzzy.

It was a code phrase that Daisy used with her parents. It meant that something magical was afoot. It was supposed to be top secret. No one was aware that Mr. and Mrs. Gates knew about Glop and Toxites. It was the only thing that had protected them. But if Clean was using the Gateses' secret code . . .

Spencer couldn't dwell on the thought for more than a second before his entire focus shifted to the spilled jug of drain cleaner in the center of the room. The thick yellowish liquid was chugging across the carpet without being absorbed. In fact, the very opposite seemed to be happening. The floor in the toy room was changing. It was as though the solid particles of the house were dissolving and liquefying.

In no time, the center of the room was gone and Spencer was staring down into the garage below. But it didn't stop there. The drain cleaner sloshed across the floor and began climbing a wall. Everything it touched instantly dissolved; the liquid ate through the house as if it were made of sugar. Soon the jug itself had melted away. But there was no stopping the destructive chemicals that had already spilled out.

Across the room, Marv's hairy arm thrust through the portal and seized Daisy, pulling her back into the safety of Welcher's janitorial closet. Spencer and Rho had their backs to the opposite wall, watching the acid drain cleaner eat its way closer to the portal.

"Looks like Clean dropped the squeegee over there." Rho pointed to one of the last remaining sections of floor in the toy room. Before Spencer could say anything, she sprinted in front of him, leapt across the gap, and grabbed the squeegee.

"Windex!" Rho shouted. Marv's hand appeared again, this time tossing a blue spray bottle to Rho. There wasn't much liquid, and Spencer didn't know what she had in mind.

The moment Marv's hand was back inside, Rho kicked

the window where Clean had opened the portal. Spencer gasped as bits of glass went flying and the portal vanished.

"What are you doing?" Spencer cried. Smashing their only escape route didn't seem like the brightest idea. Rho ignored him, stepping dangerously close to the edge. She took a deep breath, seeming to gauge the distance down to the garage. Then she leapt through the hole in the floor, landing with a clang on the dissolving roof of the automobile below.

One of the house's exterior walls had completely disappeared, exposing a blue early-June sky. Spencer couldn't tell how far into the house the drain cleaner was spreading. Beyond the toy room, he saw that his parents' bedroom was half-eaten. He assumed it would continue until the entire house was gone.

The drain clog remover was almost to Spencer's feet now. He turned his shoes sideways, balancing on the last ledge of solid floor.

"Jump!" Rho shouted.

Spencer looked down to see what Rho had done. Glopified Windex had turned a portion of the garage floor into a flat panel of glass. Rho had used the squeegee, reopening the portal to Welcher. As Spencer looked down, he could see Marv and Daisy, but they appeared to be standing sideways.

Rho slipped through the portal. The floor of the garage became the wall of Welcher. Gravity shifted and she stood up.

The thick drain cleaner was spilling down into the

garage. Spencer knew he didn't have much time. Tucking his glowing hands close to his chest, Spencer sized the jump. A bit of the floor gave out under his foot. His balance was thrown and he leapt awkwardly down.

Spencer's feet passed through the portal, but his shoulder clipped the edge, shattering the glass on the garage floor. His head slipped through just as the gateway closed. Spencer's falling momentum carried him across the janitorial closet, and he tumbled against the hard floor, coming to a stop against the far wall. Miraculously, his hands still shone with the Aura. Despite all that had transpired, Spencer had managed not to touch anything.

"What happened?" Marv asked, hoisting Spencer to his feet.

"Clean got my family," he answered. "But they're still alive. The Witches are keeping them for questioning."

"What the heck?" Daisy said. "Why am I wearing this ridiculous outfit?" She lifted a foot, wiggling the giant red clown shoe.

"You got a bit distracted in there," Rho said.

"Yeah." Daisy nodded. "It was bad. I knew General Clean was there, but I just couldn't focus. Did he say anything to me?"

"Something odd," Rho said. "I didn't catch its meaning." She glanced at Spencer for clarification, but he paled at the realization of what Clean's nonsensical message to Daisy could mean.

The Gateses might be in danger!

Spencer stared at his friend, but he couldn't bring

himself to tell Daisy. He had to get to the Gates home and make sure everything was all right.

"We have to go!" Spencer blurted. He darted through the doorway and up the stairs to the hallway. He didn't wait for the others. He didn't want to explain it in front of Daisy.

Now a half hour after school dismissal, most of the students had already gone home, but a few still lingered near the front office. Spencer didn't care if they saw his glowing hands. He had to get to Daisy's house! Clean had already taken the Zumbros. Spencer wasn't going to let him take the Gateses.

He raced past the cafeteria, rounded a corner, and passed the drinking fountain outside Mrs. Natcher's classroom. It was more than a regular drinking fountain, of course. It was the source of all Glop. Spencer and Walter had created it, and the Witches had surfaced from its depths.

Spencer knew that the Witches were somehow watching over the Glop source from afar. Every time Marv approached the fountain, Sweepers arrived within seconds to stop him. But something about it didn't seem right. The enemy Sweepers were quick to bat the janitor away from the Glop source, but they never once attempted to detain or abduct him.

Against the adversity, Marv had succeeded in taping off the drinking fountain and covering it with a black garbage bag. An out-of-order sign, scrawled in the janitor's awful handwriting, was tacked onto the top.

These were simple precautions, aimed at keeping curious students away, as if the horrid sulfuric smell wafting from the source wouldn't do that. On really quiet days in the classroom, like last week's end-of-year math exam, Spencer could hear the gentle gurgle of the Glop as it roiled in the drinking fountain.

Spencer didn't pause to listen or smell now. Desperate to reach the exit at the end of the hallway, he was sprinting by Mrs. Natcher's classroom when a sneakered foot thrust out of the doorway, tripping him.

Spencer went down hard, tucking his glowing hands close to his chest and taking the fall on his shoulder. He slid a record distance across the hard floor, finally coming to a halt as his attacker stepped out of the classroom with a satisfied sneer.

"Why are you in such a hurry, Doofus?" It was Dez, his leathery Sweeper wings tucked tightly across his back and his unnaturally muscular arms folded across his chest.

Dez Rylie was the only Rebel Sweeper. The bully had taken a potion from New Forest Academy and turned himself half Rubbish. He could fly and belch dust, but none of his special abilities could prevent Alan Zumbro from insisting that he go back to school. So Dez was once again a full-time student at Welcher Elementary School. His giant black wings looked out of place to Spencer and Daisy, but only people who had used pink soap would be able to see his Rubbish side. Dez looked perfectly ordinary to his classmates and teacher.

Spencer groaned, but not out of pain from his fall—the Glopified coveralls had protected him. The groan was from sheer annoyance at running into Dez. Spencer didn't even bother to give the Sweeper kid an answer. Dez was a nuisance, but he wasn't a threat. They'd learned to work together—most of the time.

On his feet once more, Spencer finally reached the door at the end of the hallway. He turned sideways and slammed against it. When the door didn't budge, he gave it a solid kick.

"Helloooo?" Dez said. "It has a doorknob."

"Yeah, well, I can't really touch the doorknob right now," Spencer said, extending his hands for Dez to see.

"Whoa! You're all glowy!"

"Would you just open the door?" Spencer yelled.

"No way," Dez said. "What do you think I am, your servant?"

Rho and Marv arrived, Daisy a few steps behind. She had ditched the clown shoes, tiara, and foam hand, but the Dracula cape was still tied around her neck.

"Oh, no," Daisy said when she saw who had joined them. "What's Dez doing here?"

"Not opening the door for Spencer," Dez answered.

"Why are you at school in the first place?" Daisy gestured all around them. "School's out. You should go home."

"Mrs. Natcher made me stay after to take a test."

"Then why aren't you taking the test?" Daisy asked.

"Mrs. Natcher's not the boss of me," he said.

"Where is she?" Daisy asked, peering back down the hallway toward the classroom.

"Sleeping," Dez answered. "I really like that green spray."

"You didn't!" Daisy gasped. Green spray knocked people unconscious and erased a few minutes of memory leading up to the spraying. How Dez had come by a bottle, Spencer could only guess.

"Would someone *please* just open the door?" Spencer shouted.

"I don't feel like it," Rho said. Surprised by her bored tone, Spencer turned to find her sitting on the floor, her knees tucked up against her chest. "It doesn't matter anyway. We'll never make it anywhere before the Sweepers find us."

"What's the matter with Rho?" Daisy asked.

It was Marv who answered. "Rubbish breath," he said. "Classic symptoms."

Daisy glanced down the hallway. "I don't see any Rubbishes."

"Except for the giant one standing next to you," Spencer said. "Dez, your breath is affecting Rho."

"Oh, please," he said, breathing into his hand and trying to smell it. "It's not that bad."

"Your *Rubbish* breath," Spencer said. "It's causing apathy. She's giving up, and we kind of need her right now!" If only they had vanilla air freshener. It was designed to counteract Toxite effects.

"You have to hold your breath," Daisy said.

"That's stupid!" replied Dez. "I'm not doing that."

"Hold your breath!" Marv demanded, shooting Dez a nasty glare.

25

The Sweeper kid rolled his yellowish eyes. "For how long?"

"A couple of days ought to be enough," Spencer said.

"Ha ha." Dez faked a laugh. Then he drew in a deep breath, his broad chest swelling. Daisy stepped forward and opened the door for Spencer as Marv helped Rho outside.

With Dez holding his breath and a blast of fresh air in her face, Rho revived instantly. "The truck's over there," she said.

The team raced across the parking lot toward a Glopified garbage truck idling by the dumpsters. The kids were familiar with the armored Auran trucks. The Rebel garbologist, Bernard Weismann, had commandeered Rho's old truck, and Daisy had even driven it once. This one looked much the same, but the paint was bright orange.

They were almost to the truck when Rho grabbed Spencer's arm. Pulling him aside from the others, she looked him in the eye. "What is going on?" she demanded. "What did Clean mean about his socks?"

"It's a code phrase that the Gateses use," Spencer explained. "Daisy's parents have known about Glop from the beginning. They pretend to be oblivious because it's the only way they can stay safe. But if General Clean knows about the family code, then I'm afraid he'll go after them."

"Or he may already have them," Rho said.

"It doesn't make sense," Spencer said. "Why today? They've never come after Daisy and me before."

"You were not the target," said Rho. "If Clean had wanted you, he would have taken you weeks ago. You don't

26

really think you are escaping danger, spending every day so close to the Glop source?"

"What do you mean?" Spencer asked.

"They're taking everyone," answered Rho. "All the Rebels. But someone has to be left to pay the ransom. You, Daisy, and Marv know too much. When everyone else is captured, the BEM will cut you a deal—give them the nails and the Rebels will be spared. Isn't that what General Clean said before he destroyed your house?"

Spencer gritted his teeth in frustration. He wasn't being ignored by the BEM, he was being used!

Rho's eyes flicked to the glow around Spencer's hands. "It's fading," she whispered. "We don't have time for the Gateses." She paused, then added, "You know they're already gone, Spencer."

He shook his head. Rho had spoken exactly what he felt, but the need to check on Daisy's parents outweighed any other option. "We'll be fast," Spencer promised. He had no idea how long the magical Aura would linger around his hands. He'd never tested its duration before. Usually he used the magic right after he spat.

Rho nodded and dashed off toward the truck. As Spencer drew nearer to the vehicle, he saw the driver. Sitting behind the wheel was a grumpy-looking old man with a mullet and a foam-front baseball cap. But Spencer knew the driver was only an illusion created by the Glopified windshield. As soon as the passenger door opened, he saw inside the cab.

The actual driver was a girl who looked to be no more

than thirteen years old. She had dark skin, but her hair was stark white, formed into dreadlocks. Spencer remembered that her name was Gia, derived from the colony she had originally served—Georgia.

"What took you so long?" Gia asked.

"There's been a setback," Rho said, climbing into the cab.

"We have to stop by Daisy's house," Spencer said. It was difficult to enter the high cab without using his hands. "It isn't far."

"Why are we going to my house?" Daisy asked, finally untying the Dracula cape.

"Just want to make sure everything's all right before we head to the landfill," Spencer said.

"But my parents are home."

"Good," Spencer said. "I hope so."

As Gia pulled out of the parking lot, Dez made a deep gasping sound. "Did somebody count that? I held my breath for like five minutes!"

In the close proximity of the cab, Dez's Sweeper breath was already causing Rho to wilt. "That was weak," Spencer jibed, hoping it would coax Dez into trying again.

"Oh yeah?" said the predictable boy. "Count *this!*" Dez drew in another deep breath, his face already turning red.

CHAPTER 4

"HE HAS A THING AGAINST GERMS."

The same eerie stillness that had surrounded the Zumbros' house greeted them at the Gateses'. Spencer had a sinking, sick feeling in the pit of his stomach. And Daisy's cheerful cluelessness didn't ease his guilt for not telling her why they had come.

Gia stayed in the garbage truck with Dez. It wasn't hard to convince him to stay behind, since going with Rho into the house meant he had to hold his breath. Even with his enhanced Sweeper abilities, Dez was getting light-headed.

There was one thing that Spencer could always count on when approaching Daisy's house. But this time, there was no barking black dog. Marv extended his razorblade as they stepped onto the front porch.

The door to the house was not only unlocked, it was open. Daisy pushed it inward and called for her parents.

Spencer cringed at her loud voice. Rho gave him a look indicating he should silence her. But Daisy's shout seemed to do no harm.

"Whoa!" Daisy said once she stepped inside. And, peering over the girl's shoulder, Spencer understood her surprise.

The Gateses' house was empty. Literally, empty.

The normally inviting living room was bare, the leather couch, love seat, and armchair gone. There were no lamps, no coffee table, no bookshelf. Even the large rug was missing from its spot in the center of the room.

"This is . . . unusual," Daisy muttered, moving into the next room. The Rebels followed, Spencer scanning for any sign of the enemy. Clean was definitely not here, but neither were Daisy's parents, nor any of the Gateses' belongings!

Spencer knew they were too late. General Clean had beaten them to the house, taken Mr. and Mrs. Gates, and cleared everything out. Spencer didn't understand why, but the vacant home gave him an unsettled feeling.

They stepped into the kitchen, which seemed spacious with the dining table, chairs, and barstools missing. Mrs. Gates's cherished china cabinet was nowhere to be seen, the wall looking blank where it had once stood.

Daisy stopped, swiveling suddenly to face Spencer. "I think I know what's going on here," she said.

Spencer felt his stomach twist, wondering if it would be better to quickly tell Daisy the truth or to let her come to it on her own. He braced himself.

"My parents are deep cleaning the house again," said Daisy.

Spencer exhaled, her statement a far cry from what he was expecting. "What?"

Daisy nodded. "Every now and again, my parents move some furniture around so they can deep clean the carpets."

Spencer looked at her—Gullible Gates. She didn't see the signs that were so apparent to everyone else. Daisy's parents weren't deep cleaning the house. They'd been captured!

"I better check on my Thingamajunk," said Daisy, slipping out the back kitchen door.

Spencer, Rho, and Marv stared at one another in silence. "You have to tell her what really happened," Rho finally said.

Spencer shook his head. He couldn't do that to Daisy. She wouldn't handle it well, and he needed her to stay strong. "We'll find her parents," Spencer said. "They'll be with my family and the rest of the captured Rebels. We'll rescue them. Daisy doesn't have to know."

"Take a look at this," Marv said, holding out a scrap of paper. "Found it on the countertop." The big janitor held out the note for Spencer to read.

TELL ME WHERE THE NAILS ARE AND
I'LL TELL YOU WHERE YOUR PARENTS ARE.

There was no signature. A note like that didn't need to be signed. It was definitely from Clean. It was the same bargain he'd tried to strike with Spencer. This time it was intended for Daisy. But she didn't know the location of the nails either.

"Throw that away," Spencer said. "We can't let Daisy see it."

Marv hesitated for a moment, then crumpled the paper in his beefy hand. He glanced around the kitchen for a spot to discard the note.

"The garbage can's under the sink on the right side," Spencer said. He knew, because Daisy's dad had a saying for anyone who asked where the trash can was: "It's right there, under the sink. Get it? *Right* under the sink."

Marv opened the door below the sink, but the trash can wasn't there.

"Figures," Spencer said. "The BEM even stole the garbage."

"Nope," Marv said, opening the cabinet door on the left and finding the forsaken garbage can. "Other side." But as the big janitor tossed the wadded paper into the trash, Spencer saw something he recognized.

"That textbook!" he said, pointing into the trash can. "Pull it out." For once, he was grateful not to be able to use his hands. Reaching into the garbage was nasty business.

Marv withdrew the textbook and held it out for Spencer's examination. Once more, the boy felt his spirits fall. It must have been visible, because Rho asked, "What's the matter?"

The moldy textbook in Marv's hand was much more than an ordinary book. Spencer could see short stubs of broken pencils jutting out of the pages like crooked teeth.

And there, wedged between two of the pencils, was a pink retainer.

It was Bookworm's jaw.

The Thingamajunk had a way of traveling through trash. His body changed every time, but one thing remained the same: Bookworm's head was always comprised of a dented lunchbox, fused to a moldy textbook that dangled open like a mouth.

As Marv turned the textbook over, Spencer saw the place where the lunchbox was supposed to be. There was a sticky residue around the edge of a depression. Whatever had happened to Bookworm had resulted in his head getting split in two.

There was only one way that Spencer could say it. "Bookworm's dead."

The back door opened and Daisy reappeared, her usual optimism dimmed a bit. "That's weird," she said. "Bookworm isn't out there."

Marv dropped Bookworm's severed jaw back into the trash can and quickly shut the door below the sink.

"In fact," Daisy said, "nothing's out there. The tool shed is empty."

"Maybe your parents took Bookworm for a walk." Spencer tried to sound convincing, as if the truth he'd just learned didn't make his heart ache.

"Maybe," Daisy responded.

They all stood in awkward silence for another moment, the emptiness of the kitchen akin to the feeling in Spencer's gut.

When it was clear that Spencer had no plans of breaking the news to Daisy, Rho finally spoke up. "We should get to the landfill. Spencer's Aura looks like it could run out at any moment."

They filed outside to find that Gia had backed the Glopified garbage truck into the Gateses' driveway. She and Dez were standing by a short ladder that led up to the top of the truck bed.

"Ready to un-Pan the boys?" Gia asked him as they approached the truck. That afternoon had brought bad news after bad news. Spencer was more than ready to do something good.

Gia was the first through the portal. She scampered up the ladder and dove into the back of the garbage truck, disappearing immediately. Daisy was next, but as she leapt out of sight, Spencer realized that he was going to have a problem.

"I don't think I can climb the ladder without using my hands," he said. This was getting tiresome. He couldn't wait to un-Pan the Dark Aurans so he could touch things again.

"That's what I'm here for," Dez said. The Sweeper kid jumped into the air, his leathery wings unfurling. Before Spencer could protest, Dez snatched him around the middle and hoisted him into the air. "I've always wanted to throw you in the trash!"

They were above the garbage truck now, a little higher than Spencer felt was necessary. Looking down, Spencer could see through the open hopper right into the pile of trash.

"Bombs away!" Dez yelled, releasing Spencer and spiraling down behind him.

They dropped into the garbage truck side by side and burst out through a dumpster at the landfill. Dez grabbed Spencer by the arms, and, with one flap of his wings, they were both standing on a dirty concrete platform, surrounded by a semicircle of Glopified dumpsters.

They weren't alone. Besides Gia and Daisy, who had passed through before, there were seven other Auran girls. They looked roughly Spencer's age, with brilliant white hair and three hundred years of experience. Spencer was grateful that V wasn't there. He didn't know how he would react when he saw her. Rho said V had turned to their side, but last time he'd come to the landfill, V had betrayed Spencer.

"Who's the Sweeper?" asked an Auran named Shirley. She pointed at Dez.

"He's with us," Spencer said. "Most of the time."

"Why's the boy glowing already?" Dela asked, pointing at Spencer's hands.

"Spencer activated the magic before we found him," Gia responded. "Don't know how much longer it'll last."

As if in response to her statement, the glow around Spencer's hands flickered. His window of opportunity was closing. And it wouldn't open again for another two days.

There was a disturbance in the dumpster, and Spencer turned to see Rho leap over the edge and land beside him. Marv was right behind, exiting the dumpster a bit less gracefully than Rho.

"Where are the boys?" Rho said, a hint of urgency in her voice as she scanned the faces of her fellow Aurans.

"Don't know," said Lina.

"Late to their own party," Jersey said. "Why am I not surprised?" The ten Auran girls didn't exactly get along with the three Dark Auran boys. And although they were finally all on the same side, Spencer knew it would be difficult to let go of the feud that had existed between them for so many years.

"Can't you call them or something?" Daisy asked.

"That would be far too convenient," said Sylva, clearly annoyed by the secretive nature of the Dark Aurans.

"They can't be far," Gia said. "Let's spread out and find them before Spencer's Aura burns out."

The glow flickered again, and Spencer held out his hands helplessly. The Auran girls scattered, leaving Rho with the Rebels on the concrete dumping pad. The moment the others were out of sight, Spencer saw movement behind one of the dumpsters.

Olin stepped into view, his face smudged with dirt and his cutoff sleeveless shirt filthy. His white hair was buzzed quite short, and the bronze dustpan fused around his neck looked painful.

His appearance was so sudden that the Rebels started with fright. By the time they relaxed, Aryl and Sach had also arrived.

"That's better," said Aryl, taking off the hood of his brown cloak.

"We can't stand an audience," Olin said, tugging at the Pan on his neck.

"Especially them," Sach added, gesturing toward the building where the Auran girls lived.

"Marv," Olin muttered, reading the sewn name patch on the janitor's big coveralls. The boy turned to Spencer. "Looks like my instructions for the Vortex worked," he said, pointing back at Marv. "You got your friend."

"Yep," Spencer said. "Now I'm here to hold up my end of the bargain." He stretched out his left hand. The glow was sputtering now. "We don't have much time," Spencer said. Since the power would take a few days to recharge, he would only be able to undo one of the boys. "I'll un-Pan Olin. Once he's free, Olin can un-Pan Sach, who can un-Pan Aryl."

"No need for that," Sach said. "We have a way for you to un-Pan all three of us and still keep your power to help the Rebels."

Spencer was puzzled. "It doesn't work like that," he said, surprised that the Dark Aurans seemed to have forgotten the rules that governed their own magical abilities.

Sach ignored Spencer's doubts. "Who brought the sponge?" the Dark Auran asked.

Aryl reached into his cloak and withdrew a yellow sponge about the size of Spencer's fist. He held it out, coaching Spencer on what to do. "Right hand," he said. "You have to Glopify the sponge."

Spencer held out his Glopifying hand. "What's it going to do?"

"No time for explaining," Olin said as the Aura on Spencer's fist sputtered again. "Besides, I don't think you'd like the answer. Just do it."

To speed up the decision making, Aryl gently tossed the sponge toward Spencer's outstretched right hand. Spencer's fingers closed around it, and he felt the magic flow through him, Glopifying the yellow sponge and draining his reserves.

It was done in a moment. The glow faded from Spencer's hands and the sponge shimmered slightly. It felt wet and heavy in Spencer's hand, but other than that, it didn't seem very extraordinary.

"Is it done?" Daisy asked.

Spencer nodded, discouraged. "And I've got nothing left," he said, knowing that it would be another few days before his power recharged. He looked at the Dark Aurans, feeling sorry that his promise to un-Pan them would yet again be postponed.

But Aryl was grinning. "I think you've got all the de-Glopifying power you need right there." He pointed at the soggy item in Spencer's hand. "That, my lad, is a spit sponge."

"A spit sponge?" Spencer shuddered, quickly withdrawing his hand and dropping the yellow sponge to the concrete.

"Told you he wouldn't like the answer," Olin said. "He has a thing against germs."

"Doesn't everyone?" Spencer said. "I mean, who really *likes* germs?"

"I do!" Dez said. "Germs rock!"

"You're disgusting," said Daisy.

"If by disgusting you mean amazing!" He flexed his large biceps.

"What does a spit sponge do?" Rho asked.

"Spencer," Sach said, "when you activate the magical Aura, what do you do?"

"I spit," answered Spencer.

"Right. And when you touched that sponge, your Glopified spit was infused into it," Sach explained. "Now you don't have to wait for a regeneration period. You don't even have to spit. All you have to do is wring a bit of spit out of the sponge, rub your hands together to activate the Glop, and you're at full power."

Spencer stared at the wet sponge lying at his feet. It was a brilliant tool, and it could make a huge difference in getting needed Glopified supplies into the hands of the Rebels.

But, really? A spit sponge? Could it get any grosser than that? Even if it was his own spit, Spencer didn't want to pick it up, let alone carry it around.

"What if it . . . leaks?" Spencer asked.

"It won't," Aryl said. "The sponge will only release the spit when you squeeze it with the same hand that Glopified it. To the rest of us, the sponge feels dry."

Marv bent over and picked it up. Spencer was surprised to see that the sponge hadn't left a wet mark on the concrete where he had dropped it. Still, Marv shouldn't be touching other people's spit sponges. Spencer reached out and took it from him.

"I don't know about you," Olin said, "but my neck

is really itchy. You know, I don't think I've been able to scratch it for about two hundred years."

Spencer shook his head. Here he was, worried about the germs in his spit sponge, while the three Dark Aurans were still under the curse of the Broomstaff.

Spencer held up his sponge and squeezed. A dribble of saliva ran into his left palm. He shivered, trying really hard not to think about what it was. Instead, he focused on the task ahead.

"It's time to set you guys free."

CHAPTER 5

"WE'RE IN THIS TOGETHER."

Olin was the first to get un-Panned. Spencer extended his glowing left hand and pressed it against the hard bronze. A bright magical pulse shot through the metal. There was a resounding crack, and Spencer stepped back.

Olin leaned forward. The dustpan around his neck was no longer Glopified. A jagged split down the back let the first bit of fresh air onto the bare skin of his neck. Olin reached up, taking the Pan in both hands and bending it open. It slipped away from his body, and he let it clang to the concrete pad.

His skin looked raw and painful. Huge calluses had formed on the spots where the Pan rubbed most. The rest of his body, tanned and tough from so many years in the Texas sun, was a stark contrast to the pale, tender flesh that had been hidden under the Pan.

Olin reached up and rubbed his neck with both hands. There was a huge smile on his face and he finally broke into a joyful laugh.

"Is it as good as you remembered?" Aryl asked.

Olin nodded. "Even better."

"What are you waiting for?" Aryl asked Spencer, clearly anxious to go free. "There's plenty of spit in that sponge. Once you release the three of us, we'll Glopify sponges for ourselves. Then we'll see if we can't create a few more weapons for your Rebel friends."

Spencer nodded. The spit sponge was a bonus he hadn't expected. He already felt more useful, knowing he could use his Glopifying powers without waiting for them to regenerate.

Wringing out the spit sponge twice more, Spencer quickly un-Panned Aryl and then Sach.

"I don't get it," Dez said, watching the Dark Aurans laugh and rejoice. "So they took off their weird necklace thingies. What's the big deal?"

"It's not a necklace," Daisy explained. Marv and Dez hadn't been with them on their first trip to the landfill. "It's a Glopified dustpan that stopped them from using their powers and kept them trapped on the landfill."

"What kind of powers?" Marv asked.

"Basically the same as Spencer's," said Daisy. "But they've got a lot more experience."

"Sissy powers," Dez said. "Nothing beats my wings."

Sach twisted his head back and forth, feeling the full range of motion in his neck that the Pan had denied him.

He gave a celebratory laugh and kicked his broken Pan. It skidded across the concrete pad and came to rest at the feet of someone who had just stepped out of the Auran building.

It was V.

She stood rigid, her impossibly long white hair swirling around her in the breeze. She held a slender black shovel in one hand like a staff, the butt of the rawhide-wrapped handle against the ground, with the tapered trowel above her head. In her other hand, she casually held a mug of soda, brimming with fizzy bubbles.

V's presence instantly killed the jubilation of the Dark Aurans. They stood beside Rho and the Rebels, watching the thin girl walk slowly toward them.

"Free at last," V said, gesturing to the fallen, de-Glopified Pans. "What will you do with your newfound freedom?"

It was silent for a moment. Then Aryl replied. "I suppose it's time to do what the Witches created us to do."

"What's that?" Spencer asked.

"Destroy the Toxites," said Olin. "Forever."

"You have a plan?" V asked.

Sach chuckled. "Plans," he said, "happen to be our specialty."

"I'll call the others," V said. She lifted the mug to her lips like she might take a sip, but paused when Aryl cut in.

"No," he answered, striding toward the Auran building. "We'll take it from here. Just us and the Rebels. The last thing we need are you meddling girls."

V's face darkened and she lowered her mug. With her other hand, she swung the Spade around until the pointed shovel stopped just under Aryl's chin. "It's no mystery that I don't like you boys," she muttered. "But the Witches have betrayed us all. We're in this together. We agreed upon that."

Olin stepped up, pushing the Spade away from his friend's face. "Very well," he said. "You alone. Besides, we might need your shovel."

"What about Rho?" Spencer blurted. She was standing there between Marv and Dez, looking small. Under strict orders from Marv, the Sweeper boy was holding his breath again. Not only did it protect Rho from his Rubbish effects, but Spencer liked how it silenced Dez's usual annoying commentary.

Rho stared in silent pleading at the Dark Aurans. If they were only going to trust one of the Auran girls, shouldn't it be her?

"Why not?" Sach said. "Rho took a chance on us. Without her, we'd probably still be feuding." He glanced around the concrete dumping pad, scanning for any of the other Auran girls. "Let's hurry inside," he said, "before the others come back."

V led the way into the sturdy cinder-block building. Months had passed since Spencer had been inside, but the interior was just as gloomy and dim as he remembered. They moved down a hallway and into a spacious room where the vaulted ceiling was pocked with skylights.

The first time Spencer had met the Aurans it had been here, sitting around the large circular table with thirteen chairs. V and Rho had lied to him at this table. He was counting on it to be different this time.

Olin shut the door behind them, switching a dead bolt to lock it shut. Daisy, V, and Rho were already settling into the wooden chairs when Dez took a gasping breath.

"I think you guys are trying to make me get light-hearted!"

"It's *light-headed*," Spencer corrected. "Although it's hard for an empty head to get any lighter."

"Whatever," Dez said, still panting for breath.

"Hold it," Marv demanded, one strong hand on the back of Dez's neck.

"I don't think that will be necessary any longer," V said. The spade was propped against the tall back of her chair. She set down her mug and produced an aerosol can of vanilla air freshener. She spritzed a mist across the room, and Rho instantly perked up.

"Take a seat," Marv ordered, dragging the annoying Sweeper into a chair beside him.

"I could take you down if I wanted to," Dez grumbled.

Spencer rolled his eyes as he seated himself with the Dark Aurans. "We're all on the same team," he reminded Dez. He glanced across the table at V, hoping that was really true.

"Speaking of teams," Sach said. "Last time you came to the landfill, there were more of you. Where are the other Rebels?"

There was a moment of silence before Marv answered. "This is us."

"What do you mean?" Aryl asked. "What happened?"

"The BEM is capturing the Rebels, one by one," Spencer answered. "They've got almost everyone. And those of us left are almost out of weapons."

"What about the old warlock, Walter Jamison?" V asked. "Our visions went dark after the Witches returned."

"So did mine," Spencer said. "But you wouldn't be able to see Walter anyway. When we opened the Glop source, the Witches took us by surprise." Spencer swallowed hard at the horrible memory. "Walter didn't survive."

A respectful silence hung in the room. Then Sach continued. "Is there anyone left who might be of use to our cause?"

"What about the garbologist?" Rho asked.

Marv shrugged. "Haven't heard from Bernard in a week. BEM probably got him by now."

"We have Bookworm!" Daisy said.

Spencer and Rho shared a guilty glance. Marv seemed to study the wooden tabletop.

"He's a great fighter and he can travel fast through the garbage," Daisy went on.

"I don't think we can count on Bookworm right now," Spencer finally said.

"Why not?" Daisy asked.

"Well . . ." Spencer thought about telling her the truth, but he could only imagine the devastation it would cause her to find out about her missing parents and dead Thingamajunk. "Bookworm's all the way back in Welcher,"

Spencer invented. "I don't think we have time to go get him."

Daisy nodded. "Okay," she said. "At least we know where to find him if we need him."

"I can't say I'm encouraged by our numbers," Sach said. "You're sure there's no one else?"

Spencer thought about it for a moment. "I guess there's Min and the Monitors," he said. Min Lee was a genius kid they'd met at New Forest Academy. He had organized a network of student spies across the nation who monitored their school janitors and sent reports of suspicious activity. "But they're just a bunch of regular students. I'm not sure how they'd do if we called on them to fight."

"Let's hope we don't have to find out," said Aryl. "But it doesn't hurt to list them among our allies."

"Now," Olin said, "let's get to business." He turned to Spencer. "You said you helped Walter Jamison open the Glop source?" Spencer nodded. "So you know where it is?"

"It's a drinking fountain at Welcher Elementary School," he answered. "Why?"

"Because now it's time to close the source."

CHAPTER 6

"I LOVE BINGO!"

Marv leaned across the circular table. "Believe me," he said, "we've tried to destroy the source. Hit it with all we had. BEM has Sweepers protecting it."

"The Glop source can't be destroyed," Olin explained. "But it can be closed."

"How?" Daisy asked.

"The same way it was opened," said Aryl. "With a Glop formula."

Spencer remembered how he and Walter had added every ingredient to the drinking fountain. Spit of an Auran was the final element, which was why it had been necessary for Spencer to be there.

"As long as the source is open," Sach said, "we run the risk of the Witches getting their wands back."

"The bronze nails are safe for now," Aryl cut in. "But

it's only a matter of time before the BEM finds them. If the Witches get their wands, this war will be lost."

"So that's why we have to close the source?" Daisy said.

Sach nodded. "There are a number of reasons. For every moment the source stays open, more Toxites are being introduced to the world."

"Because Toxites are born out of Glop." Spencer shot a glance over at V. She'd been recycling the nasty liquid with her Glopified pump house. But Spencer had put an end to that operation.

"Right," said Olin. "But you have to understand what Glop is, and where it's coming from."

"Where?" Aside from the source, Spencer had never really thought about it.

"You've been there before," Olin said. "The Dustbin."

Dez moaned, obviously remembering when they had intentionally gotten sucked into the Vortex. "Not that place again! It was so . . . dusty!"

Marv folded his big arms. He'd spent more time in the Dustbin than any of them. "Glop comes from the Dustbin?"

"Indeed," Sach said. "Everything ties back to the Dustbin. Think about it—when dust gets wet, what happens to it?"

"It turns to mud," Spencer said.

"The Glop source is a spillway," said Sach. "When the source is open, magic dust from the Dustbin leaks into our world. But crossing over the threshold causes the dust to weaken and destabilize. It turns into Glop."

49

"So Glop is just muddy dust from the Dustbin?" Daisy asked.

"Basically," said Aryl. "Hundreds of years ago, the Glop source opened for the first time. We don't know exactly how it happened, but as a result, thousands of gallons of Glop leaked over from the Dustbin before the source could be closed. Since that time, those thousands of gallons have been recycled over and over, sustaining life for enough Toxites to continually regenerate and cover the nation. Now the source is open once more. Each day, hundreds of gallons of new Glop are leaking into this world through that drinking fountain in Welcher Elementary. It gets absorbed into the ground and mingles with the Glop that's already here. This is causing the Toxite population to increase, since more Glop equals more Toxites."

"So, if we close the Glop source, it'll stop the Toxites?" Rho asked.

"It'll stop the new flow of Toxites," Aryl clarified. "Then we'll just have to deal with the ones that already exist here—the hundreds of thousands that continue to regenerate in the Glop that has already leaked into the earth."

"All this sounds lovely," V said. "But who knows the formula to close the source?"

"We do." All three of the Dark Aurans said it in unison.

"The Witches gave us the recipe the first time we closed the source," said Olin. "That was a long time ago. We were just kids then. But you don't forget something that important."

"You guys closed the source before?" Spencer asked.

Sach nodded. "It was a direct order from the Founding Witches. We closed the source, sealing them inside, safe and sound until the day when they were supposed to return and help us."

"Stinks to be you right now," Dez said.

"Stinks to be all of us, if the Witches have turned evil," Sach answered.

"When the Witches came back," Spencer said, "what were they supposed to help you do?"

"Destroy all Toxites forever," answered Olin.

"So there is a way?" Marv asked. It was what the Rebels had been searching for since Alan was rescued from the dumpster prison.

"Remember the Instigators from the Dustbin?" Aryl asked.

Spencer nodded, and he saw Marv's expression darken at the name. The Instigators were the rulers of the Dustbin. They had constructed a giant fortress, unleashing waves of toilet-paper mummies to wipe out any newcomers.

"The first time we entered the Dustbin," Aryl continued, "we were prisoners of the Instigators. The Witches rescued us, but as we made our retreat from the Instigators' fortress, we came across something horrible. We found the very place where Toxites originated. Three hideous nests. They were not occupied by giant beasts or monsters, but in the heart of the nests were three great brains, rotten and corrupted. Visible brain waves of light intertwined, spiraling heavenward like a beacon."

Spencer felt a chill pass through him. He remembered

what he'd seen as he rode the slipstream leaf blower out of the Dustbin. He'd looked across the wide expanse of endless dust and seen the dark fortress of the Instigators. He'd seen a beacon of eerie light rising from the heart of the black abode.

"The Instigators created the brain nests," Aryl continued, "and the Witches told us that we were the only ones who had the power to destroy them. Within us was the ability to destroy Toxites forever. The Witches called us the heroes of the Dustbin."

"So you have to go back there," Spencer said. "Back to the Dustbin."

"Eventually, yes," answered Sach. "But first, there's something we must find in order to succeed."

"We need the scissors," said Olin.

"You should have told me," Daisy said. "I have some in my backpack. I could have brought them."

Olin chuckled. "These are no ordinary scissors. They are likely the most powerful Glopified tool in history."

"More powerful than the Vortex?" Spencer asked. The deadly vacuum bag and the Spade were the strongest things he'd encountered.

"Three times more powerful, you might say," said Sach. "We Glopified the scissors together, before we got Panned. Using our combined magic, we created something that would be strong enough to sever the brain waves from the nests."

"I could probably do it with my bare hands," Dez said, but everyone ignored him.

"The Toxites are fueled by those brain nests," Olin said. "If we snip the connection, the brains will wither, and the Toxites will return to ordinary dust, never to bother another student again."

"But the Glop source must be closed when that happens," Sach added.

"Why?" Spencer asked. "If we use the scissors now, why do we even need to worry about closing the source?"

"Destroying the nests will create a lot of destructive energy," Aryl said. "We have to contain the blast in the Dustbin. If the Glop source is open, that energy will spill into our world, destroying everything in its path."

"Destruction." Dez grinned, rubbing his hands together. "Sounds cool."

"This wouldn't be the kind of destruction you want to see," Olin said. "The blast would cause the source to rip wide open. All that magic dust from the Dustbin would come through like a hurricane, turning to Glop when it entered our world. Since the dust is endless, there would be no way to staunch the flow. Earth would be completely flooded within minutes. Everything would be covered."

"Welcher?" Daisy asked.

"It would be gone," Olin said.

"San Francisco?" she persisted.

"Also gone."

"What about New York City?" Daisy asked.

"*Everything* would be flooded," Olin emphasized.

"Even China?" Daisy's eyes grew wide.

"*Everything!*" Olin said again. "China is part of everything."

"That's why closing the Glop source is our top priority right now," Sach said, getting them back on topic. "It'll stop the flow of new Toxites, make it impossible for the Witches to restore their wands, and it will protect the world from the devastation that will ensue when the brain nests are destroyed."

"Plus," Olin added, "it buys us more time to get the scissors."

"Where are they?" Rho asked. Spencer was surprised that she hadn't heard of them before, but then he remembered that the Dark Aurans thrived on keeping secrets from the girls.

"Well . . ." Olin scratched behind his ear. "We lost them."

"You created the most powerful weapon in history," V said, "and then lost it?"

"We completely underestimated the toll it would take to create something that strong," Aryl said. "The effort nearly killed us. We were left drained and vulnerable for weeks. It was months before the Glop recharged in our systems."

"When we regained consciousness," Olin said, "the scissors were gone."

"We approached the other Aurans to ask if they'd seen anything suspicious," Sach said, gesturing to V and Rho.

"You accused us!" V yelled. "You had the audacity to accuse us of stealing after you had swiped the *Manualis Custodem* for yourselves!"

"We were keeping the book safe until the proper time," Sach countered.

V shook her head, long white hair swaying. "We did what we had to do to keep you under control."

"We were weak," Aryl said. "We could barely even stand when you dragged us out to the Broomstaff!"

"If we had let you recover, you would have destroyed us all!" V said.

"Enough!" Rho leapt to her feet, slamming her hands flat against the table. "This quarrel is centuries old. Let us work together."

V and the Dark Aurans settled back in their chairs as order was restored to the room.

"Good," Rho said, seating herself once more. "Now, what happened to the scissors?"

"We don't know," Sach said, running a hand through his white hair. He shot an icy glare at V. "I'm sure someone stole them."

In response to the veiled accusation, V simply folded her arms and leaned back in her chair.

"We have to find the scissors or this will never succeed," Aryl said.

"Can't you just Glopify new scissors?" Spencer asked.

"The effort nearly killed us the first time," Olin answered. "Doing it again would surely finish the job."

"Those scissors have to be around here somewhere," Daisy said. "We can search."

"We've searched," Olin said. "We've spent the last two hundred years searching every inch of this landfill."

55

"Whoever stole the scissors," Sach said, glaring again at V, "obviously didn't want us to have them. Their first move was probably to get the scissors out of the landfill, knowing that once they were away, the curse of the Pan would stop us from ever reaching them."

"Now that we're free to leave the landfill," Aryl said, "it looks like our search parameters have opened up."

"I'll try the Silver Swiffers," Marv said.

"What kind of name is that?" Dez retorted.

"It's a retirement group," Marv said. "Bunch of old birds that worked for the Bureau back in the day. They get together on Tuesdays for Bingo."

"I love Bingo!" said Daisy. "What do they get if they win?"

"Cleaning supplies," Marv answered. "They can't let go of the glory days, and many of them illegally collect Glopified supplies. They've got a lot of old gear. One-of-a-kind stuff. They might have come across the scissors."

"Silver Swiffers," Spencer mused. He remembered hearing about them when the Rebels were picking a translator for the *Manualis Custodem*. "Wasn't Professor Dustin DeFleur part of that group?"

"The professor was dusting the floor?" Dez asked.

"No," Spencer said. "That's his name."

"I don't get it," said Dez.

"DeFleur was part of the group," Marv said. "Before he rejoined the BEM."

"He must have lost at Bingo," Daisy said.

Walter had trusted Professor Dustin DeFleur to translate

the *Manualis Custodem*. But the old professor had intentionally left out some very important parts of the handbook that
kept the Rebels from knowing that the Witches were bad.

Most recently, DeFleur had been hired as the P.E.
teacher at Welcher Elementary. He kept an eye on the Glop
source and sabotaged any work that Marv or the kids might
attempt. Spencer, Daisy, and Dez had been skipping that
class, usually sneaking down to the janitor's closet to spend
P.E. time with Marv.

"Look into the Silver Swiffers," Sach said. "I think it's
worth a shot."

"Meeting's tomorrow in southern Florida," Marv said.
"Doesn't leave me much time to get there."

"Then you'd better get on your way," Olin said. "Do we
have a truck in Florida?"

Rho shook her head. "I think Lina's parked in Atlanta.
That's our closest."

"Third dumpster from the left," Olin told Marv, gesturing past the doorway to the concrete pad beyond. "Keys
should be in the ignition. Jump through and drive the truck
wherever you need to go."

"Best of luck," Sach said. "Let's hope you have some
good news after Bingo."

Marv stood up and looked at Spencer and Daisy.
Spencer really didn't want the big janitor to go, but it would
be worth it if Bingo gave him a lead on the scissors.

"You two be all right?" he asked, rubbing a hand through
his beard. Spencer and Daisy nodded. "Stay here. Be back

tomorrow night," he said. "Don't get into trouble without me."

"Don't worry," Dez said. "We will."

"Have fun at Bingo," said Daisy. "I hope you win."

Marv nodded brusquely at Spencer, crossed the room, and disappeared into the hallway. Something about his leaving made Spencer feel alone. As he looked around the table, he realized why.

No adults.

Their Rebel friends had all been captured, and now Marv was off on a mission of his own. Spencer, Daisy, and Dez were alone with the Aurans. And while the residents of the landfill were technically three hundred years old, they sure didn't act like grown-ups.

"This is what we call *divide and conquer*," Sach said. "While Marv is off playing Bingo with the old-timers, Rho and the girls can start gathering the ingredients we'll need to close the source."

Rho nodded, using another spritz of V's vanilla air freshener to keep Dez's Sweeper breath at bay. "What do we need?"

"Basic stuff," Sach said. "A combination of six ingredients will close the Glop source." He numbered them on his fingers as he went. "Eye of Grime, tooth of Filth, beak of Rubbish, bristles of a broom, blood of an Auran boy."

"Wait! What?" Spencer cut in. He remembered that the formula to open the source had included spit of an Auran. Now blood would be required?

"So, which one of you chumps is going to die for this?" Dez asked.

"No one's going to die," Olin said. "It only needs to be a drop of blood."

"That's boring," said Dez, pretending to lose interest in the conversation.

"But the drop has to come from one of us," Aryl said, gesturing to himself, Olin, and Sach.

"What about Spencer?" Rho asked. "He's an Auran."

"And he's a boy," Daisy pointed out.

Olin nodded. "I hadn't considered it. But Spencer's blood would work too."

"That was only five ingredients," V said. "What about the last one?"

"The last ingredient . . ." Sach paused. "It might be a bit tricky to come by."

"What is it?" Spencer asked.

"We'll need a hair from the head of one of the Witches."

CHAPTER 7

"THEY KNOW I HAVE A MYSTERIOUS PAST."

W hat?" everyone cried in unison.

"How are we supposed to get a hair from the Witches?" Spencer asked. "Run up and pluck one without them noticing?"

"Nobody's even seen the Witches since they arrived," Rho said. "They've locked themselves in a room at New Forest Academy, waiting for General Clean and his Sweepers to find the bronze nails. We'll never get close enough to pluck a hair from their heads."

"Maybe we don't need to," V said, standing up. She walked around the table until she stood behind Dez's chair. Reaching behind him, she pulled a long white hair from the back of the chair. She held it out for everyone to see.

"Whoa!" Dez said. "Was that the hair on my back? I had no idea it was so long!"

60

"It's not yours, Sweeper," V said. "It's mine. I've spent a lot of time sitting in these chairs. And what a Dark Auran boy may not know is rather obvious to a girl with long hair. It gets everywhere."

She let the single white hair fall to the floor and returned to her seat.

"What are you suggesting?" Olin asked.

"If the Witches have locked themselves in a room at New Forest Academy for the last six weeks," V said, "then I'm guessing that's where we'll find plenty of hair."

"But the Witches aren't going to leave," Rho said. "The only reason they'd go out would be to get their wands."

"Then perhaps we should give them what they want," V said.

"No way!" Spencer shouted. Walter had died to keep those nails safe. Now V was suggesting that they offer them up? "Have you listened to anything we've said? If the Witches get those wands, the war is over for us."

"Relax," V said. "I'd never be such a fool to give them the real nails. But perhaps we could lure them out with some counterfeits."

"Fake nails?" Rho said.

"No, they're real," Daisy said, holding out her fingernails for everyone to see.

"That's not the kind of fake nails we're talking about," Spencer said.

"That might be crazy enough to work," Aryl said, agreeing with V for the first time.

"The nails would have to be convincing," Olin said.

61

"And the moment the Witches throw them into the Glop source, they'll know they've been tricked."

"It won't matter," V said. "All we need is a few minutes. Just enough time to slip into their empty room, collect a hair for the Glop formula, and get out. The Witches will return to the Academy in a rage, but by that time, we'll already be at Welcher, tossing the ingredients into the drinking fountain and closing the source."

"I don't know," Spencer said. It sounded risky, and Spencer had a hard time trusting any plan that V might concoct.

"I like it," Sach said. "It needs some work, but I like it."

"How are we supposed to make perfect duplicates if we don't even know where the real nails are?" Spencer pointed out.

In response, Aryl reached into his cloak and withdrew a small item pinched between his finger and thumb. As he placed it on the table, Spencer saw that it was one of the antique nails. Sach produced the next one, setting it on display before him. Olin's eyes flicked cautiously around the room before he withdrew the final nail from his pocket.

Spencer felt a chill pass through him. He hadn't seen the three bronze nails since the night Walter had died to protect them. It seemed careless to have them sitting in the open.

"Alan gave them to you?" Daisy said. In the aftermath of the Witches' return, Spencer's dad had taken the bronze nails. When he had returned, Alan had assured the Rebels that the nails were so well hidden that even he did not know where they were.

"Actually," Sach said, "we got the nails from an old Thingamajunk named Bookworm." He smiled at the look of surprise in Daisy's eyes.

She turned to Spencer. "Your dad must have given the nails to Bookworm and told him to hide them."

Spencer nodded. "That's the only way my dad could get rid of them without knowing where they were hidden."

"Your Thingamajunk is quite a remarkable creature," Olin said. "He visited us independently, delivering one nail to each of us. Instead of hiding them in the landfill, we kept them close. You don't let something as important as the Witches' wands out of your sight."

"Yet you seem to have let the scissors out of your sight." V leaned forward and plucked Aryl's nail off the table. Spencer tensed, but the Dark Aurans let her examine it, seeming to bite back a number of insults and accusations.

"Lots of intricacies," V muttered, spinning the nail between her slender fingers. "It's not going to be easy to forge something to look this old. It has centuries of character."

"So do we," Sach said. "The false nails will be convincing. I can promise you that."

The answer seemed to satisfy V, and she set the nail carefully before Aryl once more. The word of the Dark Aurans seemed to carry a lot of weight. If Sach said they could deliver, V believed him.

"How do we expect to deliver these false nails to the Witches?" Spencer asked.

"We could leave them in an obvious place and hope they stumble upon them?" Rho suggested.

"That could take days—weeks," said Aryl. "It's time we don't have."

"Maybe we can put them in a box on their front porch and doorbell ditch," Daisy said.

"I think that would seem a little suspicious," Spencer said. "Besides, I don't think the Witches will have a doorbell."

"Fine," Dez said, kicking his feet onto the table and reclining his chair. "I'll do it." Everyone turned to him, and he used his wings to shrug. "I'll deliver the fake nails to the Witches."

Spencer looked at the Sweeper suspiciously. "Why would you volunteer for that?"

"Duh," Dez said. "So we can get the stupid hair and close the Glop source."

Spencer shook his head. Dez was being a little too eager. "I don't trust him. Besides, it'll never work. People at the Academy know who you are."

"That's exactly *why* it'll work, Doofus," Dez said. "They know I have a mysterious past."

"*Traitorous past* is more like it," said Daisy. "You've double-crossed us so many times I got dizzy trying to figure out which side you were on."

"That's what I'm saying!" Dez said. "It's one of my great qualities."

"Being two-faced is not a great quality, Dez," Spencer pointed out.

"It is today," he said. "I'll show up at the Academy and they'll see that I'm a Sweeper. I'll tell them I betrayed you guys, stole the nails, and brought them to the Witches. They'll totally let me in."

Spencer wished Marv were still there to shut down Dez's bad idea. Instead, the Dark Aurans embraced it.

"We can't let you go alone," Aryl said. "You'll need backup in case something goes wrong."

"Of course something will go wrong!" Spencer cried. "We're talking about Dez!"

"Then it sounds like we'll need someone to chaperone this little mission," Olin said.

"I'll go with him," V volunteered. "No one was more disappointed by the Witches' return than I was. If we're going to hit them, I'd like to be there to witness it."

Sach shook his head. "Your hair's a bit of a giveaway," he said. "Besides, the Witches know every single Auran. They made us into what we are."

Spencer shrugged. "I can't go with Dez either. The Witches will recognize me immediately. I was there when they returned."

"I suppose that leaves Daisy," said Rho, turning to her. "How would you like to be Dez's date back to New Forest Academy?"

Dez moaned. Spencer looked at his wide-eyed classmate. Daisy swallowed hard. "My dad says I'm not old enough to date."

"Think of it more like Dezmond's bodyguard," Aryl said.

"No way!" Dez yelled. "I don't need a bodyguard. Check

65

this out!" He leapt to his feet, conjuring up a belch from deep within his stomach. When it rumbled forth, he turned away from the table, spewing a stream of black dust across the room. "Do you think someone who can do that needs a bodyguard?" He sat back down in his chair as a coughing fit struck him. "Give me a drink." Dez reached out for V's mug of soda, but she moved it away protectively.

"We can't let Daisy go in alone with him!" Spencer pleaded.

"Spencer's right," said V. "The Sweeper is too irresponsible. Perhaps a good disguise can get me into New Forest Academy." She glanced at Rho, seated beside her. "It worked for Jenna."

"It's going to take more than a disguise to fool the Witches," Aryl said. He turned to Sach and Olin. "We'd better make some spit sponges of our own, lads. We've got supplies to Glopify and false nails to forge. It's going to be a long night."

"What do you have in mind?" Rho asked.

Aryl leaned across the table. "I think I know how to send Daisy *and* Spencer with Dez."

"It'll never work," Spencer reminded. "The Witches will spot me."

Aryl shook his head. "Not this time. If my plan works, *no one* will spot you."

CHAPTER 8

"YOU GUYS READY TO DO THIS?"

Spencer slept better than he'd expected, considering that he wasn't at home in his tidy room. Netty, the Auran who had given up her bedroom for Spencer, kept a clean space and seemed to have good hygiene. He awoke feeling rested and rejuvenated, anxious to see what the Dark Aurans had accomplished during the night. He'd volunteered to work with them, but the boys had insisted that he sleep. Spencer would need his strength for the days ahead.

He caught a big breakfast at the round table in the conference room. Sylva turned out to be quite the chef. Apparently, three hundred years of cooking experience led to some pretty amazing eggs Benedict. Daisy joined him for oatmeal and toast before the two of them headed outside to the dumpsters.

Dez swooped down when he saw them exit the building.

He'd been perched on the edge of the roof, like a vulture waiting for roadkill.

"You guys ready to do this?" Dez seemed a little too excited, and slightly caffeine-riddled. Spencer wondered if he'd found an Auran stash of Mountain Dew. "This is going to be awesome! Fist bump!" Dez punched Spencer in the arm.

"Ow!" Spencer pulled away. "That wasn't my fist."

"What are you doing up already?" Daisy said. "I thought we'd have to splash you with cold water to wake you."

"Nah," Dez said. "I didn't sleep at all." He was bouncing on his toes as if he might fly off at any second. "I was flying around the landfill using my super eyesight to help the Dark Aurans find stuff."

Spencer had almost forgotten that Dez's Sweeper powers helped him see great distances, even in the dark. Not to mention the fact that he didn't need to sleep for long periods of time.

"Man," Dez said. "Those guys are way better at Glopifying stuff than you are." He slugged Spencer on the arm again. "Check this out."

Dez made a giant leap forward, his black wings bearing him aloft until he came to perch on the lip of a portal dumpster. He extended a talon finger to point. Spencer and Daisy hurried to the edge of the concrete pad to look in the direction that Dez had indicated.

Spencer froze in astonishment. Daisy clapped her hands. Before them were piles upon piles of Glopified weapons.

There must have been over a hundred brooms, and at

least as many mops. Pushbrooms, vacuum bags, plungers, spray bottles, razorblades, and dustpans. Most of it looked used and beat up, but when did cleaning supplies ever look pretty?

"What do you think?" sounded a voice at Spencer's ear. He whirled around, only half surprised that the Dark Aurans had crept up on them. The three boys looked worn and tired. Spencer could only imagine the strain of the long night.

"Where did you get all this?" Spencer asked.

Sach gestured vaguely toward the mounds of landfill trash. "That's what this place was made for, remember? For centuries, janitors have been sending maxed-out cleaning supplies to the landfill. There's no shortage here."

"We just had to give them new life," Aryl said. "A bit of magic spit and these supplies are back in action. But this time, they won't ever max out."

Spencer grinned. He didn't know what to say. For the first time since Walter's death, it looked like there might be hope for the dwindling Rebel force.

"You'll need these," Olin said, holding out a couple of tool belts. Spencer was glad to see them again. He and Daisy had donated theirs to a Rebel school in desperate need. But a mission into New Forest Academy would be nearly impossible without a Glopified tool belt.

Spencer and Daisy accepted the belts and buckled them on. The belt felt right on Spencer's hips, and he realized how much he'd missed it.

"Stocked with all of the usual," Olin explained, pointing

to the U clips that held long-handled supplies and the spill-proof pouches with smaller items.

"What about Dez?" Daisy asked, noticing that there wasn't a belt for the Sweeper kid.

"I don't need weapons, remember?" he said, still perched on the dumpster above them. "I'm a walking weapon."

"The Rebels are supposed to be destitute," Aryl explained. "If we send Dez with a belt full of Glopified supplies, the Witches will be suspicious. Remember, he's supposed to be a traitor."

"Yeah," Spencer said. "We're hoping that doesn't come true."

"Relax, Doofus," Dez said. "I'm sticking to the plan this time." He pulled a Ziploc sandwich bag from his pocket and dangled it out for Spencer to see that it contained the bronze nails.

"You gave Dez the nails?" Daisy said.

"Those are the fake ones," Sach said. "I told you they'd be convincing."

"I'm not really sure how convincing they look in a Ziploc bag," Spencer said. "They're supposed to be magic wands, not Cheetos."

"Duh." Dez stuffed the false nails back into his pocket. "I'll take them out of the bag before I hand them over."

"Which brings us to the exchange," Sach said, getting them back on topic. "The moment you arrive at the Academy, Dez will be spotted. The guards might try to take the nails, but Dez will insist that he deliver them to the Witches personally. This is important: Spencer and Daisy will need to know exactly what room the Witches have been hiding in so they can search for the hair."

"What happens to Dez after he delivers the nails?" Spencer asked.

"I doubt the Witches will befriend him, if that's what you were thinking," Olin answered. "They'll probably hand him over to the Sweepers to be kept as a prisoner."

"Probably?" Spencer said.

"Either that, or they'll order him dead on the spot," Aryl said. "We're really hoping for the first option."

"And you're okay with this plan?" Daisy asked the Sweeper boy.

"I don't care," he said. "Either way, I get to bash some heads." He knocked his fists together.

"As soon as the Witches have taken the bait," Olin said, "Dez is supposed to fight his way out of New Forest Academy."

"That's the part I like," said the muscular kid.

"One Dez, against who knows how many Sweepers?" Spencer said. "He'll never make it out of there."

"Normally, I would agree with you," Aryl said. "But we're hoping that Dez will get out the same way you and Daisy will get in."

"How's that?" Spencer asked, anxious to hear Aryl's plan that would prevent him from being recognized by the Witches.

Aryl grinned. "You'll be invisible."

Daisy's eyes grew wide, and Spencer tilted his head skeptically. "Invisible?" he repeated.

"What do you know about bleach?" Sach asked.

Spencer knew that it was a harsh cleaning chemical that took color out of fabric. The first time he'd done his own laundry, he'd accidentally used bleach instead of detergent. All of his clothes in that load had come out white.

"I know you're not supposed to get it in your eyes," Daisy said. "Or on your skin."

"Glopified bleach is a bit different," Aryl said, producing a spray bottle from the stock of Glopified equipment. "It's safe to the skin. But it has an unusual effect on any object it touches."

He kicked a rock out of the dirt, about the size of a tennis ball. Stooping down, he picked it up and held it out for the kids to see.

"Ordinary bleach takes the color out of fabric, countertops, and almost everything it touches," Aryl explained. "Glopified bleach doesn't just turn things white." He sprayed the rock in his hand. "It turns things invisible."

The stone in Aryl's hand shimmered like a mirage. Then it disappeared completely. His hand was still cupped around something, but Spencer couldn't see anything at all. Aryl made a tossing gesture, and a second later, something thudded against the dirt, leaving a small impression where the invisible rock sat.

"We're going to bleach ourselves?" Spencer asked.

"Yup," Olin said. "Bleach the color right out of you."

Spencer reached out his foot and nudged the invisible stone. He felt it move, despite the fact that no one could see it.

"How long does it last?" Daisy asked. Spencer could tell that she too had some hesitations about going invisible.

"Like other sprays, the effect will last about fifteen minutes," answered Aryl.

"That doesn't give you much time to collect a Witch's hair and escape," Olin said.

Spencer didn't like operating under a time limit. "Can't we just spray ourselves again if the invisibility wears off?"

"You can spray yourself again, yes," Sach said. "But the second time, the invisibility effect is . . . permanent."

"I don't want to be invisible forever!" Daisy said.

Aryl shrugged. "Then only use the bleach once." He held the bleach bottle out for Spencer, who exhaled slowly and accepted it.

Olin retrieved a second spray bottle. He passed it to Daisy, and she clipped it on her belt.

"What about mine?" Dez asked.

"You can't walk in there with a bottle of bleach," Olin said. "They'll know you're up to something."

"Spencer will pass you his bottle as soon as the Witches have taken the nails," said Sach. "Bleach yourself and fight your way out while Spencer and Daisy find the hair."

"Yeah, yeah," Dez said. "Enough talk. Let's do this!" He dropped from his perch to land beside Spencer.

"Wait!" came a shout from across the concrete pad. Two Auran girls were rushing toward them. The one in the back was clearly Rho, and Spencer identified V by the Spade in her hands.

"Give me a bottle of bleach," V said.

"You're not going with them," Olin answered. "Invisible or not, it's too risky that you'll be caught. The Witches can't find out that we are behind this operation. If they trace Dez and the false nails back to the Dark Aurans, they'll figure out that we're trying to close the source or take action against the brain nests."

"I won't get caught," V said. "I'll stay in the truck. They need a driver to get them to the Academy."

"Then we'll send Rho," Aryl said. "We need you to use the Spade for us. There's something in the landfill we have to get."

V gripped the rawhide handle protectively. "What do you need out there?"

"The Vortex vacuum bag," Sach answered.

"The Vortex was destroyed," Spencer said. "It was in the BEM laboratory when it got flooded. It's at the bottom of the Atlantic."

"We have another," said Sach. "There were actually three Vortices. One of them was set off in the 1980s. The BEM called it an anomaly and safely disposed of it. That was Aryl's."

"The one you're familiar with was mine," said Olin. "But now it's swimming with the fishes. That leaves Sach's, but it's at least a day's journey into the landfill, stashed at one of our hideouts."

"I had no idea there were three Vortexes," Daisy said.

"Vortices," Aryl corrected.

"Huh?"

"The plural of Vortex is Vortices," he explained. "Like mouse and mice. Child and children."

"Enough!" Dez cut in. "We get it. Like sheep and sheeps."

Spencer rolled his eyes at Dez's bad vocabulary. "Why do you need another Vortex?" he asked Sach.

"It's the only way back into the Dustbin," he said. "Once the Glop source is closed, we'll need to act fast. With any luck, your friend Marv will have a lead on those scissors. As soon as we have them, we'll use the final Vortex to enter the Dustbin and destroy the Toxite brain nests."

"Why take the time to go looking for your vacuum bag?" V asked, still clutching the Spade defensively. "You're free now. Why not save time and Glopify a new Vortex?"

"It's not that easy," Olin said. "It's a rare vacuum bag that will link up to the Dustbin. Regular Glopified vacuum bags simply charge up the bits of grit inside—it's where we get vac dust. But Aryl created the first Vortex by accident. Gia had taken hold of his Pan and ordered him to Glopify a bag. For some reason, it didn't behave like the others, but instead formed a gateway into the Dustbin."

"I punctured the bag," Aryl said. "I hoped to get pulled out of the landfill. But the curse of the Broomstaff was too strong. The Pan kept me rooted while everything around me was drawn in. But I knew I'd created a real gem. When Gia came collecting, I told her it didn't work. She gave me a second shot, and the next vacuum bag Glopified normally—full of vac dust."

"We started looking for opportunities to create another," Olin said. "Over the decades, the Auran girls ordered us to

Glopify hundreds of vacuum bags. Only three of them ever linked to the Dustbin."

"Isn't there another way in?" Spencer asked, thinking back on something Sach had said. "What about the Glop source?"

All three Dark Aurans stared blankly at him. Spencer fidgeted, wondering if he'd said something wrong. In an attempt to explain himself, he went on. "You said the Glop source is like a spillway from the Dustbin. We know the Witches came through it to get here. Theoretically, couldn't someone go into the source and come out in the Dustbin?"

Olin and Sach were shaking their heads. Aryl looked skeptical. "*Theoretically,*" he repeated. "People aren't meant to touch raw Glop. I don't think anyone could survive that."

"The Vortex is definitely the only safe way into the Dustbin," Sach said. "That's why it's worth a day's trek into the landfill to get it."

"But you need the Spade to reach it," V stated.

"Which is why you simply can't go to the Academy," Aryl said.

V pursed her lips in thought. "Fine. I'll go with you."

"How will we get to the Academy?" Spencer asked.

"I'll drive you," Rho said. "But I won't stay long. The girls and I are still gathering ingredients for the formula. We'll want to be ready to close the source the moment you return."

"Take my garbage truck," V said, pointing to the first dumpster. "It's parked in Utah. Several hours' drive, but that's probably the closest you'll get to Denver."

"Finally," Dez said, winging his way to beat everyone to V's dumpster. "You guys ready to see my combat skills?"

Spencer didn't like dividing up like this. He felt as though the Rebel force was stretched so thin they might fall apart at any moment. Walter was dead; their parents had been captured along with so many of the Rebels. Bookworm was decapitated, and Bernard and Penny were missing. Marv was in Florida playing Bingo with retired janitors, while V and the Dark Aurans headed into the landfill.

Spencer put a hand on Daisy's shoulder as they walked toward V's dumpster. Daisy had been by his side from the start. Her steady presence gave him hope and courage. Now they were walking right into the Witches' lair. They were going to New Forest Academy one last time.

Spencer zipped his coveralls and climbed into the dumpster.

CHAPTER 9

"SOME CALL ME DEZ."

Rho steered the garbage truck off the canyon road and parked in a dirt pullout about a quarter mile from New Forest Academy's entrance. Dez leapt from the cab and landed squarely on the road's edge.

"Hurry up," he said, squinting against the afternoon sun. "I've got some Witches to fool." He checked his pocket to make sure the sandwich bag with the false nails was where it should be.

"We're probably going to come across some Sweepers in there," Spencer said, digging around in his janitorial belt. Vanilla air freshener would counteract the Toxite breath, but the scent might give them away. He found what he was hoping for, grateful that the Dark Aurans had been thorough in preparing the belts.

"Put on your mask," Spencer told Daisy, stretching the elastic band of his dust mask around his head.

"You guys look like dorks every time you wear those," Dez said. Spencer didn't care how he looked. Any second now and he'd be invisible.

"When should we bleach?" Daisy asked, once she got her dust mask in place.

"Better do it now," Rho said. "You don't want to risk getting any closer while you're visible."

"The invisibility only lasts fifteen minutes," Spencer pointed out. "By the time we walk to the Academy entrance, I don't think we'll have enough time."

"Who says we're walking?" Dez extended his wings.

Spencer checked his watch so he'd know what time his invisibility would expire. Then he realized that if the bleach worked, he wouldn't be able to see his watch until it was too late.

"Help me spray them," Rho called to Dez. "We don't want the bleach to wear off on one of them before the other."

Daisy handed her bleach bottle to Rho and Spencer gave his to Dez. He didn't like the idea of the bully aiming anything at his face, but if Spencer bleached himself, he might miss a spot.

"You'll probably want to close your eyes," Rho said, which was more warning than Spencer got from Dez. Spencer managed to snap his eyes shut just as the first shot of bleach misted over his face. He heard Dez's talon clicking

79

against the trigger on the spray bottle and felt a slight tingling sensation on his skin.

"Whoa!" Dez remarked. "You actually look cool for once!"

Spencer dared to open his eyes as Dez was spraying down the rest of his body. He glanced at Daisy. She didn't have a head! Her right arm had also disappeared, and Rho was thoroughly misting away.

Spencer watched his own arms and chest disappear. Looking down, all he saw were a pair of disembodied legs. Then those, too, vanished as Dez finished the job.

Spencer was completely invisible! He took a step forward, finding his movement to be no different from normal. He stomped one foot in the dirt, observing the impression that remained under him as he stood there.

"Sweet," he muttered, his voice coming out like normal.

"Remember, just because you're invisible doesn't mean we can't hear you," Rho pointed out. "It'll be a silent operation for the two of you."

Spencer nodded, then realized that no one could see it. "Right," he answered. Then, remembering part of the plan, he reached out and stole the bleach from Dez's grasp.

"Hey!" the Sweeper protested. "Give it back!" He flailed his arms aimlessly in Spencer's general direction, swiping for what must have looked like a floating bottle of bleach.

"I have to carry the bleach," Spencer reminded him. "I'll pass it to you after the nails have been delivered."

"I knew that," Dez said, folding his arms casually.

The bleach bottle was still visible in Spencer's hand, a

rather significant detail. He held it out, and Rho used hers to spray it down. The bottle disappeared in Spencer's already invisible grip. Feeling with his other hand, Spencer found an empty loop on his belt and attached the bleach bottle.

"I'm going back to the landfill," Rho said. "I'll keep a squeegee portal open for you. Once you get the Witch's hair, use your connecting squeegee and it'll take you right back to me."

"We'll be fine," Dez said. "I'll give the fake nails to the Witches, turn myself invisible, and then run the view with you guys at the squeegee."

"Run the view?" Daisy asked.

"It's something people say when they're meeting in a secret place," Dez said, wearing an expression that was clearly aimed to make Daisy feel foolish.

Spencer rolled his invisible eyes, though no one could see them. "It's *rendezvous*, Dez. Not *run the view*."

"Whatever," the Sweeper kid said.

"If for any reason you can't make it through the squeegee opening," Rho said, "the portal in the back of this garbage truck will be your backup plan." She checked her wristwatch. "You should hurry."

"Time to fly," Dez said, holding out both arms to his invisible passengers.

"It's like a group hug." Daisy's voice drifted out of nowhere as Spencer stepped into Dez's reach.

"No," said the Sweeper. "Don't say that."

They leapt into the air, and Spencer watched Rho climb

up the side of the garbage truck and jump through the portal to the landfill.

They were alone—with only fifteen minutes of safety.

Dez cut through a stand of roadside trees and bore them over New Forest Academy's outer parking lot. He swung around, depositing Spencer and Daisy next to the entrance sign.

WELCOME TO NEW FOREST ACADEMY
HOME OF THE OVERACHIEVERS

No sooner had Dez set them down than a cry went up from the Academy's defensive wall. In the bright daylight, Spencer could clearly see half a dozen security-guard Sweepers staked out on top of the brick wall.

"Showtime," Dez muttered. "Try to keep up." He took off, running a few steps and then using his wings to glide. Spencer sprinted after him, hoping Daisy was doing the same, since he couldn't see her.

By the time Dez was halfway to the Academy's entrance, he was surrounded. Spencer pulled up short behind the enemy Sweepers, bumping into another invisible person at his side.

Good. Daisy had made it.

Eight Sweepers formed a ring around Dez. Spencer was grateful for the dust mask. Without it, he would surely be drowsy with two Filth guys at such close range. Glancing around, Spencer was grateful that General Clean was not among the greeting party.

Spencer took a deep breath. It was time for Dez to play his part.

Dez folded his big arms across his chest, not looking a bit intimidated by the fact that he was outnumbered. "Take me to your leader!" He laughed at himself. "I've always wanted to say that."

"What are you doing here?" asked one of the Filth Sweepers.

"I've got something for the Witches," Dez answered.

"Let's see it."

"I don't think so," said Dez. "This is important stuff. I'm not giving it to you. I don't even know your name."

"I'm Hal. Who are you?"

"Some call me Dez. Others call me the Midnight Terror."

Spencer rolled his eyes. He thought he heard Daisy snort beside him. Dez's acting was way over the top.

"I've never seen you before," said a Rubbish Sweeper. "I thought I'd met all of my kind."

"I used to be a student here, but I've been gone for a while," Dez said. "Ask any of the Academy teachers. They'll vouch for me."

"Where've you been?" asked Hal.

"I was undercover," answered Dez. "With the Rebels." It was silent for a moment, obvious that none of the Sweepers knew exactly what to do.

"I think he's lying," said a Grime woman.

"Only one way to find out," Dez said, innocently holding out his hands. "Take me to your leader."

Hal reached down to his belt and unclipped a Glopified walkie-talkie. The two-way radio had unlimited range, and Spencer wondered who might be on the other end.

The Sweeper took a deep breath and lifted the device to his chapped lips. But before he could press the button to speak, a woman's voice crackled through the radio.

"Bring the boy to us." The voice caused a shiver down Spencer's spine. It was the voice of a Witch. He knew it. "His offer intrigues us."

Hal swallowed hard and lowered the radio, staring at his comrades.

"How do they do that?" whispered the Grime woman.

Hal began to shrug as his radio sounded once more, the woman's voice saying, "We have eyes everywhere." The Witch's answer was accompanied by a short cackle as Hal clipped the radio back onto his belt.

"Good," Dez said, stepping forward. "Let's go."

The Grime woman moved swiftly to block his path as Hal produced a roll of duct tape from his baggy pockets. He tore off a long strip, but instead of binding Dez's wrists, he stepped around and grabbed hold of a wing. Instinctively, the boy jerked free. "Nobody touches my wings."

"You want to see the Witches or not?" Hal said.

Dez gritted his teeth and allowed his wings to be folded back. In a moment, Hal had taped the tips of his wings together, making it impossible for Dez to take flight.

An invisible Spencer and Daisy followed the group of Sweepers as they escorted Dez through the great gate of New Forest Academy and onto the school's campus.

"We should call the General," the Grime woman said quietly.

Hal shook his spiky head, bits of dust shaking out of his mousy hair. "General Clean's at the prison site. He doesn't like to be bothered when he's interrogating the Rebels."

They walked past the library and the fields in front of the rec center. Uniformed students bustled from building to building, arms laden with advanced textbooks. Was it really just earlier that school year that Spencer and Daisy had fled to the Academy seeking refuge?

Spencer brushed against an invisible person at his side. Among the hum of student activity, Daisy's voice was barely a whisper in his ear.

"They look pretty studious for the last week of school," she said. "Kids at Welcher sure don't act like this."

"They go year-round at the Academy," Spencer whispered back. "No summer break for them."

Only the brightest students were accepted into New Forest Academy. The school had been created by the BEM to raise a select generation of geniuses while everyone else was polluted by Toxite breath. There was an intense week of screening, and Spencer remembered the type of kids that were accepted. They were selfish and manipulative, each one willing to step on everyone else to get to the top. Spencer felt suddenly grateful for good old Welcher Elementary School.

They were headed to the main building. The Sweepers guided Dez up the stairs and through the front doors.

Spencer barely slipped through before the door closed, and he could only hope that Daisy had done the same.

They wound through the hallway, the Sweepers politely saying "excuse us" to the Academy students. Spencer wondered how they looked to the common eye. The students couldn't see the Toxite parts of the Sweepers. They probably looked like an ordinary group of adults leading a troublemaking Dez down the hallway.

They paused at the top of some stairs leading down into the janitorial closet. The place had once belonged to Slick, but he had been eaten by his own overgrown Grime. Perhaps the Witches had moved into Slick's old office.

Hal looked at his Sweeper companions. "Lund, Wilson, Johnson. You're with me." Three of the Sweepers stepped forward, including the Grime woman. "The rest of you get back to your posts."

Half the Sweepers moved off while Hal led Dez and the others down the dim stairwell. Spencer and Daisy followed as closely as they dared. Spencer tried to line up his footsteps with the Sweeper in front of him, minimizing the chance that he'd be overheard.

When the group reached the bottom of the stairs, Spencer was surprised to find Slick's old office still unoccupied. There were boxes and racks of cleaning supplies, but no sign of the Witches.

Then Hal stepped over to a wooden pallet with a chain rising from the center. Spencer had a sinking feeling as he realized where they were going.

The hidden parking garage.

"IT'S ALL FOR THE WITCHES."

The Sweepers stepped onto the pallet with Dez at the center. All bristling with quills, wings, and tails, there definitely wasn't going to be room for Spencer and Daisy. But if they didn't make it onto the platform, there would be no chance of reaching the Witches' lair.

Dez must have realized this at the same moment. As Hal reached up to pull the chain and activate the platform, Dez thrust his arms out, knocking the Grime woman off the pallet.

She hissed in anger, and Hal seized Dez by the back of the neck with one clawed hand.

"Back off!" Dez said. "I need my personal space!" He held his arms out, drawing an imaginary circle around himself. "This is my bubble," he said. "Nobody gets in my bubble."

But in that moment, two invisible people had done exactly that. Spencer and Daisy slipped past the Grime woman and tucked themselves deep into Dez's personal space. Spencer didn't know how Daisy was faring, but he found himself in the unfortunate position of having his face pressed close to Dez's armpit. He held his breath. It did not smell pretty.

The Grime woman stepped back onto the platform, and Hal let go of Dez's neck. The boy kept his arms outstretched, maintaining his personal bubble while shielding his invisible classmates from detection.

Hal pulled the chain, and the platform began to lower. It took longer than Spencer remembered to reach the bottom. Maybe that was because his neck was cramping and Dez's armpit was sweaty.

At last, the platform settled and the Sweepers cleared off the pallet. Spencer and Daisy waited behind for a moment, catching their breath before stepping onto the first level of the underground parking garage.

The place couldn't have looked more different from when they were there last. On the mission to rescue Spencer's dad from the dumpster prison, this level had been swarming with giant Extension Rubbishes. Now it was full of racks and shelves, spanning from one side to the other. In the fluorescent garage light, Spencer saw the eclectic collection of items on display.

There seemed to be a little of everything. There were scraps of plastic, rubber, and metal. Seashells, dirt, sand, rocks. Another shelf held dried herbs and spices.

Candlesticks, cotton balls, rotten fruit, nail clippers. The list went on—the strangest assortment of random objects.

Spencer couldn't help but wonder what it was all for. The disarray was maddening to his organized mind. The whole situation gave him the creeps.

They reached the elevator on the far wall. Spencer remembered the last time they had ridden down in it. These were freight elevators, with little more than a metal grate for a door and exposed concrete flicking by as they descended.

When they reached the bottom, Spencer knew that the Grime woman who opened the door would have to remain behind to keep it open for the others. Spencer and Daisy were the first to silently slip out as the grate door opened. The last thing he wanted was to get stuck in the elevator.

The second level was even creepier than the first. Instead of the huge Extension Filths that had battled them last time, more shelves and cabinets greeted them. This time the shelves were lined with bottles and jars.

Mysterious objects floated in various colors of solutions. Spencer recognized some common ingredients like pickles and peaches. But for every bottle he recognized, there were a dozen with unknown contents.

As they walked forward, Spencer saw a row of glass bottles that seemed to hold eyeballs and organs of some unknown creature. He heard a disembodied voice beside him whisper, "eww." It seemed Daisy was just as repulsed by the bottles as he was.

Along one side of the level, special grow lights were

shining on large potted plants. That section was enclosed with some sweaty plastic, like a makeshift greenhouse.

They reached the second freight elevator and stepped inside. The grate slammed shut and the elevator plummeted. When it stopped, a Rubbish Sweeper stayed behind to keep the door open until everyone had filed onto the third level.

Spencer didn't have to worry about Hal overhearing his footsteps here. The third level was a noisy mess! Cages lined the parking garage, some small and some large. Inside the cages were almost every type of animal Spencer could think of.

"Umm," Daisy whispered at Spencer's side. "Why is there a zoo under New Forest Academy?"

"Not to mention the creepy jars and random collections," added Spencer. He didn't worry about being overheard. There were at least a hundred caged birds making a racket above them.

They passed a huge alligator, lying still under a hot light. A group of small monkeys jumped from bar to bar in their cage, howling at the passersby. There were lions and tigers and bears.

"Oh, my," Daisy said, pointing to a cage with a long-haired yak. "I don't even know what that thing is."

It looked kind of like a cow, with dingy black hair that grew so long it almost brushed the ground. The yak stared at them, chewing its cud and rubbing a horn against the bars of its cage.

"Okay," Dez said to Hal. "I was cool with the weird

piles of stuff and the bottled eyeballs. But I've got to know. What's up with the animals?"

Spencer was grateful Dez was finally asking. He didn't know how much longer he'd be able to contain himself without bursting out with the same question.

"It's all for the Witches," Hal answered. "They're Glopifying new cleaning supplies every day. But doing so requires experimenting to get the right formula. Witches' brew," he said. "And these are their ingredients."

Dez reached out and tapped the bars of a nearby cage. "They're putting kitty cats in their Glop formulas?" The kitten in the cage shrank back in fear.

"They'll use anything to get the results they want," answered Hal. "If they had their wands, they wouldn't need all this. Until we find those bronze nails, we just have to keep carting stuff down here for their experiments."

They reached the final elevator and everyone stepped inside. As they left the zoo sounds behind, Spencer wondered how much more time he and Daisy had before becoming visible again. He hoped they were close to the Witches. Based on the last time he'd been down here, the fourth level was the bottom of the secret parking garage.

"Wait here," Hal instructed the final Sweeper. The Grime guy opened the elevator door, and Hal ushered Dez out. Spencer and Daisy fell into step behind them as they made their way across the final level.

"The Witches don't get many visitors," Hal said, his voice soft in the echoing garage. "Don't say or do anything to upset them. Got it?"

"Believe me," Dez said, "the gift I'm bringing them is going to make their day."

"It better," Hal answered.

"Have you met the Witches before?" Dez asked.

"Only once," he said. "When they first arrived."

"What were they like?" asked Dez.

"They . . ." Hal began. But his mouth seemed to grow dry, and he swallowed the rest of his sentence, an involuntary shudder passing from his spiky head to his clawlike toes.

At last they arrived. Against the far wall, in the spot where Alan Zumbro's dumpster prison had once been, was a new structure.

It was a large cinder-block room, built into the existing wall. It looked plain and drab, with nothing but a heavy-looking metal door in the facade.

"This is it," Hal said. "Ring the doorbell."

Spencer squinted to see the little button beside the fortified door. The Witches really did have a doorbell?

Dez cast one glance all around the parking garage. Spencer knew he was looking for any sign of his invisible classmates. But the Sweeper boy looked right through them. Dez exhaled slowly, rolling his head from side to side in a neck-popping motion.

Then Dez reached out one taloned finger and rang the Witches' doorbell.

"YOUR FACE!"

The doorbell sounded strangely normal. Even waiting outside the door, Spencer could hear the resounding *ding-dong* as it echoed through the vast parking garage.

"Who ordered more pizza?" came a crackly voice from within the room.

"Mmmm," said another. "Lovely thing, pizza."

"It's not pizza, you idiots!" came a third voice. "It's that boy we told them to bring down."

"A pizza boy?"

"I don't want to eat the pizza boy," said the second. "I just want the pizza."

"Is one of you going to answer the door?" the third voice demanded.

"Not me!" said the first. "I'm still wearing my nightie."

94

"You're always wearing your nightie," said the second. "I'll answer the door."

Spencer braced himself as shuffling footsteps drew closer. Then the metal door inched open just a crack. Spencer saw only a sliver of the Witch's nose, crooked and warty, but it was enough to identify her as Holga.

Holga peered through the open door, gave a bloodcurdling scream, and slammed it shut.

"She was right! It's not pizza!" she cried. "It's a . . . *visitor!*"

"No, no," said the second voice. "That can't be right. We don't get visitors."

"It's not a visitor, you ninnies!" shouted the commanding voice. "We asked them to bring him down to us!"

The door cracked open again, and Spencer saw one eye peering through the frizzy black hair of Ninfa. Then she too screamed and slammed the door shut. "It's a visitor!" she screamed. "And I'm still in my nightie!"

What followed were two minutes of absolute cacophony from inside the Witches' lair. Spencer heard water running, drawers slamming, blow dryers blowing, and the distinctive sound of hairspray. Then the door flung wide open so abruptly that Dez took a step backward.

Spencer's blood went cold. In the doorway stood all three Founding Witches. They were poised for their expected visitor, fake smiles adorning their unattractive faces.

"This better be good," Ninfa said. "I got dressed for this." She tugged at her ill-fitting black dress.

"Who are you?" demanded Belzora. She stood between the other two, a head taller and rail-backed.

This was the moment they had come for. Spencer held his breath, hoping that Dez played his part convincingly.

"I'm Dez Rylie," he said. "I brought you something." He reached into his pocket and withdrew the sandwich bag and the bronze nails. "Oops," he muttered. "I meant to take them out of the bag first." Dez used his talon to rip open the baggie. Then he upended the three nails into his hand.

In unison, all three Witches leaned forward to inspect the offering. Dez extended his hand, and Spencer saw that it was trembling ever so slightly. Spencer clenched his fists. The Witches had to take the bait! They had to!

Striking like snakes, in a deft unison movement, the Witches emptied Dez's palm. They held the bronze nails close, scrutinizing the little items under the garage's fluorescent light.

Dez lowered his hand and took a step back.

"Where did you come by these?" Holga asked, pinching her nail between thumb and finger.

"I used to be with the Rebels," Dez said. "I stole the nails from a guy named Alan Zumbro."

Spencer didn't like how Dez had incriminated his dad, but at least he hadn't blabbed about their connection with the Dark Aurans.

"How do we know they're real?" Ninfa asked.

Holga stuck out her tongue and licked the nail. "Ick!" She spat on the floor. "It tastes all bronzy."

"That's because it's made of bronze," Ninfa said. "You are so thick sometimes!"

"Are you calling me fat?" Holga yelled.

Spencer was watching for any opportunity to get inside the Witches' room. But the way the three of them were standing across the threshold made it impossible. He would have to wait until they stepped outside and then slip in before they shut the door.

"You!" Belzora yelled, pointing a gnarled finger at Hal. A series of shiny bangle bracelets jingled around her wrist. "Untie this boy's wings."

Hal nodded his dusty head. Reaching up, he jerked off the strip of duct tape. Dez stretched his wings and folded them in.

"There's only one way to know if the nails are true," Belzora said. She turned to Ninfa. "Get the squeegee."

Ninfa ducked out of sight. There was a small open space in the threshold now. Spencer wondered if he could slip past unnoticed. But the risk of bumping into Belzora was too great. In a second, his window of opportunity had closed as Ninfa returned to fill her spot, squeegee in hand.

Belzora stepped down from the doorway. She walked past Hal and Dez, drawing a bottle of Windex from the black folds of her robes.

"It is time, sisters," Belzora said, misting part of the garage wall until it turned to glass. "Bring the squeegee! We must away to the Glop source!"

Ninfa leapt down, somewhat spryly for a woman her

age. She swiped the Glopified squeegee across Belzora's glass wall, and a portal fizzed into view.

Spencer was looking directly into the empty gym at Welcher Elementary. The school day had been over for some time, and by this point in the late afternoon, only a few teachers would still be around.

Waiting for the Witches on the other side of the squeegee portal was the treacherous P.E. teacher, Dustin DeFleur. The old professor was leaning heavily on his cane, mad-scientist hair frizzing out in all directions.

"Welcome, esteemed mistresses," DeFleur said, bowing as low as his stooped back allowed him. "I received your call and used the squeegee as you asked."

Spencer turned back just as Holga stepped out of the doorway. At last, the way was open! Spencer just needed to slip the bleach bottle into Dez's hand and get inside the lair.

He fumbled for a moment, finding it difficult to locate and remove the invisible bottle from his belt. At last, it came free. Spencer took a step toward Dez, pressing the bottle into the boy's Sweeper hand. Dez's fingers closed and Spencer let go of the bleach bottle.

There was an audible thud as the invisible bottle hit the floor of the parking garage. Spencer froze. Dez had dropped the bleach! He must not have had a good grip on the bottle, and since Spencer couldn't see, he had let go too soon.

"What was that sound?" Belzora spun around, her eyes flicking across the empty garage.

Spencer looked down at the spot where he thought the

bottle might be, but it was invisible. Neither he nor Dez could pick it up without feeling blindly for it.

Then Dez Rylie made eye contact with Spencer, his mouth opening in surprise. "Dude," he muttered. "Your face!"

The fifteen minutes were up. Spencer was becoming visible again. He glanced beside him to see Daisy's face shimmering into view. It seemed to be floating in midair, since the rest of her body was still invisible.

Impulsively, Dez's wings shot out, shielding the visible faces of Spencer and Daisy from Hal, Professor DeFleur, and the Witches.

"You guys should probably hurry," Dez said to the Witches. "The Rebels aren't going to be happy when they find out I stole those bronze nails." Dez kept his wings extended, but he wouldn't be able to hide his friends for long. Spencer's arms were beginning to shimmer into view.

Holga paused by the doorway to the Witches' lair, reached back, and pulled the metal door closed. She hunched over the handle for a moment, and when she withdrew, Spencer could barely see around Dez's wing to notice that she'd used a rope to tie the handle closed.

Ninfa turned to the Sweeper named Hal. "Take the boy back up." She gestured at Dez. "If he's lying, we'll want to question him before we kill him."

"No," Belzora said, jerking the squeegee out of Ninfa's hand. She stepped closer, towering over Hal. "Forget the boy. You will go back up alone. Use this squeegee to await our return."

Without needing any further convincing, Hal took the squeegee, dropped to all fours, and galloped like a giant Filth across the parking garage.

"What about him?" Holga said, pointing to where Dez stood as a human shield for Spencer and Daisy.

"The boy comes with us," Belzora said. "If he's lying, we finish him on the spot."

Spencer almost panicked. This wasn't part of the plan! If Dez went with the Witches, he would have no chance of escaping once they discovered the nails were fake!

Spencer grabbed his razorblade, ready to flick it open and protect Dez if necessary. But the Sweeper boy took a deep breath and shrugged his shoulders.

"Sure," he said. "Let's go." Then, in a final attempt to keep Spencer and Daisy hidden from the Witches, he jumped toward the portal, buffeting Ninfa and Holga with his wings. He ushered them toward the portal and then stepped through himself as Belzora reached back and shattered the glass, leaving Spencer and Daisy alone in the parking garage.

"I'M NOT VERY GOOD AT KNOTS!"

Daisy had pulled off her dust mask and was chewing nervously on her fingernails—a very strange sight since her hand was still invisible.

"What should we do?" she asked.

Spencer shrugged, slipping his own mask down around his neck. "What we came here to do," he answered. "Dez will probably try to stall them. I just hope he doesn't get hurt. Still, I'm guessing we don't have long before the Witches figure out they've been tricked."

Spencer walked over to the metal door. Both his hands were visible now, and he grabbed the rope that Holga had tied around the handle.

Daisy giggled.

"What could possibly be funny right now?" Spencer asked, looking back at her.

"It looks like you're floating," she said, pointing at his still-invisible legs. Under other circumstances, Spencer would have joined in the laughter. It did indeed look strange to see only the top half of Daisy gliding over to join him at the door.

"I can't get it," Spencer said, fidgeting with the knots. "Holga tied the door shut."

"She must be really good with knots," Daisy said. "Mine never hold very long."

"I think the rope's Glopified." Spencer stepped back. There was an easier way to do this. He reached into his janitorial belt and withdrew a razorblade. Sliding his thumb against the button, he extended the long, double-edged blade. He put the sharp edge to the rope and pulled quickly upward. The Glopified blade sliced through expertly, and the rope fell to the floor in two pieces.

"That was easy," Spencer said, holstering his razorblade. But as he took a step toward the Witches' door, he saw movement by his now-visible feet.

The rope was alive.

The two severed pieces reared up like striking snakes. Daisy screamed, and Spencer jumped backward. But the nearest rope had already bound his ankles. He fell hard to the pavement, his Glopified jumpsuit protecting him from any pain.

The second rope slithered toward Daisy. Her razorblade flashed as she cut it once, twice! But instead of falling to lifeless shreds, each piece of severed rope grew back to its original length.

Spencer grappled with the one around his ankles, wishing for a moment that his legs had remained invisible a little longer. He couldn't pry it loose with his bare hands, and he couldn't think of any other tool that would help. In desperation, he drew his razorblade once more and sliced through.

The rope fell into four pieces at his feet, each growing and slithering after him. He and Daisy retreated across the parking garage, with eight snake ropes moving in pursuit.

One rope leapt at Daisy and she sliced it in half. Nine ropes now. Ten, as Spencer cut down another that threatened to bind his feet again.

"We have to stop cutting them!" Spencer said. "It's like a Hydra. Every time we cut off its head, it grows another."

"Ropes aren't supposed to have heads!" Daisy cried. "Do you have another idea?"

Spencer reached into his belt pouch and plucked out a pinch of vac dust. He delivered a Palm Blast directly at the nearest pair of ropes. They were pulled momentarily down but seemed to slither out of it.

"Windex!" Daisy shouted, leveling her blue spray bottle and shooting a rope as it leapt at her. The rope shimmered blue and turned to glass in midair. Then it fell to the pavement, shattering into a dozen shards.

"Windex!" Spencer repeated. The ropes had clustered together, and under Spencer and Daisy's combined spray, all were quickly turned to glass. They crashed into each other, stiffening and breaking. Some reared up and tipped, shattering into small fragments.

"Phew," Daisy said.

Spencer swiveled his Windex around his finger like a gunslinger and clipped it back onto his belt. "Good idea," he began to say. But as a strange sound drew his attention back to the pile of broken glass, Spencer realized that the idea had actually been a very bad one.

The Windex effect was short-lived on the rope, and the countless shards of glass were transforming back into their original material. As they did, each fragment of rope grew to its original length, forming dozens of new snakes.

"Oops," Daisy said, clipping away her Windex.

The two kids broke into a dead sprint for the Witches' lair, leaping over rope snakes. At Spencer's side, Daisy went down, an aggressive rope wrapping around her knees and dropping her to the pavement.

Spencer doubled back, but a single rope had lassoed him around the middle, dragging him to his knees. He grunted, gripping the attacking rope in both hands. Spencer tried to rip it away, but all he could do was pull the two ends together. In desperation, he looped the rope around itself and tied it into a tight knot.

Instantly, the rope went dead, falling loosely around his middle. Spencer gave a short cry of surprise and victory. Another rope leapt onto his leg, but Spencer was ready this time. He seized the ends and tied them off, turning the Glopified rope lifeless.

"You have to tie them up!" Spencer shouted, killing a third rope that came his way.

"I told you," Daisy said. "I'm not very good at knots!"

She was lying on the pavement, Glopified ropes winding from her ankles past her middle. She was flailing desperately, trying to keep her hands free of the ropes' grasp.

Spencer reached out and grabbed her outstretched hand, trying to hoist her to her feet. One of the ropes sprang forward, and before he could react, Spencer's wrist was lashed to Daisy's.

"This could complicate things," Spencer said, grabbing the nearest end of the rope. Daisy used her free hand to seize the other and they brought the ends together.

"Okay," she said. "Teamwork!"

"Bring your end over the top," Spencer instructed, pulling his piece of rope around. The first attempt failed, and Spencer felt more ropes entwining his legs.

"Good," Spencer said, ignoring the rope slithering up his back. "Now bring it down through the middle."

"Pull!" Daisy yelled. They both tugged their ends of the rope and the knot went tight. The rope around their wrists was limp now, and Spencer wriggled free just in time to tie up the one constricting his neck.

Once the weakness was discovered, it wasn't long before Spencer and Daisy had vanquished most of the ropes. A few of Daisy's knots slipped, but it wasn't hard to pull them tight again, choking the ropes lifeless once more.

"Come on," Spencer said, as he and Daisy outran the remaining snakes. "We've got a hair to find."

They reached the metal door to the Witches' lair, and

Spencer grabbed the handle. They had lost precious time in battling off the ropes. The Witches might return at any moment. Spencer pushed open the door, crinkled his nose at the pungent smell, and stepped inside the Witches' lair.

CHAPTER 13

"THE TIME HAS COME AT LAST."

It wasn't a pretty place, and Spencer instinctively drew his hands to his chest in order to avoid touching anything.

It was basically one large room, with a kitchenette against the back wall, adorned with a heap of leftover-crusted dishes. Towers of empty pizza boxes stood like crooked architectural columns. Lumpy-mattress bunk beds were stacked three high, and experimental cleaning supplies littered the entire room. Boxes and crates were piled up everywhere, with empty jars and bottles strewn about.

"What's that smell?" Daisy asked.

"I don't think they shower much," Spencer answered. He slipped his dust mask over his face again, but it didn't help with the smell.

"Do they even have a bathroom?" Daisy asked.

Spencer simply pointed to the only other room in the

dwelling—a bathroom that looked so germ-infested, he didn't want to go within ten feet of it.

"That's probably the best place to find a Witch hair," Daisy said.

"You check it out," Spencer said, relieved that she seemed to be volunteering. "I'll look around out here."

Daisy skirted around a dingy couch with holes in the upholstery and slipped into the bathroom. Spencer moved around by the triple-decker bunk beds, careful not to touch the blankets and sheets that appeared to be falling off. He would have inspected the pillows from a safe distance if something hadn't caught his eye.

In the center of the room, previously hidden by a tower of wooden crates, was a pedestal sink. It stood like a centerpiece in the lair, its porcelain stand rising out of the floor. But more amazing than the sink was the vast pile of soapsuds bubbling up out of the drain.

The suds blossomed over the edge of the sink like a cloud. Countless soapy bubbles, piled high and stagnant, seemed to shine with an unnatural light.

Spencer stepped closer to the shimmering sink, intrigued by its prominent placement in the cramped living quarters. He squinted at the suds, noticing what he thought was a reflection in the glossy surface of the bubbles. But it was more than a reflection. It was movement.

Spencer bent closer, until his nose was only inches from the puff of suds. He couldn't believe it. Every single tiny bubble held a scene. Some displayed buildings, others showed parks and playgrounds. People walked in and out of view, like miniature humans seen through the fish-eye lens of a surveillance camera.

In one cluster of bubbles, Spencer saw a location he recognized. It was the main building of New Forest Academy, somewhere right above them. Students were making their way through the hallways, carrying books on their way to class.

"No way," Spencer whispered, as he realized what he was looking at. It was a security system. The soapsuds were like tiny cameras scattered all around, relaying live video to the corresponding suds in the Witches' sink. No wonder the old hags never had to leave their lair. The Witches could keep an eye on the entire world from their living room!

Spencer watched the cluster of soapsuds that monitored the Academy. There was at least one tiny bubble displaying every room. Several of the larger areas were being observed from multiple angles.

His curiosity piqued, Spencer reached out and touched one of the bubbles. It stuck to his finger as he pulled it away from the other suds. Gently, he held it between his index finger and thumb. When he moved his fingers apart, the bubble grew until he could read the titles of the textbooks in the Academy students' hands. Then he pinched his fingers together again and the bubble shrank back to its miniature size.

Spencer shook his head in utter amazement at what the Witches had created. He wondered what other locations were under surveillance. Welcher? The landfill?

Daisy entered the room, a hairbrush in her hand. "I

found a . . ." she started to say. But Daisy paused when she saw the sudsy sink. "What's that?"

"This is crazy," Spencer said, pulling the dust mask down around his neck again. He stuck out his finger and replaced the tiny soapsud into its cluster of bubbles. "These are all cameras, Daisy." She stepped up to the opposite side of the sink as Spencer continued scanning. "The Witches have been watching everything."

"Bernard!" Daisy cried. Spencer hurried around the sink as Daisy carefully extracted a bubble. She zoomed in by spreading her fingers the same way Spencer had done.

The soapsud showed a dim room with a single cot in the corner. The Rebel garbologist, Dr. Bernard Weizmann, sat on the floor, his aviator cap clutched in both hands and his expression worn.

"Where is he?" Daisy asked.

"I don't know," said Spencer, "but he looks like a prisoner."

Daisy's spirits seemed to fall. "They got Bernard, too. . . ."

"Which part of the sink did you get that soapsud from?" Spencer asked.

Daisy answered by shrinking the bubble back to its minuscule size and setting it back into the cluster where she'd found it.

Spencer leaned closer to the group of soapsuds surrounding Bernard, using his body to shield what he was seeing from Daisy. If her parents could be seen in the soapsuds, Spencer wanted to make sure Daisy didn't know about it. She moved around to scan the other side of the sink.

Each camera showed a simple jail cell with a different occupant. They were Rebels—all of them. Spencer couldn't count them all. There must have been hundreds, some cells housing multiple prisoners.

He saw Earl Dodge, the cowboy janitor who had helped them in Colorado. He saw so many faces he didn't know. Then he saw Daisy's parents. Mr. and Mrs. Gates were seated side by side on the wobbly cot in their scant cell. They looked tired and afraid, thrown so suddenly into the world they had tried to avoid.

Spencer didn't pause there. He kept searching the soapsuds, desperate to find his own family. At last, he saw the faces he was hoping for. Snatching up the bubble, he expanded it between his fingers. His mom was seated on one of the cots, Max asleep in her arms. His dad was crouched, talking to Spencer's other siblings, who sat in a frightened huddle.

Spencer shrank the soapsud and returned it to its place. He couldn't bear to watch any longer. And he couldn't afford to let Daisy search the suds. This would not be a good time for her to discover that her parents had been taken too.

Spencer grimaced. Their families were imprisoned and he didn't even know where they were. Somewhere in that cluster of soapsuds there had to be a clue to the location of the prison. But there simply wasn't time to scrutinize every bubble.

Spencer had an idea. He didn't know how long the soapsuds could exist apart from the Witches' sink, but it was worth a shot. He found an empty jar on the floor, a bit of red liquid dried on the side. Mustering his strength against the germs, Spencer picked it up and returned to the sink.

Cupping his hand, he scooped up the entire cluster of soapsuds that displayed the Rebel prisoners. Trying not to pop any, he slipped the shimmering suds into the jar and twisted the lid on. The soapy bubbles ran down the inside of the jar, pooling in a fluffy mound at the bottom.

"Did you find a hair?" Spencer asked, remembering what they had come for.

She held up a pink hairbrush, clogged with gnarly black hairs. "More than one," she answered, tucking the brush into her belt.

"I don't know how you picked that thing up." Spencer shuddered. "You're braver than I am."

"I'm sterilizing myself when we get back," Daisy said. She cast one last glance at the sink of soapsuds and froze.

"What is it?" Spencer said, taking a step toward her. Wordlessly, Daisy pointed into the shimmering camera lenses.

It was a cluster of suds displaying Welcher Elementary School. Spencer saw multiple angles of the gym and cafeteria. He saw Mrs. Natcher in her classroom, still hunched over her desk even though school had been out for nearly an hour.

Then he saw the drinking fountain—the source of all Glop. The garbage sack that had covered it was ripped away, and the caution tape and out-of-order sign were crumpled on the hallway floor.

Spencer plucked out the soapsud and zoomed in by expanding his fingers. Standing before the source were the

Founding Witches and Dez Rylie. They stared into the gurgling mess of Glop, the fake bronze nails still clutched in Belzora's hand.

"They haven't done it yet," Spencer muttered, wondering what kind of delay Dez had provided them.

"Make it bigger," Daisy said. Spencer couldn't stretch his fingers any farther. Daisy reached out with both hands and gently took the soapsud from him. The sudsy bubble clung to both of her palms, and when she spread her arms, the image grew with it.

The display was so large now that Spencer could see a bead of sweat on Dez's forehead. He saw a tuft of whiskers jutting from Holga's chin and a mat of spiderweb in Ninfa's hair.

"The time has come at last," Belzora said.

Daisy jumped at the sound of the Witch's voice. It sounded hollow and far away, but at this magnitude, the soapsud seemed capable of relaying sound.

Belzora lowered her head, arm extended to drop the nails into the Glop source. Her voice was low in recitation.

> *What mighty power was in these nails*
> *Shall be for stories and for tales.*
> *For hither comes the greater power,*
> *With wands we'll shape this final hour.*

The Witch took a deep breath.

"I like that poem," Ninfa said.

Holga nodded in agreement. "It rhymes."

Belzora dropped the bronze nails into the fountain.

"YOU KNOW WHAT'S FOR DINNER?"

The bronze nails landed with three distinct *plops* in the gurgling Glop source. Far away, in the Witches' lair, Spencer held his breath and Daisy, still holding the soapsud, did a nervous shuffle.

Things were about to get very bad for Dez Rylie.

"What's happening?" Holga pushed forward to peer into the Glop fountain. "Why's it taking so long?"

"Patience, dear ones," Belzora said, though Spencer could see that she too was growing anxious.

The Glop went still for a moment, and then the fountain began to hiss. All at once, there was a burst of light and fire. The Glop source erupted as three items rose from its depth.

"Ah, yes," Belzora said, reaching down and withdrawing the first item. "There we are."

It was a wand!

Spencer felt a rush of cold fear wash over him. A combined sense of helplessness, loss, and betrayal struck him all at once. He glanced at Daisy, but she was frozen, her mouth wide in shock.

Belzora held the wand aloft. It was made of bronze, weathered and worn like the nail that had preceded it. It was twisted and tapered, just over a foot long.

By the time Spencer's shock had worn off, Ninfa and Holga had also retrieved their wands from the Glop source, which was now back to gurgling in its usual fashion.

"Feels right in the hand, doesn't it?" Ninfa asked, flexing her fingers around the bronze piece. Hers was straight like a thin pipe, with rings that formed ridges down its sides.

"It's been too long," said Holga. Her wand was the shortest and thickest. Grooves had been forged into one end, perfectly formed to her fingers.

It was over now. The Witches had their wands. Spencer was shaking his head, a sick feeling in his stomach. How had this happened?

"Boy!" Belzora shrieked, turning to face Dez. He stood as rooted as a tree in the hallway. She began to cackle. "You have earned a place at our side!" Belzora pulled Dez into a tight embrace.

"Yeah," Dez said, once she let him go. "I told you the nails were real."

"No," Daisy muttered, barely hanging on to the large soapsud. "What have you done, Dez?"

115

Spencer gritted his teeth in anger. "We never should have trusted him! I knew it!"

"What now?" Dez said, giving Holga a high five.

"The surviving Rebels will be squashed beneath the power of our wands!" Ninfa cried. "We must return to the Academy at once. Summon General Clean and his Sweepers."

"You know what's for dinner?" Holga asked.

"Pizza?" Dez guessed.

Holga shook her head. "War."

Daisy's trembling hands closed, popping the surveillance bubble. The soapy film splattered across the room, shattering the image of defeat and betrayal.

"He tricked us," Daisy mumbled. "Dez is a bad guy."

"He must have switched the fake nails for the real ones sometime during the night," Spencer said, recalling how Dez hadn't slept at all. Spencer sighed hopelessly. How Dez had managed the deception wasn't important right now. If the Witches were coming back to New Forest Academy, then it was definitely time to leave.

"Come on, Daisy." Tucking his stolen jar of soapsuds under one arm, Spencer crossed the room and pulled open the metal door. He stepped down to the parking garage pavement, cautious of all the snake ropes still littered about. The knots seemed to be holding; the ropes were lifeless and nonthreatening.

Spencer drew his Windex and misted the wall next to the spot where Belzora had made her entrance to Welcher. It turned to glass as he took his squeegee from the belt.

"Dez must have dropped this," Daisy said, picking up the bottle of bleach that had become visible.

"Not like he needed it," Spencer said bitterly. He swiped the squeegee across the glass surface, waiting for Rho to complete the portal and welcome them back to the safety of the landfill.

They waited for only a few seconds before the stripe of sizzling magic transformed into a doorway. Spencer peered through the portal.

"That's not the landfill," Daisy pointed out, looking over his shoulder.

"That's the Academy," Spencer said, backing away from the portal. "That's the main building right above us!"

"What do we do?" Daisy said.

A familiar face peeked into view, long white hair swishing as she whispered. "Quickly!" V said. "We don't have much time."

"Why are you at the Academy?" Spencer asked.

"There's been a slight problem," V answered.

"Where's Rho?" added Daisy.

"Long story. She's been injured," explained V. "The squeegee was stolen. But I got it back . . . sort of."

Spencer drew a pushbroom and stepped through the portal. He recognized the location better now. It was Director Garcia's old office. If he remembered correctly, they weren't far from the front door of the main building. It would be a straight run across campus, a quick flight over the Academy wall, and down the road until they reached the garbage truck.

Daisy followed him through the portal as V brought the squeegee handle around and shattered the glass. "Don't want anyone following us," she muttered, discarding the squeegee as Spencer moved toward the office door.

"Wait," V hissed. "There are Sweepers out there!"

Spencer took a moment to slide his jar of soapsuds into his largest belt pouch. It was a tight fit at first, but the pouches were bigger on the inside. Once the bottle was stowed, he gripped his pushbroom with both hands, ready to burst into combat.

"Where's Dez?" V asked, fumbling with a handle on her own janitorial belt.

"He tricked us," Daisy said. "He gave the Witches the real nails."

"What?" she gasped.

"It's bad," Spencer said. "The Witches have their wands."

V shook her head. "Well, that really backfired on us." She drew a new squeegee from her belt. "This should take us back to the landfill." She crossed to a tall vanity mirror and swiped the squeegee downward, opening a fizzing, shimmering exit.

The new portal was completed, filling up the mirror across the office. But again, the view through the gateway was not the landfill they were expecting. It was Welcher Elementary School!

Professor Dustin DeFleur stepped away from the threshold, a squeegee in his hand. In a heartbeat, the Witches were there, standing face to face with Spencer, Daisy, and V, in Director Garcia's old office.

"Hello again, dearie!" Ninfa gave a false smile when she saw Spencer. "I suppose it's a waste of breath to ask you what you're doing here. We've learned everything we needed to know from our little helper."

Belzora stepped aside, and Dez appeared through the portal. Spencer felt a swell of rage building inside him.

"How could you?" he yelled. Spencer hurled his push-broom like a spear, hoping to knock Dez clear back into Idaho.

It was sailing through the air, on a direct course for the Sweeper boy's chest, when Belzora's wand flashed out of the concealment of her black robe. A stream of dark dust spewed from the tip of the bronze wand, catching the push-broom midflight and reducing it to harmless particles. Then the cloud of dust vanished, leaving only a musty smell in the air.

"Oh," Belzora said. "You're surprised to see what our wands can do? You haven't seen the half of it."

Ninfa's wand spewed a gritty streamer, the magic dust instantly closing the portal to Welcher and leaving nothing but Spencer's frightened expression in the tall vanity mirror.

Belzora put a hand on Dez's shoulder. "Go quickly and summon General Clean." She flicked a channel of dust from her wand. It struck the office door and obliterated it. The dust hung in the doorway like a curtain as Dez stepped toward it. Spencer didn't want him to escape. It wasn't fair that Dez got away without punishment.

"Sorry, guys," the bully muttered. Then he stepped through the veil of dust and into the hallway. Spencer saw the open door as an opportunity. He would rather face the Sweepers out there than the Witches in the office.

Spencer grabbed Daisy's sleeve and sprinted for the exit, V jumping after them. He was just feeling like they might make it when his head suddenly slammed into a solid piece of wood.

Spencer fell back, dazed to see that the door was in its place once more. The lingering dust from Belzora's wand had re-formed the door exactly as it had been. Spencer only remembered seeing that kind of creation power once before, but it wouldn't be possible on earth.

"How did she do that?" Daisy asked.

Spencer mumbled in disbelief. "Dust."

"I think you're catching on," Belzora said. She twirled her wand between her thin hands, the bangle bracelets on her right wrist jingling. "Our wands are linked to a place of dust and raw magic. You've been there before. You call it the Dustbin."

"That means we can un-imagine anything we don't like," Ninfa said. Dust issued from her wand, decimating Director Garcia's desk.

"And imagine anything we do like," added Holga. Her wand flicked around, a small spiral of dust leaking out and forming into a cheese pizza. It landed with a splat on the office floor.

"The wands magnify the effect," Belzora said. "The magic is ours to bend and to shape. We are the rulers of the dust, more powerful here than we ever were in the Dustbin."

"You were down there?" Spencer said. "You were in the Dustbin that whole time?"

Belzora nodded. "In fact, I believe you met some of our creations." She raised her wand. "Let me refresh your memory."

The magic dust swirled and a humanoid shape appeared. It was made entirely out of quilted toilet paper, with two rolls for hands and a vacant gap for a mouth.

"You will come with me for questioning." Its voice was whispery and threatening. One of the rolls flicked out, releasing a streamer of toilet paper that lashed around Spencer's chest.

"I don't think so!" Daisy said. Her razorblade flashed, severing the toilet paper from her friend. Spencer followed up with a second blow, his blade slicing the TP mummy down the center and reducing it to dust.

"This can't be true," Spencer muttered as the pieces started falling into place.

"The TPs belong to the Instigators," Daisy said.

"Don't you get it?" V said. Spencer and Daisy turned in surprise as V strode over to stand beside the three women.

"The Witches *are* the Instigators."

CHAPTER 15

"THAT WOULD RUIN EVERYTHING!"

It was a horrible revelation, adding to the list of lies and deceit. The Instigators were the ones who had created Toxites. They had captured the Dark Aurans and performed experiments on them. . . . Spencer couldn't believe it was true, but at the same time it began to make sense. Had the Witches been evil from the very beginning?

V smirked at the look of shock that Spencer and Daisy wore.

"What are you doing?" Daisy asked her.

"Collecting my reward," answered V.

Ninfa reached out and put a protective hand around the girl's thin shoulders. "V has been a wonderful little helper."

"I thought that's what Dez was for," Spencer said.

"Don't be foolish," Belzora replied. "That boy is nothing but a nuisance."

For once, Spencer momentarily agreed with her.

"So Dez wasn't part of this?" Daisy asked, her hopes seeming to rise.

"Of course not," V said. "I couldn't trust someone like him. During the night, I swapped the real nails for the false ones after the Dark Aurans had forged them. Dez had no idea what he was really doing. Once the Dark Aurans were far enough into the landfill, I gave them the Spade, doubled back, took Rho's squeegee, and led you here."

"She *is* very clever," Holga said.

"If Dez wasn't working with you," Spencer said to the Witches, "then why'd you let him go?"

"Punishment was waiting for him outside," Ninfa said. "Sweepers deal with Sweepers. It's an internal affair."

If Dez had walked out of the office and into a trap, the Sweepers wouldn't go easy on him. At least he hadn't betrayed the Rebels . . . again. Spencer wished he had the chance to thank Dez Rylie, but he feared that opportunity would never come.

"Now," Belzora said. "What was it you came for?" She tapped her pale chin with the tip of her wand. "Oh, yes. Search them for a Witch's hair."

Spencer glanced at Daisy. If the Witches found the hairbrush, the Rebels would have no way of closing the source. That was assuming that they even survived the next few minutes.

Holga's stubby wand released a thread of dust that curled forward with tremendous speed. It struck Spencer's belt, reducing the buckle to mere particles. His belt slipped from his waist, caught in the wake of Holga's wand dust. It tumbled to the office floor in front of him and was joined by Daisy's belt a second later.

V stepped forward and rifled through the contents of both belts, shaking her head as the search turned up negative. Spencer glanced at Daisy. She stood rigid, her right hand in a fist as V stepped closer and began to inspect her coveralls. She patted Daisy's pockets before moving on to frisk Spencer.

"Nothing," V finally said. "The only hairs on them are the ones attached to their heads."

Spencer never took his eyes from Daisy. Where was the hairbrush? Had she left it behind in the parking garage?

Ninfa gave a shriek of victory, her wand tip coming around on Spencer and Daisy. A blast of wand dust shot out, forming midair into a familiar rake. Spencer tried to step aside, but the projectile rake was moving too quickly.

The wooden handle slammed into the floor directly between Spencer and Daisy. The metal prongs of the rake expanded over them, growing so quickly into bars that they knocked the two kids together.

In a heartbeat, the rake had become a cage, crushing all hope Spencer and Daisy had of escaping the Witches in Garcia's office. Spencer had been imprisoned in a rake cage before. The only way to retract the bars was to twist the rake handle.

Spencer grabbed the wooden handle that rose in the center of the cage, but he knew it was useless. The rake cage would open only if a hand from the outside twisted it.

"That's better," Ninfa said. "Hairless and trapped."

"Goodie," said Holga. "Their plan is derailed. They cannot close the source without a hair from our heads."

Ninfa nodded. "And unless they feel like blowing half the earth into dusty particles, they cannot destroy the nests while the source is open."

"That's a relief," replied Holga. "We worked too hard creating those brain nests to have some little brats destroy them."

"You created the Toxites?" Daisy whispered in horror.

"From scratch," Ninfa said, taking a curtsy.

It was one thing to know that the Instigators had done it. Now they were looking at them, realizing that the revered Founding Witches had started it all. . . . Spencer shook the bars of their cage, and Daisy looked like she might cry.

"We needed something that would dull the mind," Belzora explained. "Something that would sweep across this growing nation and infest the schools, targeting the future's greatest asset—an active mind."

"But we didn't want to take possession of a few struggling British colonies," Ninfa cut in. "During our time, America was not the world power that it is today."

"There was that whole Revolutionary War thing," Holga added.

"So we waited, tucked away in the security of the Dustbin," Belzora continued. "Wars were fought and our nation grew, while school janitors, spread across the states, fought a secret war against the very Toxites we created."

"Then, in the prophesied Day of Wickedness, when our

three warlocks felt as bitter about the world as we did, the Warlocks Box was opened," said Ninfa. "The pieces were in motion, and our Toxites were finally allowed to do what we created them to do."

"Now we are back," Belzora said. "Stepping into a world of possibilities. In a few short years, the cycle will be complete. Then we will lead the Academy students to rule over the mindless masses!"

Holga cackled. "Mindless masses!" she repeated. "Nice alliteration."

Spencer tried to process it all. The Founding Witches had created the Toxites in the Dustbin. Hundreds of years ago, they had opened the source for the first time, letting through a wave of Toxites that would continuously be recycled at the landfill. It was just the right amount of creatures, and the nation's janitors could keep them at bay until the time was finally right to withdraw. That time was now. The source had reopened and the final phase of the Witches' three-hundred-year-old plan was in effect.

"What's your part in this, V?" Spencer asked, watching her through the bars of the rake cage. He couldn't understand why anyone would side with the Witches after hearing their centuries-old scheme. "What did they promise you?"

"V has been very helpful," Belzora said. "We needed someone trustworthy to watch over the Dark Aurans. It isn't good for them to be free. Something could happen to them. Something bad."

Spencer swallowed hard. "You're going to kill the Dark Aurans?"

All three Witches burst into demented laughter.

"Don't be foolish, boy!" Holga cried.

"The Dark Aurans mustn't die!" said Ninfa. "That would ruin *everything!*"

"Why?" Daisy asked. "You don't seem to care about anyone else."

"Only the Dark Aurans have the power to destroy Toxites forever," Belzora said.

"I know," Spencer said. Aryl had told him that. "Isn't that just another reason for you to want them dead?"

"You don't understand," Belzora said. "The Dark Aurans are the only things keeping the Toxites alive. That's why the boys are the only ones who can destroy them."

"If you want the Toxites destroyed so badly," Ninfa added. "Go back to the landfill and kill your friends. If the Dark Aurans die, the Toxites die with them."

CHAPTER 16

"WE'LL FIND ANOTHER WAY."

Spencer could barely even comprehend what the Witch was saying. "No," he muttered. "You're lying."

"The Dark Aurans have been to the Dustbin before," Belzora said. "Many, many years ago. We captured them— three outstanding pupils in our village. And while they never saw the faces of the Instigators, we were there, performing experiments that would change the world."

"Olin was particularly alert and attentive," Ninfa said. "The opposite of his greatest attribute is found in the Filths that spawned from his sharp mind. We can thank Olin for the fatigue and exhaustion that the Filths exhale."

"Aryl was proactive," Holga said. "Quick to volunteer, always working hard. His mind led to the creation of Rubbishes, instilling apathy and boredom into the most eager students."

128

"Sach was unusually focused," said Belzora. "He could spend hours working on projects and finding solutions. His disciplined mind formed Grimes, exhaling distraction into every classroom."

Spencer rested his forehead against the bars of his cage. He couldn't believe it. The Dark Aurans—his friends—were the very cause of the Toxite infestation.

"Refraction Dust," Ninfa said. "That was the crowning achievement of our experiments with the Dark Aurans. The Refraction Dust extracted the boys' best qualities and created brain nests that would fuel Toxites with the opposite effects."

"Once our experiments were finished and the brain nests were formed," said Belzora, "we 'rescued' the boys from the *Instigators*. It was the only way to gain their trust."

"But we couldn't let them wander about unsupervised," Ninfa said. "Teenage boys have a knack for finding trouble. So we created babysitters for them." She pointed at V. "We picked our girls thoughtfully, careful to give them immortality but not the Glopifying power of the boys."

"That made them jealous, see?" Holga said. "Right from the start, we planted the idea that the boys were evil. We created the Broomstaff and gave V specific instructions to Pan them at the first sign of darkness."

"Then their security was assured," Ninfa remarked. "Stuck in the landfill, never growing older, our boys fueled the Toxites for centuries."

"And now we need them more than ever," Belzora said. "The Dark Aurans must keep breathing, keep thinking, keep fueling the Toxite brains until our mission is complete."

"Why are you telling us this?" Spencer asked.

"We wanted you to know what you've been fighting for," Belzora said.

"Think of the times you found yourself in combat defending Olin, Aryl, and Sach," said Ninfa. "We wanted you to know that you were really defending Filth, Rubbish, and Grime."

"Would you have changed your mind if you'd known who they really were?" Belzora asked. "It calls into question your character. Would you let your friends die to rid the world of Toxites?"

Spencer didn't even hesitate with his answer. "I would never turn on my friends," he said. "We'll find another way."

"Yes, yes," Ninfa said. "Those silly scissors."

"The Dark Aurans weren't supposed to make those, were they?" Daisy said. She'd been silent in the rake cage for so long. Now Spencer thought she sounded hopeful.

"It wasn't ideal," Holga said.

"They were just doing what they thought you had created them to do," Spencer said. "Make something powerful enough to destroy the brain nests."

"While the boys were Panned, they posed no threat to us," Belzora said. "They could make a million scissors capable of destroying the brain nests. Under the curse of the Broomstaff, they could never leave the landfill."

"But then I came along," Spencer said, drawing

courage from the fact that he'd done something to offset the Witches' master plan.

"Didn't see that coming," Holga admitted.

"Now the boys are free," Spencer continued. "They'll use the scissors and destroy the Toxites, fulfilling exactly what you said they'd do!"

"Not going to happen," Ninfa said, placing a protective hand on V's shoulder. "We know the scissors are lost. By the time you find them, we will have crushed the Rebels and Panned the Dark Aurans anew."

"You told them everything?" Daisy shouted at V. "I'm glad I never told you who I have a crush on!"

"I didn't need to tell them anything," V said, looking small amidst the three Witches. "I just had to let them see for themselves."

Spencer thought about V's statement, the truth suddenly dawning on him. "Soapsuds," Spencer said, feeling betrayed to know that the Witches had been watching their council at the landfill. He wondered where the tiny bubbles had been hidden so no one noticed them.

"Oh, he's sharp," said Holga, pretending to give Spencer a poke with her finger.

"Our surveillance suds can form themselves on any puddle of standing water," Ninfa explained. "But the Auran council room was dry. We needed V to provide a liquid surface."

"Your mug!" Spencer said, remembering how V had brought a mug to the table with her. "Those bubbles weren't from the root beer! Those were soapsuds!"

"You drank soapsuds?" Daisy seemed disgusted. "Does that mean the Witches can see your insides?"

"No," Spencer said. "V never took a single drink. That mug wasn't there because she was thirsty. It was there because she was letting the Witches spy on us!"

"What does it matter?" V shouted. "After I succeeded in swapping the nails, I knew my time was coming to an end."

"You're going to die?" Daisy asked.

"Eventually, yes," V answered. "And to me, that is welcome news." She stepped forward, her long hair swirling around her. "I regretted my choice to become an Auran." She spoke softly, even though it was obvious the Witches could hear. "Others grew up. Others moved on. Not us. I was trapped forever in this body, denied the normal life I could have lived. Instead of growing old and enjoying one lifetime, I grew bitter and resented four lifetimes. The only hope I've held on to was the return of the Witches."

V glanced back at them as if they were some kind of deliverers. "That's why I tried to give away the *Manualis Custodem* two hundred years ago. I wanted the Witches to come back. When they finally did, the other Aurans turned away, vowing to fight the Witches. I saw my hopes of ever growing old fade away. So I played along. I joined your Rebellion. But I had one more mission to accomplish."

V turned away from Spencer and Daisy, facing the Founding Witches. "You have your wands," she said. "Just as I promised. Now let me age, as you promised."

Belzora stepped forward, a smile on her face. "So much potential. You have a wonderful lifetime ahead of you," she said. Carefully, the Witch selected one of the bangle bracelets around her wrist and slipped it off.

"In the precise moment you became an Auran," Belzora said, "the years that you would have aged were siphoned away into the nearest bronze object—a Timekeeper. We prepared this bracelet for you, keeping it safe all these years—a time capsule of your life."

Belzora held out the Timekeeper ceremoniously. "You have earned this moment, Virginia. Enjoy every year." She slipped the bracelet onto V's slender wrist.

A ripple of magic crept up her arm the moment the bracelet touched her skin. V stumbled back in shock. She was growing taller, bigger. Ribbons of black hair flowed from her scalp, and her flowing locks extended to impossible lengths. Her clothes ripped at the seams, and she thrashed, crying out in agony.

"What's happening?" Daisy shouted, gripping the bars of the rake cage.

"We're giving her what she asked for," Ninfa said. "She's growing up."

V was an adult now, her hair filling half the room and her fingernails curling as they grew. She scratched at the bronze Timekeeper bracelet around her wrist, but her arm had grown too quickly, the skin swelling and making the bracelet impossible to remove.

"Not . . . like . . . this . . ." V moaned, falling to her knees as she neared middle age. Streaks of white reentered her hair, but this was the touch of old age. Her body seemed to shrivel and shrink as deep wrinkles crept across her face and neck.

She was dying.

"Stop it!" Daisy yelled, pounding on the cage. The Witches merely cackled.

"Nothing we can do," Holga said.

"As long as she touches her bracelet, the years will be returned to her," answered Ninfa.

V reached through the bars of the rake cage, her cry for help a painful moan. Daisy tugged at the bronze jewelry on her wrist, but it wouldn't budge. V's wrinkly hand wrapped around the rake handle. Using what seemed to be all her remaining strength, she twisted the handle.

The rake cage opened instantly, the metal prongs retracting into a tool that seemed capable of doing little more than raking leaves.

Daisy dropped to her knees, trying to administer some kind of aid to the dying old woman. V's shoulders were stooped now, her arms frail and bony. At last, the bracelet slipped from her wrist and landed with a tinkle on the office floor.

V was lying back, her head cradled in Daisy's lap.

"Spencer." V's voice was barely audible. With her limited strength, she lifted a finger and beckoned him closer. He knelt at her side, taking her hand in his. She was grandmotherly now, feeble and sickly. But below her wrinkly brow, V's eyes still burned with youthful vengeance.

"The scissors," she whispered. "They're . . . lost."

"I know," he said. "We'll find them."

"Lost . . . in the landfill." V coughed, an action that caused her eyes to close. "I . . . stole them. Long ago." She opened her eyes. "Find them."

Spencer nodded wordlessly. What could he say to someone who had lived a lifetime before his very eyes?

"Tell the others I'm sorry," V said. Her hand slipped away from Spencer's. She groped the floor beside her until her arthritic fingers closed around the bronze Timekeeper. She gripped the bracelet tightly as Spencer and Daisy watched the final years of V's life ravish her weak form. Her eyes closed for the last time, and the breath leaked out of her chest.

V's fingers went limp, and the bronze bracelet rolled across the office floor.

CHAPTER 17

"NOTHING PERSONAL."

Spencer looked up, his face hot with anger. Daisy was crying softly at V's side.

"You killed her," he said to the Witches, who stood watching impassively.

"Age killed her," Ninfa corrected. "Why do you care? Wasn't she a traitor to you?"

V had done terrible things against the Rebels, it was true. But none of that made Spencer feel like she deserved death. She just wanted to grow up. She just wanted to have a normal life.

"What now?" Spencer said. "You're going to kill us, too?"

"If we had a Timekeeper for you," Belzora said, jingling the twelve remaining bracelets, "we'd make you wear it."

Spencer couldn't afford to be discouraged by the fact that he was now the only Auran who didn't have a way to become mortal again. But even if the Witches had prepared a Timekeeper for him, the effect certainly wouldn't do to him what it had done to V. Spencer hadn't been an Auran for even a full year. Touching his Timekeeper might cause him to grow an inch or two, but it wouldn't kill him.

"You were never supposed to gain this power," Ninfa said. "So . . ." She shrugged. "We're going to have to turn you to dust."

"Nothing personal," Holga said. "We simply can't have a fourth Dark Auran running about. And since you're not tied to the Toxites, you're expendable."

Spencer judged the distance to his janitorial belt. V's gray hair had flowed over the top. It would be difficult to pick up without getting tangled. Belzora raised her wand.

There was a loud knock on the door.

"Pizza delivery?" Holga said.

"For the last time," Belzora cried. "No one ordered pizza!" She flicked her wand at the door, disintegrating it with a puff of dust. Hal, the Filth Sweeper, staggered in. There was a trickle of blood on his forehead, and one eye was already black and swollen shut.

"This better be important!" Ninfa snapped as Hal stood leaning heavily on the door frame. "We were about to pulverize someone."

"The Sweeper boy," Hal muttered. "He escaped. We've searched everywhere. He's gone!"

"And now you come crawling to us for help?" Belzora asked. "He was your responsibility."

"You seem useless," Holga said, raising her wand. "Good-bye."

A thick ribbon of dust shot from her bronze wand, striking Hal in the chest and knocking the Sweeper out of him. He struck the wall, slumping down, blinded by the force.

"Why didn't he die?" Holga muttered, inspecting her wand as if it had suddenly become faulty.

"Sweepers," Ninfa said. "You have to kill them twice." A second blast from Ninfa's wand hit the dazed Hal, instantly vaporizing him. Belzora followed up with a figure-eight wave of her wand, causing the door to rematerialize.

"See?" Ninfa said to Spencer and Daisy. "Quick and painless. You probably won't feel a thing as you turn to lifeless dust."

Spencer didn't like the idea of his body getting blasted into a million little particles. He dove for his janitorial belt, but the handles of the cleaning supplies were snagged in V's sea of hair.

"Not so fast!" Ninfa leveled her wand and released a blast of vaporizing dust. The magic attack passed only a foot above Spencer's head, reducing the filing cabinet to fine particles.

"You missed?" Holga shrieked. "How could you miss? He was ten feet away!"

"It wasn't my fault!" Ninfa said. "Someone bumped me!"

"Pitiful excuse," Holga said, pointing her wand at Daisy. She fired a deadly shot, but it went wide, vaporizing Garcia's office chair.

"You did that on purpose!" Holga yelled at Ninfa.

"Did what?"

"Bumped my elbow!" answered a furious Holga.

"I did no such thing," Ninfa defended. "You're just a lousy aim."

Spencer and Daisy were crawling toward the door, janitorial belts around their waists. The Witches' wand dust had disintegrated the buckles, so now a shred of duct tape held the belts in place. Spencer didn't know what good luck had caused the Witches to miss twice, but he had a bad feeling that Belzora would be a deadeye.

They were almost to the exit when Belzora stepped around her bickering sisters and lowered her bronze wand. Spencer grabbed a metal dustpan from his belt. As he gave the handle a twist, the dustpan fanned out into a round shield covering his head. He didn't know if it would be enough to stop Belzora's attack, but it was his only option.

Spencer heard the dry hiss of magic dust streaming from the wand. He braced himself, but Belzora shrieked in surprise, her arm jerking suddenly upward so that the attack obliterated the ceiling fan over their heads.

"Either they're all bad aims," Daisy said, "or we have a guardian angel."

"How about a guardian Sweeper?" said an unmistakable voice.

"Dez?" Spencer said. He'd heard the boy's voice as clearly as if he were standing beside him. But there was no visible sign of Dez anywhere.

The door to the office banged open, as though struck violently. Spencer felt an unseen hand grab him by the front of the shirt and jerk him into the hallway, Daisy flailing at his side. At the same moment, three accurate wand attacks blasted a hole in the floor where Spencer and Daisy had been standing. The Witches weren't likely to miss again.

"This way!" Dez's voice called as the exterior doors to the main building flung open.

"Where are you?" Spencer asked.

"Right in front of you, Doofus," answered Dez.

The Witches emerged behind them, wands flinging powerful dust toward the exit. Spencer and Daisy narrowly dodged again, propelled down the steps as the front part of the school crumbled.

They sprinted across the lawn in front of the rec center, much more agile than the aged Witches. Academy students were scattering, adding to the chaos as another blast from a Witch's wand tore a deep gouge in the grass.

Three Pluggers emerged from the computer labs: two men riding armored Filths and a woman on an Extension Grime. The Glopified saddles held them tight to their beasts, orange extension cords making an unnatural connection from their battery-pack belts into the Toxites' flesh.

When the Pluggers had almost reached them, one of the Filth riders was suddenly yanked from his saddle. His extension cord snapped as he was hurled through the air by some unseen force. The Extension Filth, now riderless, reared back and galloped away from the fight. It had no quarrel with Spencer and Daisy. It just wanted to soak in the Academy brain waves.

"Yeah!" Dez said. Spencer saw two footprints smash down the grass beside him. "Invisibility rules!"

Spencer turned just as Holga's wand released a streamer of destructive dust toward Daisy. He brought up his shield and leapt in front of the blast. It hit him like a thousand pounds, demolishing the shield and sending Spencer skidding across the lawn.

He grunted in pain. His shield arm was broken; he had heard the bones snap. Spencer's eyes rolled back as he fought to maintain consciousness against the pain.

Spencer didn't understand how the impact had hurt him. His Glopified coveralls should have prevented that sort of injury. Grasping at the zipper of his coveralls, Spencer realized that it had slipped an inch or two. V must not have zipped it all the way after she searched him for the Witch hair. Now his arm was shattered, and the pain was almost too intense to bear.

Invisible Dez picked off the Grime Plugger in the same manner as he had the first. That left one BEM Plugger on a giant Filth. Daisy delivered a Funnel Throw of vacuum dust directly into the beast's snotty muzzle. Its head dropped with the suction, leaving a clear shot for her mop to lasso the rider. The strings snared him around the shoulder, toppling him from the saddle.

Dez's arm suddenly became visible as it swung through the air, delivering a knockout punch to the unseated Plugger.

"It's wearing off!" Dez said, his entire shoulder and the left side of his face visible once more. His unseen arm suddenly wrapped around Daisy, while his visible one hoisted Spencer to his feet.

Spencer moaned at the pain. "My arm's broken."

"Boohoo," Dez said. "Don't be such a crybaby." The Sweeper boy took flight, his invisible wings snapping against the air as he bore his companions straight up.

Below, Spencer saw the Witches stomp their feet in a rage. Dust swirled from their bronze wands, the powdery magic forming into familiar shapes.

Brooms. Created out of thin air.

The Witches grabbed their solid brooms and took flight, soaring on an intercept course for the escaping kids. Dez angled hard and flew Spencer and Daisy out over the Academy wall. The Witches used their wands to alter course, scraggly hair blowing. The dust from their wands formed into buffeting winds that directed their in-flight brooms however they wished. The angry hags were coming in fast, their wands spurring the broom bristles to speeds that Spencer had never seen on a typical broom.

Dez halted in midair, his now-visible wings flapping to keep them aloft. The boy's legs were still invisible, and when Spencer looked down from the dizzying height, all he saw was asphalt and a few parked cars in the lot below him.

"You ready for this?" Dez asked, looking down and squinting one eye.

"What are we supposed to be ready for?" Daisy asked.

Dez grinned mischievously. "Trust fall!" yelled the Sweeper boy, suddenly letting go of Spencer and Daisy.

They plummeted side by side, a stomach-wrenching free

fall toward the blacktop below. Daisy screamed, reaching out to grasp the back of Spencer's coveralls. He couldn't help but flail to stop from spinning, an action that shot needles of pain all the way to his shoulder.

Then, *poof*, Spencer and Daisy were in the landfill, their momentum spitting them out of the dumpster to land in a heap on the trash-stained concrete pad.

"SHE HAD OTHER PLANS."

D ez appeared a split second after Spencer and Daisy, shouting like a maniac, "Close the dumpster! Close the dumpster!"

Rho stepped up and grabbed the black lid, slamming it shut with a resounding *clang*. Daisy removed the orange healing spray from her belt and carefully misted Spencer's arm. The magical solution was capable of knitting broken bones back together, though Spencer would have to endure several more minutes of pain before the spray took effect.

Dez let out a laugh and gave a victorious fist pump. "Man, those Witches never saw me coming!"

"Literally," Rho pointed out. "You were *invisible*."

"Did you guys get it?" Dez asked, turning to Spencer and Daisy. "Did you find the stupid hair?"

Spencer was just beginning to shake his head when

Daisy produced the pink hairbrush, choked with long, scraggly black hairs.

"I thought you dropped it!" Spencer said, feeling more encouraged than he had in weeks. "Where was it?" He couldn't figure out how V had missed it when she had searched them.

"It was in my hand the whole time," Daisy said. "As soon as the Witches showed up, I knew they would try to take it away. I used the bleach to turn the hairbrush invisible. Then I just had to make sure I didn't set it down or I'd never find it again."

Spencer grinned. Amid so much failure, he was thrilled that they had accomplished what they'd set out to do. "Nice work." He was amazed at her quick thinking. "You did great."

"It was nothing," Dez said casually.

"I was talking to Daisy," replied Spencer.

"Hey! I did some awesome stuff too," Dez said.

Spencer had a hard time admitting it, but they never would have escaped without Dez. "How did you get past Hal and the Sweepers?" Spencer asked, remembering that Dez didn't have bleach at the time.

"I have a skill they weren't expecting," answered Dez. "Burping."

"You belched at them?" Rho raised an eyebrow. It didn't sound like a very threatening skill.

"Yup," Dez said proudly. "I burped up a huge cloud of black dust and escaped while the Sweepers couldn't see anything."

"Only you could find a way to make burping your secret weapon," Spencer said.

"I made my way back to the garbage truck and came through the dumpster," Dez carried on. "Rho was sprawled out on the concrete. It seemed like a dumb time to be sleeping. I could have used some help."

"I wasn't sleeping," Rho said. "Someone hit me with the green spray and took the squeegee."

"That was V," Daisy said.

"I thought she went into the landfill with the boys," Rho said.

"She had other plans," said Spencer, wondering how to break the news.

"Anyway . . ." Dez said, annoyed that other people were talking during his story. "I grabbed some extra bleach from Rho's belt and went back through the dumpster. The first thing I did was make myself invisible. But then I realized that the BEM would be looking for the garbage truck, so I bleached it out, too. I drove up and parked it right outside the Academy wall. Then I made my way back to that office where you guys were. When Hal went inside to report to the Witches, I slipped through the door. That's when the Witches tried to blast you, so I knocked off their aim."

"That was you?" Daisy said. "I was starting to think they couldn't point their wands straight."

"Wands?" Rho said. She froze as the gravity of that statement struck her. "The Witches have their wands?"

Spencer nodded regretfully. "V swapped out the nails, and Dez delivered the real ones to the Witches."

"I didn't know I was helping V," Dez said. "I promise." He held up three fingers. "Scout's honor."

"You're not even a Scout," Daisy said.

Dez shrugged. "Doesn't mean I can't use their honor."

Rho's face was turning red, her hands clenched into fists. "Where is the traitor now?" She was struggling to keep her voice calm. "Where is V?"

Spencer and Daisy glanced at each other. When Daisy put her head down, Spencer knew it was his responsibility to break the news.

"V's dead."

Rho's expression softened, then sank. Tears welled in her eyes, and Spencer wondered what the loss must feel like. The Aurans had been together for nearly three hundred years. They shared centuries of memories. Prolonged time had given them the opportunity to grow closer than a family. No matter what V's betrayal had been, this was going to hurt the Aurans.

"How?" Rho finally managed, just barely keeping her emotions in check.

"She grew up," Spencer said. "She grew old."

"That old dead grandma lying on the floor in the office?" Dez said. "That was V?"

"Show some respect!" Daisy scolded.

"The Witches have Timekeepers for all of you," Spencer said. "They're bronze bracelets on Belzora's wrist. They kept them from the moment you first became Aurans. The years you should've aged have been collecting in the bracelets. When V put hers on, she aged so fast she couldn't get it off until it was too late."

Rho nodded to show that she understood. "I'll call the others," she whispered. "They deserve to know."

"In the end," Daisy said, "V wanted you to know she was sorry."

And Spencer remembered V's final message. The Glopified scissors were lost somewhere in the landfill. Spencer didn't know how they could possibly find the scissors when the Dark Aurans had searched the trash heaps for centuries with no luck. But he chose to take hope from V's last words.

"We need to get Marv," Spencer said. His Bingo game in Florida was a dead end. The retired Silver Swiffers didn't have the scissors. They'd been lost at the landfill all along!

"And we need to talk to the Dark Aurans," Spencer added. "When will they be back?"

Rho was staring off into the landfill, a vacant expression on her youthful face. "Sorry," she said, turning when Spencer paused for an answer. "What did you say?"

"I know this is hard," Spencer said. "But we have to keep going. When will the Dark Aurans get back?"

Rho swallowed and wiped the tears with the back of her hand. "They were going deep," she said. "Almost all the way to the Broomstaff. They won't be back until tomorrow night."

"Then we'll have to start looking without them," said Spencer.

"Looking for what?" Rho asked.

Spencer gazed out into the strange formations of Glop-tainted garbage in the landfill. Somewhere out there was the tool they needed to destroy the Toxite brain nests.

"The scissors."

CHAPTER 19

"WERE THE PRIZES GOOD?"

Spencer, Daisy, and Dez paused at the door to the conference room with the Aurans' round table. Rho had gone through Lina's garbage truck to find Marv and bring him back from his Bingo game with the old folks. All their efforts had to focus on finding the scissors, now that V had revealed their true location.

"Nobody say a word," Spencer said, grabbing the doorknob. "If V's mug is still in there, the Witches will be watching." He pushed open the door.

The conference room was empty. No one sat at the round table, and the skylights were dimmed by the lowering afternoon sun. There was only one item atop the large round table.

V's mug of root beer stood untouched from when she had left. As the kids drew closer, Spencer saw the fizzy bubbles. Knowing now what he hadn't before, he bent close and looked at the magical soapsuds.

He half expected to see into the Witches' lair, thinking he could look backward through the suds to see the pedestal sink and the horribly dirty living space. Instead, Spencer saw only the reflection of his face and the spacious room behind him.

It made sense that the soapsud surveillance worked only one way. The Witches wouldn't take a chance that someone might be able to look into the suds and spy on them.

Just to be sure that the bubbles weren't regular soda fizz, Spencer reached out and dipped his finger into the suds. He pinched a single small bubble and expanded it to a large view screen between his finger and thumb. An ordinary bubble surely would have popped by now, and Spencer had no doubt that the Witches were still watching the room.

As Spencer stared at his glossy reflection in the soapy bubble, Dez reached out a finger and popped the soapsud with his sharp talon.

"There," he said. "Problem solved."

Spencer gave him a disapproving glare as he gestured to the remaining soapsuds floating in V's mug of soda.

"There's more," Spencer said quietly.

"You mean, every tiny bubble is a camera?"

Spencer didn't know if they were all active. But based on what he and Daisy had seen in the Witches' sink, he didn't doubt it.

"We can't just pop all the soapsuds," Daisy explained.

"We have to dry up every ounce of liquid or the suds could reform."

Spencer picked up the ceramic mug, careful not to spill any of the foamy suds down the side. Daisy opened the door for him and he carried it down the hallway to the kitchen.

There was a pot of water coming to a boil on the stove and a package of pasta laid out beside it, but no one was around. Spencer assumed that the Auran chef preparing dinner must have stepped out for a moment.

Spencer crossed to the sink and carefully poured the root beer and soapsuds down the drain. He turned on the faucet, letting water flush the surveillance suds deeper into the pipes. Then he tore off a paper towel and carefully dried the sink and V's mug.

"There," he said. "Now we can talk in privacy."

It was a simple thing to dispose of the Witches' surveillance. If Spencer had known about the suds before, the Witches wouldn't have their wands and V's death might have been avoided.

"What do we have to talk about?" Dez asked. Discussion clearly wasn't really his thing.

"We need to make a plan to find the Glopified scissors," Spencer said, guiding his companions out of the kitchen.

By the time they arrived back at the conference room, Rho and Marv were waiting at the round table.

"Everything all right?" Rho asked.

"We had to take care of some soapsuds," Spencer said, placing V's dry mug on the table.

"Somebody's been drinking suds?" Marv asked.

"The Witches were watching us," Spencer said. "They use soapsuds like surveillance cameras."

To demonstrate what he was talking about, Spencer reached into his belt pouch and carefully slid out the jar of suds he'd stolen from the Witches' sink. He placed it on the table, and Marv picked it up.

"Those suds show the BEM prison where the Rebels are being held," Spencer explained. "I haven't had a chance to study them, but some of our friends and family are there." He glanced nervously at Daisy, but she didn't seem to suspect that he was also talking about her parents. She still thought they were safe at home with Bookworm.

Marv grunted as he examined the suds curiously. Then he set the jar on the table once more. "You've been busy," he observed.

"Yeah," Dez cut in. "Not all of us got to go play games with the old fogies."

"Speaking of games . . ." Daisy said. "How was Bingo?"

"Lucky," answered Marv. "Won blackout."

"Were the prizes good?"

In answer to her question, Marv placed a carton on the table. "Won this vintage toilet-bowl cleaner."

"Man," Dez laughed. "You got ripped off."

"Silver Swiffers claim it's a one-of-a-kind," Marv said, shrugging. "Carton's about a quarter full."

"What's it supposed to do?" Spencer asked.

"Made in 1962," said the janitor, reading the label off the carton. It had several holes in the top for shaking the deodorizing powder into the toilet bowl. "Silver Swiffers said it works like Toxite attractant. Shake a bit into the toilet and the little monsters come from all over the school. Once they climb inside the bowl to enjoy the powder . . ." Marv made the sound of a gunshot with his mouth. "Like shooting fish in a barrel."

"Why don't they Glopify it anymore?" Spencer asked. It sounded like a useful item to draw all the Toxites into one place.

"It could be like the Vortex vacuum bags," Rho said. "Perhaps only that specific brand of powdered toilet cleaner from 1962 Glopified properly."

"Dunno," Marv said, holding up the carton. "Just don't make it like they used to."

"I still think you got ripped off," Dez pointed out. "The grand prize was toilet-bowl cleaner."

Marv nodded in what seemed to be partial agreement. "I was hoping for the scissors."

"We know where they are," Daisy said, excitement in her voice.

"The scissors are lost somewhere in the landfill," Spencer explained.

"That'll take a lot of searching," Marv said. "We could use a garbologist about now."

Daisy nodded. "If Bernard were here, he'd tell us that we have to become one with the garbage. In order to find the trash, you have to *become* the trash."

"Philosophy for garbologists," Marv muttered.

"It's actually a pretty good idea," Spencer said.

"I think it's dumb," said Dez. "How are we supposed to become the trash?"

"We're not," Spencer answered. "We're going to find someone who already is."

CHAPTER 20

"HE'S DIFFERENT FROM THE OTHERS."

Spencer was taking charge. He had a plan, sort of. Rho was going along with it, even though she clearly expressed her opinion that it wouldn't work.

Marv had stayed back at the Auran building to study the jar of soapsuds Spencer had stolen from the Witches. Dez had also been left behind, though not by his choice. The Sweeper boy had gone to the pantry in search of a late-night snack when Spencer, Daisy, and Rho quietly slipped away.

V's dying words had revealed that the scissors were lost in the landfill, but churning through that much garbage would be worse than searching for a needle in a haystack. The ancient scissors might be buried under acres of rotting garbage. Not even the Spade could uncover something that long-lost.

They needed a way to quickly scour the trash, checking under every bag and bucket. They needed someone with a close connection to the garbage, someone who was one with the trash.

They needed a Thingamajunk.

"I don't understand," Daisy said, trying to keep pace with Spencer and Rho as they moved farther away from the Auran building. The moon was only a sliver overhead, and it was easy to stumble in the darkened heaps of trash.

"Why don't we just ask Bookworm?" Daisy asked again.

"He's too far away," Spencer said, wondering how long his flimsy lie would hold up.

"But we left Gia's garbage truck in my driveway," Daisy went on. "Can't we just jump through and talk to him?"

Spencer grunted in frustration. "It's not that simple," he said, dismissing her request again. He felt guilty when he caught Rho's eye. She knew that Bookworm was ruined, his garbage head cloven in two.

"This isn't going to work," Rho said quietly. "We've tried a dozen times since Daisy tamed Bookworm. The other Thingamajunks aren't like him. He was . . . special."

Spencer stopped at the top of a garbage mound. "Well, it has to work this time," he said, slipping a backpack from his sweaty shoulders. "We need the garbage on our side, or we'll never find those scissors."

He reached into the backpack and withdrew a glass bottle. He'd taken it from a weapons stash in the Auran building. It wouldn't do much good against other people, but it had a special use for Thingamajunks.

The bottle's lid was twisted tightly, but Spencer still held it delicately like it might spill. The contents looked vile. They were an organic mash of rotting vegetables, putrid chunks of meat, and wet, moldy bread.

"You didn't tell me we were having a picnic," Daisy said. Then she saw the disgusting bottle in Spencer's hand. "Never mind." She drew back. "I'm not hungry."

"This isn't for us," Spencer said. "It's for the Thingamajunks." It was a stink bomb, similar to the kind Aryl had used to spur a Thingamajunk stampede in the Valley of Tires. This bottle was small, and Spencer hoped it would attract only a single garbage creature.

"You have a gift?" Rho asked, as Spencer lifted the bottle to throw it. He nodded, resolute in his decision to tame another Thingamajunk. Then he pitched the stink bomb down the hill.

The bottle spun through the air before crashing into the bent frame of a discarded bicycle. The glass shattered, and the rotten mixture splattered across the debris below.

It was silent for a moment. A warm draft of wind carried the stench of the stink bomb to Spencer's nose, causing him to gag before pinching his nostrils shut.

"That makes Bernard's socks smell good in comparison," Daisy said, her voice higher pitched from plugging her nose.

"You've smelled Bernard's socks?" Spencer asked.

Daisy shrugged. "I lost a bet."

"Quiet!" Rho whispered. She was the only one not plugging her nose. Spencer supposed that living a few centuries in a landfill had probably numbed Rho's sense of smell.

The Auran girl was pointing down the slope of garbage, where Spencer glimpsed the slightest movement in the darkness. It seemed like nothing more than a ripple through the trash, like a snake cutting through tall grass.

The bent bicycle exploded as a Thingamajunk erupted from the garbage, devouring any scrap that was tainted by the stink bomb.

Spencer's flashlight kicked on, and the bright beam instantly highlighted the hungry beast at the bottom of the hill. "Hey!" he called. "Still hungry?"

In two thundering leaps, the Thingamajunk summited the mound, landing with tremendous force between Spencer and Daisy. The trash displaced under the creature's heavy feet, causing a shock wave that brought Spencer to his knees.

The flashlight rolled out of his hand, but the magical beam of light clung to the trash figure, illuminating its patchwork features.

Its head was a patterned couch cushion. The fabric was ripped on both sides, and the dirty stuffing jutted out like tufts of white hair on an old man's head. Atop the cushion was a pile of rotting potatoes, sprouting tubers from the spots that weren't soft and black.

Bits of the broken bicycle now comprised the body. Crooked spokes formed a rib cage, and the pedals served as hands. The rest of the body was mainly grocery bags, with a broom handle sticking out by the shoulder and a smashed-up vacuum cleaner for a leg. The bike bell was hooked on the Thingamajunk's elbow, and when it raised an arm to strike Spencer, the bell gave a cheerful *ding!*

"Back down, you cheap pile of scrap metal!" Rho's sudden outburst of trash-talk caused the Thingamajunk to hesitate, its arm lingering above Spencer's head. "You got stuffing in your ears? Get going!"

Technically, the Thingamajunk didn't have ears. But its couch-cushion head did have plenty of stuffing. "Wait," Spencer hissed at her. "You're going to scare it away."

It was obvious that Rho had more to say to the Thingamajunk, but she bit her tongue and let Spencer make his attempt at taming it.

He held out a hand. "It's all right, big fella. We're not going to hurt you." The Thingamajunk seemed to snort, its entire body illuminated by the fallen magical flashlight.

"I brought you something," Spencer said, digging in the open backpack at his feet. "Something special just for you." He held out the object. "It's a gift."

It was V's ceramic mug, empty and dry, leaving no chance for the soapsud cameras to re-form. Now the mug dangled by its handle from Spencer's fingertips, a simple offering of friendship to the angry Thingamajunk.

"You're trying to tame it with *that?*" Daisy said, peeking out from behind the garbage figure.

"You did it with an old retainer," Spencer pointed out. He wiggled the mug enticingly before the Thingamajunk. "Take it," he coaxed. "Let's be friends."

The creature grunted, and a bit of cushion stuffing

shook loose from its head. It reached out its hands, the two bicycle pedals carefully gripping the fragile mug.

"Good," Spencer urged, sliding his fingers out of the handle. "Friends?"

The Thingamajunk lifted the mug to what appeared to be eye level. It stared at the gift for one still moment. Then it brought its pedal hands together, smashing the ceramic mug into tiny shards.

The trash monster bellowed, and its vacuum-cleaner leg kicked out, knocking into Spencer's chest with such force that he went careening down the slope. If it hadn't been for the protection of his Glopified coveralls, the kick probably would have broken some ribs.

Lowering its head, the Thingamajunk plowed into Daisy, leapt clear over Rho, and landed at Spencer's feet. He scrambled to get away, knocking the Thingamajunk's hands aside with a plunger from his belt.

"I don't think it worked!" Daisy called as the Thingamajunk pursued Spencer back up the mound of trash.

"I don't understand!" Spencer gasped, ducking under a swinging pedal. "My gift was way better than Daisy's."

"Hey!" she objected. "Bookworm loved my gift!"

"I know, but why?" Spencer said. "What's so special about a pink retainer?"

"It was special to Daisy," said Rho. "It was a gift from Bernard's collection, and that made it meaningful."

"The mug was meaningful!" Spencer yelled. He'd reached his companions once more, and Rho threw a blast of vac dust to hold back the pursuing Thingamajunk.

"I told you this wouldn't work," Rho said, positioning herself to gain a tactical advantage against the downhill Thingamajunk. "We tried it after you left."

"Maybe we just need a better gift," Spencer said.

The Thingamajunk dropped into a heap of trash, escaping the vac dust suction that kept it rooted. It reappeared directly beneath Spencer, forming a new body from the surrounding trash as its couch-cushion head launched the boy into the air. Its arms reached out, catching Spencer as he fell and slamming him against the ground.

"Drop him!" Rho yelled. "Put him down, you soggy lump of disgustingness!"

The trash-talk took effect immediately, and the Thingamajunk stopped, dangling Spencer upside down by one foot.

"Let me give this a try," Daisy said, stepping forward. She cleared her throat and attempted to tame the Thingamajunk much as she had won over Bookworm several months ago.

"Listen up, Couchpotato!" It moved its gaze toward her, the pile of rotten potatoes shifting atop the couch cushion. "I've got something for you," she said. "And it means a lot to me." As she spoke, Daisy reached up and unclasped the necklace she was wearing. "My grandma gave me this when I turned eight. If you behave, I'll let you wear it. As a token of our friendship."

In one swift movement, the Thingamajunk dropped Spencer on his head and swiped the necklace from Daisy's grasp.

"Hey!" she shouted. But a second kick sent Daisy into a painful tumble. The Thingamajunk reared back and made a sound that could only be interpreted as a mocking laugh. Then the creature kicked up a pile of trash and disappeared into the landfill.

"What just happened?" Spencer asked, squinting out into the darkness.

"Couchpotato just stole my necklace!" Daisy said, rolling over to sit with a *huff* amidst the debris.

"That was a nice thing you tried," Rho said, placing a comforting hand on Daisy's shoulder. "A little while back, Shirley offered a music box that she'd kept for over two hundred years. Doesn't get much more sentimental than that."

"What happened to the music box?" Spencer asked.

"The Thingamajunk smashed it to splinters," answered Rho.

"Maybe he didn't like the song it played," Daisy suggested.

"They don't care about gifts or kindness," said Rho. "They're just mindless heaps of junk."

"Not Bookworm," Daisy said. "He's different from the others." She clenched her fists. "Bookworm is going to be so mad when I tell him that Couchpotato stole my necklace!"

Once more, Rho gave Spencer a meaningful glance, and he knew that the truth had to come out. Rho took her cue and slipped quickly down the garbage mound, leaving Spencer and Daisy alone.

"Daisy," Spencer said. "There's something I have to tell you."

"THAT'S A BIG WAD."

Daisy looked at Spencer, her big eyes already a bit watery from the recent theft of her favorite necklace.

"When we stopped by your house," Spencer began, picking his words carefully, "we found a note from General Clean."

Daisy furrowed her eyebrows. "What did it say?"

"He found out, Daisy," Spencer said. "I don't know how, but he discovered that your parents were in on the secret."

She stood up abruptly. "We have to warn them!" There was panic in her voice. "Clean might be on his way to—"

"It's too late," Spencer cut her off. "General Clean got your parents at the same time he took mine."

Daisy took a step away from him, a single tear slipping down her cheek. "You knew?" she whispered. "And you didn't tell me?"

"Your parents are going to be fine. They're imprisoned with the other Rebels," he said. "I saw them in the soapsuds we stole."

"Why didn't you show me?"

"I didn't want to upset you," Spencer tried to justify. Now every reason he had given himself seemed weak. He should have been honest with her from the start. "I just wanted to rescue them and get your parents home so you never had to worry that they were missing."

Daisy swallowed hard. "You can't fix everything, Spencer."

He lowered his head in shame. "I know. And there's more."

"More what?" Daisy asked.

"Bad news." Spencer took a deep breath. "We found part of Bookworm's head. It was in the trash can, stuffed under the left side of the sink. I don't know what happened to him, but without the lunchbox, he's lifeless. I'm so sorry, Daisy. Bookworm is . . ."

Daisy's grin cut Spencer off midsentence. Her nerves seemed to relax, and she clapped her hands together.

"What . . . ?" Spencer stammered. "Why are you smiling? I just told you that Bookworm is dead. The BEM ripped his head into two pieces. He's gone!"

"But the trash can," Daisy said. "Which side of the sink was it under?"

"Huh?" The question caught Spencer by surprise. Bookworm was dead, and all Daisy cared about was where the trash can ended up?

"What did you say?" Daisy pressed. "Was it under the right side, or the left?"

"The left," Spencer said. "I remember, because your dad always says that thing . . ."

"The garbage is *right* under the sink," Daisy completed her dad's phrase. She was laughing now, the very opposite reaction from what Spencer had anticipated. She turned and started down the garbage slope.

"Come on!" she called behind her. "We have to hurry!"

Spencer scrambled to keep up. "Where are you going?"

"To my house, of course," said Daisy. "It's time for my garbology lesson!" She broke into a dead sprint, so determined that Spencer couldn't catch up to her until they reached the concrete pad and the portal dumpsters. Daisy hoisted herself over the rim, and Spencer jumped in after her. A second later, the two kids were tumbling out the back of the garbage truck and into the Gateses' driveway.

"Would you please tell me what's going on?" Spencer asked. They approached the house quietly and cautiously, side by side as they moved up the walkway.

"Bernard's been training me," Daisy whispered, the porch steps creaking underfoot.

"Training you to do what?"

"To be a garbologist," Daisy said, like it should have been obvious. The front door of the house was still cracked open and they slipped inside to find that all was empty and quiet. Daisy moved quickly through the darkened house, and when she flipped on the kitchen light, Spencer caught up to her.

"Whenever Bernard comes by," Daisy explained, "he leaves me clues in the trash can. If it's a regular day, my dad says the garbage is *right* under the sink. But if Bernard came while I was at school, my dad says that Bernard *left* the garbage under the sink for me. Right, left. Get it?"

"Got it." Spencer nodded. "Your parents know Bernard?" Daisy had made Spencer pinkie swear not to tell a soul that her parents knew about Glop. He was surprised that she allowed Bernard to interact with them.

"Of course," Daisy said. "He's my garbology teacher. Bernard has become a family friend. And if the trash can is on the left, that means that Bernard was here when the BEM attacked." Daisy dropped to her knees and opened the cabinet below the sink. The garbage can was just as Marv had left it, tucked away on the left side.

Daisy carefully lifted it out and peered into the trash.

"What do you see?" Spencer asked impatiently.

"This might take a minute to sort out," said Daisy. "I'm already at a disadvantage since you disturbed the site."

"The *site?*" Spencer said. "It's a trash can, Daisy. Not an archaeological dig."

"Bernard leaves his clues very carefully," she said. "It might have messed things up when you dug around in here the first time."

"Technically," Spencer said, "it was Marv. I couldn't touch anything. My hands were glowing at the time."

Daisy began withdrawing items from the trash can, setting them aside in a specific manner that seemed very contrived to Spencer.

The first to come out was Bookworm's jaw. Daisy lifted the moldy textbook and examined the cover. "You can see where the lunchbox detached."

"I told you," Spencer said. "The BEM ripped him apart."

But Daisy shook her head, pulling a razorblade from the trash. "The BEM didn't touch Bookworm," she said. "The lunchbox was surgically removed from the textbook."

"What?" Spencer said. "Surgically removed?"

"Bernard disassembled him," Daisy said, pointing at the book like it should be self-explanatory. "And Bernard wouldn't do a thing like that unless he knew that Bookworm could be reassembled."

"Why would Bernard want to take Bookworm apart?" Spencer asked.

Now Daisy was pulling a variety of objects from the trash. "The house was surrounded," she said, placing a dozen blue M&M's on the floor in a circle.

"Wait a minute," Spencer interjected. "How in the world do you know that M&M's are supposed to resemble the bad guys?"

Daisy pointed to them. "They're all blue, which means they were put there for a reason," she said, sounding an awful lot like Dr. Bernard Weizmann. "Blue starts with B, which is just two letters short of BEM." She nodded. "The house was surrounded. Too many enemies for Bookworm to handle alone. Bernard knew my Thingamajunk would die to defend my house and parents. So Bernard must have cut him apart to protect him."

Spencer picked up Bookworm's moldy jaw. "Where's the other part?" he asked. "Where's Bookworm's lunchbox?"

"I don't know," Daisy muttered, perusing the remaining contents of the trash can. She reached in and pulled out a latex glove. "Ooo," she said, like she'd happened upon a real treasure.

"What?" Spencer asked, clearly not seeing things like a garbologist-in-training.

"The way the latex fingers are bunched up means that Bernard pulled off the glove in a hurry."

"How can you tell that he was wearing it at all?"

"Most latex gloves are covered with a bit of white powder to keep them from sticking," Daisy said. "Bernard wore it long enough to sweat. You can tell by the way the powdery stuff is crusted and dried on the inside."

Spencer scratched his head. "Why would Bernard wear the glove into the house, but then take it off once they were surrounded? He could have used it to slip past the BEM."

"I don't think he wanted to escape," Daisy said. "He disassembled Bookworm and abandoned his glove. He even left these behind."

Daisy reached into the can again and pulled out Bernard's distinctive key chain. It was loaded with odd charms, and dangling among them was the key to the Glopified garbage truck.

"I didn't see Big Bertha outside," Spencer said. The only garbage truck he'd noticed was the one Gia had parked in the Gateses' driveway.

"He must have parked it far away and come in on foot,"

Daisy said. "Let's see if he left us another clue." She tipped over the trash can, spilling the remaining garbage across the empty kitchen floor.

Spencer stared at the scraps of paper and bits of food decorating the floor. Daisy rifled through them carefully, unafraid of the germs that might be lurking in the mess. "Anything?" he asked.

"Yeah," Daisy said, lifting a torn piece of cardboard from the garbage. It was a yellow scrap, obviously ripped from a box of Cheerios. She held the small piece up, squinting both eyes and twisting her head slightly to the side.

"Looks like Big Bertha is parked at 5th East and Maple Street," she said.

"No way," said Spencer, dubiously. "You got all that from staring at a scrap of Cheerios box?"

"Cheerios?" Daisy seemed confused. "I was just reading the address Bernard wrote on the back of this cardboard." She flipped the scrap around, and Spencer saw the garbologist's small handwriting.

"Let's go," Spencer said. If Bernard had left them the keys to Big Bertha and a mysterious address, then they had to see it through. He grabbed Bookworm's textbook jaw and tucked it under one arm.

Daisy reached out and shoveled all the spilled garbage into a pile. "Can you hand me the trash can?" she asked.

"What are you doing?" Spencer asked.

"Cleaning up," said Daisy. "I can't leave this garbage on the kitchen floor." She reached into the pile and popped a blue M&M into her mouth.

"You didn't . . ." Spencer said, turning away. He'd seen Bernard eat stuff out of the garbage, and it looked like the practice was rubbing off on Daisy. "Is that part of your garbologist training? Picking out the edibles?"

"Don't worry," Daisy said, swallowing the candy. "We solved Bernard's clues. This isn't evidence anymore."

Spencer rolled his eyes. It wasn't destroying the evidence that had him concerned.

"Can you hand me the trash can?" she asked for a second time.

Spencer grabbed the can. As soon as he touched the edge, he felt an unmistakable squish as his finger made contact with something that should never be touched with a bare hand.

"Gum!" Spencer yelled, dropping the trash can and rubbing his fingers against his jeans. "Somebody's nasty pre-chewed gum is stuck to the inside of your trash can." He shuddered, mentally re-feeling the unexpected squish on his index finger.

Daisy shuffled over on her knees to inspect the trash can. She put her face disgustingly close to the offensive wad of gum and took a sniff.

"Strawberry Bubble Blaster," she muttered. "Bernard chews this kind."

"Well, next time he comes over you should tell him to throw his gum *in* the garbage can instead of sticking it to the side," Spencer said. "That's so gross."

"Wait a minute," Daisy said. To Spencer's horror, she

carefully reached into the can and peeled the pink gum away.

"That's a big wad," Spencer pointed out, as Daisy laid the gum across her palm.

"At least five sticks," she said. "But look." She pointed at the gum, and Spencer's curiosity forced him to bend closer than he wanted to.

Bernard's huge wad of gum was stretched flat, with a few teeth marks indenting the side. Spencer saw a small smooth spot on the edge where he'd accidentally pressed his index finger. But centered in the gum was a perfect impression of a key. And below it, another, lying like a mirror image.

"Two keys," Daisy said.

"Or two sides of one key," Spencer pointed out. "It's a mold."

"I don't think it's moldy," Daisy said. "It's only been here a day."

"No," Spencer said. "It's an impression. A mold that shows us the exact pattern of a key. Bernard must have pressed it into the gum to make a copy."

"Key to what?" Daisy said.

"I bet we'll find out at 5th East and Maple Street," Spencer said, even more anxious to go now.

Daisy stepped over to the kitchen cupboard and took out a Tupperware container. Popping open the lid, she stuck Bernard's gum to the bottom of the plastic dish and replaced the top. In the excitement, she seemed to forget about the need to clean up the kitchen. Spencer didn't remind her as they slipped out the front door and into the night.

CHAPTER 22

"I LOOKED IN THE GARBAGE."

There was nothing special about 5th East and Maple Street, except for the seemingly innocent garbage truck parked at the edge of Maple Park. Spencer hadn't been back to this area of town since the beginning of the school year. He saw the apartments nearby and remembered how Garth Hadley had once lured him into a trap of relocated Toxites. Now Garth Hadley was gone, wiped to dust by the TPs in the Dustbin. So much was different. Spencer scarcely felt like the same person.

It must have been past midnight when Spencer and Daisy stopped at Big Bertha's bumper. Their foreheads glistened with a bit of sweat from the long walk across town. They'd cheated a little, using brooms to glide when they were sure no one was watching.

Daisy dug Bernard's key chain from her janitorial belt

and inserted the key into the lock. The driver's door swung wide, buffeting Spencer with the mixed smell of two dozen tree-shaped car fresheners hanging from the mirror.

The two kids hoisted themselves into the cab and shut the door. They didn't want anyone sneaking up on them, and Big Bertha's cab was one of the safest places as long as the doors were closed.

"What are we looking for?" Daisy asked.

"This, I think," said Spencer. He picked up an envelope that was resting on the truck's dashboard. Across the front, Daisy's name was scrawled in Bernard's printing. "It's for you." He handed the letter to his companion.

Daisy ripped open the envelope and withdrew a sheet of paper. She began to read aloud.

"If you are reading this, it means I succeeded in getting caught. Your parents are in danger. I'm going to your house and I hope to be there when General Clean arrives. I wish I could save your mom and dad, but I'm afraid they'll have to get captured with me."

Daisy paused. "He knew. Why would Bernard go to my house if he knew he'd be caught?"

Spencer pointed at the letter. "Keep reading."

"I'm not sure what I'm going to do about Bookworm. If he's too strong, he could blow the whole operation. I'll try to disarm the Thingamajunk by breaking apart his head. Don't worry—I should be able to reassemble him later." Daisy began reading faster than her lips could move, and she trailed off.

"Hey," Spencer said, reminding her that he needed to hear. "Out loud, please."

"Sorry," she said, before resuming the narration. "The BEM isn't just taking prisoners. They're trying to erase all trace of the Rebels by emptying the houses of the people they abduct."

Daisy looked up, the realization finally dawning on her. "My parents weren't deep cleaning the carpets."

"I'm afraid not," Spencer said. "I think the BEM took all your belongings."

"But there was still stuff in *your* house," Daisy pointed out.

"The BEM must have been in a hurry when they took my family," Spencer said. "It didn't really matter since Clean came back to dissolve everything we owned with his Glopified drain clog remover."

"Why would they take all our stuff?" Daisy asked, horrified at the realization that the Gateses had been robbed.

"It would look a lot less suspicious to the neighbors," Spencer mused. "If a moving truck pulled into the driveway and loaded everything up, the people next door would just assume that you suddenly had to move away. They'd ask less questions when nobody ever saw you again."

"We would never move away without telling our neighbors," Daisy said.

Spencer shrugged. "It's just a theory." He pointed to the note in the girl's hands. "Let's see what Bernard says."

Daisy turned back to the paper. "I think the BEM is

trying to stop us from finding something," she read. "I'm not sure what."

Spencer knew it was about the scissors. The BEM didn't necessarily have to find them, so long as they prevented the Rebels from ever locating the scissors. It was a good strategy.

"Stealing all our possessions makes it so the Rebels can't leave any important information behind," Daisy read on. "But I'm betting that the BEM won't take out the trash. So that's where I'll leave my clues."

Daisy looked up smiling. "Everyone underestimates the garbage," she said. Then, glancing back at the note, she read on.

"I know where the Rebels are being imprisoned. The BEM is transporting them and all their stolen belongings to a tiny island off the southern coast of Florida. A master key will unlock the gate to the island, as well as the individual cells where the Rebels are trapped. Unfortunately, the only person who holds a master key is General Clean. If everything goes right today, I'll get captured at your house. I'm taking this gamble so I can get close to Clean. I'll do my best to make an impression of his master key and leave it behind for you to find. The rescuing part is up to you and Spencer. Come save us. Your friend, Dr. Bernard Weizmann, garbologist."

Daisy lowered the letter and stared at Spencer. "He didn't say anything about Bookworm's lunchbox."

"He should have left it in the garbage can with the textbook," Spencer said.

"Maybe he tried," Daisy said. "Maybe the BEM got to him before he could drop it."

"If Bernard had the lunchbox with him when the BEM attacked the house, that would mean . . ." Spencer trailed off, realizing the likely fate of Bookworm's lunchbox.

"The BEM took it," said Daisy. "Along with everything else."

"Bernard said stolen belongings were also transported to that island," Spencer said. "If we can break into that prison, we have a chance of finding the lunchbox and putting Bookworm back together again."

Daisy nodded, looking skeptical about their chance at succeeding. "This isn't going to be easy."

"We should head back to the landfill," said Spencer. "We need to talk to Marv and make a plan."

Daisy nodded in agreement. As she folded the letter, she noticed writing on the back of the page. "What's this?" She turned the paper over and read the postscript.

"P.S. If I happen to leave blue M&M's in your trash can, don't eat them. I found them rolling around under the driver's seat of Big Bertha. Don't know how long they've been there."

Daisy swallowed nervously.

"See," Spencer said. "I told you. It's never a good idea to eat garbage."

"Well . . ." Daisy shrugged. "I'm still alive." She stuffed the letter back into the envelope and placed it in the glove compartment. "What should we do with Big Bertha?"

Bernard's garbage truck no longer had an active portal

to the landfill. The lids of every dumpster could be closed to prevent unwanted visitors. But Rho's dumpster, which connected to Big Bertha, had been destroyed. The Dark Aurans had smashed it when the Rebels escaped the landfill back in February.

"Let's drive it back to your house," Spencer suggested. "That way we can use Gia's truck to get back to Big Bertha if we ever need to."

They were back at the Gates home in no time. Daisy drove Big Bertha, and she only hit the curb once. Spencer remembered fearing for his life the last time his friend had sat behind the wheel. But without a gang of Pluggers trying to run her off the road, Daisy was actually a pretty safe driver.

The kids slipped out of the truck and Daisy locked Big Bertha, tucking the garbologist's odd key chain into her belt. Spencer led the way, climbing the ladder up the side of Gia's truck until he was staring into the dark bed through the open hopper. He slid his legs over the edge and jumped down, preparing himself to come tumbling out of Gia's dumpster at the landfill.

Instead, Spencer's feet hit the bottom of the truck with jarring force. He grunted in surprise, sliding sideways through the knee-high trash. He felt his feet pass through the portal, but something was wrong. The gateway seemed to be closing before he could get through. There was pressure against his knees, and he felt like the portal might close around him at any moment, leaving his top half in Idaho and his legs in Texas.

"Don't jump!" Spencer called up to Daisy, just as he felt a firm hand grip his ankle. He was pulled through the trash, leaving Idaho behind. His head cleared the rim of Gia's dumpster just as the black lid slammed shut.

Dez dropped Spencer heavily to the concrete pad. "Good thing I was there to pull you through, Doofus," the Sweeper boy said. "I have pacific instructions to close all the dumpster lids. I was shutting Gia's when you fell in."

"First of all, it's *specific*, not *pacific*," Spencer corrected. "And I didn't fall in. I was trying to get back!" Spencer reached up and threw open the dumpster lid. He called to Daisy, and she appeared a second later.

"What happened?" she asked. Dez flew over their heads and slammed the lid shut again, perching atop the closed dumpster when he was finished.

"Where were you guys, anyway?" he asked.

"We went back to Daisy's house for clues," Spencer answered. "Why are you closing the dumpsters?"

"Duh," he answered. "We can't take any chances. We're under sage."

"Sage is an herb!" Spencer yelled. "What are you talking about?"

"The Pluggers," said Dez, pointing off toward the deep gorge that isolated the landfill from the rest of the Texas desert. "I'm talking about the nasty gang of Pluggers trying to get into the landfill."

"The Pluggers are here?" Spencer asked.

Daisy chimed in. "I still don't see what this has to do with sage."

"He meant *siege*," Spencer corrected.

"Whatever," said Dez. "At least I didn't run away when the Pluggers showed up."

"We didn't know they were coming," Daisy said. "Anyway . . . we know how to find the scissors." She held up the moldy textbook that was once Bookworm's jaw.

"Somebody wrote down the directions to the scissors in a dirty old book?" Dez asked.

"Bookworm," Daisy said. "He can search through the landfill faster than all of us combined."

"Then what's he waiting for?" Dez asked.

"The rest of his head," answered Spencer. "When General Clean attacked Daisy's house, Bernard must have taken Bookworm's lunchbox head. Rescue Bernard, and we get Bookworm back."

"Where is the weirdo garbologist?" asked Dez.

"In prison with the rest of the Rebels," Spencer said. "They're being held in a facility off the coast of southern Florida."

"Where did you guys learn all this?" Dez asked.

"I looked in the garbage," said Daisy. The Sweeper kid made a confused face.

"Where's Marv?" Spencer asked. They needed to make a plan with the janitor.

"We're all out at the gorge bashing some Plugger heads," Dez said.

"Are the Dark Aurans back yet?" Daisy asked.

"Just the girls," answered Dez. "But I guess they fight all right." He launched from the dumpster and soared in the direction of the gorge at the landfill's edge. "This way," he called down.

"Do you think Dez is different?" Daisy asked quietly, as they struggled to keep pace with the flying boy.

"Different from what?" Spencer asked.

"From how he used to be."

"We all are," answered Spencer, thinking of how much he had changed since everything had started in September. Spencer's greatest worry used to be the germs on a public handrail. Now he carried the future of education on his shoulders.

"I mean, he's still annoying," Daisy said. "And rude and disgusting. And selfish."

"Yeah," Spencer agreed. "I wouldn't count on him to jump in front of a mop attack for me."

"But I think he's finally on our side. It's almost like he cares about destroying the Toxites."

"If Dez cares about destroying Toxites," Spencer said, "it's because of the *destroying* part. He'd like to break anything he could get his Sweeper hands around. But I don't think his feelings about schoolwork have changed."

"True," Daisy said. "He never does his homework. He doesn't even do his classwork. In fact, what kind of work *does* Dez like to do?"

Spencer shrugged. "Dirty work." At least Dez was good for something.

"YOU KNOW
WHAT WE
HAVE TO DO."

The deep gorge that formed the landfill's perimeter had become a full-scale war zone. When Spencer and Daisy arrived, the Auran girls were dirty and sweating, their knuckles bruised as they gripped their cleaning supplies.

Spencer recognized the spot where they made their defense. Several months ago, the Rebels had driven a garbage truck across a magical bridge. The bridge had collapsed when unauthorized BEM vans tried to follow. Now there were only the twisted remains of asphalt and metal where the bridge jutted out and dropped a frightening distance into the gorge.

"Here comes another!" shouted one of the Aurans. Spencer saw the outlines of two girls run to assist her just as a Grime-riding Plugger leapt the final distance up the cliff wall and landed at the top of the gorge.

A razorblade sword flashed and Spencer heard it clatter uselessly against the interlocking armor that the Extension Grime wore. The large Toxite puffed its gullet, glowing green slime building into a deadly projectile. The three battling Aurans dove aside just as the acid streamed from the Grime's mouth.

Spencer saw the Plugger adjust the dial on his battery-pack belt, presumably decreasing the flow of energy that the creature was receiving through its Glopified extension cord. The electricity made Extension Toxites calm and docile. Lowering the output spurred the Grime forward in a rage. It leapt over the puddle of acidic vomit, and the rider gave a cry as the way opened into the landfill.

Marv came barreling out of nowhere, his bearlike form grappling onto the Plugger. Under the weight of the attack, the man was dislodged from his saddle, gripping desperately to his cord so he didn't get unplugged.

Marv rolled away from the enemy, a plunger appearing in his beefy hand. The rubber suction cup clamped onto the Grime's armored back, and he lifted the squirming creature into the air. He barely ducked in time, as the Toxite's long tail swung around with enough force to knock off his head. Then Marv detached his plunger, hurling the Extension Grime back over the edge of the gorge. The screaming Plugger was dragged along, now frantic to separate his belt but unable to do so in time.

"Where've you two been?" Marv asked, approaching Spencer and Daisy. He had a cut across his cheek, but the pain didn't seem to bother him.

"Long story," Spencer said. "We have to talk." He pointed back toward the Auran building.

"Kind of busy," Marv said.

Just then, an Auran's voice called out. "Incoming Rubbish!"

Spencer turned to see a Plugger on an overgrown Rubbish winging over the gorge. The Aurans scrambled to their defenses, and Spencer saw Rho crouching behind a metal garbage can.

"Trashcannons ready!" she yelled. The only trashcannons Spencer had ever seen were the ones mounted into the side of Big Bertha. They packed a powerful punch, shooting a heavy slug of high-velocity trash at whatever enemy was unfortunate enough to be in their sights.

"I have first shot!" Rho shouted.

"Second!" called Sylva, anchoring herself behind another trashcannon a few yards away.

"Third!" said Yorkie, taking another station.

They waited until the flying Plugger was halfway across the gorge. Then Rho took aim, pounding the bottom of her trashcannon and sending a wad of dangerous garbage directly at the BEM worker.

The Extension Rubbish veered instinctively, missing the debris as the trash projectiles spread out like buckshot from a shotgun. But the evasion was short-lived as Sylva took the second shot. This one slammed directly into the Toxite and rider, shredding the creature's leathery wings and sending beast and rider plummeting out of sight.

"Rho!" Spencer called, racing up to her. He was excited

to tell her about his plan to rescue Bookworm, which would help them find the scissors. But Rho didn't seem interested.

"How many left?" she called, completely ignoring Spencer.

Jersey stepped back from the gorge's edge, lowering a pair of binoculars. "Hard to count," she answered. "Looks like the far side is still bristling with them."

"You know what we have to do," Shirley said quietly to Rho.

She shook her head. "We can last a while longer. We just have to defend this stretch."

"Why aren't the Pluggers trying to get through somewhere else?" Spencer asked. He knew the gorge surrounded the entire landfill. There was no way that nine Aurans could defend it all.

"Thingamajunks protect the gorge. They stop anyone from crossing over," she said. "The Pluggers might have the landfill surrounded, but we're counting on the wild Thingamajunks to protect their part."

"Why aren't they here?" Spencer asked. He hadn't seen any Thingamajunks helping the Aurans with their defenses.

"They abandoned this stretch when we built the bridge," Rho said.

Daisy nodded. "Development always drives the wildlife away."

"Shirley's right, Rho," Jersey seconded. "We can't hold the Pluggers back forever. Even if we could, there's no telling how long the Thingamajunks will resist. If the Pluggers learn how to trash-talk, we're lost."

"We have to torch the gorge," Shirley said.

"And trap ourselves here?" answered Rho.

"We have the dumpster portals," Jersey said.

"But if the dumpsters fail, we can never leave again," Rho said resolutely.

A Filth Plugger clambered up over the edge of the gorge, drawing four exhausted Aurans to bat it back.

Rho sighed deeply and nodded. "Bring the petrol."

Jersey and Shirley ran off, and Rho finally paid Spencer some attention.

"You're going to light the gorge on fire?" he asked.

Rho nodded. "If the landfill gets overrun with BEM Pluggers, it will only complicate the search for the scissors."

"Why didn't you burn it sooner?" asked Daisy. Jersey and Shirley reappeared, each lugging a large red oil drum with the help of a Glopified plunger.

"This is Glopified gasoline," Rho explained. "The same stuff that powers our garbage trucks." She nodded for Jersey and Shirley to begin.

The two girls pried open the caps and used their plungers to tip the large containers on their sides at the edge of the gorge. Instantly, the smell of gasoline reached Spencer's nose as the liquid began chugging out, spilling over the cliff and into the deep chasm below.

"It won't burn out," Rho said. "We light this now, and the landfill will forever be ringed in fire."

The two oil drums had discharged their load. The girls tipped the cans to allow a final dribble to run out.

"That's enough?" Marv asked. Spencer shared his

skepticism. A hundred gallons of gasoline didn't seem like enough to protect miles and miles of gorge.

"There are other cans below," Rho said. "We placed them a long time ago, preparing for an event like tonight. The fire will ignite the others, and the landfill will be surrounded in seconds."

There was a sudden rush of wind overhead, and Dez landed beside the empty oil cans. "What are we doing?" he asked, sounding as if he was afraid of being left out of something fun.

Jersey produced a small matchbox. She dragged one of the matches along the textured edge of the box, and a tiny flame sprang to life. Jersey held it out to Rho. "Would you like to do the honors?"

"Sure," Dez said, plucking the match out of Jersey's fingers and tossing it over the edge of the gorge before anyone could react.

The small match touched the spilled gasoline, instantly igniting a giant flame. The blast of heat and light caused Spencer to stumble backward, shielding his face. In a second, the ribbon of fire had consumed the portion of the gorge that the Aurans had been defending. Flames licked the sky, creating an impenetrable wall that rose at least fifty feet above the cliff tops.

In the seconds that followed, there was a series of resounding *booms* as the pre-positioned gas tanks exploded. Fire sprouted along the gorge until it curled away out of sight around the mound of landfill trash.

It was as bright as daylight now, and so hot that Spencer immediately began to sweat. Rho turned to face Spencer. Her youthful look seemed dimmed, despite the brightness of the fire.

"Was there something you wanted to talk about?"

CHAPTER 24

"I DON'T THINK WE SHOULD FLY."

It was morning before Spencer got a chance to explain what he and Daisy had discovered about the BEM's island prison.

The other Aurans did not meet Spencer at the round conference table. Even with the ring of fire burning around the landfill, there was still a risk of invasion. The rest of the girls maintained the perimeter, keeping the trashcannons loaded and ready in case a daring Rubbish Plugger decided to brave the flames.

Rho joined Spencer, Daisy, and Marv in the conference room. Dez came along too, hoping that the new plan would bring more action now that the burning gasoline repelled the enemies at the gorge.

"Let me get this straight," Rho said, once Spencer was done explaining what he and Daisy had learned from

Bernard's garbology clues. "We are supposed to break into a BEM prison and rescue the captive Rebels, just so we can repair a Thingamajunk?"

Spencer nodded.

"I thought we were supposed to be looking for the dumb scissors," said Dez.

"We'll never find the scissors on our own," Spencer said. "Olin, Sach, and Aryl have been looking for two hundred years. We have to take this detour to get Bookworm back."

"Quite the detour," Rho muttered.

"Plus," Daisy added, "if we succeed, then we'll have a whole army of Rebels to help us."

"Won't be easy," Marv said, opening the jar of soap-suds that Spencer had stolen from the Witches' sink. "Been studying these before the Pluggers showed up. Lots of security to get to the BEM island."

"But the suds give us a huge advantage," Spencer said. "If we know what security they have, it will be a lot easier to get past it."

"Let's see what we're up against," Rho said, gesturing to the jar of suds.

Marv carefully upended the glass jar, sliding the foamy soapsuds onto the tabletop. He blew gently on them, using his breath to spread them out. Leaning forward, Spencer could see movement in each tiny glossy surface.

Marv squinted at the soapsuds for a moment. Then his thick fingers picked out one little bubble. The janitor took it between his hands and stretched the image so it was easy for everyone to see.

Through the soapsud camera, Spencer saw a small, wooded island in the distance. A series of buoys surrounded the land, cordoning off a section of water as they bobbed in the ocean. There was a long causeway that stretched from the soapsud viewpoint over to the BEM's private island. The bridge stood high above the water, with sturdy pillars jutting into the sea.

At the entrance to the bridge, Spencer saw a sign posted on both sides of the road. He squinted to read the printed words.

WARNING: NO TRESPASSING
AUTHORIZED VEHICLES ONLY
BEYOND THIS POINT

And then in tiny letters below:

VIOLATORS WILL FALL TO THEIR DOOM

"Hey!" Rho said, studying the image. "Those little cheaters! That's *our* trick."

"What?" Daisy asked.

"That bridge is a replica of the one we had at the gorge," she said. "It's rigged to collapse unless the tires of the vehicle are coded with Glopified paint."

"I guess the BEM was impressed when your bridge dropped a couple of their vans into the gorge," Spencer said. "They wanted to make their own version to keep us away from the island."

"You know the code for the tires?" Marv asked.

"Ours was a specific series of crosswalks you had to drive over." Rho shrugged. "Theirs could be anything."

"What if we cross the bridge on foot?" Spencer asked.

"It won't work," she answered. "If it's like ours, any footfall will trigger a collapse."

"Even if we fall," Daisy said, studying the image in the soapsud, "it looks like we'd just land in the water. Maybe we could swim over to the island."

"Nope," Marv said, shrinking the soapsud and picking up another one. "Here's the view under the bridge." He expanded the soapy bubble.

Clinging to the underside of the bridge was the largest Extension Grime Spencer had ever seen. It made the Toxites that the Pluggers rode look small. This thing was a real monster. From nose to tail, Spencer guessed it was easily the length of a football field. Each sticky fingertip was the size of a trampoline.

The monster Grime was hanging upside down. Its pale eyes were rolled back in what appeared to be peaceful slumber.

"Whoa," Daisy whispered. "How'd it get so big?"

"Can't see it now," Marv said. "But when I looked earlier, I could see the extension cord. It's plugged in to something."

"They must have been growing it for months," Spencer said.

"Big deal," said Dez. "Looks like the lazy thing is sleeping anyway. We can totally get past."

"See those buoys." Marv gestured with his hairy chin,

since both hands were occupied with the soapsud. In the distance, Spencer saw the ring of buoys sectioning off the water around the island. "Anything crosses those buoys and the Grime wakes up."

"So what?" Dez said. "I'll just fly across."

"Like this pelican?" Marv turned their attention back to the soapsud. A large bird was flying into view, winging its way innocently toward the island. The moment it crossed over the buoys, the monster Grime's giant eyeballs swiveled around. It slipped around the side of the bridge with silent movements.

The Grime held perfectly still for one second. Then its tongue shot out at lightning speed. Like a frog catching a fly, the Grime nailed the pelican in midflight. The black tongue retracted with a shower of spit, and the Grime swallowed the large bird whole. The pelican was hardly a snack for such a huge Toxite. With the island defended, the Grime resumed its position under the bridge, its eyeballs rolling back again as the extension cord soothed and nourished.

"I don't think we should fly," Daisy said.

"I fly way better than that seagull," said Dez. "I'll drop in from so high that the Grime's tongue won't be able to stretch that far."

Marv shook his shaggy head. "Fly too high and they'll spot you from the island. Element of surprise is gone and you'll never reach the prisoners."

"What's on the other side of the bridge?" Spencer asked. "What are we up against if we make it to the island?"

Marv replaced his soapsud and picked out another

bubble. Instead of expanding it between both hands, he simply enlarged the view between his thumb and index finger. "Chain-link fence circles around the whole island," Marv said. He stretched a few more suds to show multiple viewpoints of the fence rising out of the sandy beach. Beyond was nothing but a tangle of dark trees.

Spencer saw the warning signs on the fence immediately. "Oh, great," he muttered.

"What?" Rho asked.

"We met a Glopified chain-link fence at a construction site when we broke into the BEM laboratory," he explained. "It's like an electric force field that runs along the whole fence and stretches across the top. You can't even fly over a fence like that." He glanced at Dez, knowing the Sweeper boy was about to suggest the idea.

"Then how do the BEM get onto the island?" Daisy asked.

"Only one break in the fence," Marv said, fishing through the soapsuds with his finger until he found the right image. He picked up the tiny bubble and enlarged it between both hands. "There's a gate that covers the road. Right where the bridge comes in."

Spencer could see a heavy metal gate spanning the road, which provided the only gap in the island vegetation. Positioned beside the road, just inside the fence, was a tall security tower with bright searchlights that panned across the sandy beach.

"Gate's locked," Marv pointed out.

"Hasn't stopped us before," said Dez. "I'll smash that lock to bits!"

"And get fried in the process," Rho said.

"Luckily," Spencer said, "Daisy and I happen to have the key to that lock." He nodded to his friend, who then produced a small Tupperware container from her janitorial belt.

Peeling back the lid, Daisy held it out for everyone to see the contents.

Rho and Marv looked confused. Dez just chuckled. "Hate to break it to you, Gullible Gates," he said. "But that's just gum."

Daisy nodded. "Strawberry Bubble Blaster," she said excitedly. "Bernard made a mold of General Clean's master key in this gum. It should open any lock we come across."

"Brilliant!" Rho said, pulling the plastic container from Daisy's hand. "We can have a duplicate key made in no time."

"Supposing the key works and we get past the fence," Marv said. "We finally get to the prison." He picked up a new soapsud and held it out for display. "Looks like this."

Spencer studied the image for a moment before pointing out the obvious. "Those are storage units." He remembered his mom renting one when his family moved to Aunt Avril's house. The Zumbros had stowed most of their belongings, planning to dig stuff out again when they got a home of their own.

Marv grunted. "Six rows. Hundred units per row. Holding more than a thousand Rebel prisoners on this island."

Besides the Sweeper guards that patrolled the aisles, storage units didn't seem like a very secure facility. The long rows were flat-roofed, with cinder-block walls. A roll-up, garage-style door closed each unit, and Spencer saw a metal lock securing each door.

"Those doors look flimsy," Dez said, and Spencer agreed with him.

"So what's the trick?" Spencer followed up.

Marv shrugged. "Seems reasonable that a janitor would use a storage unit. Gives them potential to be Glopified."

"I'm guessing we won't be able to smash through those doors very easily," Rho said.

"We won't need to," Daisy said. "We have a master key." She pointed to the locks on the doors, her finger almost popping the enlarged soapsud.

"So all we have to do," Spencer said, "is unlock six hundred storage units before the Sweepers stop us."

"That's after we get past the collapsing bridge, humongous Grime, and electric fence," added Daisy.

"And we'll have to avoid being seen in the soapsuds," Rho said. "If the Witches spot us coming, we lose the element of surprise."

"Can they see us now?" Daisy asked, leaning forward and staring into the suds on the table.

Spencer shook his head. "Only the suds at the island are streaming an image," he said. "The ones we have are just displaying what the others are recording."

"But the Witches don't have these display suds anymore," Daisy said, pointing at the table. "We stole them."

JANITORS: HEROES OF THE DUSTBIN

"The Witches won't want the prison in their blind spot," Spencer said. "I'm sure they'll make more soapsuds to display what's happening on the island. That way, they can watch just like we are."

"Let's just pop the stupid suds when we get there," said Dez, jabbing at the air with his sharp talons.

"We're trying to be sneaky," said Daisy. "Don't you think the Witches would notice if their soapsuds started popping?"

"Look," Spencer said. "I know this isn't going to be easy. But we have the element of surprise, we have the master key, and we have my spit sponge, which means I can Glopify anything we need to help us succeed."

"Don't forget Marv's Bingo prize," Dez said sarcastically. "Magic toilet-bowl cleaner will probably help."

Dez's words, intended as a mocking jab, suddenly formed into a plan in Spencer's mind. He grinned. "Actually," Spencer said, "I think you're right."

"MY GREAT-GRANDPA HAD A GLASS EYE."

It was late afternoon and incredibly hot when Spencer found himself staring across the long bridge to the BEM's private island. After the Rebels had hopped through Lina's dumpster, Marv had driven the garbage truck off the southern tip of Florida and through a series of toll bridges and islands. Using the information they'd gathered from the soapsuds, Marv, Spencer, Daisy, and Dez had finally arrived at the BEM's private bridge.

Daisy checked the zipper of her coveralls and glanced impatiently out over the water. "He's been gone a long time. Do you think he's in trouble?"

"It's Dez," Spencer pointed out. "He's always in some sort of trouble." He didn't like how the plan started with Dez. But there was really no one else who could do the job as quickly.

Marv stomped his feet, as though testing out the new rubber boots he was wearing. "Let's get in position," he muttered, sauntering off the road and down the beach toward the water's edge. Spencer and Daisy followed him, their own boots leaving marks in the sand.

They stopped just at the point where the bridge began to rise over their heads. Squinting ahead, Spencer could see the monstrous Grime clinging to the shadows like a troll beneath the bridge. It still appeared to be sleeping, and he didn't want to go any closer for fear of awakening it.

Rho's voice sounded through the walkie-talkie clipped onto Spencer's janitorial belt. "You're still out of sight," she said. "Are you under the bridge?"

"We're here," Spencer said. He adjusted the volume, turning Rho's voice down to a mere whisper. They would need to communicate, but he didn't want the Sweepers hearing them.

"All right," she said. "I'm guessing one more step and you'll come into view of the first soapsud. Looks like it's positioned on the underside of the bridge."

Spencer, Daisy, and Marv turned their eyes up toward the bottom of the bridge, scanning the shadows for a surveillance soapsud. It had to be somewhere damp, since the bubble needed constant moisture to stay formed.

"There," Marv said, peering around the first pillar that supported the bridge. He pointed a thick finger, and when Spencer leaned forward, he saw the small soapsud clinging to a spot where the high tide left the concrete slick with mildew.

Marv reached to his belt and drew a bottle of Windex. Taking careful aim, he shot a narrow stream directly at the soapsud. The magic window cleaner shimmered blue on contact. In a second, the little soapsud had turned to glass.

Spencer stepped out in plain view of the bubble. "Anything?" he asked into the walkie-talkie.

"Nothing," Rho answered. "It won't fool anyone if they study the image. The waves aren't even moving. But it should be good enough if the Witches are just glancing over."

"My great-grandpa had a glass eye," Daisy said, tapping the glass soapsud with her fingernail. "He couldn't see a thing out of it."

Spencer turned his gaze over the water again. Now that he was sure they could fool the suds with Windex, he was anxious to get over to the island. The effect would only trick the surveillance for about fifteen minutes.

Just as Spencer was muttering his name, Dez landed heavily in the sand behind them. His black wings folded in and he strode toward them.

"Everything set?" Spencer asked.

Dez nodded. "The speedboat should be coming in fast. Any second now."

"Put these on." Marv tossed a pair of rubber boots to the Sweeper boy.

"They're not really my size," he protested. "Besides, I don't like to wear stuff that Spencer had to spit on."

They were all wearing boots that were the product of Spencer's spit sponge. It had taken him the rest of the night and well into morning to Glopify all the new gear they would need to break the Rebels out of the storage-unit prison.

Dez had just finished pulling his boots on when the sound of a motor drew Spencer's eyes across the water. Skipping over waves at high velocity, a speedboat cut across the line of buoys, heading straight for the island.

The monster Grime beneath the bridge responded immediately. Its huge eyes rolled around and it sprang into the water, extension cord trailing as it dove out of sight.

"That's our cue," Spencer said. He ran to the spot where the bridge was so low overhead that he had to duck to go under. Then, leaping into the air, he stuck his feet to the underside of the bridge. The Glopified boots responded instantly, holding him fast to the concrete. He dangled upside down, the magic of the boots making him feel as comfortable as though he were strolling down the road.

Spencer didn't wait for the others, though he heard their boots clinging to the bottom of the bridge behind him. The group sprinted forward, counting on the distraction of the speedboat to hold the Grime's interest.

"I should be flying," Dez grumbled at Spencer's side. They had considered that idea, but the huge Grime was accustomed to watching the water and the skies. The belly of the bridge was where the Grime lived. And who would be crazy enough to run straight through the Grime's personal space?

Spencer's eyes flicked out across the water. It was confusing, being upside down. The ocean and sky had switched places, two shades of blue that disoriented him. Every foot-fall gave Spencer confidence. Just as they'd predicted, the bottom of the bridge didn't register their unauthorized cross-ing. If it had, the bridge would have collapsed by now.

The invading Rebels were halfway across the causeway when the humongous Grime came out of the water. It took the speedboat in a perfect interception, catching the fast vessel in one sticky hand.

The Grime tossed the boat into the air, its whole slimy body propelling up after it. Out of the water, the motor screamed. But it silenced instantly as the Grime's wide mouth closed around the boat. The jaws snapped together, jagged teeth shattering wood and metal. Bits of speedboat showered down as the Grime completed its aerial arc and dove back into the depths.

Daisy gasped at the sight. "Those poor fishermen!"

"Relax," Dez said. "There was nobody aboard. I duct-taped the controls down and pointed the boat at the island."

Spencer said nothing. If the Grime returned to its undercling perch before they reached the island, their res-cue mission would come to a sudden end. He pushed harder, leading the group in a life-or-death race.

The moment he saw sand below him, Spencer jumped. His Glopified boots came away from the bridge, connecting once more with earth's natural gravity. It took him a second to orient, then Spencer scrambled up the beach and away from the water.

Dez and Daisy were right side up once more. Marv leapt from the bridge just as the water erupted behind them. The monster Grime twisted in the air, its sticky fingers adhering to the causeway.

It was facing them, its huge tongue flicking out to lick the edge of the bridge. The four Rebels stood frozen on the beach, barely daring to breathe. Then the Grime's big eyeballs rolled back and it made itself comfortable.

"What happened?" Spencer gasped. "Why didn't it see us?"

"Blind spot," Marv whispered, pointing directly down the nose of the Grime. Spencer had forgotten that the Grimes couldn't see directly in front of them. For little Grimes, the blind spot was a mere inch or two. But this thing was huge, and its blind spot must have been several feet across.

"Hey!" Daisy said. "Is that a seashell?" She began to move forward, but Spencer grabbed her arm. "Let go!" she demanded. "I'm on a tropical island! I have to find seashells!"

Spencer pulled a white dust mask from his belt and quickly fit it over Daisy's face. She came to an immediate halt, her eyes wide as she realized how distracted she'd been. Spencer put another mask over his face. There would be Filth Sweepers ahead, and he couldn't risk getting sleepy.

"Well, we made it to the island," Dez said.

"Now for the hard part," Marv said.

"THERE ARE NO COOKIES."

Marv plucked a shiny key from his belt pouch. It was a copy of General Clean's master key, forged from Bernard's gum mold. He drew a bottle of bleach and handed it to Spencer. Then, with the key in one hand and a bottle of Windex in the other, Marv gestured for Spencer to begin.

It was done in a moment. The last things to vanish were Marv's rubber boots. After the big janitor was completely bleached, Spencer could see only the impression of his feet in the sand.

"Only got about fifteen minutes," Marv's voice floated from nowhere. "Don't follow until Rho gives the word."

Spencer nodded to show he understood, wishing that he and the others could turn invisible too. But since they had already used the bleach once, Spencer knew that a second spray would make it so they would never be seen again.

They would have to rely on Marv's invisibility and hope his distraction would provide enough cover that the rest of them could slip in unnoticed.

Marv grunted invisibly, and Spencer saw his footprints move up the beach toward the gate.

"Let's go," Dez said the moment they were alone.

Spencer caught his muscled arm. "Give him a minute."

They waited in silence until Rho's voice whispered through the Glopified walkie-talkie. "Marv found the next soapsud. He turned it to glass and I never saw him. You're clear until you reach the storage units."

Spencer nodded to his companions and peered out from under the bridge. He was anxious to get away from the slumbering Grime under the causeway. The gate that spanned the road was open just a crack, the lock dangling ajar from when the invisible Marv had used the master key.

The three kids raced up the beach. Spencer kept glancing at the gate tower. All the enemy had to do was look out the window and they would see the intruding Rebels. But Spencer was counting on Marv to sufficiently distract the Sweepers.

They reached the gate without detection. It seemed strange to be breaking into a BEM prison in broad daylight. Spencer might have felt more comfortable sneaking around under the cover of darkness, but if all went according to plan, it wouldn't matter. The Rebels would be free before the BEM Sweepers could stop them.

"Marv didn't leave the key," Dez said, pointing at the vacant keyhole in the open gate lock.

"It's there," Spencer said. "It's just bleached." He reached over to the lock, felt the end of the invisible key, and slipped it out of the heavy lock.

"Let me carry it," Dez said, swiping for the item in Spencer's grasp. He tried to pull his hand away, but the Sweeper kid's taloned fingers caught his wrist. With the momentum of his arm, Spencer felt the master key fly out of his grasp, landing invisibly in the brush by the roadside.

"Way to go," Spencer muttered. "You made me drop it!" He and Daisy peered into the bush, but it was a hopeless search.

"Big deal," Dez said. "I thought you had a different plan to open the locks on the storage units. What about the magnet thingy?"

"I know," Spencer said, "but it wouldn't hurt to keep the master key as a backup plan in case the magnet doesn't work the way it's supposed to."

"Look." Daisy pointed toward the guard tower. Spencer abandoned his search for the master key, ducking into the bushes when he saw half a dozen Sweepers exiting the tower. He knew Marv's plan was working when they hastily turned away from the road and moved out of sight.

Spencer led his companions past the gate, pausing at the corner of the guard tower, waiting for Rho to tell them it was safe to continue. Daisy was breathing nervously at his side, but Dez just kept sniffing the air through his beaklike nose.

"Mmmmm," he muttered. "Do you guys smell that? I think somebody's baking cookies."

"All I smell is the ocean," Daisy said.

"Oh, no," Spencer groaned, realizing what was happening. He pulled off his dust mask and tossed it to Dez. "Put this on, quick."

Dez didn't bother to catch the mask; it bounced off his chest and fell to the ground. "No way. I don't want to look dorky like you two. Besides, Toxite breath doesn't affect me."

"It's not the Toxite breath," Spencer explained. "That smell you're picking up is Marv's toilet-bowl cleaner!"

"The toilet-bowl cleaner smells like baking cookies?" Daisy asked.

"It does to him," Spencer said. "Marv spread the powdered cleaner on the electric fence to draw the Sweepers away." He pointed to the exodus of Sweepers making their way hungrily to the far fence. Spencer and Daisy couldn't smell anything, but the vintage Toxite attractant worked surprisingly well on the Sweepers.

"I've got to have some!" Dez said. "Before those other guys eat it all!" He spread his wings and leapt into the air. He didn't get far, as Daisy's Palm Blast of vacuum dust dropped him to the ground.

Spencer maneuvered around the bully and strapped his dust mask over the boy's face. It barely fit over his beak of a nose. "There are no cookies," Spencer said.

Rho's voice came through the walkie-talkie. "You're clear to enter the first two rows of units. Marv's still searching for the other suds. I'll let you know when they're glass."

Spencer peeked around the corner to make sure that the Sweepers were still facing away. Then he led a sprint to the first row of storage units. The three kids stopped with their backs to a cinder-block wall.

"Let's open the first squeegee," Spencer said. "Rho's ready for us."

Dez misted the wall, but the magic Windex seemed to fizzle out, unable to transform the cinder block to glass. "Not working," he muttered.

Spencer had assumed this might happen. "The units are Glopified. They don't want us turning the walls to glass."

"Then how do we make the portal?" Daisy asked, waving her squeegee uselessly.

Spencer removed the spit sponge from his belt. This part was nasty. It didn't matter how many times he'd done it, the task was gross. As he squeezed the sponge, a dribble of his spit leaked out into his left hand. He replaced the sponge and clapped his hands together, rubbing them briskly to activate the Glop that lingered in his bodily fluids.

In a moment, both hands were glowing with a golden Aura. His right had the power to Glopify, but Spencer's left hand was the one needed for this task.

He reached out and pressed his left palm against the wall. He felt the Glop leak out of the cinder blocks, and he knew he'd succeeded as the Aura faded from his hands.

"Try it now," Spencer said.

"Why don't you just de-Glopify all the units?" Dez asked. "Then we could turn the doors to glass and break them."

"Spitting on every door would take way too long," Spencer said. "I'd have to use the sponge between each one.

Then we'd have to follow up with the Windex, and the moment we shattered one door, the Sweepers would be on to us." He shook his head. "We have to open all the units at the same time. Stick to the original plan."

"Gee," Dez said. "Sorry I had an idea." He turned his bottle of Windex back to the cinder block and gave a few sprays. As the de-Glopfied wall turned to glass, the storage unit beyond appeared to be vacant.

Daisy followed up with a swipe of her squeegee. The portal opened, connecting the cinder-block wall to the conference room at the landfill.

Spencer stared at Rho, standing states away. "The entire facility is clear," she said. "The rest of the suds are glass, so the Witches will have no idea we're here." Rho glanced at a clock on the wall of the conference room. "Marv has only about four minutes of invisibility left. Not long after that, the suds will become active again. He'll try to keep the Sweepers distracted, but you have to hurry."

Rho pushed a pair of cleaning carts through the portal. They rolled through the cinder-block wall and came to a stop at Spencer's feet.

"Whatever happens," Spencer said, turning to Dez, "do not let this portal close. In a couple of minutes there are going to be a lot of defenseless prisoners on the loose. We have to give them somewhere safe to go."

Daisy gave her squeegee to the Sweeper boy in case he needed to swipe again.

There was a rippling shock wave of magic that raced along the electric fence. "Looks like one Sweeper got too close," Spencer said. The vintage toilet-bowl cleaner was doing its job. But the powdery stuff was really old. There was no telling how long the attractant would last.

It was time to put a few new Glopified supplies to the test.

CHAPTER 27

"WE HAVE TO FIND HIM."

Spencer reached down to his belt and removed a new aerosol spray. He'd used his spit sponge to Glopify it last night. All the tests had worked perfectly, and now it was time to put it to use in the real world.

It was stainless steel polish, a convenient item for any janitor who wanted to keep metal appliances shiny and clean. Of course, the Glopified version would do more than make the metal sparkle.

"I thought we couldn't spray the locks or walls," Dez said.

Daisy hefted her own can of polish. "Are you sure this will work?" she asked Spencer. "It's not like it can open locks."

"That's exactly *why* it'll work," Spencer said, trying to boost his own confidence. "Sprays like Windex change whatever they touch. The BEM designed the storage units

212

to repel that kind of spray. The locks are basically indestructible." He held up his aerosol can. "But this is just polish. All we have to do is make the locks shiny."

Dez grunted. "I'm glad I came along to see this." His voice was thick with sarcasm. "I bet the prisoners inside will be thrilled to have shiny locks."

Spencer ignored the comment, stepping onto the back of the janitorial cart, his feet finding their familiar place on the motion-sensitive base. "You take the first three rows," Spencer said as Daisy stepped onto her cart. "I'll get the others."

She nodded to show her understanding. Then Spencer leaned forward, and the janitorial cart responded by picking up speed. He raced past the rows that he'd left to Daisy and then turned a corner, lining himself up to drive down one side.

As he sped forward, Spencer pushed the nozzle of his Glopified can, sending a mist of stainless steel polish at the metal lock in the door. Instantly, the round lock twinkled in the bright sun, polished to a glare from the Glopified spray.

Spencer moved on, driving just fast enough to get the job done quickly but accurately. The Glopified polish moistened each lock, removing any rust or grit and brightening the metal to a beautiful shine. When he was done with the row, Spencer wheeled around, doubling back down the aisle and polishing the locks on the opposing storage unit doors.

Spencer skidded around a corner, leaning hard as he blasted the polish along the next row of units. His accuracy and speed improved despite his finger growing tired from the repetitive motion of pressing the spray can's nozzle.

He didn't know how much time the task was taking. He only knew that they had to get them all before the fifteen-minute polish effect wore off. Marv was surely visible by now, and the suds would be progressively turning back into their soapy surveillance.

Spencer could see the end of the storage units. He shook his bottle to make sure there was enough polish for the remaining locks. There were maybe a dozen left, when his janitorial cart jerked to a halt with such force that he was thrown from his ride and sent tumbling across the pavement.

His Glopified coveralls protected him from the road rash, but the force still left him gasping for air, the aerosol can flung from his grasp. Spencer scrambled for the polish, but before his hand could close around it, a foot came down on his wrist.

"Did you really think you could succeed?" General Clean asked. He must have dropped down from the roof of the storage units, using his sticky tongue to topple Spencer's cart. Clean stooped and retrieved the fallen can of polish, holding it carelessly in his sticky fingers. "With this?"

"It was working," Spencer replied. "We hit more than five hundred locks before you guys even noticed we were here."

General Clean removed his foot from Spencer's wrist and took a step back toward the wreckage of the janitorial cart. "It did you no good," Clean said. "Whatever this polish was designed to do, it has clearly failed." He held up the aerosol can as if it were a child's toy. Clean gestured toward the storage-unit prisons. "Our Witches developed the formula to Glopify those locks. The prisons are quite secure. Your metal polish could never hope to open those locks."

"I wasn't trying to *open* the locks," Spencer admitted, reaching into his belt pouch for a new Glopified item to make its debut. "I just needed something shiny for my magnet."

Spencer pulled the magnet from his pouch. It was black and round, just smaller than a hockey puck.

Marv had been the first to point out that stainless steel was not magnetic. That would have been a problem if the magnet were ordinary. This one was Glopified, and Spencer's invention had a pull stronger than any regular magnet. Of course, it worked only on metal items that were shiny and polished.

The moment the Glopified magnet cleared his belt pouch, the magic activated. A silver force field shimmered like an orb around the magnet, encompassing Spencer's entire hand. The polished metal locks responded instantly. They ripped from the doors, whizzing through the air like bullets as the magnet pulled them in.

General Clean dropped to the ground, seeking cover from the flying locks, as Spencer leapt onto the wall of the nearest storage unit. His Glopified rubber boots adhered expertly to the vertical surface, and in five quick steps, he had run straight up the wall. Standing on the roof, Spencer held the magnet above his head like a victory torch.

He hoped the Rebels inside the storage units were keeping their heads low, because the magnetic locks were taking the most direct course to Spencer's hand, smashing through walls and cinder block to reach the boy on the roof.

The polished locks struck the glowing magnetic orb with a resounding *ping!* The Glopified pull drew them in from all across the compound until Spencer's hand, safe within the silvery magic, was the center of a giant ball of metal locks.

Spencer's arm slumped under the weight as the locks continued flying in. The mission was a success! All around the compound, the storage unit doors began to open. Where once a Glopified lock had kept them closed, now there was a gaping hole in each door.

On all sides below him, Spencer saw the faces of the Rebel prisoners, squinting against the sudden sunlight. It took them only a moment to realize that this was their chance for escape. The entire complex filled with the cries of the freed prisoners as they pushed open their broken doors and flooded out into the aisles. Spencer heard Marv, Daisy, and Dez directing the prisoners toward the squeegee exit.

General Clean gave a cry of rage and hurled the can of polish aside. His Grime tongue shot out, catching Spencer's arm with such force that he tumbled from the roof of the storage unit. His coveralls protected him, but in the shock of falling, Spencer had no choice but to release his grip on the magnet and its heavy payload. His hand slid out of the glowing magnetic orb, and the mess of polished locks hit the ground with a metallic thud. But the task was already done.

The aisles were now crowded with freed prisoners, and Spencer fell back into the throng. He unclipped a mop from his belt, turning back to find General Clean. But the big Sweeper was lost in the crowd.

"This way!" Spencer rallied, drawing the Rebels down the aisle to the spot where Dez would be waiting at the portal. Spencer scanned the escapees, anxious to see the familiar faces of his friends, desperate to see his family. But he saw only the nervous faces of strangers in his aisle.

The toilet-bowl cleaner had surely worn off, and whatever further distraction Marv had been attempting could not keep the Sweepers on the island from noticing that the prisoners were escaping.

The enemy approached quickly, and as Spencer ran toward the portal, he saw skirmishes breaking out on every row. The Sweepers were doing whatever was necessary to stop the Rebels from escaping. Spencer grimaced as he saw an unarmed Rebel struck down by a Filth Sweeper. Near the second row, a cluster of defenseless Rebels were attempting to overpower a Rubbish Sweeper. The attempt was short-lived as the strong Sweeper threw the Rebels back like rag dolls.

At last, the squeegee portal came into view. Dez hovered above the opening, ready to grapple with any other Sweepers that might draw near. Marv, now fully visible, stood before the portal, ushering Rebels through to the landfill. Dez must have given a few extra swipes with the

squeegee, because the portal was wide enough for three prisoners to pass through at once.

Rho was on the other side, frantically passing Glopified
weapons back through to a group of Rebel prisoners who
now stood to defend the portal.

A Filth Sweeper came rolling forward like a ball of
spikes. Spencer shouted a warning to the portal defenders as
double mops lashed out, throwing the Sweeper aside. Penny
twirled her weapons, blowing a strand of red hair from her
face.

Spencer couldn't help but grin when he saw her. Even
with borrowed mops from Marv's belt, Penny looked dangerous and agile.

Pushing past the ring of Rebel defenders and through a
mass of jittery prisoners, Spencer neared the squeegee portal. It took him a moment to find Daisy among the crowd.
When he did, his heart swelled with relief.

Mr. and Mrs. Gates were holding tightly to their only
child as Daisy led them toward the portal. They appeared
uninjured and relieved to be reunited, despite the current
danger. The image of the Gates family only caused Spencer
to wonder again if his own family was safe.

The Rebels were pouring through the magical doorway
in the cinder block. More than half of them had reached
safety, but the dwindling throng drew the enemy Sweepers
closer. Spencer pitched a Funnel Throw of vacuum dust
overhead and saw a Rubbish Sweeper go down under the
suction.

"Nice throw," said a calming voice behind Spencer. He

whirled around to find his dad, helping his mom and siblings over to the portal.

Alan Zumbro pulled his son into a sideways hug. "I think you have a knack for rescuing me from prison."

Spencer smiled. "You have a knack for getting caught."

"There wasn't much I could do," Alan said. "I had to stay with your mother. The Sweepers had the house surrounded."

"This probably isn't the best time to tell you, but . . ." Spencer swallowed. "There is no more house. Clean dissolved it with some Glopified drain cleaner."

"What?" Alice shouted as she passed Spencer's little brother through the squeegee portal. His mom looked a bit frazzled, but Spencer was proud of her for keeping it together. Alice sighed. "Your aunt's going to kill me." Then she stepped through the portal, staying close to her children.

Daisy came alongside Spencer and his dad. "I haven't seen him," she said. "I don't think Bernard is here."

"He has to be," answered Spencer, scanning the remaining faces of the Rebels. "We saw him in one of the suds." Then he remembered the unopened storage units. General Clean had attacked before Spencer had had time to reach the end of the row. He felt a sinking sensation in his stomach. Without thinking it through, Spencer took a step in the direction of the locked units.

Alan caught his son's arm. "Where are you going?"

"I didn't get them all," Spencer answered. "Bernard

must be trapped in one of the units at the end of the last row. We have to find him."

Alan reached out and unclipped a pushbroom from Spencer's belt, nodding for his son to show the way. Daisy readied her plunger, preparing to join Spencer and his dad as they pushed through the line of Rebel defenders and past the attacking Sweepers.

"Dez!" Spencer yelled. "Give us some cover!"

"You got it!" answered the flying boy. He straightened himself in midair, working up a belch. Then he ripped off his dust mask and let it out, spewing a black cloud of grit over the BEM Sweepers.

In the concealing haze, Spencer rushed forward, his dustpan shield plowing past a Grime Sweeper. A moment later, Spencer was leading Daisy and his dad on a dead sprint down the rows of storage units.

They rounded the final corner and Spencer saw the wreckage of the janitorial cart. Beside it was the Glopified stainless steel polish. He gathered up the aerosol can and sprayed the liquid over the lock on the nearest storage unit. But the lock stayed motionless. The magnet should have ripped it away!

"Look for the magnet!" Spencer called, racing the final distance and polishing each remaining lock until all were sparkling in the sunlight.

Daisy fell to her knees, scouring the aisle. The area was littered with hundreds of bent locks that were no longer attracted to the Glopified magnet. The polish had worn off and the locks were now a dull and rusty metal.

221

"It's not here!" Daisy shouted.

Of course it wasn't. If the magnet had been lying out in the open, the recently polished locks would have pulled out of the doors, flying to attach themselves to it.

"It's gone," Spencer muttered. As long as the magnet was completely covered, it wouldn't work. "Somebody must have picked it up and put it in their pocket."

"Not a pocket," answered the rich, deep voice of General Clean. "A fist." He held out his slimy hand, the Glopified magnet presumably clenched tightly between his partially webbed fingers. The Sweeper General smiled. "Hello again, Alan."

CHAPTER 28

"TO PUT TO REST OUR DOUBTS."

Spencer saw his dad's jaw tighten beneath his trim beard. To everyone else, General Clean was Reginald McClean—an ex-warlock, commander of the Sweeper forces. He was an enemy without a shred of kindness or mercy.

But to Alan Zumbro, General Clean was an old friend. He was Rod Grush, Alan's former coworker and partner. They had spent years together, working to uncover clues that would lead to the Auran landfill and the *Manualis Custodem*. But Rod Grush had betrayed Spencer's father, a decision that had led to Alan's detainment in the dumpster prison at New Forest Academy.

"When we met in my laboratory," Clean said, "you didn't believe that I would kill you." He took a silent step

223

toward Alan, his white lab coat swaying around him. "What do you think today?"

"Give us the magnet," Spencer demanded.

"Stay out of this, boy," answered the Sweeper. General Clean never took his eyes from Alan Zumbro. "I have a score to settle with an old friend."

Alan finally acknowledged the big Sweeper. "What do you want, Rod?"

"A duel," answered General Clean. "To put to rest our doubts."

"What doubts?" Alan asked.

"You doubt that I would kill you," said Clean. "I doubt that you would kill me." He shrugged. "I see only one way to resolve this."

He reached into his lab coat and withdrew a damp rag. Spencer felt sick when he saw it. The last time he'd witnessed Clean use the Glopified rag, it had caused the death of Walter Jamison. With a single crack of his damp rag, General Clean's victims vanished without a trace.

"Choose your weapon," said Clean. "And let me familiarize you with mine." He dangled the rag as if he were displaying a fine cloth. It was wrinkled and stained, the hem slightly tattered. "The rag can tear through cloth and covering, dematerializing organic flesh on contact. Anything touching that flesh vanishes with it. Not even your Rebel coveralls can protect against my rag." Clean's reptilian mouth curled in a smirk. "I learned that the night I finished Walter Jamison."

Spencer stepped forward, his teeth gritted in anger at

General Clean's casual mention of Walter's death. But Alan held out a hand to steady his son.

Spencer saw his dad step forward, the hot sun causing a trickle of sweat to drip down the side of his face. "Razorblade," Alan said, beckoning with his outstretched hand.

"This isn't a fair duel!" Daisy cried. "Sweepers have to die twice!"

"Then my opponent will have to be *twice* as determined," answered Clean.

Spencer withdrew a razorblade from his belt and pressed it into his father's hand. "You don't have to do this, Dad," he whispered.

Alan slid his thumb along the button, extending the razorblade into a two-edged sword. The metallic sound echoed between the rows of storage units.

"Your boy is right," Clean said. "You should think carefully. Do you have the mettle to kill an old friend?"

"I've thought long enough." Alan leapt forward, swinging his razorblade in a downward arc. General Clean reacted, sliding easily out of the way.

Clean sidestepped, his rag parrying a thrust from Alan. They paced as only duelers can, weapons darting and flashing in the hot Florida sun.

Spencer positioned himself beside Daisy, the two kids huddling near the wreckage of the janitorial cart. It was clear that General Clean had the advantage. Being half Grime made his movements silent and swift.

The Sweeper sprang sideways, leaping off the wall and

making an aerial whip for Alan's head. Alan ducked aside, following up with a series of sharp thrusts as the Sweeper hit the ground.

"Give me the magnet!" Alan demanded. Clean's tail swished out, and Alan barely managed to leap over it.

"You should have rescued all your people the first time," said the Sweeper. He kept his left hand closed tightly around the Glopified magnet.

Spencer reached into his belt pouch and drew a pinch of vacuum dust. Clean was drawing closer, definitely within range. A simple Palm Blast would take the Sweeper down, and Alan could easily finish him.

"How will you do it, Alan?" Clean asked. "How will you kill me?" He whipped his rag, and the damp fabric wrapped around Alan's blade as he parried the blow. "Will you stab me through the chest?"

Clean flicked the rag, angling the tangled razorblade back at Alan. The blade nicked Alan's shoulder, but he refused to let go of the weapon. Spencer saw his dad wince in pain.

"Or," Clean continued, "will you take my head?" The Sweeper tugged his rag upward, causing Alan's arm to extend. They stood face-to-face, sweat dripping from their chins.

"I don't need your head," Alan said. "I just need your hand."

With one swift movement, Alan Zumbro slipped his razorblade out of Clean's rag and brought the sword around in a deft slice. The Glopified razorblade cut through General

Clean's forearm, completely severing the Sweeper's left hand.

General Clean cried out in pain. His rag fell limply to the ground as he gripped the stump of his left arm, oozing with the pale slime of a wounded Grime. Clean staggered back, tumbling to his knees among the wreckage of the jani-torial cart. Standing only a few feet behind him, Spencer saw the gruesome wound and looked away.

Alan took a step forward, the tip of his razorblade gently touching Clean's broad chest. He needed only to thrust, and General Clean would die.

"You won't," muttered Clean. His voice was raspy and his breath short from the pain. "You won't kill me. Even if it's only the death of my Sweeper side. You don't have the nerve to stab an old friend."

Spencer saw his father hold the tip of the razorblade steady for several long seconds. The sun beat down on his bearded face, and his shirt was wet with sweat and blood.

Silently, Alan took a step back and closed his razor-blade. "Get out of my sight," he whispered.

Moving with all the speed and fluidity of a Grime, General Clean's remaining hand snatched his limp rag from the ground and tucked it into the folds of his soiled lab coat. His long tongue shot out, stealing the razorblade from Alan's grip. The Sweeper lunged backward, his wounded arm wrapping around Spencer as his tongue delivered the blade into Clean's hand. The sword extended, its smooth edge pressed threateningly against the boy's throat.

Spencer didn't even have time to gasp. His pinch of

vacuum dust fell uselessly to the ground. He squirmed against the big man's grip, painfully aware of the sharp weapon pressed under his chin.

Clean's tail lashed out like a whip, knocking Daisy back against the storage units as Alan stepped forward with his fists clenched.

"Let him go!" he demanded. Any trace of mercy that had glimmered in Alan's eyes died when General Clean touched his son. The Sweeper began a slow retreat, dragging Spencer with him.

"The magnet!" Spencer cried. "Open the storage units!"

Everyone's eyes turned to the severed hand lying on the pavement. The Grimelike fingers were still curled tightly around the magnet.

Daisy lunged for the fallen hand. Closing one eye in disgust at the task, she peeled back the sticky fingers, and the magnet rolled out of the grasp. Immediately, the polished metal locks ripped from the storage unit doors and came whizzing to the magnet in the girl's hand.

In the hailstorm of flying locks, General Clean's razorblade suddenly snapped shut. The big Sweeper leapt onto Spencer's back, knocking the boy forward onto the pavement. Spencer pushed against him, rolling onto his side, but General Clean was gone.

"Where'd he go?" Spencer staggered to his feet, gaze casting down the rows of storage units. He knew the Grime Sweepers could move quickly, but Clean's sudden departure was too fast. It was almost as if the General had vanished.

"I got the magnet!" Daisy shouted. She was holding it

steady above her head, now a dozen shiny locks bent around its magical glow. The remaining Rebel prisoners threw open their doors and stumbled out into the sun.

Spencer was still scanning the area, searching for any sign of General Clean. His father's hand on his shoulder caused him to startle.

"We have to get these last prisoners back to the land-fill," Alan said, gesturing toward the squeegee portal. Spencer nodded, finally giving up on wondering how Clean had escaped so suddenly.

"This way!" Alan said, leading the new batch of the Rebels back toward the portal.

Spencer approached Daisy, who still stood with the glowing magnet in hand. "How do I get these off?" she asked, pointing to the shiny locks that clung to the silvery orb of magic surrounding the magnet.

"Try to slide the whole thing into your belt pouch," Spencer suggested. "The locks will fall off when the polish wears off."

Daisy nodded, fighting to stuff the magnetic ball of locks into her pouch. Once the magnet was stowed, she slipped her hand free.

The recently freed Rebel prisoners were moving quickly, leaving their young rescuers behind. A shadow passed over-head, and Spencer looked up just as Dez landed beside him.

"Hurry up, you chumps," Dez said. "Not sure how much longer those Rebel defenders can keep the squeegee portal open."

Spencer nodded. They needed to get back to the land-fill.

"I'd offer to give you a *hand*," came a familiar voice from behind. "But it looks like you've already found one."

Spencer turned to see Dr. Bernard Weizmann standing in the middle of the aisle, holding General Clean's sundered hand. He twitched his pencil-thin mustache and waved Clean's slimy hand at them in greeting.

"What's with the creepy hand?" Dez asked.

"Eww," Daisy said. "Put that down!"

"I've got to *hand* it to you," Bernard said with a wink. "You must have solved my garbology clues."

Daisy nodded. "Your note was right. The Rebels are looking for something important. And we need Bookworm's help to find it," she said.

"We have his textbook back at the landfill," Spencer explained. "Did the BEM take his lunchbox when they captured you at the Gates house?"

Bernard nodded. "I couldn't ditch it fast enough. One of those Sweeper thugs threw the lunchbox in the moving truck along with everything else."

"Where did all the stolen stuff end up?" Daisy asked, glancing across the island. "Are they keeping it here?"

Bernard dropped the severed Sweeper's hand and tugged nervously at his aviator cap. "They're not keeping the Rebel stuff at all." He twitched his mustache. "They're destroying it."

CHAPTER 29

"IN CHARGE OF THE BARGE."

Spencer tried to keep his hopes from sinking. The BEM was destroying all the belongings they'd stolen from the Rebels. But Bernard had been taken only two days ago. There might be time to stop the BEM before they got to Bookworm's lunchbox. "How long have you been here?" he asked.

"They locked us up on Monday evening," answered the garbologist. "They drove us through a portal to cut down travel time."

"What about the stuff?" Spencer asked. "Where did they take it?"

"They dumped the whole truckload into a set of dumpsters once we got here," Bernard said.

The news definitely could have been worse. At least the

load was nearby. "We can find it," Spencer said, trying to recall if they'd passed any dumpsters on the way in.

"I'm afraid not," Bernard said. "The BEM just came to take out the trash."

"What do you mean?" Daisy asked.

"About a half hour before you got here, I heard some unmistakable sounds," said Bernard. "A garbage barge came in off the south side of the island. The Sweepers loaded the dumpsters onboard, and it made its way back out to sea."

"A garbage barge?" Dez asked.

"A big ship," Bernard explained. "The BEM is dumping all the Rebel belongings into the ocean."

"Well, I hope the fish enjoy my fish tank," muttered Daisy.

"That's dumb," Dez said. "The whole ocean is their fish tank."

"Forget about the fish," Spencer said. "What about Bookworm's lunchbox?"

Daisy paled at the thought of her pet Thingamajunk going to a watery grave.

"I'll catch them," Dez said, cracking his knuckles. "Which way did they go?"

Bernard shrugged. "It's only been thirty minutes since pickup. A big ship like that doesn't travel fast." He held up a finger for silence as a ship's horn sounded in the distance. "They haven't gotten far."

Dez spread his wings, but Spencer caught his muscled arm. "The fence," he said. "You'll get zapped if you try to fly over." The only two safe exits off the island were through the gate by the bridge or through the squeegee portal to the landfill.

Dez backed down, clearly having forgotten about the Glopified fence. "Do your thing," Dez suggested.

"My thing?" Spencer asked.

"You know," Dez continued. "The magic spit thing."

Spencer hadn't used his spit sponge on the fence earlier because he didn't want to ruin their element of surprise. But of course it was clear to General Clean and the Sweepers that the Rebels were escaping. By now, the Windex would have worn off on the soapsuds, so the Witches were probably watching from their dirty lair.

Spencer nodded, pulling his spit sponge from a side pouch on his belt. The others followed him past the final row of storage units until they stood at the Glopified electric fence. There was a gap in the vegetation here, and Spencer could see the beach and ocean on the other side.

He squeezed the sponge, a bit of saliva dripping onto his hand. He shuddered and tried not to think about how gross his superpower was.

Rubbing his hands together activated the Glop in his spit and a second later, Spencer's hands were glowing gold.

Reaching out, Spencer paused for a brief second. He was confident in the magic of his spit. But if his left hand failed to de-Glopify the BEM fence for some reason, Spencer had no doubt he'd be blasted to smithereens by the power racing through the chain link.

Taking a deep breath, he quickly grabbed on, the fingers of his left hand wrapping through the links of fencing.

Immediately, there was a loud *crack!* His hand was like a pebble thrown into a still pond. Magic rippled away, powering down the entire electric fence.

Spencer let go of the broken fence. "That might have attracted some attention," he pointed out. "We should hurry."

Dez instantly reached out, scooping up Spencer in one arm and Daisy in the other. His wings unfolded and he jumped into the air.

"Hey!" Bernard shouted. "What about me?"

"Two hands!" Dez answered. Spencer had the sneaking suspicion that Dez could have carried a third passenger if he'd wanted to. But Spencer knew from experience that the Sweeper kid didn't like bringing adults along. With only Spencer and Daisy for companions, Dez could do whatever he wanted without worrying about consequences.

They lifted over the BEM fence and soared above the beach, racing along the back side of the island. According to the soapsud surveillance, the buoys roped off a section of water all the way around. Spencer wondered how the dumpsters could have been delivered to the garbage barge without triggering the monster Grime that patrolled the water.

Then, adjusting himself in Dez's grip, Spencer saw that one section of buoys had been moved to create a safe runway out to sea. Rubbish Sweepers must have plunged the dumpsters and flown them out to the barge. By the time the ship was loaded, the island was under attack. Luckily, they hadn't taken the time to replace the buoys. Now, as long as

Dez didn't fly outside the lines, they should be able to make a quiet escape to the ocean.

"There!" Daisy pointed out to sea. Dez picked up the pace as Spencer spotted the garbage barge. Bernard was right, the ship was slow and hadn't gone far. It was chugging black smoke as it rode the swells no more than a half mile beyond the usual perimeter of buoys.

The large vessel was wide and flat. The deck was littered with piles of debris, spilling over the many dumpsters that had been loaded onboard. It was more stuff than the Gateses had in their house, and Spencer was sure that the belongings of several Rebel households were on their way to get dumped.

The only raised portion on the deck was a wheelhouse at the rear. The boxy room had windows on all sides, allowing the captain to see well enough to safely steer the ship.

Even at this distance, Spencer could see movement on the flat deck. "Sweepers," he said. "It isn't going to be easy to sift through all that garbage and find Bookworm's lunchbox."

"I see four Sweepers on the deck," Dez said. Spencer secretly envied the boy's super eyesight. "I'll deal with the bad guys. You two find the stupid lunchbox."

"No," Spencer said. "We should take out the captain first. We'll never get anything done with somebody watching us from that cabin. Besides, if we remove the captain, then we're in charge of the barge."

Daisy snickered. "In charge of the barge," she repeated quietly.

Spencer ignored the unintentional rhyme. "If we take over the captain's room, we can stop the ship, lock doors . . . do whatever we have to do until we can find Bookworm's head on the deck."

Commandeering the garbage barge was a bold plan, and Spencer knew it would take some smart flying from Dez. The Sweeper boy responded instantly, dropping so quickly toward the water that Spencer felt his stomach heave.

Dez pulled up just before the three of them hit the ocean. They skimmed over the tops of the waves, Spencer feeling a warm spray in his face as they drew nearer to the barge.

They were close enough to see details now. The ship had a name printed in bold lettering across the sides.

Queen Anne's Debris

Dez zoomed toward the hull of the barge. Just when Spencer thought they might slam into the side, the Sweeper boy angled upward, rising straight into the air. Dez landed on top of the wheelhouse a little less quietly than Spencer had hoped. The moment his feet hit the roof, he dumped Spencer and Daisy and folded in his wings.

Spencer held still for a moment, waiting for someone to react to their arrival. But the crew of the garbage barge weren't expecting any trouble, and Spencer guessed that their attention was lax.

"What now?" Daisy asked.

Spencer crept forward on his stomach. Gripping the

edge of the wheelhouse, he leaned as far as he dared, peer-ing through the windows to the room where the captain steered.

He saw a long panel of controls covered in buttons and switches, the ship's wheel rising in the center. There was only one person in the wheelhouse, but the sight of him made Spencer draw back suddenly.

He looked at his friends in surprise. "The captain is Dustin DeFleur!"

"WE'VE GOT
TO FIND THAT
LUNCHBOX!"

Daisy looked puzzled. "The captain is dusting the floor?" she said.

"Then it should be easy to take him down," added Dez.

"No!" Spencer rolled his eyes. He enunciated clearly so there would be no confusion. "Professor Dustin DeFleur is the captain!"

"Our P.E. teacher?" Daisy said, finally catching on.

"That chump is a hundred years old," Dez said. "This is going to be easy! All we have to do is kick out his cane and he'll fall over."

"What's he doing here?" Daisy asked. "Shouldn't he be teaching second graders how to jump rope or something?"

"School's out for the day," Spencer replied. "DeFleur must have squeegeed over here to command the barge."

"Not for long," Dez said, clearly growing impatient with

238

the conversation. "I'll slam through the front window. You two follow me in." Without leaving time for them to come up with a better plan, Dez stepped off the edge of the wheelhouse. His black wings fanned, slowing his fall like a parachute as he kicked through the front window. Grabbing the edges of the broken glass with his tough hands, Dez pulled himself through.

Below, Spencer heard the old man cry out in surprise. Trusting in his newly Glopified rubber boots, Spencer stepped over the edge. His boots instantly adhered to the side of the wheelhouse. He took three steps down, Daisy by his side, and leapt through the shattered window.

The old professor had backed against the wall, his thin cane waving at the intimidating form of Dez. "Back away!" DeFleur threatened.

"Sorry, old fart," said Dez. "We're taking the ship." The Sweeper boy reached for the control panels, but DeFleur swung his wooden cane to stop him. Concealed metal prongs unfolded from the tip of the cane, forming a Glopified rake. He thrust the handle toward Dez, but Spencer was ready for a trick from Dustin DeFleur. He'd been caught in that hidden rake cage once before: on the night of Walter Jamison's death.

Spencer's razorblade flashed downward, chopping through Professor DeFleur's wooden cane. The concealed rake fell short, the handle clattering to the wheelhouse floor in two pieces. Professor DeFleur grunted, the impact of the broken cane jarring his frail body and casting him back against the wall.

"Clean said it might come to this," muttered DeFleur, a hint of madness in his eyes. "I'm ready now."

"Ready for what?" Daisy asked.

DeFleur's wrinkly hand clawed at his shirt pocket until his fingers closed around something small. "Ready to be strong again." He lifted the item to his lips, and Spencer realized too late what it was.

A Sweeper potion.

Professor DeFleur grunted, the contents of the glass vial gone. He threw the container to the floor as a rapid change overcame him.

The old man still looked wiry and thin, but his frame now seemed tough and durable. His arthritic fingers split as dirty claws emerged. Bristling, sharp quills ripped through his linen shirt, and a patch of dusty fur ran down the back of his neck. His white hair remained frizzed out like a mad scientist's, but suddenly it was studded with short spikes.

The man's eyes, now an unnatural blue color, turned on the three kids in the wheelhouse. "Who's ready for P.E. now?"

DeFleur's voice was raspy, and Spencer felt an instant wave of fatigue fill the wheelhouse. He staggered sideways, Daisy catching his arm to support him.

"Here," Dez said, digging a crumpled dust mask from his pocket and tossing it to Daisy. "I don't need it now that the toilet-bowl cleaner wore off. I still can't believe it smelled like cookies."

Professor DeFleur charged and Dez met him head-on, the two Sweepers grappling in the center of the wheelhouse.

Daisy looked down at the mask she'd caught, noticing that the thin elastic band had snapped. "Do you have to break everything you touch?"

"You would too, if you were as strong as me," Dez replied, throwing DeFleur back as if to prove his point.

Daisy knotted the two ends of elastic together and placed the dust mask over Spencer's face, reviving him just as he was slipping into careless slumber. He jerked to his senses with a deep gasp. "Good morning!"

The old professor rushed at Dez once more, but the Sweeper boy slammed DeFleur against the barge's control panel. DeFleur bounced back with the strength of an overgrown Filth, throwing Dez against the ship's wheel.

The barge lurched, making a sharp turn that toppled Spencer and Daisy to the floor. Dez pushed back, the wheel spinning on its own to set a new course.

Professor DeFleur delivered an uppercut to Dez and rolled away. The old man lunged for the ship's horn, desperate to sound an alarm, when Daisy suctioned him down with a pinch of vac dust.

Dez rubbed at the pain in his jaw. "That wasn't so bad."

Spencer staggered to his feet. "Let's see if we can stop this thing," he said, staring at the array of controls before him. The barge's new course was taking them back toward the BEM's island. Spencer grabbed the wheel, but before he could crank it, Daisy shouted a warning from behind her dustpan shield.

Spencer looked back at Dustin DeFleur, trembling on the floor of the wheelhouse. He'd seen angry Filths use this tactic before, and Spencer immediately knew that the Rebels had to take cover. He drew a Glopified dustpan from his belt, twisting the handle to fan the metal into a circular shield. Spencer threw himself in front of Dez, pushing the bully down so they both had shelter behind the shield.

With a grunt and a hiss, Professor DeFleur shot the quills from his back. Three of the projectiles buried into Spencer's shield. A few more clattered off Daisy's defenses, and dozens of deadly quills burrowed into the wheelhouse walls and control panels.

Professor DeFleur picked himself up, straining his wiry body against the waning effects of the vac dust. He looked strange now, without his quills. Spencer thought it would make him look more human, but the result was the opposite. Already, new quills were rising from his back, short nubs that would soon be deadly spikes.

DeFleur hoisted himself over the nearest control panel. His clawed fingers smashed out the glass of another window, and he dragged himself through. The old man fell from the wheelhouse, landing in a pile of garbage on the deck below.

Spencer grabbed the barge's wheel once more, attempting to steer the ship back out to sea. "It's stuck!" he said, noting where several of DeFleur's quills had shot through the wheel, anchoring it into place.

Spencer grabbed one of the quills in hopes of pulling it free. But he drew back his hand the moment it made contact. The Sweeper's quills were edged with miniature razor barbs. Ripping the quill out of the wheel would shred his flesh.

"Forget it!" Dez said, crawling up to the broken window where DeFleur had escaped. "We've got to find that lunch-box!"

He sprang out of the wheelhouse, gliding down toward the flat deck. Spencer's idea to commandeer the barge had gone horribly wrong. Now it was time to implement Dez's backup plan. He would pick off the Sweepers while Spencer and Daisy searched through the discarded belongings on deck.

Daisy had found a pair of binoculars and was scanning over the dumpsters below. Spencer wanted to rush her, but it was smarter to take their time searching the debris from the protected vantage point of the wheelhouse.

It didn't take Daisy long. "My pillow!" she shouted, pointing down toward one of the dumpsters. "And that's our dining table!" Daisy dropped the binoculars and made for the broken window. Spencer joined her, the two kids using their rubber boots to run straight down the exterior of the wheelhouse. When they reached the deck, Spencer and Daisy paused behind the first of many dumpsters.

"My stuff was in a dumpster about halfway across the deck," Daisy said. "On the left side." Hunching down, Daisy made a stealthy dash along a row of overflowing dumpsters. Spencer followed, keeping a careful eye out for enemies on-board.

Twice, Spencer saw Dez soaring overhead. When the Sweeper boy dipped out of sight, his arrival was met with shouts and the sound of struggle.

"Okay," Daisy said, pausing between two industrial-sized

dumpsters. She peered over the rim and patted the side of the big container. "This one and that one." Daisy pointed to the dumpster next to Spencer.

"You're sure?" Spencer asked.

"Both of these containers are full of garbage from my house," Daisy answered, hoisting herself up on the rim.

"I wouldn't call this garbage," Spencer said, climbing into the neighboring dumpster. He shoved against the Gateses' leather couch from their living room.

"There's a saying in garbology," Daisy began, disappearing into the debris. "Everything is garbage."

Spencer lifted his eyebrow at the strange saying. He saw the Gateses' china cabinet, smashed to shards, the precious contents destroyed. "This is valuable stuff from your house, Daisy."

"And there's another saying," said Daisy. "All garbage is valuable." She lifted a recently discovered bedroom pillow and tossed it aside. "The BEM probably dumped all my family's stuff together. That means Bookworm's lunchbox should be here."

Spencer lifted the Gateses' discarded microwave and peered underneath. "I think you're going to make a pretty good garbologist someday, Daisy."

Her head poked over the rim of the dumpster, a smile on her face. "I hope so." Then she disappeared back into the wreckage of her home.

The search was frustrating under the hot Florida sun. Spencer was using a broom handle to pry some of the heavier items up so he could see beneath them. The wood snapped in his hands, and he stepped back as an upright piano settled deeper into the dumpster.

Standing tall, Spencer saw Dez grappling with a Grime Sweeper. Two other enemies were racing across the deck to reach the boy, but Spencer had to trust that Dez could take care of himself.

Spencer glanced out over the water. The barge was on a collision course for the BEM island. He guessed that they had less than fifteen minutes before the vessel ran aground. A sudden worry crossed Spencer's mind. He twisted sideways to look out at the sea just in time to see the barge carelessly running over the cordon of buoys that ringed the island.

"I got it!" Daisy shouted. She stood up in the dumpster, using both hands to hold a dented lunchbox high above her head. No sooner had she struck her victory pose, a big smile on her face, than an enormous Grime tongue shot out of the water beside the barge.

The sticky tongue slammed into the side of Daisy's dumpster and retracted. Spencer's instincts were fast. He drew a mop and flicked the magical strings, entangling Daisy and jerking her out of harm's way as the dumpster slid wildly across the deck.

The monster Grime rose out of the water, flicking the dumpster into the air and swallowing it in one gulp.

Daisy tumbled against Spencer, both of them protected from the collision by their Glopified coveralls.

"You got Bookworm's lunchbox?" Spencer asked.

Daisy sat up, her face panic-stricken. "I dropped it!" she cried. "Into the dumpster!"

They both peered over the edge of their container. Daisy's dumpster, with Bookworm's lunchbox, was long gone. And the huge Grime was coming back for seconds!

Striking his broken broom against the trash, Spencer soared into the air with Daisy just as the monster Grime devoured the second garbage container. Airborne as they were, Spencer saw that Dez's fight with the Sweepers had broken up. Everyone stood terrified on the deck of the barge, wondering where the ginormous Toxite would surface next.

Spencer's broom had just settled back to the deck when the Grime sprang from the ocean. It landed squarely in the center of the barge, its orange extension cord trailing off into the water. The ship was barely larger than the creature, and when its tail flicked around, it cleared off more than half the deck.

Dumpsters went flying overboard, with debris hailing down on the water like shrapnel. The Sweepers that weren't quick enough to evade the tail were swept away. Spencer could hear their cries until the moment they hit the sea. He didn't know Dez's fate, as Spencer and Daisy scrambled wildly toward the protection of the wheelhouse. There was nothing they could do about Bookworm's lost lunchbox. Now all attention turned to finding safety.

The Grime's mouth opened, a dark hole large enough to drive a bus into. Its tongue lashed out, catching a Rubbish Sweeper in midair and swallowing him down.

Daisy paused in their retreat, grabbing Spencer's arm and pointing directly at the Grime's mouth. "Look!" Spencer didn't know what she wanted him to see as the Grime hissed, seeking a new victim. "Between the teeth!"

Spencer leaned forward, squinting at the jagged maw of the amphibious creature. There was all manner of debris caught in the Toxite's mouth, but the piece Daisy had noticed was wedged just between the bottom two front teeth.

It was Bookworm's lunchbox.

"Good thing he doesn't floss," Daisy said.

Spencer was considering their good luck and wondering how long the dented lunchbox would remain lodged. Spencer had once gone a whole afternoon with a poppy seed stuck between his front teeth. But he also wasn't trying to eat a barge that day.

The monster Grime made a terrifying shriek and slipped back into the water without a splash. Spencer knew it wasn't over. The creature was probably rallying for another attack.

Dez landed abruptly beside them near the base of the wheelhouse. "We've got to turn this boat around!" he pointed out.

Spencer wanted nothing more than to sail past the buoys and out of the Grime's reach, but they hadn't come this far for nothing.

"No," Spencer said. "The Grime has Bookworm's lunch-box. We've got to get it back."

"Are you crazy?" Dez shouted.

"What's your plan?" Daisy asked.

"Maybe we could wedge the Grime's mouth open," Spencer brainstormed. "Then one of us could slip inside and grab the lunchbox."

"Not it!" Dez shouted.

"Maybe we don't have to go in at all," Daisy said. She turned to Spencer. "Do you have any stainless steel polish left?"

CHAPTER 31

"YOU'RE STILL ALIVE?"

The three kids crouched at the base of the wheelhouse, waiting for the monster Grime to resurface. If there were other Sweepers still aboard, they were making themselves scarce. The barge was still purring steadily toward the island, and Spencer guessed that they would hit land in a matter of minutes.

Spencer shook the aerosol can of stainless steel polish. He didn't have much liquid left. Just enough for two or three shots.

"You better not miss, Doofus," said Dez.

"I won't," Spencer answered. "As long as you make sure it keeps its mouth open long enough for me to get a good shot at the lunchbox." The missing piece of Bookworm's head was made of metal. A bit of polish would magnetize it and then Daisy could extract the lunchbox by wielding the Glopified magnet.

There was still plenty of danger in the plan, since Spencer would need to get close enough to the creature's mouth to get a clear shot.

"Maybe it's not coming back," Daisy whispered. No sooner had the phrase left her lips than the monster Grime resurfaced. It sprang onto the deck again, its giant orb eyes darting around as it swayed its massive head back and forth to accommodate for its blind spot.

As per the plan, Dez grabbed Daisy, and the two of them flew up to the wheelhouse. They entered through the broken window, climbing over the quill-studded control panel. Once in the wheelhouse, Daisy found the ship's horn and pulled the cord.

A bass hum pealed out over the water, and the Grime sprang to silence the sound. Its front legs squelched onto the wheelhouse, tongue darting through the shattered windows and missing Dez by mere inches.

Spencer watched from below, waiting for the perfect opportunity. Dez and Daisy were making a racket, taunting and yelling to keep the Toxite's focus on them.

At last, the Grime opened its enormous mouth and bit down on the corner of the wheelhouse. Spencer leapt onto the wall, his rubber boots sticking. He sprinted upward, trying to gauge the distance. He wanted to stand close, but not too close.

Spencer saw a glint of metal between the Grime's lower teeth. Standing horizontally on the wall, dangerously near the mouth, Spencer took aim and released three quick sprays with the stainless steel polish. He knew he had hit his target when the sun glimmered sharply against a magically polished surface.

Spencer was just about to shout for Daisy to use the magnet when the Grime pulled away from the wheelhouse, its tongue flicking out to break off the radio antenna atop the ship. The tongue retracted sharply with the Grime's sudden intake of breath. The unexpected inward draft yanked Spencer's boots from the wall, and he spiraled into the Grime's open mouth.

Spencer landed on the creature's tongue, slipping toward the back of the throat. He was instantly soaked in slime, and he gagged at the feel of it. The ship's antenna landed beside him, the Grime's teeth coming together to smash it into fragments. Clambering, Spencer drew a plunger from his belt and clamped the red suction cup to the roof of the Grime's mouth. He dangled there, resisting the swallowing pull toward the Grime's dark belly.

The abrasive chewing of the antenna must have knocked Bookworm's lunchbox free of the spot where it had been stuck between the Grime's front teeth. Spencer reached out for it, his grasp slipping on the handle of his toilet plunger.

He caught the metal lunchbox and hugged it close to his chest as he tumbled into the Grime's wide throat. The daylight that shone through jagged teeth had just disappeared when Spencer, not quite swallowed, felt the unmistakable magnetic pull of the lunchbox in his hands.

He gripped with all his might as the polished lunch-box shot out of the throat and across the Grime's mouth. Spencer braced for impact as the lunchbox hit the Grime's front tooth with such force that the jagged incisor was ripped from the creature's gums.

Spencer sailed through the opening, the tooth falling to the deck below as he trailed behind the lunchbox like the tail of a comet. He crashed through a window of the wheelhouse and saw Daisy standing squarely, the Glopified magnet in her outstretched hand.

Spencer collided with Daisy so hard that the two of them slammed against the back wall of the wheelhouse. Bookworm's polished lunchbox connected with the Glopified magnet, and Dez caught the attached items as they flung from Daisy's grasp.

"No time for cuddling," Dez said, as Spencer and Daisy untangled themselves.

"Yuck!" Spencer staggered to his feet, still dripping Grime slime onto the wheelhouse floor. "I almost got swallowed!"

"At least the Grime didn't barf while you were still in there," Dez said, pointing to the massive Toxite on the deck.

Apparently angry over the loss of its tooth, the monster Grime was shuddering. Pale sacs of luminescent acid were filling just below its gullet.

"Not good," Spencer muttered as the Grime spewed its venom across the front half of the ship. The glowing acid ate through hull and deck as the monster Grime slipped back into the ocean.

The barge creaked and groaned, pitching awkwardly in the water as it began to sink. Vapor plumed upward as the water and acid mingled, waves breaking over the deck.

"We've got to get to safety," Spencer said.

"Not the island," replied Dez. He was staring out the window, back toward the BEM's private island. "More than a dozen Sweepers on the beach."

"General Clean must have called for backup," Spencer said, leaning across the control panel and noticing movement on the beach.

"What about the squeegee portal?" Daisy asked.

"If the Sweepers are waiting for us on the beach," Spencer said, "then it means the fight in the storage units is over." He tried not to despair. "The squeegee portal must have closed. We have to find another way back to the landfill."

"What about Lina's truck that we came in on?" Daisy asked. "It's parked on the far side of the bridge."

"That'll work," Spencer said. "But we have to get to it."

"I've got an idea," Dez said. Reaching out, he unclipped a plunger from Daisy's belt and leapt out of the wheelhouse. Spencer and Daisy carefully made their way down to the deck, but Dez had gone overboard. A second later, the sinking barge was rising out of the water.

Spencer crawled over to the edge of the deck and peered down as the ship flew higher. Dez's plunger was clamped firmly on the hull, his wings easily bearing the weightless barge into the sky.

"The BEM might be able to stop you two," Dez shouted. "But I'm betting they won't be able to stop a barge!"

From the water below, the monster Grime suddenly surfaced. Its long tongue shot out, but Dez had carried them straight up to a startling height. The Grime's tongue fell short, and it dove back into the water, only to resurface again with another out-of-range attack.

"Spencer!" Daisy cried.

His attention returned to the deck just as Professor Dustin DeFleur bowled into him. Spencer skidded dangerously close to the edge of the airborne barge. The Sweeper man had regrown all his quills, and when he snarled, the hair rose on the back of his neck.

"You're still alive?" Spencer shouted. He'd assumed the professor had been swept off the deck by the Grime's tail. The old man had a knack for coming back.

"I was in the engine room," said DeFleur. "Waiting till we were out of the Grime's reach." He swiped for Spencer with his sharp claws, driving the boy to the very edge of the ruined deck. "You know what they say," the professor continued. "The captain goes down with the ship."

"You got one thing right," Daisy said. Professor DeFleur turned in surprise at her voice. Daisy thrust her pushbroom, the bristles catching the Sweeper in the chest and sending him sailing off the edge of the flying ship. "The captain goes down."

Spencer watched over the side, seeing the old man

plummet the terrifying distance to the ocean. But Professor DeFleur never hit the water. Just before his fall ended, the monster Grime leapt from the sea. It caught Dustin DeFleur in its mouth, huge jaws snapping shut. Then the overgrown Toxite settled into the water, satisfied that its defensible waters were finally safe as the high-flying barge sailed over the island.

Dez was flying fast, requiring Spencer and Daisy to hold onto the deck to avoid being thrown off. In such a position, Spencer couldn't see if the Rubbish Sweepers from the island were making any attempt to stop them.

"Get ready!" Dez yelled, though Spencer had no idea what he was supposed to prepare for. He suddenly felt his stomach in his throat as the barge went into a spiraling free fall. Daisy screamed and Spencer shut his eyes. When he felt Dez's taloned hands plucking him from the deck, Spencer opened them again. The barge plummeted the final distance, smashing into the Glopified bridge and obliterating the only vehicular route to the BEM's private island.

Dez gave a chuckle and landed on the road next to Lina's garbage truck. Daisy clutched Bookworm's lunchbox as she leaned against the smelly vehicle.

"Let's get out of here," Spencer said, climbing the ladder to the rear of the truck. When he reached the top, he unclipped his walkie-talkie and put the device to his mouth. "Rho?" he said, hoping she was there to respond.

"Spencer? Thank goodness," came the relieved reply.

"Open Lina's dumpster," Spencer answered. "We're coming back."

CHAPTER 32

"THIS ISN'T YOUR FAULT."

It was evening when the Dark Aurans finally returned from their expedition into the landfill. They crept up on Spencer in their usual cryptic manner, rousing the boy from a deep sleep that had overcome him the minute he'd returned to the landfill. Well, the minute *after* he had showered off the Grime slime.

Startled, Spencer leapt to his feet, almost knocking over the cot he'd been sleeping on. He was in a room in the Auran building. His family had been with him when he dozed off, but they weren't around now.

"Light sleeper?" Olin asked.

"Not really," Spencer answered, his heart rate slowing when he saw who it was. "I didn't even hear you guys come in."

Aryl handed him a papery vacuum bag. It looked almost

identical to the Vortex that Marv had been sucked into. "Took us a while," he said. "But we found it." This final Vortex would be necessary for their plan to destroy the Toxite brain nests. Using the Vortex would be the only gateway into the Dustbin.

"Looks like you've been busy." Sach gestured to the window. Spencer crossed the room and looked out. Penny and Marv had organized the rescued Rebels into battalions. They were deep into training, Penny demonstrating some sort of tactical move with a pushbroom. Beyond the rows of soldiers, Spencer saw a fiery glow on the horizon where the gorge continued to burn, holding back the gang of Pluggers trying to get through.

"A few things have happened," Spencer said. He didn't know if he should start with the bad news of V's death or the good news that they'd finally learned the location of the long-lost scissors. And then there was the really bad news— that the Witches were the Instigators, and that they had used the Dark Aurans to spawn the Toxites, imbuing the creatures with negative characteristics that were the opposites of the boys' traits.

Spencer decided to tell it all in the order it had happened, seating himself on the cot for his lengthy narrative. The Dark Aurans took all the news with little expression, and Spencer realized that living for hundreds of years had hardened them. They were angry, he could tell. But they'd lived long enough to learn how to bottle their emotions. Spencer had no doubt that the rage would resurface, but the boys were probably waiting until they stood face-to-face with the lying Witches.

Aryl leaned against the wall, his arms folded tightly across his chest when Spencer finished. "All this time . . ." he muttered, "and all we had to do was die."

"No," Spencer said. "This isn't your fault."

"But that's the easy answer," Sach said. "If we die now, the Toxites die with us. No one else gets hurt."

"No! That's not how we do things!" Spencer said. "The Witches used you because you were the smartest boys. Olin is sharp and alert. Aryl is always planning and proactive. And you," he turned to Sach, "you're always focused and determined."

It was silent for a moment as all three Dark Aurans stared bitterly at the floor.

"Don't you see?" Spencer said. "The Witches had to use *you* to make Toxites. They couldn't do it themselves because you're better than them. *Smarter* than them. The Witches called you the heroes of the Dustbin, and they were right. Without even knowing it, you've outthought them again. The scissors will work," he said. "We just need to find them."

There was a soft knock on the door. Aryl stepped over and quietly opened it.

"Oh, hey, guys!" Daisy said, surprised to find the Dark Aurans in Spencer's room. "Welcome back." She strode into the room and smiled at Spencer. "Bernard said the glue has set. It's Bookworm time."

Spencer rose and followed her out of the room, leaving the Dark Aurans to brood over their recent discovery.

"Have you seen my family?" Spencer asked as they moved into the hallway.

"Your dad went with Dez to check on the defenses at the gorge," Daisy answered. "Your mom and siblings are with my parents."

"Where?"

"Fast asleep inside," Daisy said. "They're not used to this kind of action."

They met Bernard Weizmann on the concrete dumping pad just outside the Auran building. The garbologist stood in his usual strange attire: tweed coat, duct-tape tie, and leather aviator cap. In his arms, he cradled Bookworm's recently reassembled head.

"What kind of glue did you use?" Spencer asked, examining the seam where the textbook had been reattached to the lunchbox.

"Superglue!" Bernard answered. "And just a little bit of chewing gum." He held it out for inspection.

It looked exactly how Spencer remembered Bookworm's head. But even though the pieces were all there, the lifeless expression made it seem different. There was no playful glint in the lunchbox, no grinning curve of the textbook.

"So, when does he actually come alive?" Spencer asked.

"Patience," Bernard said. "He's been dead for a couple of days. It's going to take a major trashfusion to get his garbage pumping again."

Spencer remembered when Bookworm had been too

sick to stand. Giving him fresh trash had immediately re-vived him. Bernard seemed to think that the same trick would work here.

The garbologist crossed the concrete pad and stepped out into the trash-littered landfill. He gave Bookworm a quick peck on the lunchbox, and then hurled the Thinga-majunk's lifeless head out into the garbage piles.

"And . . . three," Bernard counted. "two . . . one!" When nothing happened, Bernard went on, counting tim-idly. "Zero . . . negative one . . . negative two . . ."

The Thingamajunk appeared, ripping through the land-fill and running straight toward them. His textbook jaw sagged open in a sideways grin, pink retainer rattling be-tween stubby pencil teeth.

"Bookworm!" Daisy cried, holding both arms out for a big hug.

Bookworm raced past them, sprinting wildly across the concrete pad and slamming into the wall of the Auran building. He fell onto his backside, rubbing his head in con-fusion.

"What happened to him?" Daisy asked, running to her pet Thingamajunk.

"He's probably a little disoriented," Bernard said. "You would be too, if someone cut your head off and then glued it back on."

Daisy crouched next to Bookworm and patted his lunch-box head.

"Last thing he remembers was defending your house,"

Bernard said. "I disassembled him just before the Sweepers attacked."

"You're safe now, buddy," Daisy whispered to her Thinga-majunk. "We're back at the landfill."

Bookworm grunted, a noise that sounded vaguely like Daisy's name. He rested his head on her shoulder and threw one garbage arm around her.

"We need your help," Spencer said.

Bookworm perked up at the opportunity to be of service. He rose to his feet and stretched, his bodily debris crack-ing and popping. He reached up with both hands, grabbing his lunchbox as if to make sure that his head was actually in place. Then he dropped onto the knuckles of his hands, stooping like a gorilla to hear Spencer's proposition.

"We're looking for a very important pair of scissors," Spencer said. "Do you know what scissors are?"

Bookworm nodded vigorously.

"Okay," Spencer continued. "The scissors you need to find are very old. They're one of the most powerful Glopified items ever created, and they're going to help us destroy Toxites."

"The scissors are lost in the landfill," Daisy explained. "How long do you think it will take you to sort through all the trash?"

Bookworm seemed to think about it for a moment. Then he hacked something up, coughing it onto the con-crete. Bernard picked it up and smoothed the crumpled scrap. It was a postcard that showed a beautiful sunrise over the ocean.

"Think you can do it by morning?" Bernard clarified. Bookworm's form of communication took some interpreting.

The Thingamajunk nodded and held out his hand to fist-bump the garbologist for guessing it right on his first try.

"Great," Spencer said. "Thanks for doing this." Bookworm glowed at the praise.

"One more thing," Daisy said, as her Thingamajunk turned to the darkened landscape. "If you see Couchpotato out there, tell him to give my necklace back."

"I THINK HE'S AFRAID."

Dawn broke over the landfill, matching the colorful red blaze of the fire from the gorge. Most of the Rebel army was still sleeping. Meredith was in the Auran kitchen, putting her lunch-lady skills to use in preparing a giant breakfast.

Spencer and his dad rendezvoused with Daisy and Bernard at the dumpsters. Dez was still out at the gorge, where he'd spent the night picking off Rubbish Pluggers that tried to break through the fire.

"Any sign of the Thingamajunk?" Alan asked.

"Not yet," Bernard said. "Not sure where the Dark Aurans are, either. We were just waiting for you two."

Daisy crossed to the edge of the concrete pad. Cupping both hands around her mouth, she yelled Bookworm's name like a parent calling a child for dinnertime.

Mere seconds later, the Thingamajunk rose out of the nearest pile of scraps and scampered toward them. Spencer wondered how Bookworm had any energy left after scouring the landfill all night. Then he wondered if trash got tired at all.

Daisy reached up and rubbed Bookworm's head. "Did you find them?" she asked. "Did you find the scissors?"

In response to her question, Bookworm reared up and beckoned with enthusiasm. He loped off into the landfill, leaving the four Rebels to follow.

They jogged a short distance, weaving through towers of cardboard and heaps of scrap. Spencer wrinkled his nose at the rotting smell of the landfill. Despite the early-morning hour, the heat was strong. Spencer knew it would be a scorching day.

Bookworm leapt onto the hood of a crumpled old vehicle, swung around a rotting broomstick, and landed in a cleared area, gesturing proudly to his findings.

As Spencer came into the clearing, his eyes grew wide. Bookworm hadn't just found the Glopified scissors they were looking for, he'd found *every* pair of scissors in the landfill.

A pile of rusty scissors was heaped about five feet high. There must have been a thousand or more, discarded to the landfill over the course of hundreds of years. Some of the scissors were broken and bent, with only a handle or a single blade. Others were in fairly good condition, clearly much too modern to be the scissors that the Dark Aurans had Glopified so long ago.

Bernard stepped forward and picked up a pair of safety

scissors of the type commonly used in preschools. He opened and closed the yellow plastic a few times before tossing it back onto the pile. "I don't think the Thingamajunk understood us," he said.

"He just didn't want to miss anything," Daisy defended her pet. "How would he know which scissors we were looking for? He just brought us everything."

Bookworm nodded, a ripped page hanging out the corner of his textbook like the panting tongue of a dog.

"Well," Alan said, "I suppose we should start sorting." He picked up a set of kitchen shears and tossed them aside. "We're looking for a pair from the 1800s. They'll probably be wrought-iron blade and handle. Nothing fancy."

"They're not here."

Spencer whirled around to find Sach sitting on the trunk of the car overlooking the clearing. He'd missed seeing him on the way in, but that didn't surprise Spencer. The Dark Aurans had spent centuries mastering stealth.

"I was watching all night," Sach said. "The Thingamajunk brought in a lot of scissors, but none of them matched the ones we Glopified."

"You're sure?" Spencer asked. "V told me they were here. It was the last thing she said."

Sach slipped off the trunk and skidded down the trash pile to join them in the clearing. "I'm telling you," he said, his expression sober, "the scissors aren't here."

Spencer knew what this was doing to him. After learning the truth about the Toxite brain nests, the Dark Aurans knew the scissors were their only hope. The other alternative for stopping the creatures meant death for the three ageless boys.

"They have to be here somewhere," Spencer persisted. "Maybe Bookworm didn't find them all."

"Bookworm?" Daisy turned to her pet, who sat hunkered at the edge of the clearing. "Did you find all the scissors in the landfill?"

Bookworm nodded, slowly at first, and then overly fast.

"He's lying!" Bernard said. "The Thingamajunk's lying to us!"

"He wouldn't," said Daisy, shooting a questioning look at the garbage figure.

"Trust me," Bernard continued. "I know how to read trash. Look at the corners of his textbook. See the way they're drooped down?" Instantly, Bookworm perked up the edges of his mouth. "And the guilty look in his eye . . ."

"Bookworm doesn't have eyes," Spencer pointed out.

"Fair," said the garbologist. "But if he did have eyes, I bet they'd look guilty!"

"Bookworm!" Daisy turned sharply to her pet. "Are you lying to me?"

The Thingamajunk shrank down, bits of trash sloughing away as he made himself smaller and smaller.

"Are there other scissors in the landfill that you didn't bring us?" Spencer asked.

Slowly, Bookworm nodded his head, pencil teeth chattering from his guilty nerves.

"Where are they?" Alan asked, but now the Thinga-majunk drew back, shaking his head. He drummed his assortment of trash fingers on the ground.

"I think he's afraid," Bernard said.

Daisy stepped over to her pet, suddenly warm with compassion. She put an arm around his smelly shoulders and looked him in the face. "It's okay," she soothed. "Thanks for getting all those," she gestured to the pile of collectibles in the center of the clearing. "But we need you to tell us where the other scissors are. Why didn't you bring them?"

Bookworm seemed to swallow his nerves. Daisy's calm voice had a restoring effect on the Thingamajunk, and he collected more trash from a nearby pile, growing back to his original large size.

"Do you know where the Glopified scissors are?" Spencer asked, doing his best to keep the friendly tone that Bookworm responded to most readily.

The Thingamajunk nodded his head.

"Is it far?" Alan asked.

This time Bookworm shook his head, holding up one finger. Then, thinking about it, Bookworm held up another.

"One hour," Bernard said. "Maybe two."

Bookworm fist-bumped the garbologist again, while Spencer considered that every conversation with Bookworm was like a game of charades.

"Then why didn't you bring the scissors?" Daisy asked.

Bookworm made a sound that represented a savage growl. Then he worked something up from his garbage body and hacked it onto the ground.

Daisy picked up the metal road sign. One corner was bent over, but it was clearly a *Do Not Enter* sign, with a red circle in the middle.

"The scissors are somewhere you're not allowed to go?" Spencer asked. Bookworm gave a thumbs-up.

"Aha!" Sach clapped his hands. "Is it down by the old staircase? Next to the washing machine?"

Bookworm clapped his hands, apparently relieved that someone else knew about the place he couldn't go.

"What's so bad about that place?" Daisy asked.

"There's a strange Thingamajunk that lives in that region," Sach said. "Most Thingamajunks are nomadic. They wander about the landfill, churning up new trash. Not this one. He's mean as murder and really territorial. He doesn't let anyone near his washing machine. Not even other Thingamajunks."

"What's so special about the washing machine?" Alan asked.

"He lives there."

"Whoa," Daisy said. "He must be really small."

Sach and Bookworm shook their heads in unison.

"Or the washing machine is really big?" Daisy guessed.

"He's a collector, of sorts," said Sach. "We nicknamed him the Hoarder because he keeps anything that comes across his path."

"Can't we trash-talk this grouch?" Bernard suggested. "It seems to work with all the other Thingamajunks."

"Or maybe Bookworm can do the talking," Spencer said. "One Thingamajunk to another."

Bookworm shook his head wildly, grunting a few times. He actually looked scared. Spencer didn't blame him. If what Sach said about this bully Thingamajunk was true, then Bookworm was the very opposite. Daisy's garbage pet had reacted to kindness, not trash-talk. He liked watching television and eating books. He was the only Thingamajunk who had ever willingly associated with humans.

"I think it's time to pay a visit to this Hoarder," Alan said. "Bookworm, can you show us the way to the washing machine?"

The Thingamajunk was trembling, but he gave a weak nod.

Spencer tightened his janitorial belt and checked to make sure that his coveralls were fully zipped. "Should we go get the others?" He asked. Penny and Marv had been working with Olin and Aryl to make sure the Rebel army would be equipped for battle. Rho and the other girls were likely manning the perimeter defenses with Dez.

"I wouldn't recommend it," Sach said. "If we want to face the Hoarder with any sort of diplomacy, we'll be better off in a small group."

"Diplomacy," Bernard scoffed. "You really think we have a chance of trash-talking our way to the scissors?"

Bookworm gave the answer they were all fearing. He shook his head and stormed off in the direction of the Hoarder Thingamajunk.

CHAPTER 34

"HEADS."

The Hoarder's dwelling was a decent hike from Bookworm's collected pile of ordinary scissors. Depending on the positioning of the landfill, it might have been days away. The Spade literally had the power to move the ground, bringing up new landscapes as old trash piles folded under. The way the Dark Aurans had left the landfill after using the Spade actually worked out quite conveniently.

During the hike, Spencer saw a familiar forest of overgrown forks and spoons. He knew that just beyond lay the Glop lagoon and the Broomstaff. But he didn't get to revisit the old sites, as Bookworm led the group another way.

Not quite two hours had passed when they came to the staircase Sach had mentioned. It was at least fifty feet wide and more than a hundred stairs high. Spencer didn't know how the stairway had gotten there. He'd stopped wondering about the fantastical formations at the landfill. It was enough to know that the ground was saturated with Glop and the magic deformed the debris in strange ways.

The odd thing about the stairs was the way they were situated. They rose on an angle into the blue sky, leading absolutely nowhere.

Bookworm paused in the shadow of the staircase. He didn't seem eager to go any farther. Peering around the edge of the stairs, Spencer saw a wide-open field of garbage. On the far side of the field was the largest washing machine he'd ever seen.

The machine was an old model that had been tipped on its side. The dials and knobs were enormous, and the lid was the size of a football field. The machine had once been white, but rust streaked down the sides and the paint was chipping in huge flakes. The lid was a little bent, and it stood barely open, like a door ajar. Inside was impenetrable darkness.

"The scissors are inside the washing machine?" Alan clarified with Bookworm.

The Thingamajunk nodded, pointing across the field of trash to the Hoarder's spacious dwelling.

"So, who's our best trash-talker?" Bernard asked.

"Definitely not me," said Daisy. Her idea of trash-talking usually led to compliments.

"I'm guessing Sach has the most practice," Spencer said.

The Dark Auran nodded, wiping a bead of sweat from his white hairline. "I say we team up on him," Sach said. "It might be more effective if we all trash-talk at once."

"Good idea," Alan said, stepping out into the littered field. "Let's do this."

Daisy turned to Bookworm. "Thanks for leading us," she said. "You want to wait here?" Bookworm settled down into a pile of trash, his textbook mouth expressing a clear look of relief at not being asked to join the confrontation. He pointed two fingers at the place where his eyes might be, then turned them to point at Daisy.

"Okay," she said, patting him on the head. "You just watch."

Spencer waited until Daisy was ready to go; then the two kids jogged a few steps to catch up to Bernard, Alan, and Sach.

The walk across the field was long. Spencer was sweating in no time, and it didn't help that he felt exposed and watched. More than once, he caught sight of movement around the edges of the field. He thought he might have imagined it until Bernard spoke up.

"Looks like we're not the only ones interested to see how this goes," said the garbologist. Spencer saw them clearly then, other Thingamajunks spying from a safe distance.

"If anyone sees a chance to slip into the washing machine, do it," Alan said. "As soon as Sach identifies the Glopified scissors, we make a full retreat back to the Rebels."

It was eerily quiet as they approached the dwelling. Lined up on both sides of the dark entrance were more than a dozen oversized pencils. They rose straight out of the ground like trees, sharp tips skyward.

Staked onto the pointy end of each pencil was a different scrap of trash. On one stake, a deflated soccer ball tucked inside a dirty pillowcase. On another, a computer keyboard with a fringe of old shoelaces. There was a skewered toaster with flip-flops in the slots meant for bread. A lamp shade wrapped around a fake potted plant.

Spencer was just wondering what the strange trash could mean when Bernard whispered a cryptic word: "Heads."

Spencer suddenly found it hard to swallow. His skin prickled with goose bumps despite the heat. The garbologist was right. These were the skewered heads of dead Thingamajunks, posted outside the Hoarder's dwelling to deliver a very clear message.

No wonder Bookworm was terrified. This guy was more than a hoarder. He was a cold-blooded killer. Spencer was just wondering if perhaps they'd made a mistake when a shadow passed out of the washing machine and the Hoarder stepped into view.

It was, without a doubt, the largest Thingamajunk Spencer had ever seen. Its body was an assortment of trash. Scraps of metal and bags of rotten groceries formed legs and arms. The torso was mostly comprised of a wooden dining table. The creature was nearly twice the size of Bookworm; Spencer had to look straight up to see its head.

The Hoarder's mouth was the bumper of an old pickup truck. Its head was a battered lawnmower that was tipped backward, the bottom displayed outward like a face. The moment the Hoarder saw the humans standing uninvited in the entrance, the lawnmower blades spun into action, its face now a blur of movement.

Spencer and his companions all started trash-talking at once. Among his own insults, Spencer caught snippets from the others.

" . . . smell worse than dirty laundry . . ."

" . . . fender bender with your face . . ."

" . . . only thing you scare is my lawn . . ."

" . . . have a picnic on that kitchen table . . ."

The trash-talking didn't seem to have its usual effect. Instead of backing down, the Hoarder appeared to be fueled by the taunting words. The large Thingamajunk seemed to grow angrier and more aggressive with every sentence.

The Hoarder shrieked, a noise that sounded like its whirling lawnmower blades had been pressed against a chalkboard. With one swipe of its lanky arm, all five humans were knocked backward, quickly silencing the useless trash-talk.

Spencer didn't doubt the Hoarder's cruel intentions as it leaned forward to pluck the humans out of the garbage. The Thingamajunk's hand was hovering just above Daisy when a familiar bellow pealed across the trash field.

The Hoarder froze, and everyone turned to see Bookworm standing in the middle of the field on quivering legs. The Hoarder seemed to laugh at the smaller Thingamajunk. It pounced over the humans, landing awkwardly close to Bookworm.

Spencer braced himself for the worst, but the two Thingamajunks did not fight. They stared at one another for a moment, both making short grunting sounds. Then the Hoarder stretched tall on its legs and beat its chest, heavy hands pounding on the kitchen table torso.

The Hoarder stepped back and Bookworm repeated the gesture, thumping his chest while bellowing as loudly as he could. Both Thingamajunks dropped onto their knuckles and circled one another. Then they turned away and headed for opposite sides of the field.

All around, the shy Thingamajunks that had been spying now poured into sight. They whooped and grunted, making their way along the edges of the field.

Spencer was on his feet again, trying to keep up with the others as they ran to the corner where Bookworm waited by the stairs.

"What's going on?" Daisy shouted when she reached her pet. "What's happening?"

The Hoarder was crouched beside the entrance to the washing machine as the other Thingamajunks filed onto the stairway. They seated themselves on the stairs, quieting their shouts once they had settled in.

"I've never seen anything like this," Sach muttered. Spencer didn't have to ask what was about to happen. The scene was quickly taking shape. The stairway was an array of bleachers, and the field, an arena.

Bookworm had accepted a challenge to fight the Hoarder.

Daisy's pet Thingamajunk didn't look nearly as brave as he had a moment ago. His garbage body was shaking and his textbook mouth quivered.

"What did you do?" Daisy asked.

Bookworm's only comfort seemed to be in holding onto Daisy. The Thingamajunk absently stroked her head as if to reassure himself that she was safe. That was why Bookworm had rushed to their rescue. Despite his intense fear of the Hoarder, Bookworm couldn't bear to see Daisy in danger.

"You good at boxing?" Bernard asked. Bookworm shook his head. The Thingamajunk didn't seem to believe in himself.

"It's okay," Daisy said. "We'll help you fight him."

Bookworm gave a thumbs-down gesture, pointing to the host of Thingamajunks seating themselves on the staircase.

"The others won't let us help," Bernard assumed. "You have to fight this guy alone."

"What happens if you win?" Alan asked.

Bookworm brought his hands together like he was snipping an imaginary pair of scissors.

"And if you lose?"

The Thingamajunk pointed across the field to where the lifeless heads were staked on the oversized pencils.

"You can do this," Daisy encouraged. "The Hoarder might be big, but you're faster. I believe in you!" Daisy gave Bookworm a big hug.

Bernard clapped his hands together. "Now go out there and kick some trash!"

CHAPTER 35

"AND IN THIS CORNER . . ."

Spencer was seated on the fourth row of the staircase bleachers, Daisy and Sach on either side. Alan put a comforting arm around Daisy's shoulders as she wrung her hands in anxious anticipation over the impending fight.

Dr. Bernard Weizmann stood at the corner of the staircase, as close to the arena as he could get. Bookworm crouched in front of him, and the garbologist massaged the Thingamajunk's trash-bag shoulders.

"I'm your cornerman," Bernard said. "You're speedy and you're smart. We're going to use that to our advantage. I'll be spotting for weaknesses in the Hoarder and tending your injuries. Check back with me as often as you can."

At the mention of injuries, Bookworm seemed to slump down a bit. Across the arena, the Hoarder reared up and shrieked, pounding its garbage arms against its kitchen-table chest.

Spencer shifted uncomfortably in his seat. Behind them, the spectator Thingamajunks took up a wild noise. It was like an extreme sporting event, with a violent aspect that was reminiscent of ancient Rome and the Colosseum gladiators.

Like a boxing announcer, Bernard stepped forward. "In the far corner we have . . . the Hoarder! He's violent, he's mean, and he's rather ugly."

As the Hoarder's shriek subsided, Bookworm rose to his full height, Bernard staggering back as the Thingamajunk bristled his trash to look as bulky as possible. He roared and banged his chest the same way he'd done when he accepted the Hoarder's challenge.

"And in this corner . . ." Bernard shouted. "Bookworm the Brave! He's fast, he's smart, and he's shaking like a leaf in the wind!"

The arena fell strangely silent. The spectator Thingamajunks held perfectly still, not even daring to rustle their garbage bodies.

The Hoarder charged, galloping with all four limbs as it churned up trash. Bookworm, his trembling visible even from the staircase bleachers, met the charge, sprinting directly at his opponent.

The two Thingamajunks collided in the center of the arena. The Hoarder's fist pounded directly into Bookworm's chest, knocking loose more than a dozen pieces of his body. Daisy winced and the spectator Thingamajunks grunted.

Bookworm immediately crumpled to a pile of trash, re-appearing a split second later at the edge of the field next to Bernard.

"You're doing . . . great," the garbologist said unconvincingly. "Just keep your head protected. You can always make another body; just don't let him get your head!"

The Hoarder was coming, clearly anxious to squash Bookworm and reestablish its territory in front of all the Thingamajunks watching.

Bernard backed up, finding himself a little too close to the action as Bookworm ducked the Hoarder's next punch. The Thingamajunks circled a few times, Bookworm taking several desperate swings that yielded nothing but air.

"Behind the left knee!" Bernard shouted. Spencer squinted but he couldn't see anything unusual. "There's a half-gallon plastic milk jug. Looks like it's keeping his whole leg structured."

Bookworm gave a quick thumbs-up to show that he understood. Then he took a heavy punch to the shoulder, breaking off his entire arm. The Hoarder reared back, whirling lawnmower blades seeming to laugh. The one-armed Bookworm rolled between his opponent's legs and delivered a swift kick to the back of the Hoarder's left knee.

The small milk jug collapsed and the Hoarder's leg buckled. Grunting in surprise, the vicious Thingamajunk dropped to one knee.

This small victory won the loudest reaction from the spectator Thingamajunks. Several even leapt to their feet, hands slapping together in a spray of trash.

"I think we know who the crowd is cheering for," Spencer said.

"Bookworm, of course," agreed Daisy. "Nobody wants the mean guy to win."

The Hoarder turned its face to the crowd, truck bumper peeling up in an angry snarl. It was clearly a glare, and the spectator Thingamajunks reacted by falling instantly silent.

Bookworm followed up with a roundhouse kick that would have made Penny proud. But just before his foot made contact, the Hoarder reached around and grabbed Bookworm's leg in both hands. Squeezing, it broke the leg to pieces, and Bookworm went scattering across the arena.

The Hoarder stood on its injured leg. Reaching down, it seized the crumpled milk jug and plucked it out. Scooping up a handful of loose trash, the Hoarder packed it into the hole, reinforcing the leg and eliminating the weak spot.

Bookworm rose up once more, having two new arms, two new legs, and a fresh body of trash. The Hoarder leapt at him, but Bookworm turned, sprinting away across the arena.

"He's scared," Daisy muttered.

"Can you blame him?" Sach said. "If Bookworm loses, his head becomes an ornament."

The Hoarder matched Bookworm's sprint, slowly gaining. It looked like a game of cat and mouse as Daisy's Thingamajunk ran in zigzag patterns. But the Hoarder anticipated the moves, cutting the corners a little faster.

Spencer wiped his sweaty palms on his coveralls. The only two advantages that Bookworm had were speed and wits. Now it seemed they could cross one off. The Hoarder was definitely faster than Bookworm.

The Hoarder lunged, catching Bookworm's heels and dragging him into a headlock. The enemy's fist came down, slamming into Bookworm's lunchbox.

"Cover up!" shouted Bernard from the corner of the arena.

Bookworm's arms flew up to cover his head. The Hoarder continued punching, blow after blow, while Bookworm's legs flailed as he tried to wriggle free.

The repetitive pounding was shredding Bookworm's arms. Once that defense was gone, Spencer wondered how many blows he could take to the head.

Daisy leapt to her feet. "Come on!" she shouted like a soccer mom. "Get out of there!"

Finally maneuvering himself into a better position, Bookworm intentionally broke apart. He re-formed in Bernard's corner once more.

"Okay," the garbologist said. "We can't rely on speed anymore." Bernard reached up and gently grabbed the Thinga-majunk's head. The lunchbox was a bit more dented and slightly wobbly where it had been fused onto the textbook. Removing a wad of chewing gum from his mouth, Bernard tacked the lunchbox down so it didn't wiggle.

"Let's go for wit," the garbologist said. "Can you out-think this guy?"

Bookworm shook his head in despair, still jittery from his recent pounding.

"Yes you can!" Daisy shouted from the staircase. At

hearing her voice, Bookworm straightened a bit. He gave her a forced smile and turned back to the arena where the Hoarder crouched, slamming both fists against the ground for intimidation.

"Try coming up underneath him," Bernard suggested. "If you knock him off balance, you can get him while he's down." He shoved Bookworm gently on the arm, encouraging him to get back out there.

Bookworm took two loping bounds before dropping into the trash-littered arena. Spencer held his breath, waiting to see where the Thingamajunk would surface. The Hoarder didn't seem concerned, and Spencer figured it would be easy to take the enemy by surprise.

Bookworm's head suddenly appeared, rising out of the trash directly below the Hoarder. But to Spencer's astonishment, the bigger Thingamajunk seemed ready for him. The Hoarder caught Bookworm's head in one hand, holding it down to prevent him from forming.

Desperate, Bookworm quickly sank back into the arena and tried to come up behind the big Thingamajunk. The Hoarder anticipated again, swiveling quickly and seizing Bookworm's head once more.

Daisy was biting her nails and muttering nervously. Sach looked down, even his determined nature dwindling as the fight wore on.

The Hoarder plucked Bookworm out of the ground like it was picking a tulip. It tossed its challenger into the air, spun around once, and slugged Bookworm in the jaw as he fell.

The stubby pencils that served as Bookworm's teeth sprayed outward, the cover of his textbook jaw wrinkling. Bookworm sailed through the air and landed in an unmoving heap several yards away from the Hoarder.

Daisy stood up abruptly. She took a deep breath, and then started descending the stairs toward the arena.

"What are you doing, Daisy?" Spencer cried. The Hoarder was treading slowly toward its downed opponent, ready to finish Bookworm with a fatal strike.

"We were counting on Bookworm to be faster and smarter," Daisy answered. She unbuckled her janitorial belt and dropped it on the bottom stair. "The Hoarder is too fast, and Bookworm can't seem to outwit him."

Spencer didn't know where Daisy was going with this. When she reached the edge of the arena, Spencer got up to stop her.

"But Bookworm has another advantage," she said. "He has something that the Hoarder will never understand." Daisy balled her hands into courageous fists. "Bookworm cares about me!"

Then, completely unarmed, Daisy Gates sprinted out into the arena.

CHAPTER 36

"KEEP THEM CLOSED."

Spencer jumped down from the bottom stair and reached the edge of the arena. He unclipped a pushbroom and was about to head after Daisy when Bernard gripped his shoulder.

"You've got to let her go, kid," the garbologist muttered as Daisy sprinted toward the Hoarder.

Spencer shook his head. She didn't even have a pinch of vac dust to defend herself. "What's she doing?"

"She's giving Bookworm something to fight for," answered Bernard.

Daisy bent down and picked up a tin can from the field of loose trash. "Hey!" she screamed, hurling the can at the back of the Hoarder's head. It fell short, clattering against a rusty barbecue that made up part of its shoulder.

The Hoarder froze, slowly turning away from where

Bookworm had collapsed. The lawnmower blades that formed its face sped up and the bumper curled back hungrily.

Daisy suddenly seemed to doubt her courage. She took a hasty step backward, tripping in the trash and landing on her backside in the middle of the arena.

The Hoarder shrieked, its hand darting out to snatch Daisy out of the garbage. Suddenly, the trash around her erupted and Daisy Gates was scooped into the protective arms of her pet Thingamajunk.

Bookworm, revitalized by seeing Daisy in danger, leapt across the arena and rolled her out into the trash at the edge of the field.

The Hoarder didn't seem to like being humiliated by a tiny human girl in front of so many spectators. Its lawnmower face was fixed on Daisy and it dashed forward to finish her off.

But standing between the Hoarder and the girl was Bookworm. The bigger Thingamajunk didn't seem to consider Bookworm much of an obstacle. They'd been fighting for several minutes, and Bookworm had spent most of the time trying to get away.

But things were different now. Daisy was in danger.

With a running start, Bookworm jumped straight into the air. He twisted above the Hoarder's head, grabbing onto the lawnmower handle with both hands. The Hoarder's head snapped back and the big Thingamajunk fell to the arena. Bookworm swung around, kicking one of the stout wooden table legs that protruded from the Hoarder's chest. It broke free with a splintery *crack!*

The Hoarder swiped for Bookworm, but the smaller Thingamajunk evaded the blow. Snatching the broken table leg, Bookworm jumped over the Hoarder's chest and thrust it into his opponent's face.

The whirling lawnmower blades jammed on the wood, grinding to a halt. Even from a distance, Spencer could hear the lawnmower's motor groaning in protest.

With a horrible grunt, the Hoarder rose to its feet once more. Black smoke was venting from the sides of the Hoarder's head like steam blowing out the ears of an angry cartoon character.

Bookworm didn't need Bernard's coaching anymore. He grabbed the Hoarder's right arm and jerked it around, dislocating the Thingamajunk's shoulder. The rusty barbecue popped out of place, and the entire arm turned to useless rubble, falling to scraps on the arena floor.

The spectating Thingamajunks were going wild. They were leaping up and down, their weight causing Spencer to worry that the staircase might collapse.

Bookworm was winning!

The Hoarder was scraping at its lawnmower face, blindly trying to remove the table leg that jammed its deadly blades. Bookworm delivered a sharp kick to the Thingamajunk's back, using the momentum to launch himself up and grab the bumper that served as the Hoarder's jaw.

Planting his feet squarely between the Hoarder's shoulders, Bookworm leaned back, grunting mightily as he bent the bumper around the lawnmower. From his seat in the bleachers, Spencer saw sparks shooting from the lawnmower's motor.

Bookworm kicked away, leaping gracefully to land beside Daisy on the arena floor. The Hoarder reared back, shrieking one last time. Then its head exploded in a cloud of black smoke and debris.

Spencer shouted and clapped his hands together. He was suddenly thrown off balance by a stampede of Thingamajunks exiting the staircase to rush the field. They were grunting and jumping as they surrounded Bookworm, bearing him up on their shoulders and toting him around the arena.

Spencer ran onto the field, grabbing Daisy's discarded janitorial belt as he passed the bottom stair. Daisy had a proud grin on her face, watching her pet enjoy the praise of victory from his fellow Thingamajunks. Spencer was grinning too. He was just glad Daisy hadn't been eaten by the Hoarder.

"That was a brave thing you did, kiddo," Bernard said, reaching out to ruffle Daisy's hair.

"I knew Bookworm would protect me," she said.

"He's quite the hero now." Sach pointed to where the other Thingamajunks still swarmed him.

"He's always been a hero," Daisy said. "The others just didn't know it until today." She tapped her chin in thought. "I wonder if Couchpotato is here," Daisy muttered. "Maybe now he'll give my necklace back."

"Bookworm's victory won us access to the Hoarder's

dwelling," Alan said. "We should find the scissors and make our way back."

Spencer handed Daisy her belt. She buckled it on, and the humans made their way toward the oversized washing machine, leaving the Thingamajunks to their celebration.

They arrived at the dark entrance to the Hoarder's dwelling. Spencer tried to ignore the Thingamajunk heads staked on the sharp pencils, feeling sorry that there was no way to help the Hoarder's previous competitors, who had not been as fortunate as Bookworm.

The rim of the washer was much too high to step inside. Spencer followed his dad's lead, drawing a broom and drifting up past the door, which stood about ten feet ajar.

When they'd all landed, Spencer had to squint to see into the dark washing machine. The chamber ahead was vast and cylindrical. Once shiny metal, now every surface was dirtied with rotten garbage residue. The smell was awful, and Spencer automatically covered his nose.

The Hoarder had earned his name for a reason. It looked like the cruel Thingamajunk had been collecting oddities for decades.

There was a stack of microwaves that rose all the way to the roof of the dwelling. Old maxed-out cleaning supplies had been sorted into piles. There were towers of dingy books and magazines, dozens of old televisions, and stacks of discarded human clothing.

"This is great!" Bernard rubbed his hands together in excitement. "A treasure trove of trash!"

Great was not the word Spencer would have used to

describe the Hoarder's cluttered dwelling. He looked up, noticing stalactites of garbage dangling from the washer's ceiling. "It's going to take us forever to find the scissors in here," he muttered.

Sach found a propane tank in one corner. The Dark Auran inspected it for a moment. The first time Spencer had met Olin, the boy had dragged him into a field of propane tanks. The landfill Glop had tainted them, and they spewed fire from an unending source of gas.

Carefully, Sach twisted the valve. The Hoarder's propane tank must have been similar to the ones in Olin's field, because immediately a geyser of bright flame shot into the air.

"There we are," Sach said, dusting his hands together. "A little more light should help."

And it did. Spencer could see the Hoarder's dwelling more clearly now, though the messy place wasn't something he necessarily wanted to view in great detail.

"Wow," Daisy whispered. "I don't even know where to start looking."

"We should spread out and search," Alan said. "The scissors could be anywhere."

"I think I can narrow it down," Bernard said. "Every collector I've ever met has a method. There's no sense in collecting things if you stow them away and can't ever find them again. It may look like chaos to the untrained eye, but a garbologist can spot a pattern."

"What's the Hoarder's pattern?" Spencer asked.

Bernard held up a finger, as if he didn't want to be

bothered while thinking. His eyes darted around the washing machine, the garbologist's gaze dissecting the mess.

"Color variations," Bernard said. "Brighter colors in the front, darker colors in the back." Now that he mentioned it, Spencer could see the pattern. It gave a sort of ominous feeling to the dwelling. The light from the entrance was brightest at the front, reflecting on the more vibrant colors. An enhanced sense of deepening and darkening resulted from the placing of darker hues in the back.

"The scissors are black," Sach said.

"So they'd be near the back," answered Bernard. He strode deeper into the washing machine, but it was clear that he wasn't finished cracking the Hoarder's collection pattern.

"The Hoarder had a knack for symmetry," said the garbologist. "Bulkier items on both sides." He pointed to the stacks of microwaves on the right, balanced by old television sets on the left. "The items get smaller as they come toward the center."

"The scissors aren't very big," Sach said. "At the most, maybe eight or ten inches long."

"Then we can expect to find them in the middle," replied Bernard, lining himself up in the center of the cylindrical washer. The others followed him, anticipation growing as they neared the rear of the dwelling.

"And last," said the garbologist, "the Hoarder left dull objects on the floor, but he kept sharp objects in boxes."

Bernard bent down, reached into a cardboard box, and withdrew a pair of antique-looking wrought-iron scissors.

"Unbelievable!" Sach exclaimed. He stepped forward and carefully took the scissors from Bernard's hand. "After all these years searching . . ." He trailed off, cradling the long-lost scissors in his grasp.

"That was amazing!" Daisy said to the garbologist. "When are we going to learn that in my lessons?"

"Next month," answered Bernard. "I have a three-week unit on trash collecting."

Spencer leaned closer to inspect the old scissors in Sach's hand. The design was very simple, with a single pin holding the two sides together. The blades didn't look very sharp, but Spencer had learned a long time ago not to underestimate a Glopified tool.

"You're sure these are the right scissors?" Alan asked.

Sach nodded. "Exactly how I remember them," he said. "We have to keep them closed. A single snip can cause a lot of damage."

"Hold them tightly," Alan said.

"Oh, I don't intend to lose these again," Sach said. "Olin and Aryl would never let me hear the end of it." Sach curled his fingers, gripping the dull blades in a closed fist.

The Rebels made their way back to the dwelling's exit. Spencer stayed close behind Sach, intrigued by the powerful item the boy was carrying. Creating the scissors had nearly killed the Dark Aurans. Spencer could almost feel their life force emanating from the simple tool.

Spencer thought again of the bright beacon of energy he'd seen when exiting the Dustbin. That powerful brain stem was keeping the brain nests alive, fueling the Toxites to destroy the minds of students. Spencer wondered if the scissors in Sach's hand would really be strong enough to sever that connection.

Exiting the giant washing machine required the aid of Glopified brooms, since the rim was well over Spencer's head. Bernard and Daisy tapped their bristles, the magic flying them in a steep arc out to the arena where Spencer could hear the Thingamajunks still celebrating Bookworm's victory.

Spencer touched his broom to the floor of the Hoarder's washing machine and drifted up beside Sach, his dad just behind them. At the pinnacle of their flight, just as they crested the rim of the washer, Spencer cried out. A figure appeared seemingly out of nowhere, clutching to the front of Spencer's coveralls and dragging his broom off course.

The face, only inches from Spencer's, was unmistakable.

General Clean.

CHAPTER 37

"I DON'T KNOW WHO YOU ARE."

It didn't make sense! Spencer couldn't comprehend how the Sweeper had appeared so suddenly, sticky fingers holding fast to Spencer and his broom.

At Spencer's cry of alarm, Sach looked back. General Clean's long Grime tongue lashed out with unbelievable speed, sticking to the scissors in Sach's hand and pulling them free. The Dark Auran yelled, swiping a razorblade a moment too late. Then his broom's unalterable course bore him through the opening and out into the arena.

Spencer and Clean slammed into the metal door of the washing machine, the broom skittering away on its own. The Sweeper General held Spencer with the stump of his arm as he drew a plunger from the boy's belt and clamped it to the door. Kicking off, he leapt back into the Hoarder's spacious washer, hurling Spencer before him like a rag doll and towing the heavy lid behind him.

The metal lid slammed shut with a jarring *clang*. Spencer scrambled to his feet, checking to make sure his coverall's zipper hadn't slipped during his tumble.

With the sunlight blocked, Spencer strained to make his eyes adjust to the dull light of the burning propane tank. When he could finally see clearly, he found General Clean standing high up on the ledgelike rim of the closed washer. Spencer saw the stump of the man's left wrist. It was no longer oozing, and Spencer suspected that Clean's Grime half had accelerated healing.

Clean held the black scissors aloft, a malevolent grin spreading across his face. From the shadows, Alan Zumbro leapt, swiping the scissors and using his broom to propel himself downward toward Spencer.

The one-handed Sweeper yelled in rage, his tongue speeding out to snare the bristles of Alan's broom. But Spencer's dad simply released his grip on the wooden handle, trusting in his coveralls to break the fall.

Alan landed on his back on the floor of the washing machine, gripping the scissors as he rose defiantly.

"How did you find us?" Alan shouted to the figure above.

"I have your son to thank for that," answered General Clean.

"Leave Spencer out of this!"

"But I can't," said the Sweeper. "I've been at his side since yesterday."

"What?" Spencer muttered.

"Your belt pouch," answered Clean. "Larger than it looks. Once I managed to squeeze inside, all I had to do was stay quiet. I guess I should thank you for the ride. I never would have been able to get past the landfill gorge without you."

Spencer instinctively touched the pouch on the back of his belt. He remembered how Clean had been holding Spencer hostage at the storage units, standing right behind him, when the Sweeper seemed to vanish. And his reappearance seemed even more sudden, with him popping out of Spencer's belt pouch midflight and taking everyone by surprise.

"The only other thing in that pouch was a roll of duct tape," Clean said. "But I've already made good use of that." He gestured to the edge of the washing machine, where a single strip of Glopified tape already secured the lid closed.

"You'll never get out of here alive," Alan said.

"I don't have to," answered Clean. "I only have to destroy the scissors. Then the Witches' victory will be assured."

"Don't do this, Rod," Alan said softly, his voice echoing up to the ledge where Clean stood. "This isn't you."

"Everything I had," Clean's voice was a low growl, "was taken from me."

"That was ten years ago," Alan said. "It was an accident."

"It could have been yesterday. The driver of that vehicle walked away." Clean's voice was trembling with emotion. "But my wife, and my kids . . ." he trailed off. When he spoke again, the tremor was gone, replaced by a frightening calm. "There is nothing good left in this world. Only the Witches can cleanse it. They can build up a new world, where those who do wrong will be punished without question."

Alan shook his head. "I don't know who you are."

"You never did," answered Clean, his sticky hand reaching into his lab coat and withdrawing a damp rag. "I believe we have some unfinished business, Alan Zumbro."

Spencer's dad stood steady, Glopified scissors clutched in one hand while his other drew a razorblade.

Clean leapt from the high ledge, dropping soundlessly and landing only feet from Alan Zumbro. His Glopified rag shot out, but Alan pulled back, dodging the attack. Spencer unclipped a pushbroom from his belt, unwilling to stand by as Clean forced a duel upon his dad.

Spencer thrust for the Sweeper, but General Clean moved with tremendous speed, sidestepping the bristles and flicking his rag toward Alan again. The frayed tip of the rag narrowly missed Alan's hand, instead flicking directly against the scissors and sending them spiraling out of Alan's grasp.

Spencer watched the black scissors soar and heard them clatter against the metal floor of the washing machine. Clean's deadly rag could vaporize flesh, but the scissors were metal, so Spencer hoped they'd still be intact.

Instantly, Spencer moved for the spot where the scissors had fallen. General Clean went for them at the same time, but Alan Zumbro leapt forward to stop the Sweeper, his razorblade thrusting. Clean parried the sword with a swish of his rag, but Alan followed with a knee to the man's stomach.

Crawling on hands and knees, Spencer reached the Glopified scissors. They had clattered across the ground, finally resting atop a pile of moth-eaten sweaters. Spencer reached out for them, but paused.

In flight, the scissors had sprung open! Sach had stressed the importance of keeping them closed. Now they lay there like a loaded gun, and Spencer had no idea what would happen if he pulled the handles together again.

Clean's rag was now crackling with colorful energy. He whipped it forward, the fabric lengthening to reach its target. Alan ducked barely in time, the tip of the rag snapping against a beat-up dresser. Under the force of the blow, the dresser instantly cracked in half.

General Clean's rag was charging up again, but Alan raced forward. The Sweeper's tail lashed out, toppling Alan into a stack of old videocassettes. The Glopified rag cracked again, this time biting nothing but air above Alan Zumbro.

As the deadly rag retracted, Alan leapt up, razorblade thrusting into the damp fabric and twisting around. General Clean tugged, but Alan held fast, both hands clutching the sword that had entangled the tip of the Sweeper's rag.

Grunting in frustration, Clean tightened his grip, charging the rag with sizzling power once more. The two men faced off, the drawn-out rag gathering more strength with every passing second.

Spencer held the open scissors, unable to breathe for

fear of seeing his dad meet the same fate as Walter. If Alan didn't let go of the razorblade, Clean's rag would surely overpower him. Alan Zumbro gritted his teeth in determination. Spencer saw the stubborn look on his father's face that his mom so frequently commented on.

"I wonder if it's painful," Clean said. Spencer could see the magic sparking and hissing along the rag. "No one has survived to tell me."

Spencer raced forward, sliding on his knees across the metal floor between his dad and General Clean. Heedless of any risk, he thrust the open scissors upward, catching Clean's rag between the two blades. Then he pulled the iron handles together, snipping General Clean's rag in two.

But the powerful scissors did so much more than cut the fabric.

The Glopified rag all but exploded, throwing General Clean one direction and Alan Zumbro the other. Everything in line with the scissors was destroyed. It was as though the two blades continued outward, slicing through the washing machine as the scissors closed.

Spencer saw daylight overhead where the metal washer had ripped down the middle. Any of the Hoarder's collections that were unfortunate enough to be in line with the scissors were sliced asunder.

Gasping, Spencer fell back, pinching the scissors securely closed.

General Clean recovered first. Using his Grime agility, he slithered up the curved wall of the washing machine and leapt across the dwelling, coming down with teeth bared to finish the stunned Alan Zumbro.

"Dad!" Spencer shouted.

In the final second, Alan Zumbro rolled over, his razorblade fully extended. General Clean's momentum carried him straight onto the blade. Spencer winced and turned away as the weapon protruded out of Clean's back.

"You killed . . ." General Clean rasped, Grime goo oozing from his mouth. "You killed a friend."

"No," Alan said, shoving the big man aside. He rose to his feet, extracting his razorblade from the Sweeper's chest. "I killed a monster."

Spencer and his dad watched as the Sweeper half of General Clean died. The man's dark skin lost its filmy texture. His tail melted to a puddle on the floor, and his remaining hand lost its sticky fingertips. Clean's Grime eyes closed, returning to the size they were meant to be, though never to see again.

Alan closed his blade and dropped to a knee, placing a hand on the unconscious man's shoulder. "Now that the monster is dead," Alan whispered, "I'll spare my friend."

CHAPTER 38

"WHAT ARE WE UP AGAINST?"

There weren't enough chairs around the conference table. Spencer and Daisy were lucky to be seated, having been among the first to arrive at the meeting.

They had returned with the Glopified scissors just after noon. Alan had taken General Clean back with them, securely confined in a rake cage and carried over Bookworm's shoulder. The man didn't speak a word after regaining consciousness, but sat with his back to the bars, knees against his chest. The sleeve of his filthy lab coat concealed the stump of an arm. And now the ex-Sweeper was completely blind, a side effect of losing his Grime half.

Spencer glanced around the conference room at those who had been trusted to attend the meeting. Beside him were Daisy, Marv, Penny, Bernard, and Alan, representing the Rebels. Spencer considered all he'd been through with

301

them over the last year. He would put his neck on the line for any one of them, and knew they'd do the same for him.

Bookworm hunkered in the corner, and Spencer wondered if the Thingamajunk could do anything more crucial than what he'd already done in defeating the Hoarder and helping them find the scissors.

Dez was there, of course. Although he didn't care for meetings, the Sweeper kid refused to be left out of anything. He was perched above the table on a high-up truss near the vaulted ceiling.

Rho and the other Auran girls were also there, some seated and some preferring to stand. They had sent Rebel reinforcements to defend the gorge, though they reported that the attacking Pluggers had mostly dwindled off.

They only waited for the Dark Aurans. In their typical mysterious fashion, Olin and Aryl had not been seen since the expedition had returned from the Hoarder's dwelling over an hour ago. Sach had set out to find them.

Spencer glanced at the clock on the wall. If the three boys didn't show up soon, the meeting would have to start without them, though it would be hard for it to do so since they had such a critical part to play.

"I don't like the idea of holding General Clean in our building," said Gia, her white dreadlocks tied loosely back.

"I don't like the idea of holding him anywhere," muttered Penny. "The man doesn't deserve to be alive." She had been furious at Alan for bring Clean back to the Auran building. Spencer couldn't blame her, knowing how painful it must be for her to see the man who had killed her uncle.

Marv grunted in agreement with Penny. "I say toss him into the burning gorge, cage and all."

Alan held up his hand. "We have two strong Rebel guards watching Clean's cage. He's powerless and trapped."

"What if he turns back into a Sweeper?" Daisy asked.

"He doesn't have another Glop potion," Alan answered. "We searched him while he was unconscious. The only thing in his lab coat was an old pen."

"Not very threatening," Bernard commented. "Unless he plans to write his way out of that rake cage."

"One shifty move, and I finish him," Marv threatened.

"We all have to stand ready to finish him," Alan admitted. "I killed him once. And I'll do it again if I have to. But I have to believe that he might change. He was a good man once."

Spencer knew that many of the Rebels disapproved of his dad's mercy toward Rod Grush. Spencer himself didn't know how to feel about it. Clean deserved a punishment, and Alan insisted that he would get it . . . just not today.

Today, there were plans to make and nations to save. If only the Dark Aurans would show up!

Finally, the door opened and Olin, Sach, and Aryl entered, faces glistening from the heat of the afternoon.

"Sorry about the holdup," Olin said, seating himself in the single remaining chair. The other two stood behind him, Aryl leaning against the high wooden back of the seat. Spencer noticed that he had the third and final Vortex vacuum bag tucked under one arm.

"That's how you're getting back to the Dustbin?" Marv asked, gesturing to the bag.

"First things first," Sach said. "We can't worry about the Dustbin and the nests until the Glop source is closed."

Penny nodded. "Sounds like it's time for a trip to Welcher Elementary School."

"That was the holdup," said Olin. "We were just there."

"You closed the source?" Alan asked.

Olin shook his head. "We couldn't get within spitting distance of the source," he continued. "Welcher Elementary has been . . . how shall I say this?" He tapped his chin. "Remodeled."

"It was pretty old," Bernard said. "Definitely didn't meet fire code."

"Did they put in a swimming pool?" Daisy asked. "I hope they put in a swimming pool."

"Not that kind of remodel, I'm afraid," said Aryl. "The Witches know our hand. They assume we're narrowing in on the scissors. Maybe they know we already have them."

"They're beefing up security at Welcher," Olin said. "There's nothing stopping them now that they have their wands."

"What are we up against?" Penny asked.

"Reinforced walls, made to repel Glopified attacks," Aryl explained. "Alarms, traps, barricades . . . they've even added on new hallways to make it harder to reach the Glop fountain."

"How did they manage it?" Alan asked. "Welcher's a public school—in a neighborhood!"

"The BEM went in just after school let out," Sach explained. "They evacuated the building, claiming there was some sort of dangerous gas leak."

"The Bureau even blocked off the nearest roads and evacuated the closest houses," Olin said. "The neighbors weren't happy, but the BEM told them there was potential for the whole block to ignite."

"Once the area was cleared out," said Aryl, "the structural changes happened quite quickly. With their wands, the Witches could form additions to the school in the blink of an eye."

"Now they've moved an army inside," Olin said. "The place is crawling with BEM fighters, Sweepers, and Pluggers."

"I hope they're gone by tomorrow," Daisy said.

"What's so special about tomorrow?" Dez asked from his perch.

"It's the last day of school," she reminded him.

"The BEM doesn't look like it's packing up," Sach said. "Quite the opposite, actually. Looks like the Witches moved their surveillance sink into one of the classrooms. They've got soapsuds watching every inch of that school."

"So," Penny cut in. "Assuming we can even get to the Glop source, how exactly are we supposed to close it?"

Sach pointed at Rho to take over.

"The Glop source will close if we mix the right formula," Rho said. "We've already gathered the ingredients. We just have to get close enough to throw everything in."

"Lots of stuff?" Bernard asked.

Rho recited the ingredients from the list the Dark Aurans had given her. "Eye of Grime, tooth of Filth, beak of Rubbish, bristles of a broom, a drop of Auran blood, and the hair of a Witch."

"We've got the last ingredient," Daisy said. She produced the pink hairbrush that they'd stolen from the Witches' apartment. "Plenty of hairs stuck in here," she said, placing it on the table.

"Okay," said Alan. "What happens after we close the source?"

"Then it's time to destroy the Toxites," Olin said with a smirk. Accomplishing that task would be especially meaningful to the Dark Aurans now that they knew they had unintentionally helped create the creatures.

"This is a Vortex," Aryl said, holding out the vacuum bag he'd been carrying. "The smallest rip in the bag will cause everything nearby to get sucked into the Dustbin."

"Yeah," Marv muttered. "Figured that one out."

"This time," Olin said, "that's exactly what we want to happen. Sach, Aryl, and myself will get pulled into the Dustbin with the scissors. Once we've landed, we'll make our way to the heart of the Instigators' fortress and cut the brain stem, destroying the nests."

"What kind of opposition do you expect?" Penny asked.

"Lots of TPs," Marv answered. "Garth Hadley made several attempts to infiltrate the Instigators' fortress. TPs stopped him every time."

"But we have an advantage," Sach said. "The Instigators aren't there anymore. Since the Witches are in this world now, they'll have a much harder time maintaining active elements in the Dustbin."

"So the fortress might not even be there?" Daisy asked.

"Creations in the Dustbin will exist as long as the mind holding them together is alive," Olin said. Spencer remembered Garth Hadley's fortress dissolving when the man died. Without his mind, the creations just couldn't hold together.

"Fortress is a stable element," Marv said. "Easier to maintain. Moving parts are tricky."

"So as long as the Witches don't end up back in the Dustbin," Spencer said, "the TPs shouldn't be much of a problem?"

"Right," said Aryl. "They'll be slow as tar, if they're there at all."

"It's been a long time since the Dark Aurans were in the Dustbin," Rho pointed out. "You sure you'll know the way?"

"It's hard to miss," Spencer said. "Just follow the big glowing beam of magic."

"There are three nests," Sach said. "Each one is releasing a steady flow of energy. About twenty feet up, the beams twist together into a brain stem, and that's where we need to strike."

"You think the scissors are strong enough to cut the stem?" Penny asked.

"They're pretty powerful," Spencer testified. "I cut the Hoarder's dwelling in half just by closing them. We can probably snip the brain stem from a distance."

"The scissors are strong," Aryl agreed, "but we can't take any chances with the brain stem. Whoever cuts the beam will have to be right there, closing the blades directly around the stem."

"But none of that can happen until we close the Glop source in Welcher," Rho reminded them.

"How many fighters does the BEM have guarding the school?" asked Penny.

"From the looks of it," Olin said, "there are about five hundred. But the Witches have set up squeegee portals all throughout the school. They can call in reinforcements in less than a minute."

Penny mused for a second. "We have about a thousand Rebels ready for combat."

"And we have Thingamajunks." Daisy turned to Bookworm. "How many are willing to help us fight?"

Bookworm flashed all ten of his fingers twice. Twenty Thingamajunks had been so impressed with Bookworm's victory that he'd convinced them to aid the Rebels in a fight.

"Will the Thingamajunks leave the landfill?" Bernard asked the trash figure in the corner.

Bookworm shook his head and frowned. Apparently, their newfound loyalty to Bookworm was limited to the landfill they called home.

"If the Thingamajunks won't leave the landfill," Rho said, "then they won't be much help in closing the source."

"A thousand Rebels," Penny mused. "We might be able to take the school in a quick blitz."

"Won't work," said Marv. "Mobilizing a thousand troops will draw attention. BEM will see us coming and call reinforcements. They'll shut us down before we even have a chance to surround the school."

"We missed our chance," said one of the Auran girls from the back of the room. "We should have moved to close the source the moment we got the Witch's hair."

"They had their wands by then," Aryl said. "The Witches were already moving into Welcher to protect the source."

"Seems funny," Daisy said. "We finally make it to the end and we can't even get back into our school."

"Yeah," said Dez from his perch. "I spend most of my time trying to get *out* of school."

"So, what's our plan?" Penny pressed.

"We don't have a plan," Alan stated.

Spencer looked around the conference room. Even with all their heads combined, they couldn't come up with a decent plan to attack Welcher. Marv was right; an all-out blitz would result in too many Rebel casualties.

"You know who could probably come up with a great plan?" Daisy said. Everyone turned to her. "Min Lee."

At the mention of the genius boy, Dez groaned from the rafters. "Not the know-it-all again . . ."

"Who's Min Lee?" asked one of the Aurans.

"He's a friend of ours," Spencer answered.

"Does he happen to be a tactician?" Bernard asked.

Daisy shrugged. "I know he plays a lot of online strategy games."

Unclipping his walkie-talkie, Spencer tuned in to channel 28, the usual frequency he used to reach Min. Lifting the device, he pressed the button and spoke. "Min? Are you there? I hope you're not at your cello lesson, because we need you now more than ever."

Quicker than Spencer expected, Min's voice replied through the walkie-talkie. "At your service."

"We need to get inside Welcher, but the BEM has taken over," Spencer explained. "We have about a thousand Rebels willing to fight and a group of Thingamajunks that are on our side but won't leave the landfill."

"Hmmm," Min said. Spencer could imagine him stroking his smooth chin. "You won't likely succeed if you fight by the BEM's terms. You need to bring the fight to you."

"That's not an option," Spencer said. "We're trying to get to the Glop source. It's a drinking fountain in the hallway of the school."

"So, the source can't move?" Min clarified.

"Not unless all of Welcher Elementary School moves with it," Spencer said.

It was silent for a moment, and then Min replied, "Now, that would be interesting, wouldn't it?"

CHAPTER 39

"DO THEY LOOK CONVINCING?"

It was Thursday evening at the landfill. Spencer stood on the concrete dumping pad, watching the sun set over the mounds of trash. The endless fire still raged in the gorge, but all reports stated that the Pluggers had given up. They'd most likely been recalled to fortify Welcher with the rest of the BEM's strike force.

It was strangely quiet. Spencer's family was locked securely inside the Auran building with Mr. and Mrs. Gates and a few other noncombatant prisoners who had been rescued from the storage unit. His mom had put up an argument, of course, but Alan had told her they needed a leader to stay behind in case something went wrong. Alice had finally agreed, accepting specific instruction on how to use the dumpster portals to get home if they hadn't heard from the Rebel army by morning.

311

Marv had moved the army of Rebel Janitors into the preplanned position, anxious to be ready when the fighting began. They had taken the demoted General Clean, sitting caged in a Glopified rake. Toting him to the battle hadn't seemed like the best idea, but the alternative was leaving him behind with the Zumbros and the Gateses. Alan simply wouldn't let the ex-Sweeper near his family.

The Aurans had all gone with the army, including Olin, Sach, and Aryl. Even Daisy had already moved out with Bookworm. Spencer was proud of the Thingamajunk. He'd beaten the Hoarder that morning and spent the afternoon making special deliveries to the Monitors. If Bookworm was tired, he didn't show it, since Daisy's praise kept her pet Thingamajunk going.

Spencer thought it was strange not to have Daisy by his side. He wondered what the conditions would be like when they saw each other next.

That left Spencer, his dad, Penny, Bernard, and Dez standing on the concrete pad with the dumpsters. It was muggy and hot. Over the landfill, Spencer saw storm clouds rolling in. Of course, there had to be lightning.

"I thought your genius friend would be here by now," Dez said, flying in anxious circles above the dumpsters.

"Me too," Spencer admitted. "I guess it was harder than he thought to get all the Monitors together."

"We shouldn't keep the dumpster open much longer," Penny said. They were taking a risk by throwing back the lid and opening the portal. But Spencer felt it was necessary.

Just then, something stirred in the trash of the nearest dumpster. Min Lee appeared, tumbling with little coordination onto the stained concrete.

"Greetings," he said, trying to regain a look of dignity as he stood up. Immediately behind him, the trash moved again. Then, one after another, young students began pouring through the dumpster portal.

Spencer recognized most of them, though many looked different since that wild day when the school bus had flown off a cliff near New Forest Academy. The Organization of Janitor Monitors had grown as the original Monitors had brought trusted cousins and friends into the group. The network of students had spread, each member spying on the school janitor and sending reports of suspicious activity to Min.

The Asian boy shook Spencer's hand. "The Monitors are at your service."

"Took you long enough," Dez retorted.

To soften the statement, Spencer said, "It was probably tough to get everyone together."

Min shook his head. "That was not the problem. The moment I gave the word, everyone squeegeed over to my house. Bookworm's deliveries made the process quick and simple."

Spencer nodded, glad to know that the Thingamajunk's efforts had helped. Bookworm had used his unique ability to travel between trash piles in order to deliver squeegees to all the Monitors who were willing to participate. Dela's truck was already in California, so a quick drive moved it into position for Min and the Monitors to get to the landfill.

"What was the holdup, then?" Penny asked.

"The problem was finding the right costume shop. I had to visit five different stores to gather enough wigs for all fifty-seven Monitors."

"Do they look convincing?" Spencer asked.

Min made a face. "They look ridiculous," he answered. "But I'm hoping the disguise will be sufficient in the rush of battle."

"I'm sure it will be great," Alan said, though Spencer wondered how much his dad really believed in this crazy plan.

Alan put a hand on his son's shoulder. "You should get on your way," he said. "I'll close the dumpster behind you and move the Monitors into position. Give us about an hour to get set."

Spencer nodded as Bernard and Penny moved toward Gia's dumpster. Dez wasted no time, folding back his wings and diving like a falcon into the trash. Alan pulled his son close for a brief hug. Part of Spencer was surprised that the Rebels were letting him play this role. But he was the obvious choice since the Witches had encountered him twice.

Alan counseled his son to be safe, and Spencer followed the others through Gia's dumpster.

A second later, Bernard, Penny, and Spencer were climbing out of the truck and onto the Gateses' driveway. Dez was already perched on top of the cab. "Come on," he said. "Let's go already!" Spencer wondered if the Sweeper's impatience would ruin the whole operation.

"Alan and the Monitors won't be in place for at least an hour," Penny reminded.

"And besides," added Bernard, "it's going to take me some time to rig up Big Bertha." The garbologist had a smile on his face as he moved past Gia's vehicle toward his old garbage truck parked on the street.

They probably could have used either truck, but Big Bertha was a better choice. Not only was Bernard more comfortable behind the wheel, but Big Bertha's portal to the landfill was broken. Even if things went terribly wrong, the BEM wouldn't be able to use Big Bertha to reach the landfill and find Spencer's family.

Bernard rummaged through Mr. Gates's mechanics garage, finding all the tools he would need. A moment later, he fired up a work light and ducked under the back of Big Bertha, only his yellow rubber boots in sight.

Penny seated herself on the steps to the house, the front porch light illuminating her project as she unclipped a squeegee from her belt and ripped off a thin strip of duct tape.

Spencer reached into his belt pouch, feeling the pointy object resting just out of sight. The responsibility felt heavy, and Spencer was a little unnerved to be carrying the Glopified scissors. He tried to reassure himself by remembering that he only needed to make one cut. And it wouldn't be where the Witches were expecting.

CHAPTER 40

"QUITE DEMANDING, ISN'T HE?"

At half past ten, Spencer Zumbro walked up the sidewalk toward the front door of Welcher Elementary School. Unlike the stormy weather brewing over the landfill, the Idaho night was clear and crisp.

The school looked a bit different since the Witches had remodeled. Spencer could see duct tape across the doors and windows. The walls looked like they had been freshly painted, surely similar to the paint Garth Hadley had used to lock Marv out when they were in the Dustbin. The whole school had been retrofitted into a defensible fortress. Seeing it firsthand, a nagging piece of Spencer's mind doubted that they would ever get inside.

He had thought about rushing the building and using his spit sponge and left hand to de-Glopify some of the Witches' defenses. But that was foolish. The enemy would be on him in a heartbeat, and any fortifications he managed to disarm, the Witches would instantly re-create with their wands.

Spencer paused at the bottom step, just ten feet from the front door. "Hey!" he shouted. "Tell the Witches I'm here to talk!" His heart was racing, but his voice actually came out with confidence.

It took only a second for his call to be answered. The intercom speakers positioned all around the exterior of the school crackled in reply. "We see you, dearie."

Spencer swallowed hard. That was Ninfa's voice. In Welcher's dim front-door light, he saw a cluster of shimmering soapsuds just above the door.

"I'm here to negotiate!" shouted Spencer.

This time the answer through the intercom was laughter from all three Witches. "You want to close the Glop source," Ninfa said. "Not going to happen."

"Let me close the source," Spencer said, "and in exchange, I'll give you these." He pulled the antique Glopified scissors from his belt and held them out so the Witches would have a clear view through the soapsuds.

After a moment of silence, Belzora's voice came through the intercom. "You're alone," she said. "What's to stop us from sending our Sweepers out to collect those scissors from your lifeless body?"

"I'm holding the most powerful tool in the history of Glop," Spencer answered. "If anyone comes to the front door besides you, I start snipping."

"You wouldn't dare," said Belzora. "If you damage the Glop source, you may never be able to close it."

Sach had warned them of the same thing. Were it not for that risk, the Rebels might have snipped their way into Welcher. But the only hope they had of closing the source meant the Glop drinking fountain must remain intact.

"Maybe that's a risk I'm willing to take," Spencer said. To prove his point, he opened the scissors wide, angling the splayed blades directly at Welcher Elementary. He was committed now, remembering what had happened last time he closed the scissors, back in the Hoarder's dwelling.

"Let's not be hasty!" Belzora all but shouted through the intercom. "I will come out alone and we can talk about this."

Alone? Spencer's heart rate quickened. It would never work if Holga and Ninfa remained behind.

"No!" Spencer shouted. "I want the three of you together."

"Quite demanding, isn't he?" Holga's voice said in the background.

"I don't hand over the scissors until I see all three of your faces in the window," Spencer negotiated. "Then you let me in to close the Glop source."

The Witches would never hold up their end of the deal, and Spencer knew it. The moment he stepped foot inside Welcher, the Witches would take the scissors and finish him. But Spencer didn't intend to keep his end of the deal either. He just needed to get the Witches away from their sink full of soapsuds. He had to give Dez a blind spot, even if it was only for thirty seconds.

"We accept your terms," Ninfa said, her voice artificially sweet. "We will meet you at the front door in just a moment."

The intercom clicked off, and Spencer fidgeted nervously on the sidewalk. He resisted the urge to look up, trusting that Dez was moving into position high above. He wanted to glance over his shoulder to the darkened street where Big Bertha was idling nearby.

Instead, Spencer faced forward, his eyes fixed on the reinforced glass of the front door. His hand was sweating, fingers still holding the Glopified scissors dangerously open.

In the dim light, Spencer saw a face press up to the glass. He recognized the wild hair of Belzora immediately. Flanking the Witch, Spencer saw Holga and Ninfa slip into view, beckoning with crooked fingers for him to approach.

With a wave of Belzora's bronze wand, the school's front door was unimagined, disintegrating to fine dust.

"No tricks, boy," she called. "Bring us the scissors."

"I'm afraid there's been a change of plans," Spencer said. "We'll be taking the school by force."

The Witches threw their heads back and cackled. "You're going to need a bigger army!" Ninfa shrieked in hysteria.

"I've got one," Spencer muttered. "It's time to send you over to meet them."

Crouching low, Spencer placed the open scissors against the sidewalk, angling the tips just slightly into the ground.

Before the Witches could react, he snipped the blades together, cutting off the foundation of Welcher Elementary School. The thunderous rumble was like a terrible earthquake, and Spencer saw the entire school shift violently.

At the sound of Big Bertha's diesel engine, Spencer whirled around to see the vehicle peeling down the street. Squealing, it veered into the school parking lot as Bernard pressed a button, engaging the new feature that he'd installed at Mr. Gates's mechanic shop.

Glopfied Windex sprayed out the back of the garbage truck, misting half the parking lot and turning the ground to glass. Penny dangled nimbly off Big Bertha's back bumper. She had duct taped a series of squeegees together, operating them all simultaneously by holding onto one handle. She dragged the long squeegee behind Big Bertha, ripping a massive sizzling portal into the glass parking lot.

Through the magic portal, Spencer saw the dark storm clouds of the landfill. He hoped everyone was ready, because this was it!

Dez dove out of the dark sky, a Glopified plunger in one hand. He did a touch-and-go, clamping the red suction cup onto the roof of Welcher Elementary. With the school's broken foundation, there was nothing to stop the plunger from working its magic. Dez's wings bore him upward as he easily lifted the entire school off the ground. Enemy Sweepers began swarming the roof, but Dez needed to carry the building only a short distance.

Turning the structure sideways in midair, Dez Rylie

dropped Welcher Elementary School through the freshly squeegeed portal in the parking lot.

Spencer watched as the whole school vanished into the ground, sliding onto a perfectly prepared spot of the landfill.

Big Bertha swiveled around, and Penny brought her squeegee handle down to shatter the glass parking lot, eliminating any possible chance of a return journey.

Spencer stared at the spot where his school used to be. Now there was nothing left but a deep hole where the scissors had sliced. The entire school was gone, and with it, the Glop source. Spencer took a deep breath. It was a bold move to relocate Welcher Elementary. It also meant that today was indisputably the last day of school.

"Ha ha!" Dez laughed, landing on the ground beside Spencer. "Did you see that? I just picked up a school!" He flexed his biceps.

But Spencer wasn't feeling the joys of victory yet. Moving Welcher Elementary was only the first step in their plan. The real battle was yet to come.

"We should hurry," Penny said as Big Bertha screeched to a halt beside the boys. Bernard leapt out of the cab as Penny squeegeed a new, much smaller portal. The four of them stepped through, arriving safely among the Rebels just as the first bolt of lightning crackled over the landfill.

Spencer stared at the Broomstaff looming over the Rebel army. Then he turned to the hillside where Welcher Elementary School had just landed, the dust still settling around it.

Belzora had reforged the front door, and all of the

newly created defenses were locking into place. The roof was crawling with Sweepers, and a gang of Pluggers had just been sent out along the sides of the school.

Spencer took a deep breath, remembering the war that Walter Jamison had predicted would occur between the Rebels and the BEM. Walter was right.

But tonight that war would end.

CHAPTER 41

"I WANT TO WRITE A LETTER."

Spencer pushed his way to the front of the Rebel troops where Daisy and Bookworm were stationed.

"You did it!" Daisy shouted when she saw him.

"Are you guys ready?" he asked, looking over the row of trashcannons. There were a dozen big cans, wedged in the ground and carefully angled at the newly arrived school. Behind each trashcannon sat an Auran girl, experienced and ready to launch a slug of trash at the enemy's defenses. Sach, Olin, and Aryl manned the final three cannons.

Rho raced over to Bookworm, so caught up in what was about to happen that she didn't even acknowledge Spencer's huge accomplishment in delivering the school to the landfill.

"Trashcannons stand ready," she said to the Thinga-majunk. "Call your people."

Bookworm tilted his head back and bellowed. Then, dropping to all fours, he thumped his hands and feet rhythmically against the trash-strewn ground.

Spencer stepped back as Thingamajunks began forming out of the trash. Bookworm grunted instructions in a language that only the garbage figures understood. The Thingamajunks saluted and, without delay, climbed into the trashcannons.

"Ready!" Rho shouted, taking her place behind a trashcannon. "Aim!" The Thingamajunks in the cannons ducked down, their garbage heads tucking out of sight. "FIRE!"

The valley echoed with a dozen resounding *booms*. Twelve Thingamajunks went airborne, shooting through the night with the speed of deadly cannonballs.

The patrolling BEM Pluggers and Sweepers had no chance of stopping the incoming trash warriors. The Thingamajunks pelted into the side of Welcher Elementary, breaking mortar and shattering reinforced glass. Most were completely obliterated upon impact, but they quickly formed new bodies from the plentiful trash surrounding the school.

The second wave of Thingamajunks loaded themselves into the trashcannons. Bookworm stooped down, throwing his big arms around Daisy.

"You be careful out there," she insisted. "Don't do anything crazy now that you're a famous boxer." Bookworm seemed to chuckle. He gave Daisy a fist bump, then dove into Rho's trashcannon.

"FIRE!"

Once again, a volley of Thingamajunks slammed into the school, smashing defenses and pounding the doors.

Marv's deep voice rumbled across the ranks of Rebels. "Attention!"

The troops formed into four lines, a myriad of Glopified supplies bristling like spears and swords. They filed forward until they stood just before the line of empty trashcannons.

Thunder rumbled overhead as Alan Zumbro stepped out to address the army. "This is our chance to end it all!" he yelled. "If we succeed, your schools will be free. And tomorrow there will be no Toxites!"

"Listen up!" Penny shouted. "We're going to charge over there and break down those doors! Once the way is open, we send the signal, and Spencer and his team move in. We don't stop fighting! We do everything we can to keep the battle on us. You got it?"

A roar went up from the Rebel troops. They were scared; Spencer could see it. He couldn't blame them. Every one of them had experience in Toxite fighting. They'd pledged to protect their schools regardless of the BEM's orders. But fighting Pluggers and Sweepers was something different. Toxites in a school typically ran from a conflict. Sweepers ran toward it.

On the front line, Marv raised a dirty pushbroom. His voice pealed out, as loud as a trashcannon. "CHARGE!"

The Rebel troops raced forward in a tight formation, a multitude of shouts and thrusting weapons. The rear line took flight, using brooms to propel themselves above the heads of their comrades. Dez flew with them, defending against airborne attacks.

With the army's hasty exodus, Spencer suddenly felt exposed. He and Daisy were alone with the Aurans, not a single adult left to rely on.

"Let's head down to the pump house and get the others ready," Spencer said.

As they trudged closer to the mighty Broomstaff, a few droplets of rain spilled from the clouds. It was almost as if the huge, gnarly broom sensed people drawing near and brewed a storm just in case anyone planned on getting Panned. Spencer smelled the putrid stench of the Glop lagoon, bubbling and glowing.

The new pump house was very different from the old, dilapidated one Spencer had blown up on his last visit to the Broomstaff. V had sworn she would rebuild every pipe, and the Auran's determination had paid off.

This pump house was rectangular, with a sturdy door and aluminum siding. V had installed the pump and built the pipes on a single level, but the house was more spacious than its predecessor.

The lagoon surrounding the Broomstaff was for Glop drainage. Once all the magical sludge had settled in, the pump could be engaged to siphon all the raw Glop back into the earth's core. From there, Toxites would spawn from the muck, living to pollute the brains of honest students.

After today, the lagoon would be harmless, and V's hard-built pump house obsolete.

Spencer acknowledged the Rebel guards at the pump

house door. There would be two more janitors inside, watching over the cage in the corner of the pump house where General Clean sat humiliated.

Min greeted Spencer and Daisy as they entered the pump house. The other Monitors were there too. Spencer wanted to thank each one of them for their bravery in coming to this strange place, but there simply wasn't time. Penny could send the signal at any moment, and Spencer still had to get supplies into the Monitors' hands.

Min had already supplied them with brooms, latex gloves, and individual bags of vacuum dust. They were defensive weapons, not intended for the Monitors to stick around and fight.

"Okay," Spencer said, passing around a large stack of dust masks. "These masks will block the effects of Toxite breath. They'll also disguise your faces. Keep them on at all times."

Several of the Monitors were already fitting them over nose and mouth, making sure the elastic band held the mask tightly.

"We stay close together and we charge fast," Spencer instructed. "If it gets too intense, use this to help you escape." He pointed to a rack of spray bottles by the door. He and the Dark Aurans had spent a good part of the afternoon Glopifying enough spray for every Monitor.

"What is it?" asked one of the Monitors. Spencer realized that he didn't even know the boy's name. But there wasn't time to learn it now.

"Bleach," Spencer answered. "It's going to be your safest

way out of the battle. Spray it on yourself and you'll turn invisible."

"But only do it once," cautioned Daisy. "It's permanent the second time."

"The effect only lasts about fifteen minutes," Spencer said, "so get out fast and make your way back to the shelter of the pump house."

"Why don't we turn invisible now?" asked another Monitor. "We could slip into the school without being noticed."

"There are certain ingredients we need to close the Glop source," Spencer said. "One of them is a drop of blood from an Auran boy. That means I have to get to the source. Since I've already used bleach once, I can't go invisible again."

"What about the other boys?" Lina asked, pointing to Sach, Olin, and Aryl.

"We're staying here," Aryl said. "The three of us are in charge of cutting the Toxite brain stem the moment the source closes."

"We have everything we need," Sach said. He held up the scissors that Spencer had given him after cutting Welcher's foundation. Aryl clutched the Vortex that they planned to use to enter the Dustbin.

"How will you get out of the Dustbin after you've destroyed the nests?" Daisy asked.

Olin reached down and hefted a freshly Glopified leaf blower. Spencer remembered using one the last time they exited the Dustbin. The blower would create a temporary

Rip back to this world. Riding the slipstream of wind, they would easily be able to escape the Dustbin.

"Spencer is top priority," Rho said. "We've given him all the ingredients to close the source. The rest of us have to make sure he reaches the drinking fountain safely."

"Spencer," rasped a dry voice from the corner of the pump house. Spencer turned to see General Clean pressed against the bars of his rake cage, twirling a pen between the fingers of his only remaining hand. The man's voice had once been booming and deep, carrying such authority that it cause everyone nearby to cower. Now it was the pathetic voice of a defeated man.

"Spencer," the man said again.

It was quiet in the pump house, and Spencer felt all eyes on him. "What do you want, Clean?"

"Lend me a paper," he said, his sightless eyes staring vaguely in Spencer's direction.

"Paper?" Spencer asked. It wasn't the request he was expecting.

General Clean held up the pen he'd been twirling. "I want to write a letter," he rasped. "To your father."

"If you have something to tell my dad, you say it to him in person," Spencer replied.

"Hey," Gia called from the pump house door. "They just sent up the signal!"

Spencer had instructed Penny to shoot an unmanned broom into the air with a flashlight taped to it when the Rebels were ready for the Monitors to charge.

"Okay," Daisy said. "They're ready for us."

The Monitors began filing outside, pulling on their dust masks and grabbing the small bottles of bleach.

"Spencer," Olin said, catching his arm at the doorway. "Good luck over there."

"You too," Spencer said. "Next time we see each other this will all be over." Sach and Aryl nodded their support, and Spencer followed the others outside.

Spencer found Min and Daisy at the head of the group. Rho and the Auran girls mixed with the Monitors. Their height and build blended well with the young students, but the Aurans' white hair caused them to stand out like sheep on a dark hillside.

"Stay close together and move fast," Min instructed the Monitors, using a voice louder than Spencer had ever heard from him. "If our trick works, the Witches will order a cease-fire and we should get safely inside." Min pulled something shimmery and white from his back pocket and placed it on his head.

It was a wig. Cheap strands, tangled from being in Min's pocket, hung past the boy's shoulders. He tucked an itchy piece behind his ear, eyes peering out between his dust mask and white bangs.

Daisy giggled. "You look hilarious!" Her laughter dispelled some of the tension of the stressful moment. Min, however, found his costume far less amusing.

"I never thought we'd save the day wearing twelve-dollar wigs from a costume shop," Min said. He handed another wig to Daisy, who tucked up her braid and pulled it on.

Spencer looked out at the Monitors, each one now covered with a cheap white wig. Some were short, others long. In a moment, the drizzling rain had matted them all down, and Spencer had a hard time distinguishing the real Aurans from the fake ones.

He turned back toward Welcher Elementary School. The Witches, watching safely from their sink of soapsuds, would see them coming, a mess of white-haired youths. They wouldn't dare harm the Dark Aurans. Killing them would destroy the Toxites they were so desperate to protect.

Spencer was counting on the Witches' paranoia now. Being unable to identify the Dark Aurans would force the enemy to call a cease-fire. By the time the Witches realized that the children were merely impostors, Spencer intended to be standing at the Glop source.

CHAPTER 42

"STOP THE LITTLE BRATS!"

Spencer led the Monitors in a sprint across the damp trash. Daisy was at one side, Rho at the other. Min tugged awkwardly at his white wig, but Spencer knew the boy's self-consciousness over it would end the moment they reached the battle.

The remaining Aurans and Monitors stayed close, their proximity adding to the confusion of who was really ageless and who was merely wigged.

Spencer held his breath as they reached the edge of the conflict. The fight waged brutally, the Rebel Janitors struggling against the seemingly endless waves of mounted Pluggers, Sweepers, and infantry BEM workers that poured out the crumpled front doors of the school.

Spencer's pushbroom powered into the first enemy, a BEM woman with a razorblade. She went spiraling into the night sky, relieving one Rebel Janitor of the duel he'd been fighting.

The Monitors hurled their vacuum dust, their untrained tosses finding a mark only about half the time. A few of them tapped their brooms the moment they reached the battle, drifting backward and then sprinting to the safety of the pump house. Spencer didn't blame them. The Witches hadn't called the cease-fire yet, and the fighting wasn't going to get any easier.

The group of Aurans and Monitors huddled tightly, the enemy bearing in on them from all sides. Daisy barely ducked under the bludgeoning, armored tail of a Filth. Spencer brought his pushbroom around and sent the Plugger rider sailing out of his saddle. Min tossed a Funnel Throw over Spencer's shoulder, temporarily pinning the angry Toxite.

Spencer was just beginning to think that they'd made a terrible mistake, that the Witches either weren't deceived or didn't care what happened to the Dark Aurans, when suddenly Belzora's voice crackled through the intercom.

"Spare the young ones!" There was a hint of desperation in her voice. "Do not touch the ones with the white hair!"

The instructions were very clear, causing the BEM attackers to immediately draw back.

"Phew," Daisy said. "It's about time." Right then, Dez swooped low, dodging an attack from a Rubbish Plugger. His big wing flapped over Daisy's head, the force of air blasting the wig right off her head.

"Sorry!" Dez called as he winged away. But the damage

was irreparable. Daisy's sandy-brown hair was clearly visible among the group of white heads.

"Wigs!" shouted one of the Sweepers. "They're wearing wigs!" Instantly, the fight swarmed around them once more.

"Stand down!" Belzora shrieked through the intercom. "Of course they're wearing wigs, you fools! The trick is knowing which three are the real boys."

Spencer grinned, realizing that the Witches had no idea that the Dark Aurans had stayed behind. He took full advantage of the enemies' confusion, pushing his white-haired group up the crumbling steps of Welcher Elementary School.

"I didn't say to let them pass!" Belzora shrieked. "Stop the little brats! And do what you wish to those that have been de-wigged."

Daisy became an instant target, despite the fact that she'd picked up her wig and was struggling to fit it over her hair once more. She had been revealed as an impostor, and was currently the only person in the group that the BEM had approval to attack.

Daisy was plucked out of the group like a flower, a Rubbish Sweeper snatching her up. She screamed, thrusting her razorblade through the man's wing. The injury caused him to veer sharply, dropping the girl to the crowd of hands and weapons below.

Bookworm rose unexpectedly amidst the group of enemies. He caught the girl in his garbage arms, ducking his head as claws and blades slashed into his body, shredding garbage from his form.

Bookworm staggered several yards under the heavy

assault, depositing Daisy at the edge of the fight. He collapsed momentarily and then re-formed with new trash, beating his chest to challenge anyone to touch the girl.

Across the chaotic battlefield, Daisy and Spencer locked eyes. He knew she didn't want to abandon him, but the struggle had drawn her too far away to rejoin the Monitors. Spencer took a deep breath, silently wished her good luck, and then turned to enter the school.

It bothered him to be separated from Daisy. Somehow it made him feel alone, even though he was still surrounded by the Monitors and the Auran girls.

The walls around Welcher's entrance were bubbling with soapsuds. Now that everything was wet from the rain, the surveillance suds were multiplying. Spencer reached up with his pushbroom, popping dozens as he passed inside. There was no way he could destroy them all, and the suds were likely to be the thing that would ruin their plan. If the Witches found out that the Dark Aurans were not with them, they would all be in danger, wig or no wig.

The entire building was bristling with enemies. Spencer saw two active squeegee portals where Sweepers and BEM workers came through as reinforcements. They bumped into the Monitors, pushing them back and slowing them down, all the while obeying the Witches' orders not to hurt the kids.

Spencer's group, however, was under no such mandate. They pressed against the enemy with full force, latex gloves helping them slip through clutching hands. Still, many caved under the fear, quickly using the bleach and making an invisible escape back to the pump house.

The interior of Welcher Elementary looked very different. The same second-grade art projects hung on the wall, but the hallways seemed wider somehow. Barricades had been set up, most of them comprised of school desks and chairs.

There was a new hallway that Spencer didn't even recognize. He was momentarily disoriented in his own school, doubting the path he was taking toward the Glop source drinking fountain.

It was challenging to move through the school. Not only were the BEM Sweepers and Pluggers doing their best to stop Spencer's group, but Welcher itself presented a new challenge. When the elementary school had been deposited in the landfill, it had landed on a hillside. The result was a gently sloped hallway that became rather slippery as Spencer and the Monitors tracked rainwater inside.

There were only about fifteen Monitors left. None of the Auran girls had fled, and they didn't hold back in their aggression toward the BEM. Spencer and his group found themselves pinned behind a bunker at the doorway to a fifth-grade classroom. They were nearing the Glop source, but the result was a huge increase in security.

"We are at a major tactical disadvantage," Min said, peering over the top of the bunker through his sweaty white bangs.

"No kidding," Spencer said. He blindly threw a pinch of vacuum dust out into the hallway. There were so many enemies, it was impossible to miss.

Outside, there was a tremendous crack of thunder that rattled the walls. Through the window, Spencer saw a flash of lightning, bright enough to momentarily illuminate the dim classroom.

"Spencer!" It was Daisy's voice, and it took him a moment to realize that it was coming from the walkie-talkie clipped to his belt.

Keeping his head low behind the barricade, he unclipped the radio. "I'm here. Are you okay?"

"It's bad!" she yelled. "Bad, bad, bad!"

"What's bad, Daisy?" asked Spencer. "Talk to me!"

"General Clean escaped," she said. "He turned on the pump and I can't shut it off!"

"How?" Spencer cried. "I thought he was blind."

"He was," she answered. "But he turned himself into a Sweeper again!"

"That's not possible," Spencer muttered. "He'd need another potion."

"The pen," Daisy cried. "There wasn't any ink in that pen he was twirling. It was full of Sweeper potion. He had it with him the whole time! Once he turned half-Grime, he just slipped through the bars of the rake cage and took out the guards."

"Where's Clean now?" Spencer asked, half afraid to hear the answer.

"That's the worst part," she said, her voice shaky through the walkie-talkie. "Did you see that lightning bolt?"

Spencer swallowed hard, the horrible truth dawning on him the moment before Daisy said it.

"General Clean just Panned the Dark Aurans!"

CHAPTER 43

"I ADDED EVERYTHING."

Spencer sat behind the bunker in numb shock. A depression seemed to come over the remaining Monitors and Auran girls. General Clean had Panned the Dark Aurans. Now that the boys were under the curse of the Broomstaff once more, it meant they couldn't leave the landfill. It meant they couldn't go to the Dustbin. It meant they couldn't destroy the Toxite brain nests.

Spencer lifted the walkie-talkie to his lips. There was one more very important question he had to ask. "Daisy. Where are the scissors?"

The answer brought Spencer a sigh of relief. "I have the scissors," Daisy said. "I got to the pump house just in time. Sach met me at the door and passed the scissors to me just before Clean overtook him with green spray. I don't think Clean saw the handoff. Bookworm was fighting some

Pluggers and I was all alone. There was nothing I could do, Spencer. I had to run away!"

"You did the right thing, Daisy," Spencer said through gritted teeth. "Keeping the scissors safe was the most important thing."

"But Clean Panned them!" Daisy shouted. "He used a blue recycle boat to haul the boys across the lagoon. He Panned them before the green spray wore off. The Dark Aurans can't leave the landfill now," rambled Daisy. "They can't go to the Dustbin! Spencer, what are we going to do?"

"Hold onto the scissors and wait to hear from me," Spencer answered, having no idea how they could possibly recover from this blow. "We're almost to the Glop source." Without waiting for a reply, Spencer clipped the radio onto his belt once more.

He gestured to a hallway branching off from the one they were in. If possible, that juncture was even more crowded with enemies. "The drinking fountain should be right down there, across the hall from Mrs. Natcher's classroom."

"What about a blitz?" Rho said. "We make a defensive formation, keeping Spencer in the middle. Then we push until he makes it through."

"We have to hurry," Spencer said. "If news about the Dark Aurans reaches the Witches, then—"

He was cut off by cackling laughter through the school intercom. "News travels fast!" Ninfa said.

"Faster than pizza delivery!" added Holga.

Spencer looked down to see a cluster of shiny soapsuds

glimmering in a puddle of rainwater at his feet. The Witches were always watching. And they'd heard Daisy's announcement at the same time he had.

Rho reached out with her foot and stomped on the suds. She turned to Spencer, her face set with determination. "Let's go!"

The Auran girls fell into an arrowhead formation, Rho at the forefront. Spencer ducked behind them as Min and the remaining Monitors filled in the back. They charged the sixth-grade hallway with unmatched fury, BEM workers and Pluggers collapsing under the attack.

A Rubbish Sweeper lunged overhead, but Shirley knocked him out with a shot of green spray. A Filth Plugger barreled into them, trying to break their formation. Its quills sprayed in a dangerous volley, pinging against the dustpan shields of the leading Aurans.

One quill passed through the defenses, grazing Spencer's shoulder. He winced at the pain, his hand reaching up to discover a light graze. It was just enough to rip his coveralls, dampening the tear with his blood.

Spencer supposed the injury was for the better. He'd need a drop of blood to close the Glop source anyway.

Ducking his head low, Spencer pressed on at the heart of the formation. Monitors were dropping off, bleaching out and running for safety. Even two of the Auran girls retreated, though in the confusion Spencer couldn't tell who.

He could see the drinking fountain ahead, gurgling with sick-smelling Glop. Spencer sidestepped an enemy mop as more of his friends fell away. The defensive formation was down to Min and three of the Auran girls. But they were almost there!

"This is it!" Rho shouted. Gia grabbed Spencer by the arm and thrust him forward. He skidded to a halt, bending over the bubbling Glop source. Behind him, Rho, Gia, Netty, and Min stood shoulder to shoulder, desperate to give Spencer time to throw the needed ingredients into the source.

He scrambled with the items in his belt pouch, pulling out the ingredients that Rho and the Auran girls had prepared for him. The first was a slimy sphere about the size of a large marble.

Eye of Grime.

The eyeball sloshed from one corner of the plastic Ziploc bag to the other. Spencer tried not to look as he pulled open the zip seal and slipped the gooey orb into the drinking fountain. It fell into the Glop with a tiny *plop*, letting off a hiss of colored vapor as the formula began.

Next, he plucked a small hard item from his pouch.

Tooth of Filth.

It was definitely one of the buckteeth from the front of the creature's mouth. It was a dull yellow color, over an inch long, resting in the palm of his latex-gloved hand. He reached over the fountain and dropped it in. The tooth hit the swirling mixture and let off a streak of blue and gold.

Mentally reviewing the list, Spencer took the third ingredient from his pouch. It was black and pointed, about the size of a jalapeño pepper.

Beak of Rubbish.

He pinched the sharp beak between thumb and finger, dangling it out over the source. With a small splash, it landed in the Glop. This ingredient vented a plume of black smoke, causing Spencer to crinkle his nose as he drew out the next item.

Bristles of a broom.

Spencer clutched a handful of yellow straw. Rho had carefully selected the bristles from a powerful Glopified broom. They looked absolutely normal in Spencer's grasp, but when he threw them into the source, they crackled and sparked like fireworks.

Spencer wasn't very excited about the next ingredient. He reached up to his wounded shoulder and winced, holding his hand there until the tips of his fingers were red.

Blood of an Auran boy.

He reached over the source and flicked his fingers, specks of blood peppering the formula. Spencer knew there were trace amounts of Glop inside his body. It was part of the change he had undergone when becoming an Auran. Olin had told him that the Glop was most concentrated in spit and blood.

The Glop source turned a vibrant red, swirling and gurgling. Spencer stared into it, one more ingredient to complete the Glop formula.

Spencer reached into his belt pouch and drew out the pink hairbrush from the Witches' bathroom. He held it cautiously by the tip of the handle. There was no telling what kind of germs were packed into the Witches' hair. At the very least, they probably had lice.

With his gloved hand, Spencer plucked out a pinch of black hairs, almost gagging as they ripped away from the brush's bristles.

Preparing himself for what might happen when the source closed, Spencer dropped the hairs into the bubbling mixture. They vanished in a moment, incorporated into the formula.

But nothing happened.

The formula didn't hiss, smoke, or change color. The source didn't begin closing at all. It continued gurgling and swirling as though nothing had happened.

Pinching out a few more strands of hair, Spencer threw them into the Glop source. But the result was the same.

Nothing.

"It didn't work!" Spencer cried. "The source isn't closing!"

"Of course not, dearie," came a chilling reply from down the hallway. The fighting ceased suddenly, Pluggers and Sweepers falling back in respect as Belzora, Ninfa, and Holga strode out of Mrs. Natcher's classroom.

"The source didn't close because you don't have all the ingredients," Ninfa continued.

"That's not possible," Spencer said. "I added everything."

Holga clucked her tongue in mock sadness at his failure. "You didn't add a Witch's hair." She smoothed a hand over her gnarly locks, and Spencer thought he saw a moth fly out.

To prove them wrong, Spencer held out the pink hairbrush. "We took this from your apartment."

The Witches laughed again. "That's odd," Ninfa said. "Why would you take *that?*"

"Your hair," Spencer said. "We needed your hair to close the source."

"Silly boy," said Holga. "That's the brush we use to comb the yak."

Spencer froze, staring at the useless pink hairbrush in his hand. The clog of grizzly black hair . . . it was *yak* hair? He remembered seeing the strange animal on the third level of the parking garage, but he didn't expect the Witches to comb it.

"You see," said Belzora, stepping forward. "We knew you were coming that day. We knew what you wanted. We planted the yak's brush in our bathroom, and you took the bait like a rat takes cheese."

Rho leapt forward in anger. She grasped for a handful of Holga's hair, desperate to yank it from the Witch's scalp. But the moment her hand touched Holga's head, a shock wave of magic blasted her backward. Rho skidded across the hallway, cradling her hand, which was smoking with severe burns.

"We thought you might try something like that," Ninfa said. "So we used our wands to Glopify these nifty hairnets before we came out to say hello."

Spencer looked closer. Now that she pointed them out, he could see that all three Witches had their hair tucked back and secured under black hairnets like the kind Meredith used in the school kitchen.

Spencer reached down and unclipped the walkie-talkie on his hip. His backup plan was rough, but without Sach, Olin, and Aryl, he was going to have to try something desperate.

"Daisy," he called. "I need you to do something for me."

"Anything," she replied instantly.

"Oh," Holga said. "He wants to say bye-bye to his girly friend. How cute."

Spencer ignored the Witch. "Do you have any stainless steel polish left?"

"Maybe a drop," she said. "Why?"

"I need you to polish the scissors."

"The *scissors?*" Daisy clarified. "What are you planning, Spencer?"

"Just do it."

"Okay," she answered. It was silent for a few seconds as Spencer stared off with the Witches. "Got it," Daisy said.

Spencer took a deep breath and reached into his belt pouch. Pulling out the Glopified magnet, he held it high over his head.

In a moment, Spencer heard a crash down the hallway, accompanied by shouts of alarm. Another crash followed, this one sounding like crumbling bricks.

"What *are* you up to, boy?" Ninfa muttered.

The Glopified scissors suddenly appeared, ripping through the wall on a direct path for the magnet in the boy's hand. An unfortunate Filth Sweeper happened to be standing in the course of the flying scissors. The sharp blades tore through him, killing his Sweeper half instantly.

The scissors slammed into the magnet and Spencer held them close, noticing how shiny the recently polished iron looked.

"Thanks, Daisy," Spencer said. He dropped the magnet into his belt pouch, scissors still fused tightly to it, and clipped the walkie-talkie back into place.

Belzora smiled wickedly. "Your big finale," she said. "Your trickery in moving the school, the lives wasted in battle against our warriors . . . and now you've brought us the scissors." She shook her head. "You fool boy. You'll never succeed. You cannot close the source without a Witch's hair."

Spencer stared at the fountain of raw magic. The Dark Aurans had warned him against doing this. He had no assurance that it would work, but at this point, it was the only risk left to take.

"The Glop formula said we need a hair from a Witch's head." Spencer's eyes darted up to Belzora's face. "But the recipe never said the hair had to be detached."

Spencer Zumbro reached out, wrapped both arms around Belzora's middle, and lunged for the Glop fountain. They went in together, sucked headfirst into the gurgling, bubbling source of all Glop.

"TO THE NESTS!"

Spencer was falling. All around him were grit and haze and dust. He felt alone and cut off, once again in that horrible place of endless gray.

He was in the Dustbin.

Somewhere nearby, Spencer could hear Belzora free falling, too. They had separated the moment they'd passed through the Glop source, the Witch kicking away from the boy who had pulled her in.

In the course of his dizzying tumble, Spencer finally managed to discover which way was up just before he hit the ground. The impact didn't hurt, and Spencer wasn't sure if that was due to his protective coveralls or to the nature of the powdery dust that formed his landing spot.

He scrambled to his knees, trying to locate Belzora before she had a chance to attack him. The Witch was standing several feet away, the tops of her tall black boots just above the soft dust.

Behind her was the Instigators' fortress and, rising at its heart, the bright beam of the brain stem emanating upward from the Toxite nests.

The fortress walls were made of black stone, topped with battlements and studded with turrets. The place looked like the ancient castles Spencer had seen in history books at school. Spencer remembered that familiar things could be formed from the dust, and he wondered where the Witches had lived to see such castles as the one before him.

The Dark Aurans had said that the fortress defenses would be down as long as the Witches weren't inside the Dustbin. Spencer clearly hadn't thought of that when he had pulled Belzora in with him. And if one Witch weren't enough to reanimate the TPs, Spencer suddenly saw Ninfa and Holga drop into the dust beside Belzora.

"Well," Holga muttered, dusting herself off. "I certainly didn't miss this place!"

"We barely got through the fountain before the Glop source closed," Ninfa said, straightening her hairnet. She really didn't need it anymore. The task had been accomplished. Spencer had succeeded in using Belzora to close the source!

The lead Witch was raising her bronze wand when Spencer's hand thrust into his belt pouch. Hoping wildly that the scissors were no longer magnetized, he gripped the handles and pulled them out.

The polish had indeed worn off, and the scissors

snapped open. Without delay, Spencer pointed the blades directly at the Witches and snipped the scissors closed.

His aim went high as a TP formed out of the dust, lassoing his arm and jerking it up. As the blades closed, the scissors sliced through the top of the fortress wall, crumbling the black stone to dust.

TPs were forming all around him, but Spencer had nothing to lose now. He was alone in the Dustbin and his sole purpose was destruction. He opened and closed the scissors again, cutting two dozen TPs in half.

Spencer's arm came free as the TP who'd lassoed him disintegrated. He raced toward the fortress, his feet churning through the powdery dust.

Spencer saw the three Witches through an ever-growing sea of TP mummies. The old hags must have sensed the recklessness of his charge and seen the careless abandon in his eyes.

Their bronze wands flicked out, channeling creative dust and forming it into solid brooms. "To the nests!" Belzora shouted, swinging a leg over her broomstick and striking the bristles against the dusty ground. Ninfa and Holga followed, three dark figures flying over the crumbling wall of their fortress.

Spencer couldn't worry about the Witches. At the moment, he had a few hundred TPs to fight and a fortress to destroy.

Turning the scissors on an angle, Spencer snipped a huge chunk out of the wall, obliterating everything in his path. He raced into the fortress, finding the place to be a mazelike network of walkways and staircases.

A two-ply TP leapt from an overhead catwalk and landed deftly beside Spencer. The toilet paper binding the mummy's face parted and the whispery voice issued a command to rally the others.

"The boy must die! He must not reach the brain nests!"

He might have said more, but Spencer's left hand flashed from his belt, extending a razorblade and slicing off the head of the paper figure.

TPs crawled like spiders on the walls, covering every stair and pathway as Spencer pressed deeper into the fortress. He was nearly unstoppable, wielding a razorblade in his left hand and the highly destructive scissors in his right.

Spencer felt disoriented in the Witches' fortress of interlocking catwalks. He forced himself to ignore the pathways, focusing instead on the ever-present beam of energy surging from the brain stem at the center of the fortress.

There was no beating this enemy. Despite Spencer's path of wanton destruction, the TPs continued to re-form from the grit in the air. He shouted in frustration, walls and tunnels crumbling in his rage.

An unusually fast TP blindsided Spencer, knocking him to the ground and sending his razorblade clattering. The boy brought his scissors around, but the two-ply lassoed his wrist, causing the next snip to go amiss.

They wrestled, Spencer painfully aware that the hosts of toilet-paper mummies were closing in on him. He wasn't strong enough to overpower the two-ply that grappled with him, and if he didn't regain control of the scissors, all would be lost.

Spencer cried out in desperation. He needed help! He needed someone to show up and save him. Staring into the hazy air, he wished with all his heart that help would arrive.

A razorblade suddenly slashed through the two-ply's back, causing the mummy to crumble to dust. Spencer whirled around, snipping the scissors to decimate the TPs crowding behind him. When he turned back, Spencer saw his timely rescuer.

It was Walter Jamison.

CHAPTER 45

"GO AND FINISH THIS."

Walter wasn't real, of course. Spencer had created the familiar old warlock from the magical haze of the Dustbin.

Walter stepped forward, his bald head shiny with sweat. He smiled at Spencer and reached out a hand to help him up.

There was an emptiness to this fake Walter. He could never be the real thing, but Spencer latched onto this image of his past, using the warlock's presence, however artificial, to give him strength.

"Come on," Walter said. His voice was exactly how Spencer remembered it. After all, Walter's voice only existed as an outward expression of the boy's imagination.

They raced forward, Spencer slicing through TPs with the Glopified scissors while Walter Jamison cut them down with the razorblade sword. Spencer moved with renewed determination, strengthened by having a companion in this numbing land of oppressive dust. As long as he kept his mind on the old warlock, Spencer's imagination would continue feeding the image and the magic dust would keep Walter by his side.

They were close now. Spencer could feel the pulsating heat of the brain stem. When he looked up, there was only one more high wall between him and the multicolored beam.

An archway stood in the wall just before them, sealed off with a heavy door. Spencer aimed backward, snipping the scissors to destroy any TPs behind him while Walter shoved open the heavy door.

Under Walter's imagined strength, the door swung open with surprising ease. The warlock reached back, pulling Spencer through the archway.

Spencer found himself at the bottom of a dim, enclosed stairwell. But there was something different about the air.

There was no dust here.

"This is a safe zone," Spencer explained to Walter. It wasn't necessary, but it helped make the replica warlock feel even more real. "Garth Hadley's building in the Dustbin was like this. It's designed to vent all the dust away, forming a noncreative zone so the TPs can't form inside and take over."

The air was the same here. It made sense that the brain nests would be in a dustless area. That way, nothing could take shape around the nests without the Witches' approval.

As they stood in the shadowy stairwell, Spencer saw TPs developing outside the archway. The mummies couldn't re-form where he was standing, but Spencer knew that nothing would stop the TPs from racing through the arch to get him.

Walter stepped up to the door. "You're close to the end, Spencer," said the warlock. "Go and finish this."

"Can't you come with me?" Spencer asked. The false Walter could, of course. He would do nearly anything that Spencer could imagine. And that was what scared the boy. Spencer had known all along he would face the end alone. Not even a figment of his imagination would provide him the comfort of companionship.

"I don't know if I can do this," Spencer whispered. "I don't know if I can win."

Walter reached back, and Spencer felt the comfort of the man's hand on his shoulder.

"Winning doesn't mean we all go home safe," Walter said. It was an old conversation, Spencer's imagination bringing it to his remembrance at this crucial time. "Victory will come to those who fight for what is right," Walter continued. "It won't come without its fair share of pain and suffering. No victory comes without sacrifice. But it will come. We just have to stay the course."

Walter grinned, his hand slipping from the boy's shoulder as the first TPs reached the archway. The warlock stepped out to face them alone, his razorblade shining in the steady, hazy light of the Dustbin.

Grabbing the heavy door, Spencer slammed it closed just as the first TP knocked into Walter Jamison. Spencer ripped a strip of duct tape from his belt and slapped it over the door's edge. The replica of Walter wouldn't last long, now that Spencer needed to focus his mind on other things. The warlock would disintegrate to dust once more, a painful reminder that Walter Jamison really was dead.

Taking a deep breath, Spencer began a slow ascent up the stairs. He expected the Witches to come barreling down on him at any moment. But the only sound was the steady thrum of the brain stem and the soft scuff of his shoes on the stone stairs.

The staircase deposited Spencer on a narrow walkway. The path curved, the wall forming a ring like the rim of a giant cup. The brain stem rose at the very center, surrounded by a column of dustless space as high as Spencer could see.

Afraid of what he might see, Spencer carefully stepped over to the edge of the wall. He peered down, readying himself to see the nests where the bright beam of energy originated.

Far below, in the pit formed by the ring of the circular wall, Spencer beheld the Toxite brain nests.

They were unlike anything he'd ever seen: three giant brains, nestled closely together. Each was roughly the size of a boulder, larger than a van, sitting cradled in a divot of hardened dust.

Spencer identified them immediately. The one on the left was a grayish-blue color. It looked dry, covered in a thick layer of dust, like a shelf that had never been wiped off. Rising through the spongy brain material was an assortment of sharp quills. The largest were as thick as Spencer's

forearm and taller than he was. A blue energy seeped from the brain, rising like a vapor to swirl into the single multi-colored brain stem.

The middle brain seemed softer than the others. It trembled like an overset yellow gelatin, streaks of green and orange lacing through it. A sticky, pale goo oozed from the brain, pooling in the nest around it. From this one, strands of yellow energy twisted upward.

The final brain was almost entirely black. From his viewpoint looking down, Spencer thought it seemed to be made of toughened leather. At places, the leathery material appeared to be stretched too thin, cracking slightly to let out a hiss of black smoke. The brain exuded ribbons of red light that rose to join the others.

Filth, Grime, and Rubbish.

The fueling brains of all Toxites pulsed just fifty feet be-low Spencer. The blue, yellow, and red energies tangled to-gether into a single brain stem about twenty feet up. That was the spot. That was where Sach had said to use the scissors.

Spencer glanced at the pointed object in his right hand. He didn't doubt the scissors' power. He'd just used them to carve a path through brick and stone to get here. It seemed almost strange that something so small would be capable of destroying Toxites forever.

Spencer unclipped a broom from his janitorial belt and stepped up to the edge of the wall, his toes hanging over as he looked down. The low vibrations from the brain stem caused his ears to buzz, and Spencer's face was damp with sweat from the heat of it.

He judged the distance. Angling his broom just right, Spencer gave it a light tap on the wall, just enough to send him drifting into range.

No sooner had his bristles touched the wall than the entire broom turned to dust in Spencer's hand. He reeled, almost falling into the pit of brain nests. Pinwheeling his arms wildly, Spencer stumbled back to the walkway, heart racing.

The Witches were there. No, the Witches were *everywhere*.

There must have been nearly a hundred of them, suddenly appearing along the walkway all around the wall. They were replicas, of course, like the one Spencer had made of Walter Jamison. It was a distraction tactic, aimed to throw Spencer off course. And it was working.

Spencer lowered the scissors and snipped at the approaching Witches on his right. The blades sliced through them, reducing their forms to dusty vapor.

"Which ones are real?" said thirty Belzoras in perfect unison. "We enjoyed your game with the white wigs. But now it's our turn to play."

Spencer snipped through the Witches on his left, but the ones on the right were already re-forming.

"But how can you . . . ?" Spencer stammered. "There's no dust in here!"

"We're not limited like you," answered twenty versions of Ninfa. "Our wands let us create wherever we like."

Of course. If the Witches' wands could summon dust in the real world, they certainly wouldn't have trouble in a noncreative zone inside the Dustbin.

Spencer cut down a dozen more copies, hoping to trap one of the real Witches between the scissor blades. The attempt was useless, and the group of decoy Witches continued a steady pace toward him.

Spencer paused. This was a distraction, a tactic meant only to stall him from doing what he had come to do. Spencer turned back toward the brain stem. It was so close! He didn't have another broom, but if he jumped, he would have one shot at lining up the scissors and snipping through the beam.

A line from Spencer's recent conversation with Walter Jamison played back in his mind. *"Winning doesn't mean we all go home safe."* Spencer took a deep breath. *"No victory comes without sacrifice."*

Ignoring the myriad of Witch replicas on the walkway, Spencer sprinted three steps, vaulted over the edge, and flung himself toward the glowing brain stem.

The moment his feet left the wall, Spencer realized his mistake. The Witches, the *real* Witches, were waiting for him, hovering on brooms right next to the spot he needed to cut.

His course was set, Spencer's momentum from the leap carrying him straight toward the enemy. He opened the scissors, taking aim just as Belzora's wand flashed.

The Glopified scissors exploded in Spencer's hand. He felt the metal ripping apart as the shock of the destruction knocked him against the wall. The Witches cackled in victory as Spencer fell to the nests below.

The scissors were gone, blown to useless particles before Spencer ever had a chance to touch the brain stem.

CHAPTER 46

"IS HE SMART ENOUGH?"

Spencer groaned, his vision temporarily blurred from the jolt of his fall. He was lying on his back, nestled between the giant Grime brain and the leathery Rubbish brain. He couldn't move, or didn't want to. Spencer stared up at the gently twisting ribbons of energy, watching them swirl together at the spot he had failed to cut.

The Witches drifted upward, their replicas dissolving as the three of them stood at the edge of the wall, staring down at Spencer in unmasked victory.

Spencer looked up at them, his heart sinking. This was it, then. This was where he would die—here, nestled uncomfortably among the brains he had failed to destroy.

"What are we waiting for?" Holga shrieked. "Let's finish the little whelp!" She lowered her stubby bronze wand, but Belzora grabbed her wrist.

"Has he come all this way for nothing?" Belzora's voice echoed down the pit to where Spencer lay.

"What are you suggesting, Sister?" Ninfa asked.

"I see an opportunity before us," Belzora continued. "An opportunity that the Instigators would never pass up."

"Yes!" Holga shrieked, catching on. "Yes, yes, yes!"

Spencer knew he had to move. What the Witches were planning was horrible, unthinkable! He rose to his knees, sliding in the slimy spilled residue from the Grime brain.

Belzora was using her wand, rearranging the configuration of the brains in the pit below. The Filth brain slid past Spencer, sharp quills narrowly missing his arm. He scrambled out of the way as the Grime brain wobbled to a new place, dust re-forming into a hardened nest below it.

Spencer was standing in a newly formed vacant spot. He felt the dust firming below his feet, mounding up a curved edge to form another nest. There was no oversized brain to occupy this new indentation, just Spencer staring hopelessly up at the Witches looming over him.

Holga's stubby wand angled downward, a streamer of magic dust taking shape into a fibrous rope. Spencer backed up as the rope landed coiled at his feet. But he knew Holga wasn't offering him a way out. He'd seen a rope like this before.

Rearing up like a snake, the long rope had bound Spencer's hands before he could reach his belt. The rope continued coiling around the boy, securing his arms and making its way down his legs.

As the rope cinched his knees together, Spencer lost

balance and fell onto his side. He lay there, wrapped like a bug in a cocoon, with only his head exposed.

Spencer knew the Witches weren't going to kill him. The boy's agelessness was about to become very important to them. What the Witches were planning was worse than anything Spencer could imagine.

"Is he smart enough?" Holga asked.

"He has proven to be," answered Belzora. "Almost, he outthought even us."

"Will he survive the procedure?" asked Ninfa, though the tone of her voice implied that she didn't care either way.

"The Refraction Dust will be tailored to his mind," answered Belzora. "His strongest traits will be deflected into a new brain. And spawning from that opposite trait, a fourth Toxite will rise!"

Spencer wriggled helplessly in the divot that would soon become a brain nest for his own personal Toxite. He thought of Olin, Sach, and Aryl, feeling betrayed to discover after so many years that the Toxites had been born from their minds. It seemed worse for Spencer, knowing beforehand what the Refraction Dust would do.

He wondered at the damage he would cause the world. This fourth Toxite would spread like the others, infesting schools and rotting the minds of hardworking students. Spencer didn't know what his greatest strength might be.

Was it responsibility? Loyalty? Trustworthiness? The opposite of any one of those traits would be detrimental to society.

Belzora leaned forward, her face a multicolored glow from the bright brain stem. She raised her bronze wand. At her right, Ninfa extended her wand so the tip was touching Belzora's. Holga did the same from the left, the three wands now united as one.

Belzora's voice echoed down into the pit, reciting some ancient verse in a low voice.

> *The boy that here before us lies*
> *Shall fuel these monsters till he dies.*
> *From his mind, refracted traits*
> *Turn scholars into reprobates.*

Dust was swirling around the wands, entwining the Witches' arms. It was brewing, building, with stabs of color lancing through the magic grit.

Spencer shouted something, but his heartbeat was pounding so loudly in his ears that he didn't even hear his own voice.

The Witches extended their arms, the Refraction Dust mounting to a peak before it raced down the three wands, a terrible ribbon of haze on an unstoppable course toward the tethered boy.

"Spencer!" a familiar voice shouted from above. Spencer thought for sure he had imagined it, but as his eyes turned skyward, he saw the unmistakable outline of Dez Rylie's Sweeper wings.

"No!" shouted the Sweeper boy as the bolt of Refraction

Dust streamed forward. Dez folded back his wings and went into a vertical dive toward the brain nests.

Spencer knew Dez would never reach him in time. The Refraction Dust was traveling too fast.

Then, at the last possible second, Dez Rylie did something entirely unexpected. His wings snapped out, covering Spencer protectively. He clenched his jaw, his face upturned proudly, as the Refraction Dust struck him directly in the chest.

CHAPTER 47

"YOU THINK YOU HAVE WON?"

Dez's body went limp as it absorbed the Refraction Dust in midair. His head rolled back lifelessly, and Spencer saw the boy's leathery wings begin to disintegrate. The force of the blow sent him into an out-of-control spiral, and Dez's body struck the brain stem at the exact point where the energies flowed together.

Dez dangled there for a moment, as if the brain stem held him aloft. His body was glowing deep hues of azure, amber, and crimson. Pulses of energy seemed to jolt through his body, sending blasts both up and down the brain stem.

"Dez!" Spencer shouted, but it was clear the boy couldn't hear him. It made Spencer sick to see him dangling there, to know what Dez had done for him.

Suddenly, the brain stem seemed to buck, pitching Dez out of the energy beam. He fell limply, landing with a thud on the hardened dust beside Spencer. Dez didn't move, his body still and smoking.

"Dez!" Spencer shouted again. "Wake up!" He wasn't dead, right? Dez couldn't be dead! The Sweeper half of him was clearly gone, but the boy still had one more life. Didn't he?

A sound overhead drew Spencer's attention. The three Witches had collapsed on top of the wall, suctioned down by a skilled Thumb Shot of vacuum dust. Daisy Gates appeared, Glopified leaf blower strapped to her back and a broom in her hand.

She tapped the bristles against the wall and drifted down toward the brain nests. As she drew nearer, Spencer saw the look of absolute worry on her face.

"What happened?" Daisy dropped onto the hardened dirt and ran over to Spencer.

"Dez took the hit for me," Spencer said in disbelief. Daisy grabbed both ends of the rope binding Spencer and tied them together. Immediately, Spencer felt the rope's grip loosen, and he wriggled free as Daisy knelt down beside Dez.

Daisy lowered her ear to the boy's face, listening for breathing. He looked so much smaller now that his Rubbish half was gone. Spencer barely remembered what regular old Dez was supposed to look like.

"He's breathing," Daisy said, unclipping the orange healing spray from her belt. "Where should I spray him?"

"Everywhere," Spencer said. Dez didn't look so good.

His shirt was charred and smoking, his arms and hands blistered and burned from the energy of the brain stem.

Daisy sprayed a quick mist of orange over the boy's entire body. Then she rocked back on her heels to wait for the effect.

"We can't stay here," Spencer said. "The Witches almost made a new Toxite out of me. And I'm afraid they'll try again as soon as they get up."

"What about the scissors?" Daisy asked.

Spencer lowered his head in shame. "The Witches blew them to bits before I had a chance to use them." He stared up at the eternally rising brain stem. "I guess we lost."

There was a loud squelching sound directly behind Spencer. He whirled around, instinctively drawing a mop from his belt.

The Grime brain was doing something strange. It was convulsing, the slime around it slurping as it rocked back and forth. Silver scales began forming all over the soft brain matter, shimmering like coins at the bottom of a fountain. And the Grime brain wasn't the only one having a reaction.

"Why's it so dark?" Dez shouted, suddenly sitting bolt upright as the orange healing spray worked its magic. "Hey!" The movement seemed to alert him to the fact that his wings were missing. He reached his arms around, slapping his own back. "Who took my wings? Why can't I see?"

Spencer and Daisy glanced at each other, sharing a look of sheer relief that the boy was alive. Neither wanted to break the news about his Sweeper death, and they decided they didn't have time to do so anyway, with the Toxite brain nests behaving so strangely.

The Rubbish brain was changing texture. Instead of the leathery black hide, bright colors started to emerge. Spencer saw what looked like feathers forming on the sides of the massive brain.

The Filth brain was shaking, throwing off the layer of dust that had coated it for so long. The deadly quills snapped off, clattering to the ground like discarded arrows. Tufts of soft fur pressed through the folds of the brain, creating a fuzzy blue exterior.

"We've got to get out of here," Spencer said, looking up to see if the Witches had recovered.

"Spencer?" Dez shouted, groping blindly with both hands. "I hear you, Doofus! Where are you? Why can't I see anything?"

Daisy slipped the leaf blower from her back. They'd used a device like this one to escape the Dustbin last time they came. She flipped a switch and pulled the trigger, releasing a bolt of air straight into the sky. The leaf blower kicked back, burying itself in the hard dirt. Daisy's hair whipped in the upward current.

"The Witches are going to want a ride out of here too," Spencer said. He didn't know how to stop them. The Rip would be open for only a few minutes. If they paused to fight the Witches, the Rip would close and they would be trapped in the Dustbin forever.

"That's okay," Daisy said. "The Witches can come.

Bookworm should have moved the Vortex into position by now. We'll be ready for them!"

Spencer had no idea what she was talking about, but there wasn't time to ask. He turned and grabbed Dez by the arm, hoisting the boy to his feet.

"Stay close," he said. Keeping one arm around Dez's shoulder, he stepped with the bigger boy into the whirling slipstream.

They were immediately airborne, carried up by the rushing current of Glopified wind. Daisy entered just below them, keeping her arms and legs tucked close as she flew.

They blew past the Witches standing at the top of the wall. Spencer caught a brief glimpse of their shocked faces, and his escape tasted even better. He saw Ninfa turn to the leaf blower buried in the dust. She raised her wand to pulverize it, but Belzora caught her hand. Spencer had been right. The Witches weren't willing to destroy their only way back to the real world. Instead, the three old hags joined hands and stepped into the slipstream, flying upward in pursuit of the escaping kids.

Rising parallel to and alongside the brain stem, Spencer saw new colors flashing and dancing amid the column. He didn't understand exactly what had happened when the Refraction Dust struck Dez, but the result seemed to be changing the Toxite brain nests into something entirely new.

"Oh, man!" Dez suddenly yelled, as something important seemed to occur to him. "I died, didn't I? My Rubbish half is dead!" He gasped, a look of genuine fear on his face. "I'm blind!"

Flying in the slipstream alongside Spencer, Dez touched his unseeing eyes. His fingers had returned to normal, chubby and dirty.

"The good news is," Spencer said, trying to soften the revelation, "you have to die twice to really die."

Dez threw his head back and groaned. "I didn't want to die!"

"You saved my life," Spencer said, trying to help him understand that his Sweeper half had not died for nothing.

"Seriously?" Dez yelled. "I died saving *you?* I barely even like you!"

"Thanks?" Spencer said, not sure how to take that.

"My eyes!" Dez moaned. "I'm blind forever!" Then he began whining about all the assets he had lost. "And my talons, and my muscles, and my amazingly awesome wings . . . argh! I can't even burp dust anymore!"

"Look on the bright side," Spencer said. "At least you have a normal nose again."

"My beak was better!" Dez swung a punch at where he thought Spencer was, completely missing. "Chump," he grumbled. "Even my death perception is off."

Spencer rolled his eyes. "It's actually *depth* perception," he said. And of course it was off. Dez was completely blind!

"Whatever." Dez glared out over the Dustbin, even though he couldn't see anything.

The Rip came into view overhead. Beside it, the glowing brain stem continued to rise into what seemed like infinity.

Daisy's voice drifted up from below the two bickering boys. "The Witches are coming in fast!"

Spencer looked down, glimpsing Belzora, Ninfa, and Holga rising quickly through the slipstream below Daisy. They had used their wands to fashion brooms, taking advantage of the extra speed to catch up to the three kids.

"We're almost there!" Spencer shouted down to Daisy. "Don't let them get you!"

Daisy screamed, and Spencer saw Belzora's wrinkly hand close around the girl's ankle. Before he could do anything, Spencer was emerging from the Vortex vacuum bag.

It was suddenly pouring rain, and Spencer found himself on his hands and knees in the mud beside Dez. Thunder pealed and lightning flashed, illuminating the giant Broomstaff looming above them.

They were on the little island at the center of the Glop lagoon. The Vortex was a soggy mess lying in the mud, and the garbage figure of Bookworm loomed over it. Marv was there too. And Penny, and Bernard.

Alan Zumbro helped his son to his feet. But there wasn't time to explain anything as Daisy suddenly appeared through the small hole in the Vortex.

Belzora was still clinging to the girl's foot, but she released her grip at the surprise of her sudden surroundings. Bookworm seized her by the shoulders and slammed her against the rough wood of the Broomstaff, her bronze wand slipping from her wet grasp and landing like a stick in the mud.

Ninfa and Holga appeared out of the Vortex almost

simultaneously. Aided by the element of surprise, Marv and Penny knocked the two wands aside and threw the Witches against the Broomstaff with their sister. Bernard raced around the wooden trunk, spooling out a long strip of duct tape to secure the three hags in place.

"What?" Holga shrieked, wriggling against her bonds. "You can't do this!"

"We have wands!" yelled Ninfa, her hand straining for the bronze tool in the mud. "We'll strike you all!"

Alan stepped forward, tucking a heavy bronze dustpan behind each of their thrashing heads. Lightning crackled overhead, this time only inches from the bristling tip of the Broomstaff.

All around them, the Glop lagoon was swirling and churning in a great whirlpool. Most of the magical substance had already been pumped back into the earth. In a few more moments, the lagoon would be dry.

"You think you have won?" Belzora screamed. "The brain nests live on! Our Toxites will never—"

The Witch's sentence was cut short as a deafening clap of thunder accompanied the brightest bolt of lightning so far. The electricity hit the tip of the Broomstaff, illuminating the whole shaft with a terrible magical glow.

The bronze dustpans snapped, curling like collars around the necks of the three Witches. The force of the blow rendered them all unconscious, frying the duct tape and causing them to collapse into the mud.

The lagoon slurped loudly as the last chug of Glop was pumped away. Toxites would be springing up all over the country, and the lagoon would begin its long process of filling once again.

Almost immediately, the storm broke. The rain slowed to a mere drizzle, and the thunder gave a soft farewell rumble.

Marv retrieved the three wands from the mud and tucked them in his belt. Now that the Witches were Panned, they would be held under the same curse that had governed the Dark Aurans for so many years. They would be doomed to wander the landfill, unable to perform any sort of magic unless under someone else's orders. And once the Rebels took the wands back to Welcher, the Witches would never be able to reach them again.

Spencer stepped over to the motionless form of Belzora and rolled the woman onto her side. There was something he needed from her before she ran off to live out her life in the rotting landfill. Spencer grabbed the twelve remaining bangle bracelets and slid them off Belzora's wrist.

The Timekeepers.

The Aurans deserved to have them. Not the way V had received hers, but in their own time and their own way. If they were careful, the Aurans could age however they liked.

Spencer stood up, the bronze bracelets tinkling softly in his hand. "We have to find the Dark Aurans," he said. "They could be in danger." Last he'd heard, General Clean had transformed back into a Sweeper and Panned them.

"They're fine," Alan said.

"A little sheepish to admit that they got Panned again,"

Bernard added. "They're certainly anxious for you to use that spit sponge and get them out of it."

"What about General Clean?" Daisy asked.

"Ran off," Marv said. "I would have too, if I looked like that."

"What do you mean?" Spencer asked.

"I don't know what happened down in the Dustbin," Alan said. "But there's something you have to see."

CHAPTER 48

"WHAT'S THE OPPOSITE OF ME?"

The battle for Welcher Elementary School was over. As Spencer approached the transplanted school, he noticed a few Rebels sifting through items that had fallen to the mud, collecting any discarded Glopified supplies that might be useful in the uncertain days ahead. Bernard moved off to help them, always anxious to discover treasures among the trash.

There was no sign of any BEM workers. Extension cords and battery packs littered the battlefield, but the overgrown Toxites that the Pluggers had been riding were nowhere in sight.

"When did the battle end?" Spencer asked.

"Hasn't been long," said Marv. The big janitor had a guiding hand on Dez's shoulder. The kid kept shrugging it off, but every time he did, he would stumble on something.

Dez's blindness was going to create a dependence that the rough kid would have a hard time adjusting to.

"About twenty minutes ago," Penny said, leading them up the crumbling steps of the school.

"The moment the change occurred," said Alan.

"What change?" Daisy asked, but no explanation was needed.

The hallways of Welcher were full of Extension Toxites. Abandoned in the battle, the creatures had naturally headed into the school, seeking their favored habitat. Now they sat lazily in the hallway, not bothering anyone.

But something was definitely different about the Toxites.

The Filth looked fuzzy and blue, its sharp quills replaced by the kind of fur that you wanted to pet. Its previously feral eyes were now big and watery, looking shy when it blinked. Its ears had grown long and floppy, hanging down along the side of its head. And the Filth's clawed feet had been replaced by padded paws.

"What?" Spencer couldn't help but exclaim. Daisy began to giggle wildly at the sight of the cuddly Filth.

"What's so funny?" Dez demanded, wanting to make sure that no one was laughing at him while he couldn't see.

"The Filth . . ." Spencer stammered. He didn't have words to describe it. "It's a . . . a . . ."

"A dust bunny!" said Daisy, still unable to control her giggles.

Down the hallway, Spencer saw a winged Rubbish glide forward and perch on the edge of an overturned table. But the Rubbish didn't look at all like a Rubbish anymore.

It had feathers! Bright, colorful feathers! Instead of a bald vulture head, it had a beautifully craning neck. When its emerald beak opened, Spencer expected the dry croak of a Rubbish. What came out instead was a whistling birdsong.

Spencer turned to Dez in astonishment. "What did you do?"

"Who, me?" Dez asked. "What are you talking about?"

A long Grime scuttled into view. The creature was no longer slimy, but covered in shimmering silver scales. Instead of being slender and agile, the Toxite was so plump it waddled. Its eyes didn't bulge the way they used to. Instead, it blinked slowly, staring cautiously at the humans standing in the hallway.

"And that's not the best part," Penny said. "Check this out." She bent forward and whistled softly, patting her knees as though she were calling a dog.

Instantly, the transformed Toxites swarmed toward her. The Grime rubbed its head against her leg while the Filth licked her face. The feathered Rubbish tried to perch on her shoulder, cooing softly.

Penny shrugged. "They're friendly!"

"They're more than friendly," Alan said. "Rho said she thinks their breathing has been reversed."

"No way!" Daisy exclaimed. "So the Grime will actually make me focus?" She dropped close to the new Grime, her face only inches from its scaly nose.

"What's six times eight?" Penny asked her.

"Forty-eight," she answered without delay. "Give me something harder."

"What's the square root of 154?" Penny asked.

"Whoa, not *that* hard," Daisy answered. She reached out and touched the Grime's pointed nose. "But I definitely don't feel distracted."

"And I feel wide awake," Spencer added. The floppy-eared Filth was sniffing at him, but the creature's breath actually seemed to give the boy a boost of energy.

"You've got to be kidding me," Dez said, finally catching on to what was happening. "All the freaky monsters turned into cuddly pets? That's so lame!"

"It's your fault," Spencer said.

"No way," replied Dez. "If I knew where you were standing, I'd punch you for saying that."

"I'm serious," Spencer continued. "The Toxites changed because of you."

"I don't know what you're talking about," said Dez. "They only change when I crush them under my fist of doom!"

"Not this time," Spencer said. "This time it was your brain that changed them." He turned to the others, all the pieces finally fitting together as he explained what had taken place at the brain nests.

"The Witches had me pinned," Spencer said. "They were charging up their wands with Refraction Dust, planning to use my brain to create a fourth Toxite. But Dez . . ." he grinned, slapping a hand on the boy's shoulder. "Dez took the blow for me. The Refraction Dust knocked him into the brain stem."

"And the opposite of Dez got infused into the existing brain nests," Alan finished.

"What's the opposite of me?" Dez asked defensively.

"Studious," answered Daisy.

"Focused," offered Penny.

"Interested," said Spencer.

"Okay, okay," Dez waved them off. "So that's what Toxites do now?" He moaned. "Oh, man! I just made school so boring."

"Actually," said Alan Zumbro, "I believe you just saved school."

"Yeah," Dez said. "I definitely did *not* mean to do that."

"But you *did* mean to take the blow for me," Spencer said, recalling the moment when Dez had spread his wings and absorbed the Refraction Dust. "Thanks."

The Dez that Spencer had met a year ago would never have done such a thing. They might not have transformed him into a scholar, but Spencer counted it a huge success that they'd transformed him into a friend.

"Don't count on me to do it again, Doofus," said Dez. "I'm blind forever because of you! You totally owe me one."

"Yeah," Spencer said. "I guess I do." He looked at the boy's sightless eyes. "I have an idea that might make us even. I'll see what I can do."

"You can't do anything cool," Dez grumbled. "I can't believe I saved you."

For a moment, Spencer was glad Dez couldn't see them all smiling. That was as close as anyone got to getting a "thank you" from Dez Rylie.

CHAPTER 49

"IF YOU MAKE A MESS, CLEAN IT UP."

Min and the Monitors were waiting in Mrs. Natcher's classroom with the Auran girls. Spencer and Daisy came in, guiding Dez through the open doorway.

Across the hallway, Spencer couldn't help but notice the smashed drinking fountain. What had once been the Glop source now looked plain and ordinary. The Witches' pedestal sink, still brimming with surveillance soapsuds, stood in the corner of the classroom next to the bookshelf.

"I must admit," Min said, when Spencer had finished recounting the story, "I wasn't counting on Dez's brain to save the day."

"Hey," Dez protested. "It was my muscles. I totally stopped that stupid Refried Dust."

"*Refraction* Dust," Min corrected, before Spencer could say anything.

"What will you guys do now?" Daisy asked Min.

"I will personally see to it that each Monitor makes it home safely," Min replied. "They have acted with extraordinary bravery today, and we are fortunate that no one perished."

The Monitors nodded, looking shell-shocked from the night's battle. Some of them were still wearing their white wigs, too afraid that someone would attack if they removed them.

"Bookworm can help move squeegees again," Daisy volunteered her pet. "He might even be able to talk some of the other Thingamajunks into leaving the landfill. He's very respected—for a guy made out of garbage."

Min accepted the offer with a nod, ushering the Monitors out of the classroom to begin the task of returning them to their homes.

"Thanks for everything," Spencer said, catching Min by the arm at the doorway.

"I will have my Monitors inspect their schools for these newly transformed Toxites," Min said. "I will be anxious to find out if the change affected all of them."

Daisy smiled nervously and shook Min's hand. "Write me?" she said.

"Of course," he replied.

Spencer rolled his eyes, telling himself that the feelings in his stomach did not come from jealousy. Then Min and the Monitors were gone.

"I have something for you," Spencer said, facing the nine Auran girls. They were dirty and battle worn, their white hair still matted from the storm around the Broomstaff.

Spencer reached into his belt pouch and withdrew the bangle bracelets that he'd taken from Belzora. Studying them closer, he discovered a name etched onto the inside of each one.

"These are your Timekeepers," Spencer said.

"All of them?" asked Rho.

"All but mine," Spencer answered.

"What happened to yours?" Gia asked.

"The Witches didn't know I was going to be an Auran," Spencer said. "They didn't make me one."

"I thought the years were captured in the nearest piece of bronze," Rho said.

"Yeah," answered Spencer. "But there's no way to know what that was for me. The circumstances weren't ideal when I became an Auran. Basically everything around had been sucked into the Vortex."

"I thought the Timekeeper killed V," said Shirley, a hint of concern in her voice.

"It did," Daisy admitted. "Because she couldn't take it off."

"If you keep these safe," Spencer said, "and touch them for only a moment at a time, you should be able to age at whatever pace you choose."

Rho stepped forward, her gloved hand outstretched. "I'll take it," she said.

Spencer sifted through the bracelets until he found the one inscribed with *Rhode Island*. He dropped it into her palm. The latex glove prevented any contact with her skin, and Rho remained the ageless girl she'd always been. Her fingers curled around the Timekeeper, and she dropped it into her belt pouch.

After seeing Rho survive the bracelet, the other girls lined up to get theirs. Spencer literally gave their lives back to them, one at a time.

New Jersey for Jersey. *South Carolina* for Lina. *Connecticut* for Netty. *New York* for Yorkie. *Delaware* for Dela. *Pennsylvania* for Sylva. *New Hampshire* for Shirley. And *Georgia* for Gia.

The Auran girls quietly filtered out of Mrs. Natcher's classroom, wanting time to contemplate the decision they would have to make.

Rho was the last to leave. She hung back, and Spencer could tell she had something to say to him and Daisy. "When I met you two," she started, "I never would have thought I could owe you so much. A fraction of my age, and yet I leaned on you for wisdom." Rho pulled them both into a hug.

"Remember when you were Jenna?" Daisy asked. She gave a nervous laugh. "That was weird."

The memory made Spencer blush. He was almost embarrassed to have had a crush on Jenna. He'd quashed his feelings for Rho a long time ago. She was just so . . . old.

"Are you guys having a group hug?" Dez asked. He pretended to gag.

"Where will you go?" Spencer asked.

"I was thinking of settling down," Rho said, releasing

them from the hug. "Maybe I'll try middle school for a while. If I don't like that, I can always bump up to high school or college."

"Will we ever see you again?" Daisy asked.

"I think that can be arranged," answered Rho with a smile. "Who knows, maybe I'll even be in your class next year."

She gave them one more squeeze and vanished down the hallway. Spencer's attention turned back to the three bangle bracelets in his hand.

North Carolina, Maryland, and Massachusetts.

"Are those for us, mate?" came Aryl's unmistakable voice from the back of the classroom.

Spencer and Daisy both jumped in surprise to find the three Dark Aurans sitting behind Mrs. Natcher's desk.

"Whoa," Dez said. "I didn't even see you guys come in . . . thanks to Spencer."

"Didn't expect you would," Sach pointed out.

"We didn't either," said Daisy. "And we can see fine."

"That's what happens when you have a few hundred years of practice sneaking around." Olin smirked. "The window was open." He pointed over his shoulder to where Mrs. Natcher's paisley curtains fluttered in the post-storm breeze.

"Let's get you out of those Pans," Spencer said. "Again."

"Hey," Sach said. "That's not funny. We let our guard down for one second and what happened?" He paused like he was waiting for an answer. "No, seriously," Sach said.

"What happened? We don't remember a thing. Just woke up with an old familiar Pan around our necks."

"General Clean hit you with the green spray," Daisy said. "He had a Sweeper potion hidden in a fountain pen, and he turned himself back into a half-Grime."

"Ha ha!" Olin laughed. "Now, isn't that ironic?"

"Why?" Spencer asked, failing to see the irony.

"Sweepers have to die twice," Olin explained. "But since Clean already lost his first life, now he has to remain a Sweeper until he dies."

"He probably wanted that," Spencer said.

Aryl chuckled. "He definitely didn't want what he got."

"What do you mean?" asked Daisy.

"Let's just see if we can find the old General," Sach said, stepping over to the sink of soapsuds by Mrs. Natcher's bookshelf.

Sach squinted at the foamy suds, fishing a few out with his finger until he found the viewpoint he was searching for. Taking the tiny soapsud between both hands, Sach stretched the image for everyone to see.

Through the fish-eye lens, Spencer saw the muddy hill leading up to the forest of oversized utensils. It wasn't far from the Broomstaff and the spot where Welcher had been deposited. The hill was bare, aside from the bits of scrap and trash that littered all of the landfill. Then Spencer saw a figure moving against the muddy slope. When Sach zoomed in even closer, Spencer realized that it was General Clean, trying desperately to climb away from the battlefield.

"It wasn't hard for us to escape once he looked like that," Olin said.

Spencer shook his head in amazement. The Sweeper slipping in the mud didn't look anything like the terrifying General Clean. With the Toxites' recent transformation, Clean's Grime half had been affected. Now the man was heavy and round, his stomach stretching out of his white lab coat. In proportion to his torso, Clean's legs and arms looked small and comical.

His face and neck were covered in silver scales that sparkled in the faint moonlight. Clean's tail was half the length it used to be, swishing rapidly back and forth like that of an excited dog.

The Sweeper man was scrambling up the hillside. But the task looked very challenging with his missing left hand and portly belly. He toppled back, his stubby legs failing to support his weight. Clean rolled down the slope and came to rest on his posterior, kicking and flailing like a turtle on its back.

"That's the great General Clean?" Spencer asked in disbelief over what his eyes were seeing.

"What?" Dez said. "What does he look like?"

"He looks like a giant disco ball with legs," Daisy said.

"The Sweepers changed just like the rest of the Toxites," Aryl said. "I have a feeling General Clean won't be bothering schools anymore."

Olin grinned. "Now every time the Sweeper General takes a breath, he'll actually be helping students focus."

Spencer couldn't help but chuckle at the way that had

played out. General Clean had dedicated his life to bringing down education. Now, with every breath, the Sweeper would have no choice but to build it up.

"That's not going to make him very happy," Daisy pointed out. "I think Clean would rather be blind than help education. I'm sure he won't stay a Sweeper for very long."

"He has no choice," Sach answered. "His first life ended in the Hoarder's dwelling. If he dies again, it will be permanent."

Looking into the soapsud, Spencer saw that Clean had managed to rise to his feet once more. He glanced nervously over his shoulder, as if afraid of pursuit. Then he began another attempt at scaling the muddy slope, apparently hoping to find refuge in the forest of utensils.

"What will happen to the BEM now that Clean has . . . changed?" Spencer asked. He couldn't imagine the Bureau keeping that pitiful figure in command.

"They'll pick a new leader," Aryl said. "Someone else will take his spot in overseeing janitorial work in schools across the country."

"It might take a while," said Sach, "but the Bureau of Educational Maintenance should return to what it once was—an organization established to maintain a positive learning environment for students in schools."

"But the Toxites have all transformed," Daisy pointed out. "The BEM won't have any creatures to fight against."

"You're right," Olin said. "Instead of fighting Toxites, the Bureau will feed them. Instead of scaring them away, they'll make sure the new Toxites are comfortable and plentiful in each school across the nation. Every new Toxite breath is a boost for education."

Sach gestured once more to the bubble in his hands. The ridiculous new version of General Clean had reached the top of the hill, and his shimmering tail flicked back and forth like an excited puppy's. Sach pushed his hands together, reducing the image to a tiny soapsud. Then he re-placed the bubble in the sink of foamy surveillance. Aryl tapped the metal Pan around his neck, a not-so-subtle re-minder that Spencer needed to free them once more.

Pulling out his spit sponge, Spencer dribbled a bit of sa-liva into his left hand. His palms came together, and the Glop ignited, turning his fists to golden spheres. He released Sach first, touching the bronze Pan with his left hand. Then, using his own spit sponge, Sach freed Aryl while Spencer un-Panned Olin.

"What are you guys going to do now?" Daisy asked the three boys as they kicked their fallen Pans aside.

"Well," Aryl said. "I've been Panned twice, and I'm kind of afraid if I stick around here, it could happen again. I think I'm ready for a trip to the city."

Olin nodded. "I'd say it's time we try McDonald's."

"It'll be nice to eat a hamburger that doesn't already have a few bites out of it," Sach said. "We've been living off trash food for far too long."

The Dark Aurans headed for the hallway, true freedom at their fingertips.

"Wait!" Spencer said. "Your Timekeepers."

The boys turned back, studying the three remaining

bracelets in Spencer's hand. They looked at each other, as if to reaffirm some previously made commitment.

"You hold on to our Timekeepers," Aryl said.

"What?" said Daisy. "But you'll never age. Don't you want to grow up?"

"We do," Sach said. "And that's exactly why we need you to keep the bracelets."

"I don't understand," said Spencer.

"Everything is changing," explained Olin. "After Dez's Refraction, the Toxites are actually going to *help* society."

"My bad," Dez said.

"But the critters are still tied to us," Sach said. "Dez changed their natures, but the brain nests will continue to exist only while we're alive."

"It's our fault the Toxites came to be in the first place," Aryl said. "We gave those monsters almost three hundred years of corruption. The least we can do is give another century or two for these new Toxites to undo the damage."

It was noble of them. Spencer knew they would probably rather age with the others. But the Dark Aurans were determined to right the wrongs they didn't even know they'd caused.

"Why me?" Spencer asked, curling his fingers around the bronze bracelets. "Why do I have to keep them?"

"If we hold onto them, the Timekeepers will be a constant temptation to go back on our commitment," Sach said. "We trust you to keep them safe."

"And when you get old," said Olin, "you can pass them to your children, and they can pass them to their children, and so on. We'll come get them eventually, when we feel like education is ready to step out on its own."

"Maybe you didn't hear," Spencer said. "But I don't have a Timekeeper. So I guess you'll be getting the bracelets from me, even if it's three hundred years from now."

"A lot can happen between now and then," Aryl said. "Things that are lost can always be found."

Spencer slid the bronze bracelets into his belt pouch. "Take care of yourselves," he said. "Don't eat too many Big Macs." The Dark Aurans grinned, Olin and Aryl slipping out the door. Sach paused at the threshold, reaching back to shake Spencer's hand.

Sach's voice was soft, his words deliberate and reflective. "The Witches once called us the heroes of the Dustbin. They said we were the only ones with the power to change the fate of the Toxites." He glanced across the room toward Dez. "The Witches were wrong." Then he slid silently out of the room.

Spencer, Daisy, and Dez stood in silence in their old classroom. If Spencer hadn't personally seen the school move, he might have thought he was still in Welcher, Idaho.

Sach's words lingered in Spencer's mind, the implication thick. Something else had transformed the Toxites— something the Witches would never have predicted. Spencer's bravery had led him into the Dustbin. Daisy's loyalty had rescued him. And, most surprisingly, Dez's self-lessness had changed the Toxites forever.

They had done it. What they had accomplished was

even better than destroying the Toxites. Spencer looked at his comrades and grinned.

They were the heroes of the Dustbin.

"We better get going," Alan said, appearing in the hallway and leaning into the classroom. "You kids have school in the morning."

"Umm . . ." Spencer said, pointing at the relocated building. "I think school might be cancelled."

"What?" Daisy cried. "They can't cancel the last day of school! There was going to be ice cream!"

"Daisy's right," Alan said. "First rule of janitorial work: If you make a mess, clean it up." He glanced down the hallway. "The Rebels are almost finished up out here; then we'll be ready."

"Ready for what?" Spencer asked.

"We're going to put the school back where we found it," Alan said. "And hopefully we'll get back to Welcher in time for you three to catch a bit of sleep. It's still a school night."

Dez rolled his head back and groaned. "School never gets cancelled. Next time, I'm moving Welcher all the way to Antarctica."

CHAPTER 50

"YOU'LL NEED TO HIRE SOME GOOD JANITORS."

It was a sunny day in Welcher, Idaho. Young students laughed and joked, running across the playground and into the school, totally clueless to the fact that the entire building had traveled halfway across the country and back last night.

Anyone who took a moment to pause and study the school would quickly realize that things were out of place. The school hadn't quite settled back onto its proper foundation, and many of the walls were cracked and crumbling. The morning news had attributed the damage to a very localized earthquake. But these weren't details that a student stopped to notice on the last day of school.

Spencer, Daisy, and Dez were standing in the school's back parking lot. Much of the asphalt was broken up from its brief time as a glass portal. Marv had put up some orange cones to stop parents from driving into the wreckage.

"I'm not going inside with these on," Dez said. "I can't believe how dorky I look!"

"You should just be glad you can see at all," Daisy said. "They're not that bad."

"Not that bad?" Dez repeated. "I look like somebody who loves science or something. And everything has a weird bluish tint."

"You're welcome," Spencer said.

Spencer had come up with the idea to Glopify a pair of safety goggles. They were large, and the plastic they were made of was slightly rubbery. The bluish goggles were secured behind Dez's head with a stretchy black elastic. Maybe Spencer could have hunted around for a more stylish pair, but it wouldn't hurt Dez to look a bit nerdy.

"This does *not* make us even," Dez continued complaining. "These are ridiculous." He tugged at the strap behind his head.

"But they work," Spencer said. As long as Dez was wearing the safety goggles, his eyesight would be restored. But the minute he slipped them off, Dez would go blind once more.

"Ugh! They make me feel like . . . like . . ." Unsure how to express his feelings, Dez simply belched.

"That's disgusting," Daisy said. "Why do you always do that?"

Dez shrugged. "I don't know. It's just a habitat I have."

Spencer bit his tongue. Dez was already going to have a rough day with his new goggles. Spencer didn't need to rub it in by teaching him that *habitat* was not the same as *habit*.

"I'm going in the back door," Dez said, shielding the

sides of his goggles with both hands. "I'll see you chumps in Mrs. Natcher's classroom."

Keeping his head ducked low, Dez pushed open the back door to the school and went inside, breaking the rule that encouraged students to start their day through Welcher's front doors.

"Dez," Spencer muttered, once the boy was gone. "I still can't believe what he did for me in the Dustbin."

"I've been thinking about that," Daisy replied. "I was wondering what kind of Toxite you would have created if the Witches had succeeded with the Refraction Dust."

"I wondered that too," Spencer said. "If the fourth Toxite would have exhaled the opposite of my best trait, what would it have done?"

"That's easy," said Daisy. "It would have made kids into cowards."

"Cowards?" Spencer repeated.

"That's what I think," Daisy said. "You're the bravest person I've ever known."

Spencer smiled, feeling humbled by the praise. He *had* done some pretty courageous things. He wondered what might have happened if Daisy had been on the receiving end of the Refraction Dust. She was the most honest, loyal friend a person could ask for.

Daisy followed Spencer around the side of the school so they could enter in the crooked front doors. They paused when they saw the banner hanging above the entryway.

Farewell, Principal Poach

Spencer wondered when the PTA had found time to hang the sign. The school had been missing until about four A.M.

"Farewell, Principal Poach?" Daisy said. "Is he graduating from elementary school too?"

Spencer shrugged. "Why don't we ask him?" He pointed to the sidewalk where the round principal was making his way toward the school, huffing and puffing, his face red.

"Such an old, unstable school, full of rowdy, unstable kids," said the principal, his terribly nasal voice ringing out in the morning air. "Nothing like my new job."

"New job?" Spencer asked as the principal paused at Welcher's bottom step.

"Yes. I'm leaving Welcher Elementary. A very prestigious position at another school has opened up," he said. "It's an elite private school. You ruffians have probably never heard of it."

"Elite private school?" Daisy repeated.

"It's called New Forest Academy," said Poach, a twinkle of excitement in his watery eyes. "It's going to be lavish! I'll have my own luxurious apartment on a beautiful mountain campus. No more five-minute commute to work. No more misbehaving students. And I hear that they'll actually call me *director*." He grinned. "*Director Poach*. It has quite a ring to it."

Principal Poach checked his watch, realizing that he'd arrived less than ten minutes before the bell rang. Then he gathered his strength and mounted the three stairs, entering Welcher Elementary School presumably for the last time.

"Better hurry inside," said a voice behind the kids. Spencer turned to see his dad standing with his hands in his pockets.

Spencer thought his dad had gone home. Well, technically, the Zumbros didn't have a home since Aunt Avril's house had been liquefied. But his family was supposed to be staying with the Gateses.

"What's going on?" Spencer asked his father.

"Just looking over my new school," Alan Zumbro answered.

"Welcher?" Daisy asked.

"Didn't you hear?" Alan clapped his hands together. "I'm Welcher Elementary School's new principal!"

"Dad, are you serious?" Spencer didn't know what to say. If his dad really got the job, then the Zumbro family wouldn't have to move away from Welcher. That gave Spencer comfort. The little Idaho town felt more like home than anywhere he'd been.

"Just found out myself," said Alan. "It's been a few years since I've taught school, but my résumé was . . . diverse."

"The school's still a mess," Daisy pointed out. "You'll need to hire some good janitors."

Alan smiled. "Already taken care of," he said. "Marv will be Welcher's head janitor. And Penny took a job to be his assistant."

Spencer felt relieved. Sure, this was his last day at Welcher Elementary, but he had four younger siblings with years ahead of them. Spencer would feel much more comfortable knowing that his dad, Marv, and Penny would be safeguarding the school.

Alan checked his watch. "You two better get to class. One more tardy and Mrs. Natcher might not let you graduate from elementary school."

Spencer and Daisy quickly made their way into the school. The cleanup from last night's battle had been hasty. Spencer still saw Grime slime spattered on the walls and little piles of spent vac dust on the floor. The additional hallways had probably been a real surprise for everyone.

They were almost to the classroom when Spencer heard a distinctive voice.

"Pst! Daisy!"

It was Bernard Weizmann, crouching behind a hallway trash can as though he were trying to hide.

"What are you doing here?" Daisy whispered, rushing toward him. Spencer knew for sure that they would be tardy now. Even as he thought it, the bell rang, officially starting the last day of school.

"I have a little surprise for you," said the garbologist.

Spencer made his way over to them as the strange man bent over the trash can and shouted into the garbage, "Okeydokey! Come on up!"

Bookworm rose up, his body a bit thinner than usual due to the limited amount of garbage in the trash can. Spencer glanced both directions down the hallway, sure that someone would see the Thingamajunk.

"Hey, big guy," Daisy said. "You know you're not supposed to follow me to school."

Bookworm nodded sheepishly, then extended his trash arm, a special item dangling from his thumb. It was Daisy's pendant necklace that had been stolen when they had tried to tame that other Thingamajunk.

Daisy smiled and reached out, sliding the delicate chain off of Bookworm's thumb. "You got this back from Couchpotato?"

Bookworm nodded.

"Thanks," she said. "I'm glad it's still in one piece. Last time this necklace broke, it took months before my dad got around to fixing it."

"Looks high quality," Bernard said, squinting at the piece of inexpensive jewelry. "Fake gold chain with a tarnished bronze pendant. Well, I'm sure it has sentimental value."

Spencer's heartbeat quickened, and he took a hasty step toward Daisy. "It's bronze?" he whispered, trying not to get his hopes up.

"I always thought it was gold," Daisy said, holding it before her face for closer inspection. "But I'm not very good at identifying metals."

"Garbology lesson thirty-two," Bernard said. "We'll get there."

"Daisy," Spencer said. He reached out for the necklace, then drew his hand back. "You were wearing it that day."

"What day?" Daisy asked.

"It broke when you were fighting with Leslie Sharmelle in the air vent above the classroom." Spencer was speaking fast now. "Right before I . . ."

"Became an Auran," Daisy said, finally realizing the importance of it all. She stared unblinking at the necklace her grandma had given her. "You think my necklace is your Timekeeper?"

Spencer swallowed hard and held out his hand. "There's only one way to find out."

"Are you sure?" Daisy asked. "Remember what happened to V?"

"V's Timekeeper held nearly three hundred years," Spencer said. "Mine only holds about nine months. What's the worst that could happen?"

"Growing pains," Daisy said.

"Or," said Bernard, "you could rip your pants." Bookworm laughed at the garbologist, but Spencer was too intent to pause for humor.

Daisy shrugged and dropped the necklace into Spencer's palm.

It happened so quickly that Spencer didn't even have time to cry out, though the experience was rather painful. It was a pins-and-needles kind of pain that spread down his legs and through his arms.

Spencer's pants didn't rip, but the hems were suddenly one or two inches higher, his ankles exposed. His toes curled painfully in the ends of his too-small shoes. His fingernails were the worst part, growing suddenly long and untrimmed.

Spencer's pure white hair darkened until it was once more that chestnut brown he had grown up with. Nearly a year's worth of growth caught up to him in a second, his hair turning shaggy over his ears and forehead.

"Look at you," Bernard said. "All grown up . . . I'd say you're definitely ready for junior high school."

"All this time," Spencer said, passing the necklace back to Daisy, "you had my Timekeeper."

"Well, Couchpotato stole it for a while," Daisy said. "Good thing Bookworm got it back." She closed her hand and gave the Thingamajunk a fist bump. Excited by the praise, Bookworm followed up with a fist bump for Bernard and one for Spencer.

The door to Mrs. Natcher's classroom opened suddenly, the familiar smell of cooked cabbage wafting out. The stuffy old teacher stepped into the hallway, her brow furrowed as if she couldn't wait to disapprove of something.

Bookworm saw her and leapt across the hallway. Landing only two feet away, he extended his garbage hand to fist bump the teacher.

Mrs. Natcher fainted.

ACKNOWLEDGMENTS

Well, that's it! I really hope you enjoyed the final book! It's hard to believe that the story is over. I had so much fun creating the world of Janitors and telling this tale!

You might be wondering why I don't keep going with these characters. Will I ever write a sixth book about Spencer and Daisy? I don't think so. The ending that you just read has been planned for several years.

Even though Janitors is over, I hope to write many new series for years to come. And I hope you'll enjoy them just as much!

The great team at Shadow Mountain made all this possible. Huge thanks to Chris Schoebinger and Heidi Taylor. You've supported me from the very beginning and given me great professional and personal attention.

And thanks to Karen Zelnick, Michelle Moore, and everyone else who helped with marketing, touring, and other publicity.

Richard Erickson deserves a thanks for art direction, and of course, Brandon Dorman for his incredible covers and illustrations. The art in all five books has surpassed my expectations. I'm happy to let people judge these books by their covers!

Thanks for all your editorial work, Emily Watts.

ACKNOWLEDGMENTS

Sometimes I think I know what I'm saying, but it really make sense doesn't. You've done a great job interpreting those moments!

I had the fun opportunity to narrate the Janitors audiobooks. Big thanks to Kenny Hodges, fellow percussionist and producer extraordinaire! And to Oscar (co-producer). There are a lot of crazy voices in my head. Thanks for helping me keep them straight!

Thanks to all the book stores that have hosted my signings. Also teachers, librarians, and administrators for allowing me to present at their schools.

To my mom and dad, who have always believed in me and encouraged me to do what I love. I've put to use some talents that I never knew would be useful!

And the biggest thanks to Connie. You've heard every possible version of these stories and helped me find the best. It's been so much fun to share this adventure with you. Thanks for taking care of reality so I can live in my books.

To my Rebel readers: You are the best! Thank you so much for your excitement about this series. Toxites may be vanquished, but there is no end to mess making.

Keep cleaning!

1. Glopified bleach makes you invisible. If you could turn invisible, where would you go? What would you do while no one could see you?

2. If the Dark Aurans die, so do the Toxites. Instead of considering that option, the Rebels take a different route to destroying Toxites. What are some other situations in which the easiest solution may not be the best one?

3. The Witches use soapsuds to spy on everyone. If you had surveillance suds, who would you want to spy on? Why?

4. Spencer learns that the Toxites were created from reflecting the Dark Aurans' best traits. What is one of your best traits? What opposite effect would a Toxite have if created from you?

5. The Timekeepers are bronze bracelets that hold the years of the Aurans. If you had a Timekeeper, would you use it to age? Or would you stay young forever? Why?

6. Bookworm is losing the fight against the Hoarder until Daisy puts herself in danger and gives him something to defend. What things do you find important enough to defend?

7. When Alan had the chance to kill General Clean, he decided to spare him because he hoped he might change.

Have you ever forgiven someone you thought should be punished? How did it make you feel?

8. In the Dustbin, Spencer re-creates Walter Jamison to inspire him to reach the end. Who inspires you? Why?

9. Of all the characters you have met in the Janitors series, who are you most like? Why? Who is the most different from you? Why?

10. This is the end of the Janitors series. What do you think will happen to Spencer, Daisy, and Dez in the future?

GLOSSARY OF GLOPIFIED SUPPLIES

Agitation Bucket. Keeps small Toxites trapped, causing them to grow angry and dangerous.

Bleach. Spray this on yourself for temporary invisibility. But be warned, the second time is permanent.

Boots. The Glopified rubber soles allow you to walk on walls and ceilings.

Bridge. Rigged to collapse if an unauthorized vehicle attempts to drive over.

Broom. Tap the bristles against the ground to fly high above your enemies.

Caution: Wet Floor Cone. Be careful where you step! This yellow cone will turn the floor to liquid.

Chalkboard Eraser. Throw this against any surface to detonate. A paralyzing cloud of chalk dust will fill the area.

Coveralls. Wear this outfit to protect your body from most injuries. Make sure your zipper's up!

Drain Clog Remover. Quickly liquefies anything it comes in contact with.

Duct Tape. Indestructible and fingerprint sensitive. Only the fingerprints that stick it down can peel it up.

Dust Mask. Fit this securely over your nose and mouth. Breath normally; the mask will provide pure air under any conditions.

Dustpan. With a twist of the handle, your dustpan fans out into a circular shield.

Extension Cord. These cords cause Toxites to grow dangerously large. Plug one end into the wall and the other end into the creature.

Fence. Dangerously electric, the fence stops anyone from breaking though or climbing over.

Flashlight. Use this bright beam to illuminate nearby magical items.

Garbage Truck. This armored vehicle has many magical features. Make sure you read the operator's manual before you drive!

Gasoline. Used to fuel the Glopified garbage trucks, this gasoline will never burn out.

Glass Cleaner. Spray this blue liquid on anything and it will instantly turn the object to glass.

Green Spray. Spraying this will momentarily knock out your enemies. When they wake up, they will have no memory of who sprayed them.

Ink Remover. Spray this on any written text. An identical copy of the ink can be transferred onto a separate paper.

Latex Glove. Wear this to escape from enemies. You will slip easily through their grasp.

Leaf Blower. Turn on the blower to release a high-speed current of destructive air.

Magnet. This magnet forcefully attracts any metal that has been treated with Glopified stainless steel polish.

Mop. Swing this at your enemies. The strings will stretch out to entangle them.

Orange Spray. Spray this on any injury to accelerate healing. Smells like citrus!

Paper Towels. Unroll carefully, folding the paper towels to form a map that will lead you to the Aurans' magical landfill.

Pink Soap. Use this to wash your face. After a slight tingling sensation, Toxites will become visible.

Port-a-Potty. Climb inside and shut the door. It is an entrance to a secret BEM laboratory.

Pushbroom. Send your enemies flying out of control by striking them with the bristles.

Rag. General Clean's weapon of choice. When flicked just right, the rag obliterates any person it touches.

Rake. Slam the wooden handle at your opponent's feet. The metal rake will extend to form a cage around your enemy.

Razorblade. Small enough to fit in your pocket, the razorblade can extend to a full-length sword with a flick of your thumb.

Recycle Bin. Climb aboard! These blue bins make excellent boats.

Rope. These snakelike ropes work to tie you up. Cutting the rope only causes it to regrow and multiply.

Rug. Drape this over the back of an Extension Toxite to make a comfortable saddle. It will hold you in place!

School Board. This magic piece of wood regulates who can become the next warlock.

Scissors. The most powerful Glopified tool ever created. The scissors have the power to cut anything.

Soapsuds. Used for surveillance, each soapsud acts as a camera, enabling the Witches to view their opponents from a safe distance.

Sponge. Absorbs the magic spit of Aurans, allowing them to use their powers more frequently.

Squeegee. Swipe any glass surface to open a portal to a new location.

Stainless Steel Polish. Instantly causes any metal to become shiny and magnetic.

Supply Cart. Stand on the back of the cart and lean forward. Using your weight to steer, you can drive at extreme speeds.

Toilet Bowl Cleaner. A vintage brand from 1962, the smell of this cleaner attracts Toxites.

Toilet Brush. Twist the handle to activate the spinning brush. Makes a great propellor under water!

Toilet Plunger. Clamp the red suction cup onto any freestanding object. No matter how heavy the object is, you'll be able to lift it.

Tool Belt. Strap this tightly around your waist. The belt can hold many Glopified supplies, making them weightless and invisible.

Trashcannon. These trash cans will launch a deadly, high-powered projectile of compact garbage.

Vacuum Dust. Throw a pinch of vac dust to temporarily suction your enemies to the floor.

Vanilla Air Freshener. Use this sweet-smelling aerosol to counteract the effects of Toxite breath.

Vortex Vacuum Bag. Rip a hole in this vacuum bag, and everything nearby will be sucked inside.

Walkie-Talkie Radio. Use the radios to contact BEM, or Rebel Janitors, across long distances.